Kate Thompson was born in Belfast. She came to Dublin to study French and English and had a successful career as an actress and voice-over artist before ditching the day job to write full-time. Kate divides her time between Dublin and the West of Ireland, is happily married and has one daughter.

SEX, LIES AND FAIRYTALES

Lottery winner Cleo Dowling lives her dream in Kilrowan with her painter husband, Pablo. But the dream turns into a nightmare when Pablo is commissioned to paint a portrait of a Dublin 4 princess. Bestsclling author Pixie Pirelli gets invited to all the chat shows. But she's forced to trade in her glittering career for a quiet life in the sticks. And who is La Londonista and why is she trying to sabotage Pixie's career? Hazel MacNamara has a host of celebrities in her organizer. Which of them will dazzle at the Kilrowan Arts Festival — the must-attend event of the Irish social calendar? Will it be film star Rory McDonagh? Will it be literary diva Colleen? Or will it be — shhh!

Books by Kate Thompson
Published by The House of Ulverscroft:

LIVING THE DREAM

KATE THOMPSON

SEX, LIES AND FAIRYTALES

Complete and Unabridged

CHARNWOOD
Leicester

First published in Great Britain in 2005 by
Bantam Press, a division of
Transworld Publishers
London

First Charnwood Edition
published 2006
by arrangement with
Transworld Publishers
The Random House Group Limited
London

The moral right of the author has been asserted

British Library CIP Data

Thompson, Kate, *1956 July 23 –*
    Sex, lies and fairytales.—Large print ed.—
Charnwood library series
    1. Lottery winners—Ireland—Fiction
    2. Booksellers and bookselling—Ireland—Fiction
    3. Art festivals—Ireland—Fiction 4. Artists' spouses
    —Ireland—Fiction 5. Large type books
    I. Title
    823.9'14 [F]

    ISBN 1–84617–506–2

Published by
F. A. Thorpe (Publishing)
Anstey, Leicestershire

Set by Words & Graphics Ltd.
Anstey, Leicestershire
Printed and bound in Great Britain by
T. J. International Ltd., Padstow, Cornwall

For Francesca

Acknowledgements

Thanks go to:

All at Ballynahinch Castle Hotel — what a joy to do research there; to the people of Roundstone (including Fluffy; sorry, sweetheart!); to Hazel Douglas for allowing me to live in the most beautiful place in the world; to Emmet Bergin for the fishing lore; to Vincent Woods for his help with the Gaeilgeoir stuff. To the real-life star of the Kilrowan Festival for allowing me to use him — again! To Zoe Conway, Donal Lunny, Sharon Shannon and the *Tribunals* show for allowing me to drop their names. To my fans for the *fantastic* letters! To Madge MacLaverty and Robert ☺. To all in Transworld: Kate Brader, Beth Humphries, Nicky Jeanes, Laura Sherlock, Larry Finlay, Ed Christie, Patrick Janson-Smith, Garry Prior and Garry Perry. To Gill and Simon Hess, and Declan Heeney in Dublin. To Ali Gunn and Stephanie Thwaites in Curtis Brown. To the staff of bookshops everywhere, and especially to Susan Walsh and Seamus Duffy. To Marian Keyes and Cathy Kelly, for reading a first draft — love as ever. To Francesca Liversidge — who appears in the book in the guise of Deborah — and to whom *Sex, Lies and Fairytales* is dedicated.

Finally, to Malcolm and Clara, my most dearly beloveds: thank you both for everything.

1

PR consultant Hazel MacNamara was having a bad day, and it hadn't even officially started yet. Her brand new Wolford lacetops had snagged on the edge of her waste-paper basket, she had a bitch of a hangover, and her assistant, Renée, had just phoned in sick for the second day in a row. An alarm was going off in the solicitor's office across the road *again* and she knew it would go on until the bastard solicitor finally showed up for work. When she booted up her computer, the list of things to do that was staring her in the face was actually *longer* than her face. She had a charity event to organize, she had the recording of a commercial to supervise, and after she'd got rid of the spam — delete, delete, *delete* — in her inbox, she had at least a hundred e-mails clamouring for her attention.

Her mobile went off. Jesus! It wasn't even nine o'clock yet! Caller display told her that it was Mick, her ex as of ten hours ago. He could go boil his head. She was never going to take a call from him again. How had she not *realized* what a tightwad he was before now? She'd sat across the table from him in the restaurant last night watching as he counted out *change*! It had made her so mad that she'd extracted a wad of notes from her wallet, slung them onto the table and high-heeled out of the joint. Then she'd gone home, opened a bottle of wine and had a good

1

bitch with one of her BFs down the phone. She had to admit to feeling a little stung when Erin had told her she'd never liked Mick in the first place, but they agreed ultimately that Mick had been A Bad Thing, and that it was time for Hazel to move on.

She switched off her phone, making a mental note to investigate the 'blocked senders' facility, and then put her head in her hands as the frenzied strains of an angle grinder rose from the forecourt below. Ow. Fresh hell! What she needed was —

Coffee. Very strong.

Ha, ha, Hazel — your day just got worse. There was no Illy left; she'd have to have tea. In the kitchen she filled the kettle, jabbed the 'on' switch, and went back into the office. The answering machine was blinking at her nervously, as if it sussed she was in a bad mood. She wished she could've phoned in sick, like Renée. That was the bummer about being the boss — you had to show up, hangover, flu or Ebola virus notwithstanding. But at least being the boss meant that she could show up in her dressing gown if she felt like it. Hazel worked from home, and her office was just downstairs from her bedroom. She was an escapee from commuter-belt hell, and knew that she must count her blessings. She sat down at her desk, reached for a Post-It pad and a Nutcracker PR pen and pressed 'play'. Five messages had accumulated since she'd fled the office yesterday.

'Hi, Hazel — Suki here at On-Line Studios . . . ' 'Hazel, hello — it's Jim here, ringing

2

about your tax returns . . . ' 'Hi, Hazel — I'm PA to Dominic Forrest, and we're opening an exhibition by . . . ' 'Hazel, hi! Finbar de Rossa here. We met at the post-première party of . . . ' 'Ms MacNamara? My name is Hugh Hennessy. I got your number from the Golden Pages, and I'm phoning to see if you might be interested in handling the PR for the Kilrowan Arts Festival this year? Perhaps you might call me on . . . '

Finally came the automated voice, which she automatically parroted. *End of messages!*

Hazel looked down at the be-doodled Post-It, and drew a circle round the word 'Kilrowan'. She'd never been there, but she'd heard of it. Kilrowan was a small village in the west of Ireland, and since her assistant — Renée's — mother had moved to the locality a couple of years ago, Renée was full of gossip about it.

The gossip centred around the hordes of media types who descended lemming-like upon the joint in the summer months. They went there in their Beamers and Saabs for sailing and golf and scubadiving and for the cultural highlight, which — as in most thriving summer communities — was the annual week-long Arts Festival. Kilrowan was famous, too, for its colony of creatives — the village was the haunt of artists and writers and musicians, and trustafarians who fancied themselves as being all three rolled into one.

At last. The alarm over the road finally shut up, the angle grinder had taken a tea break, and the pressure on her temples eased a little. Hazel pressed the 'play' button on the machine again,

3

and systematically deleted each message after she'd made certain she'd got the info right. She did not, however, delete the last one. She wasn't sure why. Maybe she just liked the sound of this Hennessy bloke's voice.

She entered his details in her organizer, made a pot of tea and knocked back a couple of Panadol. And then she did something that was going to change her life. She picked up the phone to Hugh Hennessy.

★ ★ ★

Pixie Pirelli was holed up in a suite in Ballynahinch Castle Hotel. She was on the run. Nobody knew she was there — not even her agent, not even her editor. Hopefully the press was equally unenlightened as to her where-abouts. She'd had major, *major* flak with them since she'd split up with her boyfriend. Pixie had found out about the castle in a book called *Greatest Escapes of the World* (or some such) and right now she had a burning ambition to become as consummate an escape artist as David Blaine. Actually, strike David Blaine: he was rubbish. Make that Houdini.

Oh, heavens! Here she was, trying to escape, and she was still mentally editing her own thoughts. That was the one drawback about being a writer — you never, *ever* stopped working. Only yesterday, when she'd been strolling by the river in the grounds of the castle, she'd been trying to find the most apposite words to evoke the beauty of her surroundings.

4

And once she found the words, she had to scribble them down in her notebook with the pen she always carried.

She'd tried to leave the pen behind once, hoping that its not-being-thereness (consult thesaurus) might sabotage her compulsion to write. But an entire novel had come into her head that day, and by the time she'd raced back home to write down her ideas, the novel had vanished into the ether. So Pixie was like Mary and her Little Lamb except that: Everywhere that Pixie went, her Pen was sure to go.

The problem for Pixie was that she couldn't simply *enjoy* life: she had to write it down. She envied those lucky people who could go off on holiday and send postcards home with scribbles like 'Words cannot describe the beauty of the Maldives' (or Martinique or Mauritius or wherever), because it was her job to *find* those words.

Pixie Pirelli was an author who'd got lucky. Except her real name wasn't Pixie, nor was it even Pirelli. Her name was plain Jane Gray. She'd been advised by an expert that 'A Brilliant Book' by Jane Gray wasn't going to get as much press as 'A Brilliant Book' by Pixie Pirelli, and the expert had been right. Pixie's books danced onto the bestsellers' shelves in bookshops and shimmied straight out of the doors, earning her a lot of money in royalties in the process.

And if that's all her job had entailed — if plain Jane Gray could sit in front of her laptop and tip-tap out Pixie's novels — life might be very rosy indeed.

But people wanted to see Pixie and they wanted to *meet* her. They didn't want to meet boring Jane Gray, who probably worked tapestries in her spare time. They wanted to meet Pixie, with her glittering career and her scintillating social life. So when Jane appeared before the public eye, she pulled on Pixie's persona — as well as Pixie's dazzling array of designer threads. She was a complete and utter media consultant's dream. She posed for photographers with a smile as big as Kylie's, she flirted with chat show hosts — even the rebarbative ones (no, Strike 'rebarbative' — too obscure — sub. 'smarmy'). And she signed copies of her books until her nail extensions ached.

That's why she'd gone AWOL. Her latest book had waltzed straight onto the bestsellers list at number one, and she was so exhausted by the concomitant publicity that she'd even allow herself to get away with the word 'concomitant'.

How glad she was that she'd found this haven! Ballynahinch Castle was one of those splendid places that weren't too intimidating. She'd had holidays in more exotic and more luxurious places — the kinds of hotels where you had your own private infinity pool and staff salaamed you everywhere you went and there was a platoon of butlers, beauticians and bell boys on standby to pamper you (she especially hated the butlering because she'd much rather unpack her own underwear thank you very much). But once you'd visited one of those resorts, you'd visited them all.

And that's something Pixie thought was really strange about herself — she found those utopian resorts rather boring. She'd had herself deposited on a small desert island in the Maldives by launch once, to spend a day alone in a Bounty Bar 'paradise'. The resort on the main island had packed a cool-box full of delicacies and champagne and exotic fruit for her, but she had stupidly left her book behind (the one she was reading, not the one she was writing) and she had thought she might go insane with boredom. Tom Hanks in *Cast Away* couldn't have boarded that launch much faster than she did when it finally showed up.

So when she'd read about Ballynahinch Castle, she'd booked herself in. She'd jumped on a plane to Galway, and a driver had met her at the airport and driven her here through some of the most astonishing scenery she'd ever gazed agape at. And now she was sitting having coffee in her suite, admiring the view of the river beyond the big picture window and actually smelling that coffee for a change. She really *had* escaped, and boy did she need to. Everywhere she went in London there was evidence of the ex love of her life gazing moodily at her from the posters advertising his latest film, and there was evidence, too, of the woman who'd stolen him from her smiling triumphantly down from the posters advertising *her* latest film. Negotiating the tube was like negotiating the halls of Hades.

Ballynahinch wasn't the only good thing about this corner of the world. Pixie had discovered, during the four days since her arrival, a nearby picture postcard perfect fishing village called Kilrowan. She'd fallen so totally in love with it that she'd decided she was going to rent an apartment or a cottage there, to start work on her next novel.

She wasn't sure how her agent would feel about her cutting herself loose from the chain gang of authors who were currently dragging themselves and their books the length and breadth of the UK for publicity purposes, but she *had* to do it. Otherwise she would drive herself mad guffing on about herself to all-comers, and the new novel would never get written.

The person she felt sorriest for on these author tours was the PR girl, Camilla, who travelled with her and held her hand. Poor Camilla had to listen with a smile stapled to her face as Jane — or rather, Pixie — trotted out 'amusing' anecdote after 'amusing' anecdote about herself. Camilla had heard them all before on many, many occasions. When researchers on television chat shows came out with that staple question: 'Well! Have you any amusing anecdotes for us?' Pixie wanted to scream down the phone that nothing, *nothing* even remotely amusing had ever happened to her in her life. But these days people weren't interested in her amusing anecdotes. They just wanted to hear all about the affair between the rapacious film star Sophie Burke and He-Whose-Name-Must Not-Be-Spoken and how it had affected her life.

The sound of the phone jangled her back to the here and now. She set down her coffee cup, feeling guilty. Oh, no! Could someone have tracked her down? Should she ignore the call? But no worries. When she picked up, the reassuring brogue of the hotel receptionist came over the receiver.

'Ms Gray? Just to let you know that your ghillie is here. He's waiting for you in the lobby.'

'Thank you. I'm on my way down now.'

Her ghillie! Last week she wouldn't have had an idea what a ghillie was. But since coming to Ballynahinch she had learned that a ghillie was the man who helped out the tourists who came here on fishing holidays.

This was more like it, she thought, as she drained her coffee cup and took a last bite of shortbread. Jane Gray was going to forget all her troubles by spending a peaceful morning on the lake in a rowing boat, being tutored in the arcane art of fly-fishing by a local ghillie, and — oops! What if he was gorgeous? He could be the inspiration for the hero of her next novel (her last book but one *Westwood Ho!* — had featured a scuba-diving instructor).

As she rummaged in her bag for notebook and pen to slip into the pocket of her padded gilet, a twinge of conscience made Pixie switch on the mobile phone that had been turned off for the past four days. The phone told her that her message memory was full, and the single message she peeked at practically screamed at her from the screen. It was from her agent. WHERE R U? she read.

And Jane Gray felt just like a child playing

truant as she typed in 'Gon fishin!', pressed 'send', then turned her cell-phone off.

★ ★ ★

It was Friday of the Saint Patrick's Day weekend, and the bookshop had been busy since the middle of the afternoon, when the denizens of Dublin 4 had started rolling into town. A consignment of books had been delivered earlier, and Cleo Dowling, the proprietress of the shop, longed to be able to slit open the boxes and align the contents on the shelves. It was one of the aspects of her job she loved the most. Every time a delivery arrived she felt a bit like Julie Andrews in the song, except:

> Shiny new jackets and unblemished pages,
> Slim books by poets and fat books by sages,
> Bestselling titles with loads of bling bling —
> These were a few of *her* favourite things!

The very smell of the books, the touchy-feeliness of them, the embossed titles on the front, the enticing blurb on the back and the smooth uncracked spines, all combined to give her a little adrenalin rush. She supposed she felt about books the same way as some women feel about shoes or handbags. Different strokes! Give her Bantam over Bally any day. And on the days when a longed-for or much-heralded title finally emerged from its nest of cardboard and protective polystyrene, Cleo was often tempted to shut up shop, race home and curl up with the new arrival in front of the fire.

'Down for the weekend?'

She'd asked people that question over and over today. Her customers this afternoon were mostly those absentee residents of Kilrowan who only ever spent a handful of weeks here. Christmas, maybe; the occasional bank holiday weekend; a week or two in summer. They were here to chill, to escape from the bedlam that Dublin City now resembled.

She didn't blame them. The last time Cleo had been in Dublin had been a couple of months ago, when she'd driven up with her artist husband Pablo for an exhibition opening. She had barely recognized the city where she'd lived in a past life. Although gridlock had made the traffic virtually stationary, everyone was rushing, and everyone was *barging*. The city centre was crammed with snarling people who all looked at you as if they resented your very existence. Staff in newsagents' behaved as if they wanted to kill you when you proffered money for your *Hello!* magazine, supermarket checkout operators had been replaced by zombies, and the taxi driver who'd taken them to the gallery had definitely been a psychopath.

She supposed her new antipathy to the city had a lot to do with the fact that she'd downshifted to a sleepy village. Kilrowan in the winter was the sort of place where you'd half expect to see dust devils or tumbleweed rolling towards you along the deserted main street, and if you saw anyone out and about after midnight it gave you as much of a surprise as if a stranger

11

in a Stetson had just ambled into town.

The summer Kilrowan was as different from its winter sister as it was possible to be. They had to erect traffic lights on the main street to deal with the congestion, and tourist buses rumbled through the joint every five minutes. Cleo did a roaring trade then.

Trade today hadn't been half bad, either, come to think of it. Pixie Pirelli's latest book was flying off the shelves, and Cleo made a mental note to order more copies.

'Hello,' she said to a well-dressed refugee from Dublin 4. 'Down for the weekend? Welcome back.'

'Thanks, Cleo. How've you been keeping?'

'Grand. You?'

'Stressed. What can you recommend for some light weekend reading? Something escapist would be good.'

'Try the new Pixie Pirelli.'

'Oh — that's out already, is it?'

'There you go.'

Cleo indicated the dump bin that she'd set up by the cash desk. It was full of Pixie's new bestseller, with gratifying dents where all the sold copies had been. Her backlist titles — *Westwood Ho!* and *Venus in Versace* — had dents too. Pixie must be coining it.

The new Pirelli had a classy cover: the kind you'd reach out an automatic hand for. The author's name was prominent, and Cleo often wondered what it must feel like to walk into a bookshop and see your name all over the place, and maybe even a cardboard cut-out of your

12

standing sentinel against a cash desk.

'Thank you,' she said, sliding a twenty-euro note into the till and producing clinkety change. 'Enjoy your weekend!'

She turned her attention to the display in the window. The cardboard cut-out of the writer Colleen was looking a bit grubby. Colleen was so famous that she needed no other name — a bit like the French author Colette — and because she had a house in Kilrowan and was one of the village's most famous exports, her cut-out had practically taken up permanent residence in the bookshop window display.

Cleo reached for a packet of Cif Double Action wipes. She wondered as she exfoliated Colleen's cardboard face whether the diva herself would descend on Kilrowan for the bank holiday. She and her lover, Margot (who also happened to be Cleo's sister), spent most of their time these days on the island they'd bought in Clew Bay. But even the famously reclusive Colleen couldn't hack being completely cut off from the rest of the world, and they'd occasionally bestow a visit on Kilrowan in the manner of potentates on walkabout in some remote Himalayan village.

Since Margot and Colleen had shacked up together, Cleo had seen very little of her sister. She had — according to an interview with Colleen in the *Irish Times* — made herself indispensable as her lov*air*'s interface with the real world, handling all her business affairs and issuing pronouncements to the press when Colleen was too fatigued to give interviews.

13

Because she was very beautiful — and because she was officially Colleen's muse — they were often photographed together. The most recent shot doing the rounds of trade mags showed them with their arms wrapped around each other, perched on a cliff on their island, gazing out to sea with enigmatic expressions, like Greta Garbo in *Queen Christina*. Pablo had drawn horns on Margot's head.

Colleen's latest *magnum opus* was due to hit the shelves soon. You'd be sure to need more time than a bank holiday weekend to wade through *that*, Cleo conjectured, as she finished wiping what looked like a jam stain off Colleen's chin. She'd read in the *Bookseller* magazine that the book had 892 pages.

'Oh, look, Abigail! The new Pixie Pirelli's out.'

A couple of girls had just come into the shop. They were young, beautiful, tanned, gym-toned — they were flawless, actually — and they had identical Victoria Beckham hairstyles. They were both sporting smart/casual: designer trainers, T-shirts with provocative slogans (T-shirts in March!), jeans with exclusive labels, and Gucci shades doubling as hair-bands. They were *rich*.

So was Cleo, but she'd never really got used to the fact. Being rich made her feel like a bad actor, or an impostor. It wasn't that she was uncomfortable or guilty about being rich, it was just that she didn't really know how to *behave* like a rich person. Neither did her husband, Pablo, she supposed. But at least he earned his money, through his paintings. Cleo had just got rich by chance when she'd won the Lotto.

14

Her lottery euros had paid for this bookshop when it had come on the market a year or so ago, and she had never been happier. Owning her own bookshop had been the ultimate wish fulfilment for her, and sometimes she still pinched herself when she realized that she, Cleo Dowling, bookseller and millionaire, was living her dream.

She lived her dream best when the shop was quiet, and she could sit on her stool by the cash register, reading — or writing one of the erotic short stories that Pablo loved so much. She'd embarked on a novel once, and it had been shite. Cleo had learned then that it was one thing to love *reading* books, quite another to love *writing* them. She enjoyed writing the stories though, and enjoyed it even more when Pablo acted them out. They got up to some extraordinary shenanigans in the bedroom of number 5, the Blackthorns, which was where they'd set up home.

'Nice cover.' The Posh-haired princesses were examining the jacket of Cleo's sister's book. 'Never heard of her though. Margot d'Arcy? Who she?'

'Dunno. Looks boring, anyway.'

Margot's slender novel, *Proust's Sewing Machine*, had been published quite recently. It had gone out under the aegis of the literary publishing house that handled Colleen, and Cleo suspected that Colleen had threatened to throw a diva strop if they didn't publish her lovair's novel as well. Cleo had only sold two copies of Margot's book in as many months, but she always had to remember to display it face out on the shelf under 'New releases' in case her sister came into the shop to spy on it.

That was one of the disadvantages of living in a village where so many residents were writers. You had to be careful not to offend anyone by making sure that their newest offspring was prominently displayed. If you didn't, they came in and did it themselves, anyway. She could see them on the security camera, surreptitiously transferring their books from where they were languishing in sheltered housing under the disadvantaged letters of the alphabet — 'R, S & T' — to the shelves where all the bestsellers hung out together, like a clique of the most popular members of the golf club.

The princesses who had just come into the shop were hanging in the 'New Releases' section, helping themselves to loads of glossy titles in hardback. Cleo had felt so sorry for the girl who'd come into the shop earlier to ask piteously when the new Pixie Pirelli would be out in more affordable mass market format that she'd given her a free copy.

'*The Shops*! Excellent. I'm buying this.'

'Don't you already have it?'

'I lost my copy. Ha! I'll leave it open at the page on vouchers so that Mother will hopefully take the hint and allow me to choose my birthday present myself. I am *so* tired of having to return every single thing she buys me. You should have seen the ostrich-skin bag she got me for my birthday. It was *beyond* hideous.'

'I know what I'm getting for *my* birthday.'

'Oh? Tell!'

'Daddy's come up with a brilliant idea. He's going to commission Pablo MacBride to paint my portrait.'

'Oh — that *is* a brilliant idea.'

What? No, it is *not*! thought Cleo. That, sweetheart, is a *ferocious* idea, and I will do my double damnedest to make sure it does not happen. This streamlined baby was going nowhere *near* Pablo MacBride. To her reasonably certain knowledge, Pablo had never had a portrait commissioned by a woman under the age of thirty, and she didn't want temptation in the form of this particularly succulent nymphette posing for him. Miss Abigail might be over the age of consent, but she had the unsullied appearance of jailbait. Cleo would have to do a little, very subtle, dissuasion when the princess's daddy approached her husband with his chequebook.

'Maybe I should ask Daddy if he'd think about getting one done of *me*,' said the other princess.

Not if I can help it, sister!

With a big fake smile, Cleo accepted the hundred-euro note that was being proffered over the counter, and handed back two euro and forty-six cents in change. She was glad to see that it went into the Cancer Research Box that she kept by the cash register.

'Enjoy your weekend.'

'You too!'

Mm hm, Cleo thought grimly as the shop door closed on the two gorgeous designer denim asses. The way things were looking, a portrait by Pablo MacBride was set to be the new must-have status symbol for the *jeunesse dorée*, and if Cleo was to divert attention from the delicacies that might soon be on offer on Sèvres porcelain to her complete ride of a husband, she was going to have to work very, very hard indeed on a new short story.

2

'Why don't you come down? Have a look around the village, get a feel for the place?'

Hazel found herself smiling. What was it about Hugh Hennessy's voice? That soft Galway brogue was very seductive.

'I suppose I could. It's the bank holiday weekend, though. That means the roads will be busy.'

'It also means you'll have longer to spend here.'

'True.' Hazel had planned to spend the weekend in Wicklow with that prick Mick, but since he was now ancient history, the plan was too. She had nothing better to do — and because she was very good at making decisions, she didn't deliberate for very long on this one. She'd go.

'OK. I'll leave work a little early, throw some stuff into a bag, and hit the road. I could get to Kilrowan at around ten o'clock.'

'Cool. I'll have supper waiting for you.'

'No worries. I can get something to eat at the hotel.'

'What hotel?'

'I'm sure there's a hotel in the village, isn't there? It's a very popular tourist destination, after all.'

'There are a couple of hotels and some B&Bs, but none of them bother staying open in the

19

winter months. It doesn't make financial sense.'

'Oh. Where'll I stay, then?'

'You can stay in my house. There's plenty of room.'

'Oh.' Oh fuck. She couldn't stay in the house of someone she hadn't even met. What if he was a serial killer, like that taxi driver who'd just been arrested?

'I'm not a serial killer, if that's what you're thinking.'

'Oh — no! Of course you're not.' She could phone Erin, tell her where she was going and leave his name, number and address with her.

'Phone a girlfriend,' he suggested. 'Tell her where you're going.'

'Actually,' she said, 'that's just what I was thinking. I hope you don't mind.'

'Not at all. I'm glad to hear it. Means you're as sussed as I'd hoped you'd be. I'll e-mail directions, and you can phone if there's a problem.'

'Oh-*kay*. Well, I'll see you later, then. Around ten o'clock.'

'I'm looking forward to meeting you, Hazel.'

'Likewise.'

The sound of the phone being put down was like a wake-up call. What was she *doing*, driving to the other side of Ireland on a rainy bank holiday Friday to stay with someone who — for all she knew — might be the Connemara equivalent of Leatherface in *The Texas Chainsaw Massacre*? What was she doing, judging someone's character solely on the basis of his voice? He could be a better voice-over artist than

20

the top dog she'd worked with recently on the Grant & Wainwright commercial. He could be a consummate conman. She remembered the silky voice of the psychopath who'd skinned the girls in *The Silence of the Lambs*, and how plausible *he* had sounded. She, Hazel MacNamara, the most clued-in gal she knew, was behaving like the girl in the scary movie who goes down into the basement when she really should know better.

But she was intrigued. She'd talked at length to Hugh Hennessy, and had been impressed not just by his accent, but by his acumen.

The Kilrowan Arts Festival had been flagging in recent years, and Hugh wanted to inject it with new blood, give it a facelift. The Dublin 4 crowd had hijacked the occasion, and it was his intention to wrest control back into the hands of the people who actually *lived* there. He also wanted to make sure that the world knew about the festival, because America was still afraid of flying since the horror of September 11, and tourism was down. Kilrowan needed to put itself firmly back on the tourist map after another winter on the skids. The job wasn't worth a whole lot of money to her, but it might be more interesting than some of the stuff she'd been working on recently. The new Grant & Wainwright campaign was wrecking her head: the marketing manager kept rewriting her copy.

She speed-dialled Erin, filled her in, and asked her advice.

'Simple,' said Erin. 'Google him.'

So she did. She googled the Kilrowan Arts

Festival and its organizer, Hugh Hennessy, whose mugshot was displayed on the site. He was a good-looking son of a bitch. The site didn't carry much information on him, apart from the fact that he owned stables and had been running the festival part-time for eight years now, but she learned a little more about the event. Colleen, the famous author, had instigated a literary award for best short story by a woman, and Pablo, the famous painter, donated a painting each year to be auctioned for charity. The end of each festival was marked by a ceilí in the village hall. A ceilí! How quaint!

There was also a list of 'Friends' of the festival, who had donated money. If you donated more than 500 euros, you were promoted to 'Best Friend'. Several celebrities were featured on the 'Best Friends' list, and Hazel found herself thinking of ways to hook others. Her organizer was full of contact numbers for celebs, and each number she inserted made her feel like a big game hunter bagging a trophy. The big plus about an arts festival was that it had kudos. Celebs would open a supermarket or a golf club for loadsamoney, but they'd open an arts festival for free.

She pressed redial.

'Well? What do you think?' said Erin. 'He's a fit-looking motherfucker, isn't he?'

'Did you google him too?'

'I did.'

'So what do *you* think?'

'Seems kosher enough.'

'Mm. I reckon so, too. I'm gonna go.'

'Go, girl. If you're not back by midnight on Monday I'll send out a search party. You do know, incidentally, that bodies have been turning up in bogs in Connemara?'

'Are you winding me up?'

'Yep. What are you going to wear?'

'Oh — country stuff. You know.'

'Have you *got* any country stuff, city girl?'

'Yes, actually.'

'Real country stuff? Like Barbour and green wellies?'

'Near as dammit. I've a great pair of walking boots.'

'Better pack some jodhpurs, too.'

'Jodhpurs?'

'Yeah. In case you fancy a ride.'

'Get off the phone, Erin.'

★   ★   ★

Once she finished tying up loose ends at work, Hazel dashed into her bedroom and packed her suiter. She wished she had time to shower and change, but the loose ends had taken her longer than she thought, and she really wanted to get on the road before the traffic started building up. She packed her walking boots (baby blue suede — she hadn't been able to resist them!), her leather jacket, her Indian Rose jeans and her Alberta Ferretti tracksuit. She packed a little black dress, vertiginous heels and dangly earrings in the event of dinner out somewhere smart. She packed night attire and underwear and her fabulous Lulu Guinness make-up bag

23

— the Toblerone one that all her friends coveted. She packed her book — the new Pixie Pirelli — and then unpacked it and replaced it with something that would lend her more artistic credibility: a heavyweight novel by Colleen that she hadn't managed to finish yet.

Once she hit the road it was a five-hour drive from Dublin — through pretty uneventful scenery until Connemara hove into view. The tedium of the drive and the blathering of the evening radio was punctuated from time to time by flippant text messages from Erin. 'Bet u pact ur agent provos' was a fairly representative sample.

And, in fact, Hazel had.

*   *   *

She rolled into Kilrowan village at half past ten. Once she'd got through Galway the drive had been tough going — the road through Connemara was a long and winding one, and she'd always hated driving in the dark. She was feeling tired now, and hungry, and she'd murder a glass of wine. She was also dying for a pee.

There were posh cars parked bumper to bumper in the village. They all had this year's Dublin registration plates, and they looked pretty damn incongruous against the background of unpretentious fishermen's cottages that lined the main street. Hazel drove past cosy-looking pubs, homely-looking shops and a post office that looked like the one Postman Pat set out from to deliver to Granny Goggins and the gang. A couple of cats blinked at her from windowsills, and a dog with 'Hello Kitty' hair accessories was trotting along the pavement, looking as if it was on an important assignment. She passed the last straggle of houses to find the sea on her left, about half a mile distant. A full moon was reflected on the water, lending the surface the appearance of beaten silver, and there were stars up there too in the night sky. She couldn't remember the last time she'd looked up to see stars in the jaundiced city sky.

Hugh had told her to take the first road to the left about a mile and a half outside the village, but when she came to the turn off she wasn't certain whether she had the right one. It was more of a track than a road, with a strip of grass growing down the middle. She pulled over and reached for the map he'd e-mailed her but before she could consult it, something happened that gave her a fright.

There was a man sitting in the dark on a five-bar gate directly opposite the passenger window. He was wearing a greasy gabardine tied at the waist with a length of baling twine, a woolly knitted hat and wellington boots. And there was a rifle propped up against the gatepost. Jesus H. Christ! She tried to pretend she hadn't seen him, but he raised a hand in jaunty salute at her. Oh no! Now he was getting off the gate and coming round to the driver's side. He bent down and looked at her through the window, then made a 'roll down the window' gesture with his hand. Oh, God. What should she do? Should she just drive on? But she couldn't do that — his

25

elbow was resting on the roof, and if she drove off suddenly he'd topple over. There was nothing else for it — she'd have to talk to him. She pressed the button, and the window slid down.

'Grand evening,' said the man.

'Yes!'

'Is it lost you are, ma'am?'

'I was looking for the equestrian centre.'

'Ah. The old Hennessy house. It's Scar you're looking for, so?'

'Scar?'

'Young Hugh.'

'Well — yes — I am looking for a Hugh Hennessy.'

'Then you're on the right track. Just head straight down there until you come to the big gates. You can't miss them.'

'Oh. Thank you very much.'

'You're welcome, ma'am.'

And with that the man stood back to allow her to proceed on her way. She could see him in the rear-view mirror as she turned and drove in the direction he'd indicated, clambering manfully back onto his gate.

Scar? The old Hennessy house? Um. OK, Hazel. It looks like you've reached the bit in the movie where you peer at the screen from behind your fingers and tell the stupid heroine not to go there.

Her phone rang.

'Yes?'

'Is that you, now, Hazel? I can see headlights.' It was Hugh Hennessy's voice.

'Um. Yes.'

'I'll put plates in the oven.'

He was gone. Hazel gulped, changed gears and continued on down the track, wondering if she should put the car into reverse.

She passed between two big wrought-iron gates to see a gracious Georgian house looking down at her. At least, it had once been gracious, but it appeared as if it had been allowed to run to seed a bit. Ivy was climbing all over the walls, the paint on the door was peeling, and a couple of panes in the big bay windows were cracked. It was a horror film scout's dream.

Oh, shit. What had she done? She picked up her phone and just managed to text Erin with 'Fone in 10!' when the front door of the house opened and Hugh Hennessy, tall, dark and loose-limbed, stepped through. He stood there, silhouetted against the golden light that spilled from the doorway, and raised a hand in greeting. Hazel slipped her feet into her heels, opened the car door and got out, still holding her phone in her hand and wishing it was a gun.

'Hi!' he said. 'Tough drive?'

'Yeah.'

'In that case you'll be glad to know that there's a casserole in the oven and a bottle of red breathing. Let me help you with your bags.'

'Thanks.'

She ducked back into the car to throw the switch that released the lock on the boot, and when she emerged, Hugh had opened it and was hefting her bags out. She suddenly felt embarrassed by the girly Lulu Guinness confection that he'd hooked with one finger. He swung the lid of the boot back down, then gestured to her to precede him up the steps and through the front door. There was a glorious smell of cooking wafting up from the end of the corridor.

'Nice to meet you at last,' said Hugh. He shut the front door behind him, then turned to her, extending a hand.

'Likewise,' she said, taking his hand. Good handshake, she noticed. 'Great smell.'

'Thanks. I like to think I do a mean casserole. Expect you'd like to freshen up before dinner?'

'Yes, please.'

'I'll bring your bags up.'

'Thanks.'

She followed him upstairs to the first floor. The room he showed her to was furnished eighties-style. There were pictures of pop stars on the wall, and postcards proliferated. There was also a big, framed collage of family photographs.

'Excuse the décor. This was my sister's room. I've only recently taken possession of the house, and the place is a bit of a mess.'

'This was your childhood home?'

'Yes. I moved back in when my father died.'

'Oh. I'm sorry to hear that. And your mother? Is she still . . . '

'No.'

'I'm sorry,' said Hazel again.

'It was a long time ago. I'll let you get on,' he added before she could say anything more. 'The bathroom's at the end of the corridor. Come on down to the kitchen when you're ready. It's in the basement.' He set her suiter on the bed and then he was gone.

Hazel waited until she heard his footsteps hit the bottom of the stairs before heading to the loo. The bathroom was old-fashioned, with vinyl wallpaper and a suite in an unattractive shade of avocado green. It was, however, scrupulously clean — apart from a patch of mildew in one corner of the ceiling.

Back in the bedroom she took in the rest of her surroundings as she unpacked her bag. Hugh's sister had clearly had a thing about clowns. There were clown ornaments and clown stuffed dolls, and there was even a laundry basket with a be-ruffed clown's head as a handle. Hazel found the notion of sleeping there with a load of clowns ogling her mildly disturbing.

As she plonked Colleen's weighty tome on the table by the bed, she saw that a little jug of fuchsia had been set there. There were also a couple of back issues of Country Life and a basket of stuff that had been purloined from hotels — the usual suspects: sewing kit, shoeshine sponge, shower cap. How thoughtful!

Moving to the collage, she studied the photographs of friends and family. They told her that Hugh's sister was a little older than he was. She had been a devastatingly pretty teenager, and was clearly cracked about all things equestrian, because a lot of the photographs had been taken at gymkhanas, and featured her holding aloft trophies and rosettes. One rather spooky shot showed a family party. Hugh was dressed as a vampire, his sister as a witch, and another boy — his brother? — was made up to look like a werewolf. In the background a woman dressed as Morticia Addams was holding a Hallowe'en lantern aloft. She had Hugh's cheekbones, and there was a look of him too in her solemn gaze. Hazel took her to be the children's mother.

Another photograph featured the three kids on horseback. Hugh was the only one looking directly to camera; sister and brother were racing ahead in a blur of motion. Hazel wondered if the brother was as good-looking as his siblings. In the only photograph to feature the children in a formal pose, a clown sticker had been stuck on his face.

Before going back downstairs, Hazel took a final look at herself in the mirror. She checked her make-up and bumphed her hair about a bit, but decided against spritzing herself with scent. Freshly applied scent said too much.

Once in the basement, her nose told her the way to the kitchen. The room took up the greater part of the lower ground floor, and it was homely and unpretentious and warm from the Aga. A couple of Labradors came to greet her, and one of them jumped up and put its front paws on her thighs.

Hugh turned from where he was karate-chopping baked potatoes. 'Down, Honey!' he said, then: 'Sorry about that,' he added. 'She's a bit over-enthusiastic.'

'No problem!' said Hazel, suspecting she sounded rather too bright. She didn't know many dogs, and this one had just pulled a thread in the cashmere of her Lainey Keogh skirt. She realized she probably looked a bit stupid, standing in what was quintessentially a country kitchen in her designer gear and high heels. Hugh was dead casual, in jeans and open-necked shirt.

'Sit down,' he said, indicating the kitchen table, which had been set for two. He ambled over to where a bottle stood open on a shelf above the Aga, poured wine into two glasses and handed her one. Then he raised his in a toast. 'To the reinvention of the Kilrowan Arts Festival,' he said. 'Here's hoping you can work your PR magic on it.'

'Here's hoping.' She mirrored his gesture, and took a very welcome gulp of wine. 'Thanks for the little touches, by the way.'

'Little touches?'

Oh, God! What a stupid way of putting it! 'The — um — flowers and the magazines and stuff.'

'You're welcome.'

Hugh set his glass down on the table and moved back to the Aga. He reached for a pair of oven gloves, and took a casserole dish from the oven. The gorgeous aroma intensified, and the dogs sniffed the air. The only sound in the room was the sound of their tails thumping against the flagstoned floor.

Hazel felt the need to say something — anything. She tended to talk too much because she found prolonged silences unnerving. 'Why were you karate-chopping the potatoes?' she asked.

31

'It's the best way of making sure they stay fluffy inside, according to Nigel Slater.'

'Are you a fan of his?'

'Yes.'

'I'm more of a Nigella Lawson gal, myself.' Ow. Why had she said that? Nigella Lawson always conjured up images of sucky, slurpy, sexy stuff.

'How was your journey down?' he asked politely, as he ladled food onto plates.

'Pretty uneventful. Until the last minute, that is. I stopped to check on directions, and an ancient lunatic with a rifle jumped out at me from a gate.'

'That'd be my stable hand Benjy, out after a fox.'

'Oh! Oh, I do beg your pardon! I'm terribly — '

'No need to apologize.'

'Why was he sitting on a gate?'

Hugh gave her a quizzical look. 'You're very 'city', aren't you? Country people sit on gates all the time. Sometimes they shoot the breeze if there's anyone around worth shooting it with; more often they just sit and ruminate. Or 'stand and stare', as in the W.H. Davies poem.'

' 'What is this life if, full of care, we have no time to stand and stare?' '

'You know it? I'm impressed.'

She didn't tell him that the only reason she knew it was because she'd used it in an advertising campaign for an upmarket country house hotel once.

'Excuse me,' she said, as her phone whispered

to her from her bag. Hazel had opted for the 'cicada' ring tone, because it was soothing. Any other mobile tones she'd sampled jangled her nerves, and she was stressed enough as it was, most days. As she'd expected, Erin's name was on the display.

'Hazel MacNamara,' she said in her crispest PR voice.

'Hi, hon. You been hacked to pieces by a chainsaw yet?'

'Oh, hello. How are you?'

'It's not me you should be concerned about. How's life down in the basement? Been there yet?'

'Well, yes, actually. That's fine. Yes, two o'clock on Tuesday is perfect.'

'What's his address, again? Elm Street?'

'I'm sorry, I can't talk right now. I'm just about to sit down to dinner.'

'Let me guess. Liver and fava beans washed down with a nice Chianti? Heh heh heh.'

'I'll talk to you then.'

'Whatever you do, don't go in the shower.'

'Goodbye.' Hazel pressed 'end call' with a clumsy thumb. Except it wasn't 'end call' she pressed — it was 'loudspeaker mode', and for several mortifying moments the sound of Erin doing a bad imitation of the shower scene theme from *Psycho* echoed around the kitchen.

'I take it that was the friend you asked to phone to make sure you hadn't hooked up with the serial killer?' said Hugh, setting a plate in front of her.

'No!' she said, before she had time to think. 'It

33

was em — business.'

'I see,' he said laconically.

Hazel stuffed her phone back in her bag, and busied herself with the buckle, wanting to strangle Erin. The buckle was being recalcitrant, and her fingers were clumsier than ever. She finally managed it, then leaned against the back of her chair with a big sigh. 'Thank God for a decent supper,' she said. 'That drive's left me stressed to the nines.'

'Take it easy, Hazel,' said Hugh, taking up the wine bottle. 'And let me pour you a little more Chianti.'

★　★　★

The first thing Hazel saw when she woke the next morning was the little jug of fuchsias on her bedside table. The second thing she saw was the alarm clock. She hadn't set it before she went to bed last night — or, more accurately, this morning — and it was now nearly ten o'clock. Dear God in heaven, that was bold of her! She was here in a consultative capacity, after all, and should, strictly speaking, be keeping business hours.

She shrugged her robe on over her pyjamas (she'd opted for brushed cotton PJs rather than one of her flimsy nightgowns. She hadn't wanted to give Hugh Hennessy any come-hitherish notions), then ran down the corridor to the bathroom — but when she tried the door, it was locked.

'Oh, sorry!' she said.

'I'm just finishing shaving,' came Hugh's voice. 'There's a loo in the cloakroom downstairs, and the kettle's on for coffee.'

'Thanks!'

In the downstairs cloakroom, Hazel peed, washed her hands, and splashed cold water on her face. She peered at her reflection in the mirror above the wash-hand basin and wiped a mascara smudge from under her eye. She'd been too tired to do her usual meticulous cleansing routine before she'd gone to bed last night, and had just done the face-wipe/moisture-slap thing.

The cloakroom was full of country stuff — wellie boots, raincoats, umbrellas, walking sticks, a chainsaw, dog leads. Hugh had said he'd take her on a guided tour of the village today, and he planned to bring the dogs along as part of their constitutional. Honey was overweight, apparently, and needed regular exercise.

She'd decided that she quite liked Honey, who had sat gazing up at her as she ate casserole (very good) last night, giving her big pleading looks which Hugh instructed Hazel to harden her heart to. She wasn't sure about the other one, though, Prue. She had kept giving her mistrustful glances. She'd ask Hugh if she could have Honey to walk this morning. Walking the dogs! What a splendidly country thing to do. And she could wear her pristine new walking boots!

She whistled a little tune as she let herself out of the cloakroom and shimmied down the hallway.

''Don't worry. Be happy.'' Hugh was coming down the stairs.

'Sorry?'

'That's the tune you're whistling.'

'Oh. Right.'

'Coffee?'

Hazel had planned on showering and getting made up before she had breakfast, but he'd spotted her barefaced now, and he hadn't passed out or looked appalled, so she must pass muster. What the hell!

'Coffee sounds good.'

In the kitchen she said hi to Honey, and hunkered down to make a bit of a fuss of her while Hugh spooned coffee into a cafetière. Prue just gave her a disdainful look, as if to say: What are you doing in my master's kitchen in your night attire, slut?

She ignored Prue. 'How long have you been living here?' she asked Hugh.

'I moved in around six months ago, after my father died.'

'Where were you before that?'

'In the mews across the yard.' He indicated through the window a mews house on the other side of the stable yard. It was typical of its kind, whitewashed, with a half-door and geraniums in troughs on the windowsills.

'Oh, it's charming!'

'It was convenient for work.'

'In the stables?'

'Yeah. I've to be up at the crack of dawn every day to muck out.'

'Oops. I feel guilty, now, for being a lie-abed this morning.'

'Was Honor's bed comfortable?'

36

He'd told her last night that his sister's name was Honor. She was married now and living abroad, as was his brother Harry.

'Yes. It was fine,' she said. 'It's a long time since I've slept in a single bed.' Oh, *Jesus*! Where had *that* come from?

Hugh refrained from comment, and poured coffee. 'Help yourself to milk and sugar,' he said.

She sat down at the table, wishing he might talk some more. He was a man of few words, she'd noticed, except when it came to the subject of the Kilrowan Arts Festival. Their conversation last night had centred around that, and ideas for fund-raising.

'Are you going to carry on living here?' she asked him now. 'It's a very big house for one person.' Hel*lo*! She might as well have said: Will you marry me, please, so that I can move in here and have your babies? What was she *on* today?

'I plan to.'

'It'll take a while to do up.' And what was the subtext here? I could help. You could do with a feminine touch? *Stop*, Hazel! 'Do the stables do good business?'

'It's like everything in Kilrowan. We do great in the summer, but everything takes a downturn in the winter. Still, that has its advantages. Gives me more time to spend with the horses.'

'You must love riding.' Eek!

'Yeah. I'm passionate about animals.'

A silence fell. Hazel flailed around for something else to say. 'It must be fantastic to earn a living doing the thing you love.' Wow! Inspired! 'I suppose you were the kind of person

37

who learned to ride before you could walk?'

'I was.'

'Your sister too, to judge by the photographs in her bedroom.'

'Yeah. Well. She was horse mad until the accident happened.'

'She had a riding accident?'

'No. The accident that killed our mother. She swerved to avoid a runaway horse and the jeep overturned. My sister never got back up on a horse after that. It was her mount. Gigi.'

Hazel's hands flew to her face. 'Oh, God! Oh — what a totally tragic story.'

He nodded; looked down at his knuckles.

Hazel felt just awful; keenly aware that no words were adequate. She felt an impulse to reach out and take his hand in hers, but that was too intimate a gesture. Silence buzzed loudly in the room, and then, thankfully, the awkwardness was dissipated by the sudden arrival of the lunatic who'd accosted her the night before. He breezed in through the back door and wiped his boots vigorously on the doormat.

'Morning, ma'am!' he greeted her. 'You found him, so. Mister Scar, sir, Christabel's baulky. Will I tether her?'

'Yeah, Benjy, please do. And get on to O'Flaherty.'

'Will do. Give's a mug of that there coffee, and I'll take it out to the yard.' He took a mug from the mug tree by the kettle, advanced to the table, and started pouring.

'Sit down and join us, why don't you?' invited Hugh.

38

'No, no, no, now. I'm sure you've important things to be discussing. I'll get on.' Benjy helped himself to milk and three spoons of sugar, then he saluted the pair of them and went back outside.

Hazel felt a little bewildered. It must have shown in her expression, because Hugh gave her one of his rare smiles.

'You're wondering why Benjy called me Scar?'

'Yes,' she admitted. 'That's exactly what I'm thinking.'

'It's my nickname,' he said. 'Has been since the accident. I was in the jeep when it overturned. I was thrown clear, but I had a close encounter with a vicious *cheval de frise*.'

'*Cheval de . . . ?*'

'A spiked fence. I was lucky to get away with just a scar. I could have been impaled.'

'Jesus!'

'I knew the kids in the changing rooms would be calling me Scar behind my back, just as they called the fat boy Blubber, and the lad with eczema Flaky. Kids are vicious buggers. So I pre-empted them by telling them to call me Scar to my face.'

'That was very brave of you,' said Hazel.

'Not really. Before the accident I was Poncy Percy. My middle name is Percival, for my grandfather. Anything was better than Poncy Percy, and Scar gave me street cred. The nickname stuck.'

Wow. For Hugh, these few sentences constituted an oration. She'd learned more about him in the past minute than she had over dinner last night. 'How very clever. Does everyone call you that?'

'All my old school friends do.'

'Scar's a much cooler nickname than the one I was landed with at school. They called me Loo-lah. Get it?'

'Um. No.'

'From 'nuts'. You know — Hazelnut. And actually, it turned out to be a real misnomer. I was one of the more sensible ones. I even ended up being head girl.'

'Your parents must have been proud of you.'

'Mm.'

Hazel didn't want to talk about her parents. She found them highly embarrassing. Her father was a professional clown and mime artist, and her mother had been a singer in a punk rock band: Hazel had been named for the punk rocker Hazel O'Connor. And of course school open days had been a nightmare. Her parents would turn up with multicoloured hair and piercings, wearing outrageous clothes. Bringing friends home was disastrous: her mother would play punk rock albums really loud, and sing and dance along to them. Walking down Grafton Street was a no-no because she would more than likely run into her father disguised as a living statue, and her friends would throw small change into the hat at his feet just to wind her up. No wonder she'd ended up working in a proper job.

She drained the last of her coffee and got to her feet. 'I'd better get my shower out of the way,' she said. 'And then we can hit the village. I'm dying to see it.'

'I hope you won't be disappointed. It's very small, and it'll be crowded with Patrick's Day visitors.'

'Tourists?'

Hugh looked despondent. 'Sadly, no. Mostly people down *from* Dublin for the weekend. Tourist numbers are way down on last year and the year before.'

'Well, I'm going to change all that,' said Hazel with mock-hauteur. 'Come next August, Kilrowan, Connemara, is gonna *rock*!'

She turned and left the kitchen. In the hallway, Prue was lying at the foot of the stairs, chin on paws, eyeing her belligerently. Hazel thought it mightn't be a bad idea to try and get the dog on her side.

'Hi, Prue!' she said brightly.

But Prue kept her head firmly on her paws. And as Hazel side-stepped her, she heard the bitch growl.

3

It was bank holiday Sunday, and the bookshop had been busy. Cleo was nearly sold out of Pixie Pirelli, and she'd sent off an e-mail to the distributors to order more copies in. She was just about to shut up shop and turn the Open sign on the door to Closed, when the land line rang. It was Pablo.

'Hey, baby! Guess what date it is?'

'What date is it?'

'It's our wedding anniversary! I only just realized.'

'It is?'

'Yep. It's a year to the day since we did the barefoot on a beach thing. Let's celebrate!'

'Yay! Ballynahinch Castle! You book it, and you'd better — oh. Bummer.'

'What's wrong?'

Cleo lowered her voice. 'I was just about to shut up shop, but someone's come in.'

'Tell them to go away.'

'No. She looks nice. I'll allow her to browse for five minutes.' She smiled at the woman who'd just come into the shop, then resumed her normal tone. 'Have we left it too late, d'you think? For Ballynahinch? It *is* the Patrick's Day weekend, after all. They're probably booked out.'

'I'm sure they'll sort something for us. We're their best customers.'

The observation was more than likely true.

Neither Pablo nor Cleo was remotely interested in matters culinary, and they ate out a lot — either in the restaurant attached to O'Toole's, the local pub, or in the posher Ballynahinch Castle. Or else they ate in bed, or had sandwiches on the go. Cleo did a mean egg sandwich with diced rashers.

'OK. Go for it,' she said.

'I'll book a room while I'm at it. That means I won't have to worry about driving home.'

'Good idea. I'll see you at home in half an hour. Any phone calls, incidentally? Any messages?' The tone of Cleo's voice was deceptively casual. She had said nothing to Pablo about the conversation she'd overheard in the bookshop a couple of days ago, when the posh totties had chatted about having their portraits painted. She was curious to know whether anyone had approached him about a commission.

'I dunno. I haven't checked the machine. I've been in the studio all day.'

Pablo's studio was at the bottom of the garden of number 5, the Blackthorns. It was one of those Scandinavian timber constructions, and he'd had it built to spec because he'd wanted it flooded with light. The underfloor heating made the joint exceptionally cosy, which was good news for Pablo, who often worked wearing nothing but a sarong. It made Cleo laugh to see him set out on chilly mornings in a big beaverskin coat and boots to cover the sixty or so yards to the end of the garden, knowing that underneath he was half naked. Sometimes he didn't bother with the beaverskin and just sprinted the distance. She'd love to know what the neighbours thought, but of course in winter they rarely had any neighbours because the houses were all unoccupied.

'Did you get any good work done today?' she asked him now.

'I got some work done. Whether it's 'good' or not is debatable. I finished *Margot with Pig*.'

'Is she going to like it?'

'She's going to love it. I put her smiling with feral, pointed teeth. And I gave her bigger boobs, and the pig looks as if it's smitten.'

'The pig being a metaphor for . . . ?'

'For whatever you damn well please, babe. Now get off the phone. I want to get on to Ballynahinch so we can celebrate our anniversary in style. Or would you rather go and overnight in the health spa?'

This suggestion met with a deathly silence.

'Sorry. Bad joke,' said Pablo. 'Bye.'

Cleo put the phone down, then opened her till drawer and finished doing the cash. She'd taken a lot today. Good. That would cover dinner tonight. It was weird how she still thought that way — calculating the cost of an evening out, even though she was a lottery millionaire. She still entertained middle-class values about most things, and rarely bought expensive or designer items unless they were in a sale.

She hummed along to the Mozart that was playing over the sound system, then decided that she ought to turn it off as a hint to her browser that she was about to shut up shop. She shot the

44

woman a look. Then she shot her another one. There was something familiar about her, something *déjà-vu*-ish . . . Ah, but of course. She was probably famous — and there was nothing unusual about *that* in Kilrowan. The villagers had become quite blasé about the number of famous people who roamed the village streets — or, more accurately — street. Loads of famous people had holiday homes here, and movies were always being made in the vicinity. One of her favourite books ever — *Mimi's Remedies* — had been adapted and made into a film here, and because the director had needed hordes of extras, Cleo had even had a part in it.

The browser was taking her time. She replaced a book about household emergencies on a shelf, and reached for another one.

OK. It was time for a hint or two. Cleo reached under the counter, killed the Mozart and flicked off the light switch that illuminated the window display. The display was looking good. When she'd learned from a reliable source that Colleen would not be in town over the bank holiday, she'd substituted Pixie Pirelli's cut-out for Colleen's and —

Eureka! *That's* who it was. The woman riffling through the household emergency section was none other than Pixie Pirelli! And it was no wonder that it had taken Cleo so long to recognize her. In person she was much less glamorous than her cut-out. The Pixie in the window stood arms akimbo, smiling a great big smile and wearing a Roberto Cavalli-looking outfit, and shoes that were no more than a pair of heels and a couple of ribbons. This flesh and blood Pixie was dressed in jeans, walking boots and a puffa jacket, and she sported a baseball cap — presumably to complete the disguise. The poor thing would badly need to wear a disguise, Cleo conjectured, after all the recent brouhaha in the press about her love life.

'Excuse me?' she said now. 'You're Pixie Pirelli, aren't you?'

The other woman turned to her with a slightly guarded expression. 'Yes. Yes, I am,' she said. 'Would you like me to sign stock for you?'

'Oh, please!' Cleo shimmied out from behind the cash desk and moved to Pixie's dump bin.

Pixie approached, and her guarded expression became animated when she took in the dents. 'Oh, how fabulous,' she said. 'Look at all the dents! It's selling well for you, is it?'

'It's flying,' said Cleo happily. 'And I wish I'd ordered more in. If I'd known that you were coming, I'd have baked a cake, as they say.'

'No problem. If you have copies by next week I'll be delighted to come back and sign more.'

Pixie produced a sparkly pen from her backpack. It was the exact same shade as the jacket of her book, Cleo noticed. She'd also noticed that Pixie was quite posh. She spoke in a rather jolly hockey-sticks English accent that reminded her of Helena Bonham-Carter, but there was nothing remotely gung-ho about her. She was very pretty, even without make-up, and she used the peak of her baseball cap as someone else might use a hand to hide behind.

'Are you here on holiday?' Cleo asked over her

46

shoulder as she carried a stack of Pixie's books over to the cash desk.

'Yes. But I'm investigating the possibility of staying on — perhaps renting somewhere for a few months. Kilrowan looks like the kind of place where I could get a lot of work done.'

'Oh, it is. Loads of writers come here to work. And painters, too. The joint's famous for being inspirational.'

'I hear it's quiet, off-peak, too. That's what I want. Somewhere with few distractions.'

'Well, you've hit on the right place. Nothing ever happens here.' That wasn't exactly true, thought Cleo, remembering the events of the year before last, when *Mimi's Remedies* had been in full swing. She opened a copy of *Hard to Choos*, turned to the title page, and held it open for Pixie to sign. Pixie's signature took her a nano-second. 'Wow. You sign fast. But your signature's changed. I seem to remember that when I ordered signed copies of yours from the distributors in the past, you put little 'o's instead of dots over all your 'i's.'

'It's had to change. I sign so much stock now that I don't have time to do the 'o's. Four 'o's adds vital minutes when you're signing thousands of copies. I used to put kisses, too, and 'Love, Pixie', and even smiley faces sometimes, but when I saw my PR girl drumming her fingers on the table during a stock-signing session, I knew I had to give up the personal touches. Now I just sign and run.'

Cleo reached for another copy of the book.

'But hang on,' said Pixie. 'I don't have to do

that, today, do I? I'm not running anywhere. Give me that copy back and I'll put in kisses for you.'

The signed copy of *Hard to Choos* was reopened, and Pixie jotted XXX below her name. Cleo thought of the kinds of inscription that Colleen habitually scrawled on her flyleaves. 'Doubt not your soul!' was fairly representative.

'Would you happen to know of any place I might rent here on a short-term basis?' enquired Pixie, sparkly pen shimmering over another title page.

'Off season? Yeah. There are masses of rentals going begging. In fact, the place next door to me is empty right now.'

'Oh? Perhaps you could let me have a contact number?'

'Sure. It happens to belong to another writer, actually. She bought it as an investment.'

'Another writer? Who might she be?'

'Colleen.'

'*Colleen?*' Pixie's signature faltered. 'Oh.'

'Do you know her?'

'Um. We were introduced at the London Book Fair once.'

Cleo knew Pixie didn't need to elaborate. She hadn't said 'we *met* at the London Book Fair once', or 'we *hung out together* at the London Book Fair once'. The word 'introduced' said it all. Colleen would have no truck with Pixie and her ilk. She soared alone like the literary eagle she was.

'I could put in a phone call to her if you like.'

'Oh! Thank you very much. I'd really

appreciate that.' Scribble, scribble, scribble, XXX. 'There. We're done.' Pixie put the last *Hard to Choos* on the top of the pile. 'What's the house like?' she asked.

'It's lovely — if I say so myself. It's built to the same spec as mine. Underfloor heating, self-cleaning, massive picture windows, fantastic view — '

'Goodness! You don't have to say anything else. I'm sold.'

'I'm heading home now. Why don't you come along with me and take a look?'

'Well — that's terribly kind of you. Are you sure you don't mind?'

'I don't mind at all.' Cleo was actually quite chuffed by the notion of having Pixie Pirelli as a neighbour. 'Just let me wrap up here.'

She went into the back room to turn off the electricity and get her coat, and when she came back out, Pixie was standing by the till with the household emergency manual in her hand. 'May I buy this?' she said.

'No purchase necessary. It's yours.'

'Oh, no — I couldn't possibly — '

'Please take it as a thank-you for signing stock for me. Anyway, the till's turned off.'

'That's jolly decent of you.'

'You're welcome. Have you some kind of problem?'

'Sorry?'

Cleo indicated the household emergency manual.

'Oh — this?' said Pixie. 'No, it's actually for research purposes. One of the characters I'm writing gets a bad electric shock.'

'Ah.' Cleo held the door of the shop open for Pixie, then locked up while Pixie perused the bookshop window from the outside.

'The display looks lovely,' she said. 'Thank you for putting my cut-out in.'

'You're welcome again.' Cleo shot Pixie a curious look as they set off down the street together. 'It must be a really weird feeling to go into a shop where there's a big cut-out of you in the window.'

'It is,' agreed Pixie. 'It's rather spooky, actually. I used to love browsing in bookshops, but it's become something of a trial for me since I became a celebrity — albeit a very minor one,' she added hastily. 'I get paranoid in case booksellers think I'm spying on them to see how prominently my titles are displayed.'

'Really? Most writers I know don't have a problem with that. Some of them throw virtual tantrums if their books are displayed spine instead of face out.'

'Do they? I just feel so grateful that my books are even in stock. Ooh. Look at him.' Pixie had been distracted by a fisherman mooring his boat down by the pier.

'That's Martin Mulholland.'

'He's terribly handsome, in a kind of rugged, macho way, isn't he? Sorry — do you mind?' Pixie took her pink pen and a notebook out of her bag and scribbled something down. She gave Cleo a look of apology as she tucked the tools of her trade back in her bag. 'I have to write stuff down as soon as I see it, otherwise I forget,' she said. 'I'm always sneaking off to the loo at parties so I can jot details down.'

'Does that mean that Martin will feature in your next book?' asked Cleo with a smile.

'Maybe. But I'll call him Seamus Moynihan, or something like that — ' Pixie's delicate nostrils flared ' — and I'd have to lose the fishy smell. Let's see how he might look. 'Seamus Moynihan was standing at the prow of his fishing boat. His long black hair streeled behind him in the wind that was blowing a bitter north-easterly'. Or maybe I'll give him a break and make that a 'balmy south-westerly'.'

'Lucky Martin! Will he get the girl?'

Pixie laughed. 'I don't know. I don't know too much about her yet. She'll announce her arrival fairly soon, I've no doubt.'

'Are your characters based on real people, Pixie?' Cleo had based her first short story on a fantasy figure, who — not long after she'd written it — had become reality. Her husband, Pablo.

'Not often. They're fairy tales, really, for grown-ups. Although in my last novel, one of my put-upon heroines tells a despotic head of accounts to get her 'enormous fat arse back up the stairs'. How I cheered when I wrote those words! I was getting vicarious revenge on all the mealy-mouthed staff in accounts departments I'd ever had to grovel to in the days when I was broke. But the disclaimer on the back of the title page lets me get away with it.'

'The 'all the characters in this book are

51

fictitious, and any resemblance to actual persons' thing?'

'Mm hm. Oh, look,' remarked Pixie. 'There's that gorgeous dog.'

'You naughty, naughty girl!' said Cleo. Her dog, Fluffy, had rounded a corner with her latest boyfriend. 'I washed her just the other day, and now she's gone and rolled in somebody's flowerbed again.'

'She's yours? I've noticed her a lot about the village. She followed me halfway along the bog road earlier today.'

'That's how she picked me up, too, when I first came here. She's a complete tart. Here we are.' Cleo turned onto the path that led to number 5, the Blackthorns. She let herself in, and held the door open for Pixie.

'Oh, it's lovely!' Pixie stood in the hallway looking around her, clearly impressed.

'I'll give you the guided tour, if you like. Downstairs first.'

The stairs led down to the sitting room. Cleo had furnished her house with lots of big comfortable sofas and armchairs. There were cupboards for all her books, but she had acquired so many that they had overflowed. New shelving had had to be put up, and her coffee table was piled with glossy tomes — mostly travel books.

'It's so *homely*,' said Pixie.

'Yes, isn't it? I love it. When I first moved in here I acted on that maxim beloved of interior designers — you know? 'Have nothing in your house that you do not know to be useful, or believe to be beautiful.' It was all Zen and 'rigorous simplicity'. But after it burned down I decided I wanted a more homey feel.'

'Your house burned down? How frightful! How did it happen?'

'Fluffy knocked over a candle.'

'Goodness. Did you have to rebuild from scratch?'

'Yeah.'

'That must have been very stressful for you. I have builders in, in my house in London, and the noise is unspeakable.'

'It wasn't really a problem. I just ran away to the continent for a year and left the lads to it.' Cleo could tell by Pixie's nonplussed expression that she was wondering how Cleo could afford to be so *flaithiúlacht*. 'I'm really rich, you see. I won the lottery.'

Pixie clapped her hands. 'Oh! How wonderful!' she said. 'I could put you in a book.'

'I'll sue.'

Pixie's laugh was interrupted by a voice from behind her.

'Hey,' said Pablo, emerging from the kitchen. He was barefoot, his hair was damp from the shower, and he was carrying a bottle of wine and a glass of red. He looked devastatingly sexy, and Cleo found herself wondering if Pixie might put *him* in a book, too. Her hands had moved automatically to the buckle on her bag the minute she'd set eyes on him; however she'd clearly decided against taking notes, for she stuffed them quickly back into the pockets of her puffa jacket.

53

'Pablo, this is Pixie Pirelli.'

'I know. I recognize you from your cut-out in the shop window. Nice to meet you in the flesh instead of cardboard.' Pablo put down the bottle, then strolled on bare feet towards Pixie with his hand outstretched. Cleo saw Pixie blush as she took it. No wonder! Pablo had the ability to turn women into puddles. 'Cleo *loves* your books,' he continued. 'I took your last one away from her just before she got to the last chapter, and she fought like a tigress to get it back from me.'

'What a lovely compliment.'

'Pixie's here to have a look round,' said Cleo. 'She's thinking of renting number 4, next door because she's after some peace and quiet.'

'Then you've come to the right place. Will you have a glass of wine?'

'I'd love one. Thank you.'

Pablo moseyed into the kitchen and returned with two more wineglasses. 'Cheers!' he said, when he'd poured.

'Cheers! Good health to you both.'

'How about that tour of the house, Pixie?' said Cleo. 'Bring your wine with you. Pablo — will you phone Colleen and tell her she has a prospective tenant?'

'Sure.'

'Follow me, Pixie. We'll start with the kitchen . . . '

And Cleo led Pixie from kitchen to study to bedrooms one, two and three, and by the time Pixie had seen the state-of-the-art bathroom, she'd made up her mind.

'It's perfect!' she said, as she followed Cleo

back downstairs. 'And so good to know I'll have such lovely neighbours.'

Back in the sitting room Pablo was talking on the phone, lounging on a couch and doodling on a sheet of paper. 'Fair enough,' he said into the receiver. 'I'll pass that on. *Slán*, Colleen.' He slung his phone onto the coffee table, then turned to Pixie. 'Well, it's yours if you want it, Ms Pirelli. I wrote all the details on here.' Pablo handed over the A4 sheet. 'You just pay the rent into Colleen's bank account each month. And if you need help with anything, you've only to ask. I know the joint inside out.'

'Pablo used to live there,' explained Cleo. She didn't feel the need to elaborate. Pablo had lived there in the days when he was Colleen's lov*air*, and Cleo didn't like to talk about the war.

'Thank you both so much!'

There came a loud thwacking noise from above in the hall, and Pixie looked puzzled. 'Whatever's that?'

'It's the dog flap,' said Pablo. 'Cue Fluffy.'

And Fluffy made her entrance, careering down the stairs and smiling broadly.

'Hey, Fluff,' said Cleo, hunkering down to scratch the dog's ears. 'It's into a bath for you again. Sometimes I think you roll in flowerbeds deliberately because you just can't get enough of Jacuzzi mode.'

Fluffy sniffed Pixie's ankles and said hello before moving on to flirt with Pablo. 'D'you mind if I ask you something, Pixie?' he said, picking Fluff up and nuzzling her. 'How did you come by the crazy moniker?'

55

Pixie looked surprised. 'I was christened it.'

'Oh. Sorry,' said a suitably chastened Pablo.

'Joke!' returned Pixie. 'My real name is Jane Gray. I was advised to dream up something that would better suit a chick-lit writer, and when I saw a Pirelli calendar on the wall of my local garage I just knew it was for me. The next day I spotted an ad for a Pixies album, so I put two and two together and came up with a name that was fun and sexy.'

'Like your books,' remarked Pablo.

'I like to think so. But surely you haven't read any of them? They're strictly girly books.'

'I've read all the sex bits.'

'Oh!' Pixie choked on her wine. 'No! You haven't?'

'Have too,' said Pablo, equably. 'There's some great stuff in there. You must have fun writing it.'

'On the contrary,' said Pixie. 'I find it *excruciating*. Every time I write a sex scene I can't help thinking all the time about my parents, and how they'll feel when they read it. They're frightful prudes, and even though they're secretly very proud of me I know I'm something of an embarrassment to them. I wish I could get specially edited copies for them, with all the sex cut out.'

'Couldn't you just not write the sex?' asked Pablo.

'Get real, Pablo,' said Cleo. 'Sex sells. Anyway, don't they say that there are only three subjects worth writing about under the sun? Sex, death and — um. What's the third one?'

'Revenge,' said Pixie in a surprisingly grim

voice. And Cleo saw the knuckles of the pretty little manicured hand that was holding the wineglass go white.

'Revenge. Of course. 'Revenge is sweet'. Who said that?'

'Byron,' answered Pixie, without missing a beat. 'The quote is actually 'Sweet is revenge — especially to women'. It's from *Don Juan.*'

Aha, thought Cleo, as she contemplated the expression on her new neighbour's face, the plot thickens. Pixie Pirelli may not much like writing about sex. She probably wouldn't much like writing about death either, come to think of it. But it looked as if she might have no problem at all writing about revenge . . .

★ ★ ★

A couple of hours later, Pablo and Cleo walked into the dining room of Ballynahinch Castle to see Pixie sitting on her own at one of the window tables.

'Poor thing,' said Cleo. 'She looks lonely. I know this is meant to be a romantic *dîner-à-deux*, but don't you think we ought to ask her to join us?'

'I've no objection at all to her joining us,' said Pablo. 'Hey, Des — ' this to the hotel manager, who was passing — 'would you mind setting a third place at our table?'

'By all means,' said Des — efficiency personified — and a waiter was summoned and issued with instructions.

Cleo made her way over to Pixie. At a big table

adjacent to her small one, half a dozen loud Americans were swapping fishing stories.

'Hello,' said Cleo. 'Will you join us for dinner?'

Pixie looked a little mortified. 'Oh, no! Thank you so much for the offer, but I couldn't intrude on your wedding anniversary.'

'You won't be intruding, honestly. Sure, Pablo and I have bugger all to say to each other.'

'But don't you want a romantic evening, just the two of you?'

'Romance works better in novels than in reality, in my experience. And I'm pretty certain you don't want to spend the next hour being subjected to endless fishy tales.' Cleo nodded in the direction of the Americans. 'Come on over.'

'I'd like to. If you're really sure?'

'Sure we're sure.'

So Pixie picked up the notebook and pen that had been lying beside her plate and followed Cleo over to the table, which was being reset for three.

'You could take notes on us,' remarked Cleo. 'Observe at first hand what couples get up to on an anniversary. Maybe if you're lucky, we'll have a blazing row. What am I having?' she asked Pablo, reaching for the menu. They always tried to guess what the other was having every time they went out to dinner, and they more often than not guessed right.

'You're having the crab and the sea bass,' said Pablo.

'Right again. And you're having oysters and rack of lamb.'

'Correct.'

'See? We're like an old married Golden Years couple. We could go on *Mr and Mrs.* There's nothing romantic about us at all.'

Cleo suddenly realized that Pixie's smile was looking a little forced. Oh, shit. She'd forgotten that the writer had just been through a particularly humiliating and very public split with her actor boyfriend. She'd better change the subject.

'What did you do in real life before you started writing, Pixie?' she asked, deftly shifting gear. 'Didn't I read somewhere that you were a model?'

'Oh, don't believe everything you read in the papers! They spice everything up to make me sound more glamorous than I really am. I'm far too small to be a model.'

Pixie *was* small, Cleo had observed. She wasn't used to looking down at very many people.

'I was actually a hand model,' said Pixie.

'A hand model?'

'Yes — you know when you see a picture of a hand in a TV commercial or in a magazine?'

'You mean like in an ad for nail varnish or something?' asked Pablo.

'Well, yes — but hand models do much more than that. I've had my hand photographed coming out of other people's sleeves.'

'Um. Explain?'

'Well, even the most fabulous-looking models can have not very nice hands, you know. So the shot is set up with me hiding behind the model, and holding the flower or the champagne flute or whatever it is she's meant to be holding. They have very clever strategies for disguising the fact that it's not the real model's hand — like draping a silk scarf over the arm.'

'Really?'

'Mm. I've been in some very famous ads. I was the hand in that ad for Gala Chocolates.'

'No! I *loved* that ad,' said Cleo.

'What a weird job,' remarked Pablo.

'Yes. It felt rather silly, sometimes, but it was better than being a foot model. I had a friend who was a foot model, and she said there was something profoundly humiliating about having your feet photographed.'

'Does it pay well?' asked Pablo.

Pixie shrugged. 'Not as well as being a bestselling novelist.'

'Yeah. That must be a blast!'

'Beats writing obituaries.'

'You don't sound convinced.'

'Well, I *love* actually sitting down and writing my books. But I do find touring and doing endless interviews rather gruelling. I'm actually playing truant at the moment.'

Pixie sounded more than ever like the head of a hockey team who's done something very naughty indeed. 'What do you mean?' asked Cleo.

'Well, I was asked to be a guest speaker at a convention of chick-lit novelists, and I said no. It's the first time I've ever said no to anything. My agent practically needed smelling salts when she heard the news, and I don't think I'm my editor's flavour of the month either right now.'

'I kind of know how you feel,' said Pablo. 'About the gruelling thing. I feel like a complete impostor when I have to go on chat shows.'

'Pablo's a painter,' explained Cleo. 'He's quite famous in Ireland.'

'How super. I wrote a novel about a painter once.'

'*Venus in Versace?*'

'The very one.'

'What kind of — er — stuff — no! What kind of *subjects* do you paint, Pablo?'

'Anything. Anyone. I'm a complete whore.'

'I'm sure you're not!'

'I am,' said Pablo. His tone was affable enough, but Cleo knew from experience that this was a touchy subject.

'It's considered in some circles to be very prestigious to have a portrait of yourself by Pablo,' she said quickly. 'He's done the Taoiseach and — oh, look! There's Hugh Hennessy — and who's that with him? She looks like Stella Tennant.'

Hugh had come into the dining room accompanied by a woman who looked as unapproachable and as haughty as a catwalk queen, all decked out in snooty designer black, shoes that *had* to be Manolos, and elegant, dangly earrings.

'You are such a nosy parker, Cleo Dowling,' said Pablo. 'You should apply to become official village gossip.'

Cleo stuck her tongue out at him. 'See?' she said to Pixie. 'We're having a row already.'

There came the sound of a discreet cough.

'Excuse me?' said the hotel manager, who had rolled up with a bottle of fizz in an ice bucket. 'Since I understand it's your wedding anniversary, Mr and Mrs MacBride, the champagne's on the house.'

'Oh, thank you, Des! How thoughtful.'

'You're staying with us tonight, I understand?'

'We are indeed.'

'You're very welcome.'

'Thank you.'

'Tell me this,' remarked Des, as he stripped the foil from the bottle, 'I was in London last week, Pablo, and I dropped into Tate Modern. Have you seen . . . '

And Cleo thought, as Pablo and Des swapped stories about Britart and the champagne was popped and poured, what an excellent idea it was that they had booked in. She couldn't think of a better way of celebrating their wedding anniversary than in a four-poster bed in Ballynahinch Castle . . .

Across the table from her, Pixie was jotting something down in her notebook. 'Sorry,' she said, when she saw Cleo looking. 'I just wanted to make a note of the puddings on the menu.'

'Why would you want to do that?'

'I always crib delicious ideas from menus. Food is important in books.'

'I bet it is.' In the very first erotic short story she'd ever written, Cleo had dreamed up a rather novel way of serving up ice-cream. 'Especially since food has become the new sex. Sales of Ben & Jerry's must have gone through the roof since — ' under the table Pablo directed a smart kick at her ankle — 'oh. Fuck. I'm sorry.'

'It's OK,' said Pixie with a shrug. 'He can feed Sophie Burke all the fucking Ben & Jerry's in the world for all I care.' It was strange to hear Pixie use the 'F' word. It was a clear indication of how much she must hate her ex. 'That would take care nicely of her size 6 figure.'

★   ★   ★

Pixie was watching her boyfriend, the Brit-pack actor Jonah Harrington, lounging on a beach on a reality TV show. She had enlisted the support of her most trusted friend, Mariella, to help her get through the endurance test she faced. Mariella had tried to dissuade her from watching this evening, but Pixie had insisted. 'It's going to be all over the papers tomorrow, and forewarned is forearmed. I might as well know what to expect when the press come baying for fresh blood.'

When Jonah had announced that he'd been invited to participate in a reality show that went by the name of *Celebrity Castaway*, Pixie had been horrified that he was even *considering* getting involved. But Jonah had been adamant. He was convinced that *Celebrity Castaway* would raise his profile and kick-start his flagging career. But Pixie had had a feeling that there was another incentive for Jonah to accept the invitation. An actress with whom he had once filmed a very steamy bed scene was also appearing on the reality show, and Pixie suspected that Jonah hadn't needed to act very hard when he'd exchanged sizzling screen kisses with the bootylicious Sophie Burke.

Her suspicions had proved to be well founded.
Jonah and Sophie had fallen into each other's
arms like long-lost lovers on the very first day
they'd been cast away, and now Pixie was
suffering public humiliation of the most
grotesque kind. She'd got through the past few
days with the support of Mariella and her agent
and her PR people, but watching the show was
making her feel as if cockroaches were crawling
over her skin.

'No!' she whimpered, as Jonah spooned
ice-cream into Sophie's trout pout, then kissed
her with evident relish. 'No!' she cried, as Jonah
smeared ice-cream all over Sophie's silicone
cleavage and proceeded to lick it off. And 'No!'
she howled as Sophie and Jonah disappeared
into their makeshift tent, taking the tub of Ben &
Jerry's with them. (Ben & Jerry's had been
Jonah's luxury of choice on the desert island.
Sophie's had been La Perla underwear.)

'OK. That's it,' said Mariella firmly, zapping
the television off. 'You're not to torment yourself
with any more of this. I am booking you into that
Irish castle, and you are getting out of here for a
few days, Pixie. Start packing now.'

And Pixie, tragic-eyed and waif-like, had done
exactly as Mariella had instructed.

★   ★   ★

'I'm sorry,' said Cleo again.

'You mustn't worry.' Pixie sounded categorical. 'I'm tougher than I look, honestly. When I

64

certified as an advanced scuba diver, my instructor wrote me a note on her underwater slate that read 'I can tell you are a fighter'.'

Scuba-diving was a tough sport, Cleo knew. She found it hard to imagine tiny Pixie sporting great big flippers and laden down with tanks and weight belts. 'And are you?'

'A fighter?' Pixie smiled. 'Do you know the Kurt Weill song *Mack the Knife*?'

'The one that goes 'Oh, the shark has pretty teeth, dear'?'

Pixie nodded. 'It's my theme tune.'

And Cleo thought, as Pixie raised her champagne flute to the happy couple and toasted their anniversary, that she would not like to get on the wrong side of this woman. Pixie might have a sugar-coated exterior, but under the carapace of sweetness there clearly beat the heart of a huntress.

4

Hazel walked into the dining room in Ballyna-hinch Castle Hotel with Hugh Hennessy, feeling a little apprehensive. There were some seriously moneyed individuals hanging out here, and she wondered if she'd pass muster. She was glad she'd packed her little black dress and her heels and the dangly earrings she'd found in Claire's Accessories. Her handbag was a fake Prada that she'd got while on holiday in Thailand, and nobody had ever suspected that it wasn't the real thing.

Now, as she strolled towards the table in the wake of the *maître d'*, she was glad to see that she was on the receiving end of some seriously flattering looks. She could breathe easy. She'd got away with it again! She looked a million dollars in an outfit for which she'd forked out less than one hundred euros.

Every single thing she'd packed to bring to Kilrowan had been a sale purchase — apart from the Lulu Guinness make-up bag, which had been a present from Erin. The brilliant thing about sale purchases was that most shoppers tended to ignore anything that looked rubbish on a hanger. Hazel's eye told her that what might look forlorn on a hanger could actually look fantastic on a flesh-and-blood woman. She lurked in the Brown Thomas Designer Room like a big cat scenting prey — especially around the end-of-sale time when most of the gear reminded her of dogs in the pound, whimpering to be taken home. She'd see another shopper dismiss a shapeless looking dun-coloured shirt or a tired-looking skirt, and knew it was time to pounce. She'd emerge from the changing cubicle to study the results in the shop-floor mirror, and she could never stop herself from feeling a tad smug when she spotted the shopper who'd rejected the shirt or the skirt looking sick with themselves for not having tried it on.

But then, they mightn't have looked as good in it as Hazel. Hazel was one of those enviable people who would look good in a bin bag. She'd actually had to *wear* a bin bag on a couple of occasions, when, as a child, she'd been dragged along to her mother's punk rock gigs. One of her earliest memories was of safety-pinned rockers cooing over her and telling her how cute she looked in black plastic.

The *maître d'* drew out a chair for her, and she sat down and accepted a menu. 'Looks good,' she said, scanning it.

'You won't be disappointed,' said Hugh. Then he raised a hand in greeting to someone on the other side of the room. 'Hey. Pablo. Cleo.'

Hazel looked over her shoulder to see a table with three people — a man and two women — sitting at it. One of the women looked vaguely familiar.

'Pablo — the painter?'

'Yes. He donates a painting to the festival every year to raise money for charity.'

'I read that on your website. It's very generous

67

of him. His paintings are fetching a lot of money.'

'I don't think it's too much skin off his nose. He's very prolific.'

'Who are the women?'

'One of them's Cleo Dowling, his wife. I don't know the other one. Hi, Cleo!'

A pretty, bubbly-looking woman was approaching the table. 'Evening, Hugh!' she said. 'How's it going?'

'Great, thanks. You?'

'Excellent form.'

Cleo cocked a look of enquiry in Hazel's direction, and Hugh obliged. 'Cleo, this is Hazel MacNamara, who's going to be handling the PR for the Arts Festival this year. Hazel, this is Cleo Dowling, who owns the Kilrowan bookshop.'

'Good to meet you!' Hazel extended a hand.

'Likewise,' said Cleo, mirroring the gesture. 'So. *Professional* PR this year! That'll be a first. How can we afford it?'

'Colleen donated a very generous lump sum,' said Hugh. 'Hopefully a big injection of cash will reap dividends.'

'Have you come up with any ideas yet?' Cleo asked Hazel.

'Well,' she replied, launching into PR speak, 'we were thinking along the lines of a theme to lend the festival a more distinct ethos. The very words 'Arts Festival' have a kind of nebulous ring to them, and a theme can define a more specific focus.'

'Hazel thought a parade might be a good way of kicking things off this year,' said Hugh. 'A kind of scaled-down version of the Macnas parade in Galway.'

'Well! I'm impressed,' said Cleo. 'It'll make a change to have somebody actually oversee events. Last year the festival just sort of — happened. What kind of a theme had you in mind?'

'I've been thinking along the lines of a 'Maritime' concept. I know it's stonkingly obvious since Kilrowan's a fishing village, but sometimes obvious is the most astute route to go down. Let's keep our fingers crossed that the media think so too.'

'Wow. Will we get to go on the *Late Late*?'

Hazel shook her head. 'Wrong time of the year. But I'd say we stand a very good chance of getting a slot on *Nationwide*. I have a friend who works on the show.'

'Hazel has a list of celebrities she's going to approach about making appearances,' said Hugh.

'Cool. Like who?'

'I can't divulge names until I receive confirmation that they'll be attending. But celebrities are always a big draw, and that'll certainly heighten our profile. An endorsement by a celebrity's invaluable publicity.'

'But won't they expect loadsamoney for showing up?'

'Generally speaking, not for something like an arts festival. Arts festivals are prestigious cultural events, and it does a celebrity no harm to get involved.'

'Talking of celebrities,' said Cleo, 'there's one

sitting at our table.'

'I *thought* I recognized the face from somewhere,' said Hazel. 'Who is she?'

'She's Pixie Pirelli, the chick-lit writer.'

'Ah, of *course*. Didn't I see her large as life in your bookshop window earlier today. What's she doing in Kilrowan? Is she on some promotional tour?'

'No. She's coming here to live for a while. She's looking for somewhere peaceful to write her next book.'

'Hey presto! Will she be around at festival time?'

'Could be.'

'I wonder if she'd be interested in taking part? Maybe do a writing workshop or something?'

'Watch out. You don't want to put Colleen's nose out of joint,' said Hugh. 'She's used to being the literary star of the festival.'

'And she *despises* chick-lit,' added Cleo.

'But if we're expanding, widening our horizons,' said Hazel, 'it can only be good to diversify. There's room for everything and everyone — and the more people we reach, the merrier. Would you happen to know anybody stellar who might be interested, Cleo?'

Cleo looked pensive. 'There's Deirdre O'Dare. She sometimes comes back to Ireland in the summer to visit her parents in Wicklow. She might be persuaded to make a diversion to the West Coast.'

'Who's Deirdre O'Dare?'

'Oh, I suppose she's not actually that well known. She's a screenwriter, and screenwriters are very behind-the-scene type people really, aren't they?'

'We could have a screenwriting workshop as well,' said Hazel. 'Could you e-mail her? See if she might be interested?'

'Sure I could. I could ask her if Rory might come as well.'

'Rory?'

'Her husband's Rory McDonagh.'

'Rory McDonagh? The film star Rory McDonagh?'

'Yep.'

'Well, that'd be a real coup! Rory McDonagh's about as stellar as they get. He'd eclipse anyone on *my* list, that's for sure!'

'Pablo's looking for you, Cleo,' said Hugh.

Cleo took a look over her shoulder at Pablo, who was waving at her from the other side of the room. 'Oh — I'd better go,' she said. 'Our starters have arrived. Maybe see you later in the drawing room for coffee?'

'Absolutely,' said Hazel.

She watched as Cleo negotiated her way back to her table. She was feeling quite excited by this project, now. Pixie Pirelli would attract media attention from Ireland and the UK, but if they could persuade Rory McDonagh to make an appearance at the festival, they'd get international coverage. And if — *big* if — he agreed, he'd be a magnet for other celebs.

'They're having champagne over on Cleo's table,' said Hugh. 'They must be celebrating something.'

She smiled at him. 'Ha! I've just thought of a

new collective noun. A celebration of celebrities! Maybe we should order some fizz, too.'

'We've nothing to celebrate yet,' he pointed out.

'Ah, but I'm a very positive individual. I'm a Chinese Year of the Tiger.'

'Oh? I haven't a clue about that stuff.'

'What year were you born?'

'Nineteen seventy-one.'

'Before or after the twenty-sixth of January?'

'Before.'

'That makes you a Dog.'

'What would I have been if I'd been born after the twenty-sixth?'

'A Pig. Pigs and Tigers are very different types.'

'And Dogs and Tigers are?'

'A marriage made in heaven.' Oh, *doh*, Hazel! 'A marriage made in heaven, when it comes to business, that is,' she said, hastily.

Oh — make things worse, why don't you?

★ ★ ★

Back at Cleo's table, Pablo and Pixie were tucking into their starters.

'Well?' said Pablo. 'Did your nosy-parkering get you any results?'

'Yes, actually,' said Cleo, giving him a look of mock-hauteur. 'Her name's Hazel MacNamara, and she's a PR person. She's been taken on board to heighten the profile of the Kilrowan Arts Festival.'

'How can the Arts Festival afford PR?'

'Apparently Colleen donated a big lump sum to start the fund-raising ball rolling. I'd better cough up a few bob, too, I suppose,' she said, laying into her crab salad. 'It's amazing the way those PR people speak, you know. It's like a foreign language. All 'focusing' and 'concepts'. Her eyes lit up with dollar signs when I told her about my film star connections. She's hoping to attract a celebrity element.'

'You have film star connections?' asked Pixie.

'Kind of. A friend of mine's married to Rory McDonagh.'

'Rory McDonagh? The film star Rory McDonagh?' The words came out in a squeak.

'The very one,' said Cleo.

'Swoon! What's he like?'

'He's gorgeous. Very laid-back, great sense of humour, devilishly sexy — '

'OK. Enough already,' grumbled Pablo. 'You can't go waxing lyrical about another geezer's sex appeal on our wedding anniversary, Cleo. How insensitive can you get!'

'Oops. Sorry, honey!' Cleo reached over and covered his hand with hers momentarily. 'Anyway, the reason she was interested is because she wants to turn the Arts Festival into a stellar event. She's going to try and get loads of celebs to attend. She asked me if you'd be around, Pixie.'

'I'm not really that much of a celeb — ' began Pixie.

She was interrupted by a voice that came from behind her. 'Excuse me? You're Pixie Pirelli, aren't you?'

73

A girl was standing by their table, holding a copy of *Hard to Choos*.

'That's me,' said Pixie.

The girl held the book out to her, with an apologetic expression. She was mute with embarrassment.

'You'd like me to sign that for you?' prompted Pixie.

'Yes, please!'

Pixie took the proffered book, produced her pen, and turned to the title page.

'I'm so sorry to intrude,' said the girl, finding her voice, 'but I'm a big fan of yours, and I couldn't believe my eyes when I saw you come in earlier. I went straight up to my room to fetch my copy of your book, and then just stood dithering in the doorway of the dining room for ages before I plucked up the courage to come over.'

'I'm very glad you did. What's your name?' asked Pixie.

'Natasha,' said the girl. 'I started your book this afternoon, and I just can't put it down!'

Pixie smiled at her. 'Which bit have you got to?'

'The bit where Charlotte's swimming and she spots the goats eating her clothes. It's so funny!'

'Oh — I loved writing that bit!'

'And I just *adore* Alex and Finn. Is she going to end up with — no! Don't tell me!'

'I wouldn't dream of spoiling the ending for you,' said Pixie, finishing signing with a flourish and handing the book back to Natasha. She smiled again at the bright-eyed expression on her fan's face as she mouthed the words Pixie had inscribed.

'Thank you so much!' said Natasha. 'I'm off back upstairs now to finish it. Good luck with the next one. Goodbye, Pixie!'

'Goodbye, Natasha. It was lovely to meet you.' And Pixie turned back to Pablo and Cleo and picked up her fork.

'Um. Excuse me?' said Cleo. 'You were about to say something about not being that much of a celebrity?'

'Well, compared to somebody like McDonagh I'm not,' said Pixie, self-effacingly.

'Do you mind it?' asked Pablo. 'When people come up to you like that?'

'No. My fan base is my life blood.'

'But you looked a bit — um — *defensive* when she first approached you,' said Cleo.

'That's because you can never predict what someone's going to say to you. I've had people come up to me and say the most monstrous things. They feel that because I'm in the public eye they've every right to say whatever they like. Someone came up to me recently and told me she'd chucked my last book in the bin because she took exception to the sex scenes. And then you get the superior ones who say things like: 'You're Pixie Pirelli, aren't you? I never read your books myself, of course, but would you mind signing for my niece/god-daughter/second-cousin-twice-removed?''

'And do you?'

'Of course I do. With gritted teeth. But it gives me a lovely warm glow when I get a reaction like

Natasha's. If I can make people laugh and cry the way I do when I'm writing, then the book has done what I intended it to. It's helped someone escape.'

'Do you really laugh and cry when you're writing?' asked Cleo.

'Oh yes,' said Pixie. 'My — ex — boyfriend came into my study once and found me abject with grief.'

'Wow,' said Cleo. 'So you identify with all of them?'

'They're my best friends,' said Pixie, with a little laugh. 'That's how sad a person I am.'

'I don't think you're sad at all,' said Pablo. 'I think it must be a fantastic feeling to earn a load of money from making up stories. Better than painting portraits of dick-head politicians with pigs.' He slurped back an oyster.

'It is a fantastic feeling,' agreed Pixie. 'But I'm always scared that things will take a dive. The chick-lit genre's way overcrowded, and heaps of writers are looking for an escape route. I have a friend who was so convinced that Magic Realism was going to be the next big literary thing that she made the mistake of branching out.'

'It didn't work out for her?'

'No.'

'Why not?'

'She was motivated by cynicism. She wasn't writing from the heart.'

'That PR woman, Hazel, was wondering if you might do a writing workshop for the festival,' said Cleo. 'How would you feel about that?'

Pixie frowned. 'I don't know,' she said. 'I don't

know if I could *teach* anyone to write. And — horror of horrors! What if they came up with something that was truly awful, and I had to criticize them? I'd *hate* that.'

'I can relate to that,' said Pablo. 'Remember that time I did a painting workshop for the women's group, Cleo?'

'When you told Colleen that her owl was exceptionally lifelike?' Cleo started to laugh.

'I'd hardly call that a criticism,' said Pixie, looking puzzled.

'It wasn't an owl,' said Cleo, laughing harder now. 'It was a horse looking over a wall. But Pablo mistook it for an owl *perched* on a wall. Oh, dear, I'm sorry!' She wiped tears of laughter away from her eyes with the corner of her napkin. 'It was nearly as funny as the time that make-up girl ordered her to wipe off her lipstick.'

'What?' said Pixie. She was looking even more puzzled now. 'Somebody ordered *Colleen* to do something?'

'Yes. A make-up girl mistook her for an extra in a film that was being made here. *Mimi's Remedies*. Oh, I'll never forget the expression on Colleen's face!' Cleo picked up her knife and fork again, in an attempt to regain her composure.

'Why did Colleen paint a picture of a horse looking over a wall?' asked Pixie. 'I would have expected her to paint something a lot more abstract, like a picture of her soul or some such.'

'She was trying to find her inner child,' said Pablo. 'She wanted to produce the kind of painting she might have done as a six-year-old.

Actually, a six-year-old might have done better.'
He sloshed wine into their glasses. 'Cheers.'

'Savage!' said Cleo. 'In a posh joint like this
you're meant to wait for the sommelier to pour
the wine.'

'Bollocks,' he returned. 'I'm not hanging
about waiting for him to notice when my glass is
empty.'

Cleo slanted him a look, then turned back to
Pixie. 'By the way, I invited Hazel and Hugh to
have coffee with us in the drawing room, after
dinner. She might run some other festival ideas
by you then. Would that be OK?'

'Certainly,' said Pixie. 'But she's not too
fabulous, is she? I find that PR people are often
quite fabulous. They're usually called Camilla or
Cressida, and they're so very sussed — and I'm
not sussed at all.'

'She didn't *seem* too fabulous. Although she
looks quite intimidating.'

'There she goes now,' said Pablo. 'Off to the
jakes.'

The three of them watched as Hazel
MacNamara high-heeled her way across the
dining room. They weren't the only ones who
were watching her. The heads of most of the
other diners in the room turned, too.

'I bet that bag's Prada,' said Cleo.

'What is it about women and labels?' said
Pablo. 'You're complete suckers. Who gives a
tinker's toss whether a bag's Prada or not?'

'It's a status thing. A label says 'I can afford
Prada or Gucci or Chloé because I am a
high-achieving individual'.'

'Sorry? Doesn't that make it more of a loser thing?' said Pablo. 'Doesn't that say 'Hey — I am an absolute prat because I forked out thousands of euros for this bag when I could have had a fake for a fraction of the price'? And anyway, how do you know which label's which?'

'Because the label's usually scrawled all over the product. Remember those awful Louis Vuitton bags?'

'And that ghastly Burberry check?' said Pixie. 'They really shot themselves in the foot when soap opera stars started wearing Burberry all over the place.'

'And footballers' wives,' added Cleo.

'And their babies,' said Pixie.

Pablo sighed a big sigh of incomprehension. 'It's all a pile of pants. I think it'd be much cooler to go round sporting bags with 'Fake Louis Vuitton' on. It would tell people you were no sucker. And how can you tell fakes from the genuine article, anyway?'

'We can't,' said Pixie and Cleo simultaneously. And then they looked at each other and laughed. And in that moment, Cleo Dowling knew that she was really, really going to like Pixie Pirelli.

★ ★ ★

In the dining room after dinner Hazel and Hugh joined Pablo and his two dates for coffee. Hazel moved in on Pixie, and Pixie knew she was in for a good schmoozing.

'Pixie Pirelli?' she said. 'I *love* your books.'

'Thank you! Thank you very much.'

79

'I hear you're coming to Kilrowan to live for a while?'

'That's right.'

'Will you be here in August, d'you think?'

Pixie started doing mental arithmetic — something she wasn't very good at. 'March, April, May, June, July, August,' she said, ticking the months off on her fingers as she counted them down. 'Let's see. It usually takes me around six months to complete a first draft, and the builders should be finished by the end of August — at least they've *promised* to — so, yes, I should still be here then.'

'You have builders in?' Hazel pulled a sympathetic face.

'Yes. That's why I'm coming over here to work.'

'You poor thing. I've been hearing some horrific builders stories lately.'

'Oh, I'll get revenge on them if they don't deliver. I'll put some loutish builders in my next book.'

Hazel smiled. 'I'd love to be able to get revenge like that.'

'Yes,' agreed Pixie. 'It can be very satisfying. You'd better not cross me!'

This time Hazel's smile looked a little more guarded. 'Ha ha,' she said. 'Did Cleo mention my idea about the workshop to you, incidentally?'

'Yes. I'm not sure about it, actually — I don't really feel qualified to instruct people. And workshops are really about work in progress. You'd need to do a series of them, and to be honest, I wouldn't have the time.'

'In that case, how would you feel about making an appearance? Something along the lines of 'An Audience with Pixie Pirelli'.'

''An Audience with Pixie Pirelli' sounds very grand, doesn't it? That'd be more Colleen's style. Wouldn't 'An Evening with Pixie Pirelli' be better? And could we keep it very informal?'

'Sure. Whatever you want,' said Hazel. 'How about a question and answer format, where you could take questions from the floor?'

'That sounds more like it. I'd be happy to do that.'

'So I can say with a reasonable amount of confidence that best-selling author, Pixie Pirelli, will be making an appearance at this year's Kilrowan Arts Festival?'

'You may. It'd be an honour and a pleasure.'

'Thank you. Let me give you a card.'

And as Hazel pulled out her Filofax, Pixie thought that, as well as being an honour and a pleasure to appear at the Kilrowan Arts Festival, it might also help to get her back in her agent's good books after skiving off the chick-lit convention. The Irish market was much smaller than the UK one, but if Hazel MacNamara was as efficient as she appeared, the Kilrowan event might attract overseas media interest.

She studied the card that Hazel had handed her. Nutcracker PR, she read. Hm. Clever name. It would appear that Hazel MacNamara was the business.

'Thank you,' she said. 'I'll certainly do

everything I can to make a worthwhile contribution to the Kilrowan Arts Festival.'

'Delighted to have you on board!' said Hazel.

★ ★ ★

An hour or so later, Hazel and Hugh took off, and Cleo and Pablo announced that they were going to bed.

'I'll go up, too,' said Pixie. 'I've an early start tomorrow, and it'll be a busy day.'

'Oh? What are you up to?' asked Cleo.

'Well, I'm travelling back to London, and I'll have builders to negotiate with.'

Cleo's jaw dropped. 'You mean you can talk to your builders on a bank *holiday*? You must be paying them a fortune.'

'It's not a holiday in the UK,' Pablo reminded her.

'And it certainly won't be a holiday for me,' said Pixie, looking glum. 'I'll have to phone my agent and my editor and explain to them why I went AWOL, and then I'm going to have to drop the bombshell that nobody's going to want to hear.'

'And that's?'

'That I'm holing up in a remote Irish village to write the next book.'

'Why is that a problem?' asked Pablo. 'I'd have thought they'd be delighted that you're starting another bestseller.'

'They won't be delighted that I'll be unavailable to make appearances in the UK media circus. That's for sure.'

They moved to the lobby to get their room keys.

'Did you enjoy your dinner?' enquired the receptionist.

'Yes, indeed, thank you. I'll be back,' said Pixie.

'Oh? I thought you were leaving us tomorrow?'

'I am, but I'm taking a place in Kilrowan for a few months, so I'll definitely manage several more visits.'

'We'll look forward to seeing you again, so,' said the receptionist, handing over their keys with a smile.

'Oh, look!' said Cleo, clocking Pixie's room key. 'You're in the room next to ours. The river view is fantastic, isn't it?'

'Yes,' said Pixie, unbuckling her backpack. 'Oh, my notebook! I must have left it in the dining room. I'd better run back and get it.'

'Damn right,' said Pablo. 'I'd say there's a lot of classified information in that notebook.'

'Well, good night, you two,' said Pixie, backing towards the dining room door. 'I'll get in touch when I arrive in town next week.'

'Do,' said Pablo. 'And remember — if you've any queries about the house, just let me know. I seem to remember that the washing machine was a bit temperamental.'

'That's very kind of you — but you may regret your offer, because you probably *will* hear from me. I'm a complete Luddite and technophobe. Good night!' she said again. 'Happy Anniversary!'

'Thanks,' said Cleo, and she and Pablo turned

and walked towards the stairs, hand in hand.

Pixie watched them go, then went back into the drawing room to wait until the coast was clear and the happy couple would be ensconced upstairs. She didn't need to go into the dining room and ask about her notebook, because it was safely tucked away in her bag. The reason she had lied about it was because she hadn't wanted to watch Pablo and Cleo go through the door of their bedroom together while she, sad singleton Jane Gray, a.k.a. Pixie Pirelli, turned the key in the lock of her own room and went through all by herself.

5

Pixie phoned her agent from the airport the next day.

'Pixie! Where have you been?' yelped Natalie. 'I've been out of my mind with worry!'

'Didn't you get my e-mail telling you that I was going away for a few days?'

'Yes. But you never go away! Are you all right?'

'Of course I'm all right, Natalie. I simply needed space to myself for a while.'

'I thought you might be having a nervous breakdown. Where did you go?'

'Connemara.'

'Connemara? Where's that?'

'It's on the West Coast of Ireland.'

'Oh. In other words, the back of beyond.'

'Yes.'

'Well, did it work, darling?' Having got over her fright, Natalie had reverted to her usual blandishments. 'Did you have a good break?'

'Yes. So much so that I'm going back.'

'What?'

'I'm renting a place there for the next six months.'

'But — ' Natalie was yelping again.

'I can't stay in London, Natalie. If I do, the builders really *will* give me a nervous break-down.'

'Christ. We need to talk. I'll phone Deborah

and arrange a lunch meeting for later in the week.'

'I'm afraid I shall be back in Ireland later in the week.'

'*What?*'

'I'm booked on a flight to Galway on Wednesday.'

'Good God, Pixie! That only gives us tomorrow, and I've meetings back to back.'

'How about Wednesday? I'll be running, but I could fit you in if you come out to the airport. We could have lunch there.'

'The airport? Lunch in the *airport*?'

'It's just a place, Natalie. Not a fatal disease.'

A big silence came down the phone, and then, 'Bugger it. Let's make it tomorrow, then. I'll cancel some meetings. The Criterion?'

'Jolly good.'

'Your PR people are not going to like this, Pixie.'

'Maybe not. But *I* am.'

'I'll get straight on to Deborah.'

'Bye, Natalie.' Pixie ended the call and immediately speed-dialled another number.

'Charlie Sedgewick,' came the response.

'Charlie — it's Pixie here.'

'Hey, sunshine! You're back?'

'I'm on my way, mate. How's my gaff looking?'

'It ain't lookin' robin, Pixie.'

Robin? *Robin*? Oh, yes! Robin Hood = good. Charlie, her foreman, had one of the strongest cockney accents she'd ever heard, and in order to work out what he was talking about she had to concentrate very hard indeed. Otherwise she'd

86

be parroting 'Sorry?' endlessly. Pixie had taken a crash course in rhyming slang when she'd first hired him, and any time she spoke to him she affected a kind of 'Matey Mockney' because she felt that her posh voice put her at a disadvantage. She also took care to put in a few swear words, to prove that she was one of the lads. However, she had a strong suspicion that it didn't wash, and that the workmen sent her up rotten behind her back.

'Oh, botheration — I mean *bugger* that.'

'And the patio rories had to go back. Wrong size.'

She hadn't a clue what the rories were, but that they were the wrong size was clearly a bad thing. 'Are you there now?'

'As we speak, darlin'.'

'OK. Give the lads the rest of the day off, and tomorrow too.'

'Two days off? It'll still cost you, Pixie.'

'I don't give a Donald Duck what it costs, Charlie. I'm on a plane to Ireland on Wednesday, and I need my gaff to myself so I can pack.'

'You're the guv'nor.'

'You said it. See you later.' Darn, she thought, as she hung up. She should have made that 'Baked potata'. She leaned back in her seat feeling dizzy. Calling shots was exhausting, and she wasn't used to it.

Her mobile bleated at her. Natalie.

'Hello, Nat.'

'I spoke to Deborah. She'd be delighted to join us for lunch tomorrow.'

'Oh, good.'

'How does one o'clock sound?'

'One o'clock's perfect.'

'I've asked Deborah to join us at half-past, so that you and I can have a chinwag first. I'll see you then, darling!'

'Looking forward to it! Byee!'

Pixie put the phone down wondering exactly how 'delighted' her editor, Deborah, would be to have her schedule disrupted by the demands of a neurotic author. But she guessed that Natalie would have got the wind up her, because Pixie had never thrown a diva strop before. Not that politely suggesting to do lunch in a hurry was what might ordinarily be described as a diva strop, but Pixie was always so compliant and so very biddable.

Her phone rang again. It was her web master. 'Oh, hello, Rufus! How are you?' Rufus was an awfully sweet computer nerd who styled himself 'Ranch Tiger' on the web pages he designed.

'Never better, Pixie,' said Rufus. 'I'm just phoning to remind you that you need to update your website.'

'Oh — thank you. The builders completely put it out of my head. I'll write a newsletter now and e-mail it to you this evening.'

'Thanks, Pixie. Talk soon.'

Pixie put her phone away, and took her laptop out of her computer case. She sat with her fingers poised above the keypad for a moment or two, then: 'Plenty happened this month,' she typed. 'I'm thrilled to say that *Hard to Choos* went straight into the bestseller list at number one and . . . '

Twinkle, twinkle twinkle . . . Thank goodness she had a job that meant she could work anywhere! Pixie hummed happily as her fingers scooted over the keypad. Her flight was delayed, and the other passengers around her were frazzled and stressed-looking, but it didn't matter to her because she could just take the tools of her trade out of her backpack. Some writers weren't so fortunate, she knew. Some writers had to isolate themselves in a precise location in order to come up with the goods, but Pixie had learned the knack of writing any time, anywhere. She'd had to, simply because there were usually so many other demands on her. Pixie wrote on trains and on aeroplanes. She wrote in waiting rooms and in restaurants. She normally hired a driver to transport her, because that meant she could very productively write in the passenger seat, while other commuters fulminated in gridlock. The only place she couldn't write at the moment was, ironically, her own home.

What would it be like to work in Connemara, she wondered, with that wildly distracting view? She'd just have to turn her back on it. And then she wondered what on earth she could put in next month's newsletter, if she wasn't attending newsworthy book launches and awards ceremonies and stock signings? Would she have to begin it by saying 'I have moved to Kilrowan where absolutely nothing ever happens'? Maybe she'd have to start *inventing* events? Oh, no. She couldn't! That would be too much like hard work — a bit like writing a novel with herself as the protagonist.

But the monthly newsletter was important, because the statistics Rufus sent her showed that people revisited the site especially to check it out. Hits peaked on the day it was published and she'd had mail from people thanking her for keeping her site updated. She knew from visiting other authors' sites that some of them languished for months without being updated. The most important reason to keep the site fresh was because the feedback she got via her readers' e-mails told her what people wanted from her books. And Pixie aimed to deliver.

Purr, purr . . . her phone was at her again. Mummy.

'Hello, Mummy!'

'Jane. You sound awfully noisy. Where are you?'

'I'm in Galway airport. My flight's been delayed.'

'Poor lamb. But I expect you're getting some work done?'

'Yes. I'm writing my newsletter.'

'Oh, good. At last I'll be able to keep up with all your goings-on. We haven't seen you for ages, Jane, and your father and I were hoping we might have a visit from you soon.' Pixie's parents had retired to Gloucestershire. They lived in a village not far from Prince Charles's country seat, Highgrove, and were terribly proud of the fact. 'How about next weekend?'

'Oh, Mummy, I'm sorry, but I'm going back to Ireland. I've fallen in love with a village in

90

Connemara, and I'm booked on a flight on Wednesday.'

'Goodness! This is very sudden.'

'I know. But I have to get out of my house. I simply can't get any work done there, and Connemara has everything I need. Peace, quiet, and a room with a view.'

'It *is* just a village you've fallen in love with, Jane?'

'What do you mean?'

'It's not another unsuitable man that's dragging you away?'

'No, Mum. There's no man.'

'I'm glad to hear it. When I think of what that hateful Jonah person did to you — '

'Mum. Please. I'd rather not be reminded of him.'

'But you will take care, won't you? You won't ever allow yourself to — '

'Mum! It's finished. It's in the past.'

There came the adenoidal announcement that her flight was boarding. Commuters all round Pixie started gathering together their bits and pieces and hurtling like lemmings towards the departure gate.

'I'd just hate to think that — '

'Sorry — my flight's been called, Mum. I'd better go. I'll phone you this evening, all right?'

'Very well. But have you really thought through this Connemara thing? It seems a rather radical thing to do, darling.'

'Yes. I have thought it through, and it's the right thing to do. You and Daddy could always come and visit. I've heaps of room.'

'There's an idea. We've never been to Ireland.'

'Do think about it. Now I'd better turn my phone off. Bye, Mum. Talk to you later.'

Pixie switched off her phone, then returned her attention to her newsletter. Tip tap tip tip tip, she went, and finally: 'Wish me luck in my Connemara adventure!'

Then she shut down her laptop and made her way to the departure gate, the last — and least perturbed — passenger to board the plane.

★　★　★

The Criterion was a fabulous restaurant. Pixie always felt like a princess when she ate there. It had been astute of her agent to choose it.

Natalie was there already, studying the menu.

'Darling!' She rose to her feet when she saw Pixie. 'You look amazing. That break clearly did you the world of good.'

'Thank you, Nat.' They observed the air kiss ritual — mwah, mwah — and then the waiter appeared unobtrusively and helped Pixie off with her coat. 'You look jolly good, too,' she said, taking a seat.

'Hey,' said Natalie, laconically. 'Now, let's get down to business before Deborah gets here. What's all this nonsense about buggering off to the arse-end of nowhere, darling? You must know that it's going to upset your PR people. Camilla bent over backwards to explain your no-show at the chick-lit convention, and now she's going to have to cancel all the other PR opportunities she's lined up for you.'

'I have to get out of my house, Natalie. It's as simple as that.'

'So you're doing the clichéd writer's thing of renting a little Irish cottage and waiting for the muse to descend?'

'No. I'm renting a rather fabulous house with underfloor heating and picture windows and a fantastic view of the sea.'

'But you could rent a fabulous penthouse with underfloor heating and picture windows and a fantastic view of the Thames!' Natalie sent her a smile in which appeal was mixed with reproach. 'I appreciate that you can't work from home, darling, but why not simply stay on in London?'

'Because I spread myself too thinly when I'm in London. I'm on a treadmill of talk shows and panels and literary events, and I'm not getting enough writing done.'

'But you know how important your image is, Pixie. Marketing is *essential* to keep your profile high.'

'To the extent that I don't have time to write any actual books to market?'

Natalie gave her a sceptical look. 'Sweetheart, you work so *fast*! There'll always be a book to market.'

'I work too *hard*, Natalie. And the pressure's mounting, all the time.'

'That's because the competition's so fierce. Take your eye off the ball and you could lose your readership like that!' Natalie snapped finger and beautifully manicured thumb together.

'I *have* to put a lid on it for a while. I'm fed up being competitive. I'm not competitive by nature, you know that. The publicity thing has always been hard for me, but I do it because I'm a good girl, and good girls do what they're told. I'm taking a sabbatical from being a good girl.' Pixie hoped she looked as mutinous as she felt.

'Are you saying that you're not happy being a bestselling author? Have you any idea how many people would *kill* to be in your shoes?'

'On the contrary. I've every idea. But something happened recently to make me take stock. I met another author — who shall remain nameless — at the London Book Fair, and she was moaning — actually *moaning* — about the fact that her book had only gone to number two in the bestsellers instead of number one. And I thought that if I ever heard myself talk like that — like a peevish brat — I would have to get out of the literary rat race for ever. It could turn me into a horrible person.'

'But you're *not* a horrible person, Pixie. You're an absolute pussycat.'

'I know. That's why I have to take a break before I turn into a rabid lynx.'

Natalie regarded her gravely, then heaved a sigh. 'You're set on this, aren't you?'

'Yes. I am.'

'OK.' From the way Nat was tip-tapping her nails on the table, Pixie knew she'd conceded defeat. 'Let's examine the practicalities. How will you manage editorially?'

'E-mail. Telephone. FedEx. Connemara's not Bogotá.'

'You'll miss your cosy sessions with Deborah.'

'Yes. I will.'

Pixie and Deborah habitually worked together in Pixie's study during the editing process. Pixie adored these sessions because writing was, in the main, a very solitary profession.

'And you'll miss your social life.'

Pixie shrugged. 'I haven't been going out much anyway, since the split with Jonah.'

Natalie curled her lip. 'You're so much better off without him, sweetheart. You know that.'

Pixie felt sudden tears prick her eyes. She couldn't cry here in the restaurant — she couldn't! She picked up her bag and got to her feet. 'Excuse me, Nat. Gotta pee.'

In the loo she shut the door on her cubicle as two women simultaneously emerged from theirs.

There came the sound of handbags being unclasped, and the spritzy hiss of scent.

'Be an angel and lend me some of your *papier poudré*, darling. I'm very shiny. By the way, did you clock who's sitting at the table in the corner?'

'Who?'

'Pixie Pirelli.'

'Who's she?'

'You mean you don't *know*?' And the Shiny One launched into the story of Sophie Burke and He-Whose-Name-Must-Never-Be-Mentioned. Finally: 'The press had a field day,' she concluded.

'How utterly ghastly for her!' Another hissy spritz. 'Mm — I love your scent. What is it?'

'It's an original concoction. George brought it back to me from Paris when he was there on his last business trip. Which reminds me, did you

95

know that the Chanel boutique on . . .'

And the voices receded as the ladies who lunch let themselves out of the loo.

Pixie remained sitting on the loo in torment. People were *still* talking about the reality TV débâcle, even though the ratings were down. She had not watched *Celebrity Castaway* since the evening Mariella had decided to pack her off to Ireland, but its grubbiness seemed to cling to her, and her skin still went all cockroachy when she remembered the Ben & Jerry's incident.

She let herself out of the loo, reapplied her lipstick and made an effort to recover her sang-froid, but on her return to the restaurant some minutes later she still had difficulty keeping her head held high as she passed the lunching ladies. Resuming her seat opposite Natalie, she said: 'May we have champagne, please?'

'Of course. Any particular reason?'

'I want to look as if I'm celebrating. I want to look as if that bastard dumping me was the best thing that ever happened to me. I want to look as if I have a life. Ha, ha, ha!' Pixie threw back her head and laughed as if she hadn't a care in the world.

'What are you laughing about?'

It was Deborah's voice.

Pixie jumped up to greet her editor.

'Mwah! Mwah! Big hug!' said Deborah.

'It's lovely to see you.'

It *was* lovely to see her. Pixie's editor was the warmest and wisest and wittiest in the world, and Pixie was very lucky to have her. Some authors moaned about their editors and accused them of 'interfering' with their work, but Pixie anticipated her editorial notes the way a dog anticipates its dinner. She loved the challenges that Deborah would set her, and worked hard to implement her suggestions. Sometimes she'd say: 'Oh, no! I *can't* do this! I don't know how!', but Deborah would just reply: 'You can, you do know, and you shall do it.' And Pixie did.

'I've a present for you,' Deborah said now, reaching into her pretty raffia basket and producing a gift-wrapped book. She handed it to Pixie and said: 'We'll miss you. But I understand that a gal's gotta go where a gal's gotta go.'

'Thank you,' said Pixie, undoing pink ribbon. The book under the glittery gift wrap was *The SAS Survival Handbook*, and the subtitle read: *How to Survive in the Wild, in Any Climate, on Land or at Sea.*

'When I heard you were abandoning the metropolis for the wild West of Ireland, I thought that this might be the best present you could get.'

'Oh — what fun!' Pixie leafed through the pages. 'This is *fascinating*! Look, here's a section on setting traps. And there are instructions for skinning small animals. Sundried worms! Ooh! And did you know that you can extract water from an animal's eyes by sucking on them? Thank you so much, Deborah. This could come in very handy.'

'When are you off?' asked Deborah.

'Tomorrow.'

'Ireland is officially an island, isn't it?'

'Yes.'

'Have a look at the page I marked.'

' "Islands are especially challenging to the survivor," ' read Pixie. ' "The feelings of loneliness and isolation are acute.' Uh-oh.' 'No worries. I'm always at the end of a phone,' said Deborah.

★ ★ ★

That evening, Pixie went to her friend Mariella's house for supper. Mariella was a writer she had met at an awards ceremony a couple of years ago. Mariella hadn't minded at all that Pixie had won the award that night, because Mariella had won it the year before. Mariella routinely hosted evenings where writers could get together to share and solve each other's problems. She had a big, comfortable house in Hampstead, she was married to the editor of a successful publishing company, and she had two adorable children. She also bore a striking resemblance to Nigella Lawson. Mariella had it all, really, but nobody could be jealous of her because she was so generous.

Tonight several other women writers were due, but Pixie had been invited to come early because she wanted to have a heart-to-heart with Mariella before she left London. She'd told her about her escape plan earlier over the phone, and had made her promise to come over to Ireland and visit.

'Come in, come in!' Mariella shut the front door behind her, then pointed towards the sitting room. 'In there. Fire. Comfy chair. Glass of wine.'

Pixie did as Mariella instructed her, and accepted a glass of red. 'Has she been voted off yet?' she asked.

Mariella shook her head. 'No.'

'Oh! What was she wearing last night? Swimsuit or bikini?'

'Do you really need to know?'

'Yes. Please, Mariella. Be honest. I need to know everything.'

'Thong.'

'Oh! Was she still reading my book and making snide remarks about it?'

'I'm afraid so.'

'Wearing those sexy little spectacles that make her look intelligent?'

'Yes.'

'Did they kiss?'

'Yes.'

'Did he feed her ice-cream again?'

'Yes.'

'The bastard!' Pixie couldn't help it. She started to cry.

'Oh, God, Pixie!' said Mariella, moving to the armchair and hunkering down at her feet. She took hold of her friend's hand and allowed Pixie to cry and cry. When it got to the hiccuping stage, she handed Pixie a tissue and said: 'Does it still hurt so much?'

'Yes,' said Pixie. 'It hurts so much that if I put it in a book no-one would believe it.'

'Can't you write it all out of your system?'

'I'll have to try. That's one of the reasons I'm

absconding. I need to write at full throttle without any distractions.'

'Put him in a book and make awful things happen to him. Make people pelt him with eggs. Make a monkey of him.'

'No. Everyone will know who I mean. It'll look as if I'm a mean-minded bitch getting revenge.'

'Why shouldn't you get revenge? He treated you appallingly. He made Matt Damon on *Oprah* look like a model of restraint.'

'I could get revenge on *her*. I could make her fart in public. I could give her warts.'

'You could push her over a cliff.'

'No. That's too dramatic — she'd like that. I'll be more subtle. I'll give her a job as a balding lap dancer in a sleazy club.'

'That's my girl! Feeling any better?'

Pixie nodded. 'You're better than a shrink, Mariella.'

Mariella gave Pixie's hand a reassuring squeeze. 'I know it's an awful cliché, darling, but time really does heal. And there are lots of other gorgeous men out there who are much more worthy of your love.'

'I guess. You're so lucky, Mariella, to have found Timothy. Was it love at first sight between you two?'

'Yes, it was, pretty much. Was it love at first sight between you and Jonah?'

Pixie pondered a moment, then gave a little shrug. 'You know, sometimes I wonder if I ever actually *loved* Jonah. I'm not sure that all the tears I've been crying haven't been tears of rage and humiliation.'

'Maybe you're right. You can't genuinely have loved him if you're wondering about it.'

'He just seemed such idyllic boyfriend material. Glamorous, sexy, fun. And he was preposterously romantic — he completely swept me off my feet. But at the end of the d — Oh! No! I mustn't use that expression! It's the laziest phrase in the world. *When I allow myself to think about him*, Mariella, I'm not sure he was right for me. I think warning bells started going off when he made the decision to appear on that show.'

'To be perfectly honest, darling, he always struck me as being an egocentric shit.'

'Oh? Why didn't you *tell* me?'

'Do you honestly think you'd have listened? Infatuation is, if anything, even blinder than love.'

Pixie pondered again. 'I wonder if he and Sophie are really in love, Mariella? Or do you think the whole sorry shambles was just a massive PR stitch-up?'

'Whatever. Who gives a toss. Anyway — they deserve each other. Their egos combined would make Everest look like a pluke. Are you all cried out now?'

Pixie nodded.

'Good.' Mariella got to her feet. 'From the painful to the mundane,' she said. 'Will you come into the kitchen and help me unclingfilm the food?'

'Sure.' Pixie stood up. 'How many are coming this evening?'

'Just three. Cathy and Marian have gone off

on holiday together.'

'So it's just you, me, Isabel, Dilys and Dominique?'

'Yep. Don't mention Dominique's book, incidentally.'

'Oh, God. I'd forgotten about that. It completely bombed, didn't it?'

'Yes. So we're not allowed to talk about the war this evening.'

Pixie gave a little grimace. 'That won't be easy. We share an editor, remember?'

Poor Dominique Masterson was the writing colleague who had recently spread her literary wings, and ill-advisedly branched out into Magic Realism. *Publishing News* had predicted that she'd alienate her fan base, and they'd been right.

'Have you read it?' asked Mariella.

'No.' Pixie shook her head. 'I'm scared to. Have you?'

'No.' Her friend moved to the door. 'But I've tried.'

In the kitchen, Mariella set about carrying dishes from fridge to table and asking Pixie questions about her holiday in Connemara, and as Pixie unclingfilmed dishes she filled her friend in on Cleo and Pablo and Hazel and Hugh Hennessy.

'So you've nice neighbours? That's good to know.'

'The Arts Festival sounds as if it could be fun, too. Oh! That reminds me. Guess who helps subsidize it? Colleen!'

'*Colleen!*' Mariella made an 'impressed' face.

'You're keeping *very* illustrious company, my dear!' The doorbell rang. 'Now, if that's Dominique, Pixie, please remember not to mention the book.'

Uh-oh. The fun starts here, thought Pixie, as Mariella made for the front door. The whole point of these evenings was to gripe about indifferent reviews, undeserved advances and supermarket discounts. Tonight would be like a wine appreciation session with no decent wine, or a dinner party without dinner, or an Ann Summers get-together with Tupperware instead of sex toys. Tonight, Dominique's book would be the elephant in the corner that everybody pretends not to see.

★ ★ ★

It was after midnight, and Pixie and Dilys and Dominique were sharing a taxi home. Dominique had — as Pixie had anticipated — been in pretty uncommunicative form, but the wine had mellowed her, and over supper she'd come up with some scandal about an actor she'd met at the BAFTAs. Scandal was Dominique's specialized subject — before she'd defected to Magic Realism the plots of her novels had been driven by thinly disguised celebrities behaving badly.

'So you're off tomorrow, Pixie?' said Dominique now. 'I'm not sure I could hack the isolation of being cast away in some godforsaken spot in Ireland.'

'Talking of castaways, darling,' Dilys said, adopting a sympathetic tone, 'how are you managing? Is it OK to talk about it?'

'I'm getting there. But I'm glad to be escaping. There aren't that many satellite dishes in Connemara, so fewer people will have watched that hateful show.'

'How much longer is it running for?'

'I'm not sure.'

'It finishes on Saturday,' said Dominique.

'Are you a fan?' asked Dilys.

'Good God, no!'

But the denial was too pat. Pixie suspected that Dominique watched the show along with its several million other devotees, and she couldn't blame her.

'I'd probably have tuned in if it hadn't been for that Burke cow,' Pixie admitted. 'That kind of car crash TV's addictive. And it could have been worse, you know.'

'How do you mean?'

She gave them a rather pained smile. 'They offered to fly me to the island.'

'To appear on the show?'

'Yes.'

'I don't believe you! Why?'

'They wanted to spice it up even more. They wanted to see me give him hell. They wanted fur to fly. Maybe they even thought I'd beg him to take me back. I told them where to go.'

'You've pulled some pretty silly stunts in the past to promote your books,' observed Dominique, quickly adding 'Well, we all have,' when she saw Pixie flinch.

'True. But while I may be a media darling, I draw the line at being a media whore. I'd have

104

compromised myself bigtime if I'd accepted that offer.' Pixie shook her head. 'Anyway. Enough about that wretched show. Why don't you two pop over and visit me in Ireland? I've two spare rooms.'

'If you're there to knuckle under and get a book written we wouldn't want to intrude,' said Dominique. 'I know I hate it if I'm on a roll and someone turns up to distract me. Have you any idea what you're going to write?'

'Yes,' said Pixie firmly. 'It's all there in my head. I just need to turn on the tap and it'll all flow out through my fingertips.'

'You make it sound so easy,' sighed Dilys. 'I hit a wall last week and I can't unblock myself.'

'Try writing a diary,' suggested Dominique. 'I often find that helps get the flow going again.'

'I'm going to have to do something. I have a deadline to meet. When's your deadline, Pixie?'

Pixie looked apologetic. 'I don't have one. I'm ahead of myself.'

'Good God! How?'

'I write fast. And I've a suspicion that the next book's going to be the fastest I've ever written.' She tried to keep the venom from showing.

The taxi was pulling up outside the door of Pixie's house. There was a cement mixer squatting in the small front garden, and a skip standing sentinel outside the front door. 'Well, here I am,' she said. 'Building site, sweet building site.'

She leaned over and kissed first Dilys, then Dominique.

'Good luck in Kilrowan, Pixie.'

'Don't get too lonely.'

'Keep in touch, won't you?'

'I will. Bye, Dominique! Bye, Dilys!'

And the taxi pulled away from the kerb and left Pixie rooting for her keys outside the house that would not be home until the bastard builders moved out.

★   ★   ★

The next day, Pixie's usual driver took her to the airport.

'How are you going to get about, in Ireland?' he asked, as he loaded her bags onto a trolley.

'I'll buy something second-hand and sell it on when I'm ready to come home.' Pixie stood on tiptoe and gave him a kiss on the cheek. 'Thanks, Stan. I'll see you in six months or so!'

With an effort — for she was really very small — she pushed the trolley through to the check-in desk and heaved her cases onto the conveyor belt. Pixie had packed with care. Seven pairs of brushed cotton pyjamas, one for every day of the week. Her flowery flip-flops. Three pairs of sweat pants, several T-shirts and her favourite dressing gown. A couple of smart outfits and a couple of glamorous ones: you never knew. The *Concise Oxford*, *Roget's Thesaurus*, and her *Dictionary of Slang*. She knew that she'd need rain gear, but she'd buy that in Galway. There was no point in packing too much.

She was early for her flight — she'd go into W.H. Smith's and help herself to some magazines. Scanning the shelves, she saw that this month's *Writers' Forum* carried an interview with Dominique Masterson. Pixie turned to the relevant page and read the words 'Dominique's Brave New World' above a photograph of the author with all her wrinkles (No. What did the face-cream ads call them?) her *expression lines* airbrushed out. She was reclining on a chaise-longue, wearing a white peignoir and a dreamy smile. There was a bowl of white tulips on the table beside her, and a stack of volumes of Magic Realism. Márquez, Allende, Rushdie. Not a chick-lit title in sight.

The other magazine that Pixie picked up was *Heat*. She leafed through it as she went to join the queue for the checkout. Oh! There *they* were, on their island! She shut the magazine immediately.

But later, on the plane, she couldn't stop herself from opening it again. It was like trying not to scratch an itch. *She* was golden of skin, hair and thong, smiling radiantly over her shoulder as she ran along a beach. He was wearing his best 'I am a sexy actor' face.

Pixie wrenched her eyes away from the magazine and looked down through the porthole at the emerald blanket that stretched beneath her. Ireland! The country that would be her home from home for the foreseeable future, the country where she'd be sure to make new friends, the country where she would construct her novel in the form of a fairytale that had lots of sex in it. And possibly a death or two. And revenge? Oh, yes, thought

Pixie as she extracted her pen from her bag. There'd have to be *shed loads* of that too . . .

★ ★ ★

Once the plane had landed at Galway airport, the stewardess was surprised when she happened upon an issue of *Heat* that had been discarded in business class to find that snot, stubble and pimples had been scribbled all over the faces of film star Sophie Burke and her handsome new squeeze, Jonah Harrington. There were speech bubbles, too, coming out of their mouths. Jonah was saying: 'I am a first-class shit', while Sophie's sanguine declaration read: 'And *I* am a *TOTAL SLAPPER!*'

6

'Our new neighbour's moved in,' said Pablo.

Cleo had arrived home from work to find him sloshing red wine into a glass. 'Yeah?' she said.

'I thought we might call over with a bottle as a housewarming present.'

'Good idea. Have you spoken to her?'

'No. But I saw her this morning doing jumping jacks in her sitting room.'

'Jumping jacks? That's a weird thing for someone to do when they first move in somewhere.'

'It's a pretty weird thing to do, full stop. Glass of wine?'

'No, thanks. I fancy a cup of tea.' Cleo wandered over to the kettle and switched it on. 'Any news?'

'Yeah. I had a phone call from the wife of some man who wants me to paint a portrait of his daughter as a twenty-first birthday present.'

Nooooo! 'Oh?' Cleo tried to sound uncon-cerned. 'Who is he?'

'A Mr Jay. His wife said she'd met me before at some exhibition opening, but I don't remember her. They have a holiday home here.'

'Are you going to do it?'

'Of course. I quoted her such an unrealistic price that she agreed without even bothering to haggle.' Pablo yawned. 'Another sucker bites the dust.'

'Will you put in a pig?'

'At that price I think she deserves more than a pig. She deserves an orang-utan as well.'

Trying not to show that she was thinking hard, Cleo busied herself with tea-making business. 'Pablo?' she said, taking care not to meet his eyes. 'Remember when we decided to get married, you mentioned the possibility of giving up doing your 'quirky' stuff? Remember you said you'd love to tell all the oh-so-happening people who want a portrait by you to piss off?'

'Did I?'

'Yes. Why don't you?'

'Why don't I what?'

'Do it.'

'What? Tell all my oh-so-happening clients to piss off?'

'Yes.'

'There's one very simple, two-word answer to that question, sweetheart.'

'And that is?'

'Professional suicide.'

'But we don't need the money!'

'Hello? Is there anyone in there? What would I do if I gave up work?'

'Go back to the kind of painting you did before you started churning out your 'quirky' stuff. I came across one of your old sketchbooks the other day. There was some really lovely stuff in there.'

Pablo gave her a 'get-real' look. 'You mean go back to doing work that was critically and unilaterally panned?'

'Oh. Was it?'

'Yep.'

'But you loved doing it, didn't you?'

'I'm not sure it would be a good idea to invite the critics to a retrospective shooting party, darling.'

'Oh. It's just that the quirky stuff seems to be — well — depressing you. You take so little joy in it.' Cleo fetched a mug from the cupboard.

'It doesn't depress me quite as much as some of the people who buy it.'

'This Mr Jay being a case in point?'

'Oh, yeah. The wife sounded like a Dublin 4 matron from hell. I can just picture her creaming herself as she tells all her friends — ' he put on an exaggerated Dublin 4 accent — ''Oh, I've hired the artist Pablo MacBride to paint Abigail's portrait for her twenty-first'. What's the betting that I get phone calls within a matter of weeks from more matriarchs wanting portraits of their princesses?'

'You've become terribly cynical about it, darling. If it's making you bitter and twisted, why don't you just give up?'

'Hey, Ms Moneybags. You're talking about my livelihood.'

'But we don't need the money.'

'You've already pointed that out, thanks. Tell me this. What am I supposed to do if I give up painting? Take up flower-arranging? Sit around and gossip with my friends all day and paint my nails instead of canvases while my wife goes and plays shop?'

'That's not fair! I don't play shop.'

'But *I* play at being a painter? By the same

111

argument, Cleo, I could ask you why you bother to work your ass off in a bookshop that brings in a derisory income when you've stocks and shares and portfolios earning you thousands?'

'You know why. It's because I love it.'

'I rest my case.'

'But you don't love your painting.'

'Who told you that?'

'I just guessed — '

'Guess again, little Cleo. I may not love the subject matter, but I love the act of creation. If you took my painting away from me, I'd be a husk. An emasculated husk, at that, who allows his lottery millionaire wife to fund his lifestyle. I don't think you've put a lot of thought into this, Cleo.'

It was true. Her argument was spurious in the extreme. It had just been a stupid knee-jerk reaction to the notion of the Posh-haired princess sitting for Pablo. He deserved an apology.

'I'm sorry. You're right.'

Pablo knocked back his wine, then poured the remains of the bottle into his glass, giving a pissed-off shrug when he saw that the level didn't reach the halfway mark. He took another bottle from the rack. An entire bottle of wine, and it wasn't even half-past six yet! But Cleo sensed that now was not the time to lecture him on his drinking.

'Are you sure you won't have a glass?' he asked, cutting the foil.

'Oh, I may as well.'

She put her mug back in the cupboard,

thinking that joining him in a glass of wine might placate him a little. He'd been narky, lately, and Cleo had put it down to the fact that he was unhappy in his work.

The sketchbook she'd come across the other day had been full of drawings that had been executed before Pablo had embarked upon his career as Court Painter. The drawings were mostly of ordinary people with no airs, no attitude, and no status symbols to display (in a recent portrait he'd painted, the sitter had insisted on wearing his chain of office). But the beauty of the sketchbook was that the people who animated its pages had character, and the drawings had soul.

Back then, Pablo had been resolutely anti-monarchy. But nowadays the more he shied away from doing society portraits the more society clamoured to be painted by him, and the higher his asking price had risen. Cleo knew that each commission he accepted filled him a little more to the brim with self-loathing, and she felt utterly powerless to help him. She'd noticed that he'd taken to using the self-portrait that hung in his studio as a dartboard, and she suspected that he was often sorely tempted to similarly use the portraits he production-lined.

And then she was reminded of their wealthy new neighbour, and she hoped *she* wouldn't ask Pablo to paint her portrait. He'd be certain to put something like a fluffy kitten in, and while Pixie might be a romantic novelist, Cleo suspected that she would have very little truck with any fluffy kittens and roses nonsense.

'Should we phone Pixie before we call round next door?' she asked now.

'Have you a mobile number for her? I don't imagine the land line's been connected yet.'

'Oh. No, I don't.' She watched Pablo's beautiful painter's hands as they worked the corkscrew. 'When is this Abigail girl sitting for you, by the way?'

'Sometime next month.' He pulled the cork, poured and handed her a glass.

Cleo took a sip, then set her glass aside as Fluffy trotted into the room, announcing her arrival with clickety claws. 'Oh, hello, darling,' she said, hunkering down to ruffle her. 'How was your day? Did you go hunting? Did you hang with your friends? Did you take sweets from strangers? I bet you did, you naughty girl. You have a very guilty look about you.'

'I took her for a walk on Lissnakeelagh earlier. She's covered in sand, I'm afraid.'

'That's all right. Any excuse for a bath. We'll put you in the Jacuzzi, later, sweetheart, as a special treat. And guess what? I found you new hair accessories today, in Breda's shop. Look!' Cleo reached for her bag and produced a see-through plastic wallet full of tiny plastic grips. Glittery grips with flower and bird and butterfly motifs, elastic bobbins with hearts on, and stars, and silly little frog-shaped combs.

'She loses them all over the place, you know. You could fill a landfill site with the plastic crap she leaves all over the village.'

This observation was true. But the fact of the matter was that everyone in the village knew and

114

loved Fluffy, and they tended to fix her mislaid hair accessories back on the bitch when they saw her sitting in her favourite spot on the harbour wall.

'I know.' Cleo made an apologetic face. 'But she looks so pretty! Don't you, darling? Hey — let's try this one, Flufflet. It's for your fringe.' She piled Fluffy's little mane of hair on top of her head and secured it with a bobbin that had daisies attached. 'There! Who's a gorgeous girl?' she said, standing up and admiring her handiwork. 'Doesn't she look adorable?'

'She looks like something by Jeff Koons.'

'Don't be horrible! She'll wow all the boys when she struts her stuff later.'

'Just like her mistress.' Pablo slanted Cleo a look of deliberation and set down his glass. He stretched a hand out to her and pulled her towards him. 'Come here, you. Fancy a ride?'

'Maybe.' She gave him a provocative look. 'What time is it?'

'Around half-past six,' he said, sliding a hand under her T-shirt and unhooking her bra.

'Then, yes,' she said.

'What's the time of day got to do with it?'

'My organizer told me this morning when I accessed it that I was to ride my husband at half-past six.'

'Did it mention a location?'

'Yes,' said Cleo. 'The downstairs shower room.'

'Then I think you'd better be a good girl, little Cleo, and do what your organizer tells you. Do you know that there's a big smut of newsprint on

115

your chin?' He rubbed the area below her lower lip with his thumb.

Cleo gave a little gasp. 'Oh! Are you telling me I'm smutty?'

'You're a very smutty little girl indeed. You could do with a good scrub-up.'

He reached down and took her hand, and then started pulling her towards the shower room. 'Come along,' he said, 'resistance is futile.'

Shutting the door behind them, he pushed her up against it. 'Now,' he said, with a tug at her T-shirt. 'Let's give you a thorough examination to see if there's smut anywhere else. Arms up. Hmm. So far, so good. Pristine girly flesh that — mm — tastes quite as succulent as it looks.'

His fingers moved to the zip on her jeans. 'You might help me out here, madam. Step out of your jeans, please. Thank you indeed — you are most accommodating. And what pretty knickers you have on! They're so pretty it's almost a shame to take them off, but — ' he pulled at the ribbons that Agent Provocateur had so considerately included in their design — 'off they must come. Now. Something tells me that location-specific inspection is required here.' He let the lacy confection fall, then knelt at her feet. 'This is rather intriguing! How very, very sweet . . . What's wrong, sweetheart? Why are you going all wriggly on me?'

'Pablo!'

'What?' he said, withdrawing. 'Do you want me to stop?'

'No . . . '

'Very well. I'll continue at your behest.'

116

'Oh!'

Some minutes later, when Cleo was on the brink of orgasm, Pablo said: 'Location-specific inspection complete. You may turn round now.'

Feeling faint with arousal, Cleo did as he asked.

'You are so very compliant, sweetheart! What makes you such a good girl? But — alas! What have we here? How did a handprint find its way onto your bottom, darling? What have you been up to? Perhaps you're not such a good girl after all. In fact, I think you are most definitely in need of a good going-over with a loofah. Into the tub with you now, for an invigorating shower.' He led her to the shower stall, and checked the gauge. 'Excellent. The pressure's on high.'

And Pablo joined Cleo under the power shower without even bothering to remove his clothes.

★ ★ ★

Pixie had set up her laptop on a table by the window in her study. She sat with her back to the window so that the fabulous view didn't have the power to distract her.

She had arrived in Kilrowan yesterday evening, and familiarized herself with her new home. The caretaker had very kindly left essentials in the fridge, turned on gas and electricity, and set a fire. Pixie had sat by the fire last night watching Irish television channels, then gone to bed at eleven o'clock and set her alarm for seven.

The first thing she did upon waking was to switch her mind into work mode. She lay under her duvet for nearly an hour, allowing her characters to walk into her head and introduce themselves. 'Ha! You think you're pretty smart, don't you?' she told one expensive blonde. 'You'd better not get too uppity with me, miss! Meet your *maker*!' This was how she started every writing day.

After she'd performed her mental roll call, she got out of bed and put on sweat pants and T-shirt to perform her SAS exercises. Whilst browsing through a second-hand shop one day, she'd come across a manual that contained an exercise programme for commando training, and she'd worked her way up to quite a high level of fitness.

Exercise was important for her because she knew that without it pounds and pounds of flab would creep up on her during all the hours spent sitting in front of her computer screen. The exercises were old-fashioned ones — sit-ups and press-ups and jumping jacks — and she was religious about doing them. Afterwards she'd have a shower, change into her brushed cotton pyjamas, and make something to eat. Smoothies, usually, or freshly juiced carrots and broccoli. She ate while her computer booted up, and then she started work. At four o'clock she'd have a banana and a glass of milk, and at seven o'clock she'd revise the day's work and do a word count. Pixie routinely notched up two or three thousand words a day.

It was now half-past seven, and she was filing

away her word count when the doorbell went. It was one of those naff 'ding dong' ones. Going upstairs to answer the front door felt a bit weird — it was the other way round in her London house.

Pablo MacBride and Cleo were standing on the doorstep. Pablo held out a bottle of wine. 'Welcome to Kilrowan,' he said.

'How very kind. Thank you!' said Pixie, taking the wine from him. 'Come in. The kitchen's downstairs — but you know that, of course.' She led the way, talking over her shoulder. 'Fantastic day, wasn't it? I'm so mad about that view that I have to keep my back turned to it in case it distracts me.'

'I know what you mean,' said Cleo, as they crossed through the sitting room. The view, in all its glory, was framed in the picture window. 'I do hope we haven't disturbed you, Pixie. Were you on your way to bed?'

'Oh, no. I've just finished work. I never leave the house when I'm working, so I always work in pyjamas. It's the most comfortable option.'

'What if you need to go out to the shops?'

'The shops? What for?' Pixie padded across the kitchen floor on her bare feet and located a corkscrew.

'For food.'

'Oh.' Pixie looked perplexed. 'I hadn't thought about that. I have my food delivered to me in London.'

'You could ask Breda Shanley if she could organize delivery,' said Cleo. 'She runs the local general store.'

'That'd be handy.' As she stripped away the foil on the neck of the bottle, Pixie couldn't help noticing that there was a distinctly post-coital look about Cleo and Pablo, and that their hair was damp. She found herself wondering if she'd ever wear a post-coital look again. She remembered — *No! Don't go there! Don't allow him back in!* 'Oh — fiddlesticks!' The corkscrew had an unfamiliar working method, and she was making a mess of uncorking the wine.

'Here. I'll do that for you,' said Pablo, taking bottle and corkscrew from her. He removed the cork expertly, then raised an eyebrow at her. 'Any chance of wineglasses?' he asked.

'Ah. Of course.' Pixie started hunting through cupboards. 'Wine-glasses, wineglasses — yes! Here we are,' she said, finally hitting on the right one.

'Haven't you got the hang of things here yet?' asked Cleo.

'Not really.' She moved into the sitting room and set the glasses down on the coffee table.

'There's a list of guidelines blu-tacked to the back of the cupboard under the stairs,' said Pablo. He poured wine into the glasses and handed them round. 'And of course, it goes without saying that if there's anything you can't manage, I'm always next door.'

'Thank you very much. Where do I get fuel for the fire, incidentally? There was a fire set when I arrived last night and there's a basket of . . . um. What do you call those black things that burn?'

'Briquettes,' said Pablo, as if he were instructing someone in a foreign language.

120

'They're called peat briquettes, and you'll find bales of them and bags of coal in Breda's shop.'

'Oh. How on earth will I get coal down the stairs?'

Pablo laughed. 'I can tell it's going to be an eye-opener living next door to you,' he said. 'The quintessential helpless woman!'

Pixie bridled a little. 'I'm quite tough you know. I do SAS training exercises every day.'

'I know. I saw you this morning, doing jumping jacks. You looked very fetching.'

'How could you have seen me?' Pixie felt a blush coming on. 'We don't overlook each other.'

'Ah, but you overlook our garden,' said Pablo, 'and that's how I saw you — on the way to my studio.'

'Where is your studio?'

'*Là-bas!*' He indicated with an expansive gesture of his arm the timber-built house at the bottom of the garden of number 5.

'Oh,' said Pixie. 'I thought that was a shed.'

'It's where I work.'

'Very well, then. I shall most definitely lay off doing my exercises in front of the view.' She raised her glass. 'Cheers! No — how do you say it in Irish? Sláinte?' She pronounced the word 'slaynt'.

Cleo laughed. 'It's pronounced 'Slawncha'.'

'Slawncha!' echoed Pixie.

'About fuel,' said Pablo. 'There's an outhouse for storing it. I'll bring you a load of bags of coal, will I? I'm assuming you don't have a car.'

'Thank you again. I'm obviously going to be awfully beholden to you two. I don't have a car yet, but I'm thinking about picking up a second-hand runaround in Galway.'

'Do you know about cars?'

'Not a thing,' admitted Pixie.

'Then I'll come with you. Make sure you don't get ripped off.'

Yikes. Pixie hoped that Cleo wouldn't be pissed off at Pablo for making the offer about the car. There was only so much attention a man could pay a woman who wasn't his wife, after all, and Pablo was so very, very sexy. If he were *her* man she wouldn't allow him to jaunt off to Galway with a virtual stranger. For all Cleo knew, she, Pixie, could have the hots for Pablo, bigtime.

'I watched some of your Irish television last night,' she said, changing the subject. 'There was a peculiar programme on where all the gorgeous, intelligent women seem to end up with losers challenged in the looks department. All the female characters were complete pushovers.' Like I once was, she could have added.

'I watched that, too,' said Cleo, 'and the same thought struck me. It's weird one, all right.'

'It's a peculiarly Irish thing, I think,' said Pablo. 'Irish men are so insecure that they have to give the impression that it's their charm and quirkiness that women find attractive. They obviously feel they don't have much else going for them.'

'Well, the ones in that programme certainly didn't. I was appalled to see a beautiful girl in bed with someone who was clearly a charlatan with a pretty low IQ.'

'You've got a lot going for you, darling,' said Cleo, 'and you're an Irish male.'

'Yes. You must be the exception that proves the rule,' remarked Pixie.

Pablo shrugged. 'Maybe. But the reason that I have so much going for me, as we are all aware, is because of the famous trademark 'quirkiness' of my paintings. They're nearly as quirky as the male characters on Irish television.'

The looks that were exchanged between Cleo and Pablo were borderline meaningful. Pixie suspected an attempt to defuse was necessary. 'So. Am I likely to find myself a quirky Irish man while I'm here?' she asked.

Cleo looked dubious. 'Most of the eligible ones around Kilrowan have been snapped up. I got lucky, with Pablo.'

'Why are you talking about me as if you'd won me in some kind of lottery?'

'You know how good I am at winning lotteries,' said Cleo with a smile.

'Yeah. Well, some of us have to earn our money through honest — ' he paused, reflected — 'or should that be *dishonest? —* labour.'

Pixie sensed a testiness here. 'Were those your paintings on the wall of your sitting room?' she asked quickly.

'Are you mad?' said Pablo. 'The only painting of mine that hangs in our house is a nude portrait of my inamorata that was painted in a spirit of true love in the early days of our courtship.'

'Might I see some of your work?' asked Pixie. 'With a view to buying something?'

'Don't you think that's rather a reckless proposition? You might hate them.'

'Actually,' put in Cleo, 'I think Pixie might like the one of Ballynahinch Castle. It's got a fairytale princess astride a pig, Pixie.'

'Sounds intriguing. What inspired that one?'

'Well,' said Pablo, 'the fairytale princess was inspired by Mrs MacBride here.'

'And the pig?'

'The pig,' said Pablo, 'is me.' And he gave Cleo a fiendish smile and knocked back the contents of his glass in a single gulp.

Uh-oh, thought Pixie. Despite the post-coital bloom, there was clearly something amiss here. A little voice in her head spoke up. *Is there material here for a storyline?* it asked her in cajoling fashion: whereupon a second voice instantly made itself heard. *No! These are nice people. These are your new friends, and you are not to steal their lives and put them in a book. Shame on you, Jane Gray, for even thinking that way!*

* * *

When the housewarming wine was finished, Pablo and Cleo extended an invitation to Pixie to join them for dinner in O'Toole's.

'That's very kind of you,' said Pixie, 'but I can't be bothered changing out of my pyjamas. I'm nice and cosy in them, and I think I'll have an early night.'

She let them out, made herself a rudimentary supper, and watched television in the kitchen while she ate it.

She could choose between a re-run of *Friends* or a documentary on RTE about the current Irish political climate. Pixie would much prefer to watch *Friends*, but she decided she ought to clue herself in a little more on what was going on in her host country.

She learned that a series of tribunals had been set up to investigate corruption in Irish politics. Goodness! Ireland seemed to be as corrupt as the Dominican Republic. A former city manager had served time for fraud, a former Minister for Justice was in the slammer on similar charges, a former prime minister was languishing in disgrace on his private yacht — and that was only the tip of the iceberg. The banks were at it too!

When she saw archive footage of a young man walking free from a murder charge, sneering at the camera and giving the people of Ireland the V sign, she decided she'd learned enough, and wondered seriously if it had been such a good idea to come here. She turned over to *Friends*, but it was an episode she'd seen loads of times ('The One Where the Monkey Gets Away'), so she turned off the television, took her laptop into the sitting room and turned that on instead.

She went to her favourites, clicked and waited for her home page to materialize into view. She wanted to make sure that Rufus, her web master, had updated the newsletter as per her instructions. Everything present and correct! Good.

Then she turned to her 'Books' page, to see if the new covers were featured. Her backlist had been rejacketed recently, and she'd sent Rufus j-pegs of the new look. Yes. All her titles were on display in their lovely new clothes.

Pixie had had half a dozen books published in nearly as many years. She'd started writing when she realized that she wasn't going to be a hand model for ever. No matter how much expensive hand cream she slathered on at night (she slept in cotton gloves), her hands would sooner or later start to show signs of ageing, and once that happened her career would be over. She knew she'd have to get cracking on some other way of earning a living.

So she'd attended a series of workshops on creative writing, and at one of those workshops she'd met a woman called Lorraine Lavelle, who was giving a talk in her capacity as a bestselling novelist. Pixie told Lorraine rather shyly that she'd written the first draft of a novel, and asked her if she'd mind taking a look at it. Just three weeks later, she'd had a phone call from her . . .

★   ★   ★

Jane Gray was in a tizzy. She was due to see Lorraine Lavelle, to seek advice on her attempt at a novel. She'd made sure to arrive early, and now she was standing outside Lorraine's charming mews house, clutching a big bunch of Vendella roses and hoping she didn't look like a stalker. She didn't want to ring the doorbell until exactly half-past four, which was the time they'd agreed upon. Lorraine hadn't entered into discussion on the phone. She'd just told Jane to come to her house, so that she could return the manuscript that had been posted to her.

The second hand of her watch hit twelve, and Jane pressed the doorbell. Nothing happened. Should she knock? Maybe the bell wasn't working? Or had Lorraine forgotten that she was coming? She was just about to try the knocker, when the door opened and Lorraine Lavelle said: 'You're bang on time!' Jane thrust the roses at her, and Lorraine accepted them with a gracious 'How kind.'

The author was wearing a loose cotton frock with a pretty cardigan over it. She had embroidered slippers on her feet. Her abundant dark hair was piled up on top of her head and held in place with a tortoiseshell jaws. She had a pen hooked onto the neckline of her dress, she had reading glasses perched on the end of her nose. She looked exactly the way Jane thought a bestselling novelist ought to look. 'Come in!' she said.

Jane followed her down a whitewashed hallway, the walls of which were covered in original paintings. Classical music was playing somewhere. As they passed the door to the kitchen (there was a gorgeous aroma of something spicy cooking), Lorraine poked her head through and said: 'Tea would be lovely when you've got a minute, Maggie! And could you put these beautiful roses in water for me?' She passed the roses through the door, and then they carried on down the hall to what was clearly Lorraine's study.

'What a wonderful room!' said Jane.

The room had floor to ceiling shelves, all

crammed higgledy-piggledy with books. There was a noticeboard bristling with Post-Its and postcards, an enormous desk covered in reference books, and a gleaming laptop resplendent on a Turkish prayer mat. There was a couch piled with squishy cushions, a comfy chair with a cat curled up on it, and a vase of delphiniums perched on a plinth. Light cascaded into the room through french windows, beyond which was a small garden, gaudy with geraniums in pots.

'Is this where you work?' Jane asked.

'Yes. I love it. Sit down — I'll shift the cat.' Lorraine picked up the unresisting cat and set it on the floor, where it sat blinking sleepily. 'Did you have trouble finding the place?' she asked. 'I'm afraid my directions aren't the best, and there are no obvious landmarks.'

'No.' Jane didn't say that she'd actually recced Lorraine's house the previous day because she was anxious that she might indeed have difficulty finding it. She was glad she had. It was in an out-of-the-way corner of Islington.

'Maggie, my housekeeper, will bring us tea shortly. But while we're waiting, I might as well tell you that I thought your novel — Oh. Excuse me.' The phone was ringing. 'I'll have to take that. It's my husband.'

She picked up the phone and spoke into it. 'Hello, darling,' she said. 'Yes, I booked tickets. Will you phone Jocelyn? Make sure we get a window table? The place is sure to be crowded after the show. Mm hm. Mm hm.'

And as Lorraine talked on the phone, Jane

looked about her and thought being a writer was very probably the best job in the world. How perfect Lorraine had made her workspace! How fantastic to be able to come downstairs in the mornings in your own home and fix yourself coffee before embarking on your novel! How wonderful to sit in front of a computer and let stories and characters flow out of your head onto the screen!

A woman came in with a tray of tea things and set them down on a side table. Lorraine mouthed 'Thanks!' at her, and the woman smiled at Jane on her way out of the room. How wonderful to have a housekeeper bring you tea and smile at you!

'I'll meet you in the foyer. Quarter-past seven. Bye, darling,' Lorraine was saying now, and Jane thought: How wonderful to have a husband whom you called darling! How wonderful to go to a show together and have dinner afterwards at a window table! How wonderful to be Lorraine Lavelle!

'Sorry about that,' said Lorraine, putting down the phone. 'Tea?'

'Yes, please.'

Lorraine sat down on the couch beside the tea table, and started to pour. Jane noticed a pile of pages on the couch, with the topmost bearing the legend 'Miching Mallecho — a Novel by Jane Gray.' Her stomach lurched.

'Milk? Sugar?' said Lorraine, pouring tea into cups. They were the prettiest china cups imaginable, with a pattern of roses clambering over them.

'Just milk, please,' said Jane.

'It's China.'

'Oh. Then I'll pass on the milk, thanks very much.'

Lorraine finished pouring and handed her the cup.

'Thank you so much for agreeing to see me,' Jane said. 'I can't believe you can be so generous with your time.'

'I'm not going to be *that* generous. I'm going to the theatre this evening and I'll have to chase you off in an hour so that I can tart myself up. Now. Brass tacks. Your novel's a mess.'

Oh!

'*But* — and it's a big but — it has potential. So I'm going to tell you how you can make it right. The first thing you're going to have to do is decide whether you want to write something literary or something commercial — '

'Oh, commercial, please. I don't want to starve in a garret!'

'Good. Now you've a better idea of who you're writing for. That's a start. Where did you get your title, incidentally?'

'It's from *Hamlet*.'

'It's the reason I agreed to read your book. I found the title intriguing, but it's wrong. You need something with more instant appeal.' Lorraine started to leaf through the pile of A4 pages. 'You have some good ideas, Jane, and a lot of the incidents are very funny, but you compromise yourself by the kind of language you use. Look at this! 'A venerable cedar tree'! When was the last time you were walking down the road and found yourself thinking 'Oh, look at that venerable cedar tree'?'

'Um. Never.'

'I thought not. You've got to write the way you talk. You may love big recondite words, but your reader's not going to thank you for using them. *Never* use the word 'recondite' in a book, incidentally. And I noticed you're a little over-fond of adjectives. A good rule of thumb is to go through your book striking a red pen through any adjectives or adverbs you find.'

'*All* of them?'

'Not all. But most. Look at all these. 'She stated *matter-of-factly*', 'He informed her *knowingly*', 'She smiled *kindly*'. You don't need them. They're extraneous. Take a knife to your baby!'

'Oh!'

'That's the best advice you'll ever get. Now, see here? You're telling, not showing . . . '

And Lorraine sat there on her gorgeous cushiony couch and gave Jane Gray a masterclass in the art of writing popular fiction.

After an hour, she looked at her watch and said: 'Time's up.'

'You've been so *kind*. Thank you so much, Lorraine, I can't tell you — '

Nor *could* she tell her, because Jane was quite inarticulate with gratitude as she made her way to the front door, carrying her precious manuscript. She wished there were more variations of the words 'thank you' so that she could stop sounding like a parrot as she dallied on the threshold of Lorraine Lavelle's house, hanging on her every last syllable.

131

'You'll want to know what the next step is?' asked Lorraine.

'Yes, please!'

'Polish it, polish it, and polish it some more. And when you think it's in good enough nick to show to an editor, put it away in a drawer for at least a week *without* sneaking looks at it, and then take it out and *don't send it*. Polish it even more, instead.'

Jane was nodding earnestly. 'Which publisher should I approach?' she asked.

Lorraine took the pen that was hooked onto the neckline of her frock and said: 'You don't mind if I scribble it on your manuscript?'

'Not at all.'

'Deborah Millen,' wrote Lorraine in block capitals, followed by a phone number.

'Deborah's my editor,' she said. 'You can mention my name. Bye, now. I've really got to dash.' She made to move back indoors.

'Goodbye, Lorraine. And tha — '

'Just one more thing, Jane.' Lorraine paused before shutting the door to her fabulous mews house.

'Yes?'

'You might want to think about changing your name.'

★ ★ ★

And that was how plain Jane Gray had become Pixie Pirelli, writer of glittering chick-lit. It had taken six months of hard, hard graft, and she often despaired when she thought that she might never get there. Because every spare moment of Pixie's life was now spent working at the coal-face of her novel. She sacrificed evenings out with friends for it, she sacrificed holidays, she even sacrificed watching *Friends* on telly.

She remembered how she'd looked around Lorraine Lavelle's study, picturing the writer sitting serenely at her desk with a cup of China tea, words tripping out through her fingers onto the screen, and realized now how wrong she'd got it. Writing was — that great word! — *gruellingly* hard work, both physically and mentally. And emotionally, too. Some days she closed down her laptop feeling as though she'd been put through a mangle.

And then had come the day when she'd wrapped her baby up in brown paper and sent it adrift via FedEx, wondering if it would ever come back to her, and feeling like Moses's mother.

The waiting game had been the most painful one of her life. Weeks went by before she picked up the phone and heard the words: 'Hello. Is that Pixie Pirelli?'

She was just about to say: 'Sorry, wrong number. It's Jane Gray,' and put the phone down, when she heard the voice say: 'It's Deborah Millen here, from Princessa Publishing. I'm interested in meeting you with a view to publishing your novel.'

And Pixie Pirelli had burst into tears.

★ ★ ★

Now she sat gazing at her babies on the 'Books' page of her website, admiring them. How pretty they were! And how pretty she looked in her author photograph! They'd flown a photographer all the way from Italy to photograph her, and as Pixie had had a rash of truly horrible spots on her chin on the day of the shoot, he'd had to do some judicious airbrushing. He'd photographed her sitting at her laptop wearing wifty-wafty chiffon and a big smile, polished pinkies twinkling across the keyboard.

She wondered now as she sat in front of her laptop what her readers would think if they could see her the way she really worked: in her pyjamas, drinking milk and eating bananas. The glass from which she'd drunk her milk earlier was still sitting by her laptop, alongside her banana skin.

Pixie shut down her computer. She took the glass into the kitchen and stuck it in the dishwasher, and dropped the banana skin in the bin.

And then she went to bed.

7

When Hazel got back to Dublin from Kilrowan after the bank holiday, she phoned Erin to arrange lunch.

'Dish the dirt!' said Erin. 'What's this Hugh geezer like?'

'I'm not dishing any dirt until we meet up. Anyway, there isn't any dirt to dish.'

'Spoilsport,' said Erin. 'How about a long lunch on Saturday? Fitzers'?'

'Fitzers', Saturday is good.' And Hazel hung up the phone.

It was true that there had been no dirt to dish. Hugh (or Scar as she occasionally thought of him — why was that name so sexy?) had been the perfect gentleman, and Hazel found this slightly perplexing because men tended to come on to her bigtime. It wasn't as if she *wanted* him to come on to her — no, no. It was just that it was — well — *unusual* that he hadn't.

After she put down the phone to Erin, Hazel sent an e-mail to Hugh to thank him for the um — *pleasant* — weekend, and to reassure him that she would get cracking on a PR manifesto ASAP. She'd been thinking a lot about it.

She knew she was going to have to start writing begging letters to celebrities. Experience had told her that out of sixty letters only ten might receive responses, and of these ten maybe only three would be positive. The next stage was cold calling. Hazel had, in the past, had numerous humiliating experiences cold calling celebs, pleading with them to participate in various events. One diva had been so outraged that Hazel had had the temerity to approach her about driving a vintage car as part of the St Patrick's Day parade that she'd instructed her agent never ever to take a call from Nutcracker PR again.

A standard response from celebs' publicists was: 'Unfortunately my client is unable to contribute at this time.' This could be translated as 'He can't be arsed', 'She is sunning herself in the Maldives', or 'He's in rehab'. And if you bypassed the publicist, you very often got a chilly 'How did you get my home number?' from the demigod/goddess you were prostrating yourself in front of.

Why bother inviting such grief? The cold, commercial truth was that every event needed a buzz factor, and celebrities could always be depended on to provide it. Hazel had got so good at her job that she didn't even find the humiliation humiliating any more. After all, celebrities were just another commodity to be graded and traded, and you couldn't allow a mere commodity to faze you.

She sent mail, then set about checking the contents of her inbox. Nothing very interesting — no spam, thank Christ — her blocker seemed to be doing the trick. Then she saw an unfamiliar name. Cleo Dowling. Who on earth was she? On opening the envelope, her memory was jogged. Of course. She was the owner of the bookshop in Kilrowan . . .

'Subject: Arts Festival', she read.

Dear Hazel,

I e-mailed Deirdre O'D. She'll be in Ireland around the same time as the Kilrowan AF is on, and while she hasn't the time to do a screenwriting work-shop (she has three kids), she says that Rory might be glad to contribute for sentimental reasons. Anyway, she said it was cool to let you have her e-mail address. It's dod@jollyrogerenterprises.com, so feel free to drop her a line. Hope this helps.

V best,

Cleo.

Well, well, well. Rory McDonagh! Another celebrity scalp to add to her address book. Baiting her hook with a Big-Fish-in-a-Big-Pond name like his would guarantee that some of the smaller fry might bite. Hang about . . . Big fish, small fry? This 'maritime theme' palaver was clearly infiltrating her subconscious.

Hazel reached for her organizer, opened it, then clicked on the section marked 'ex-directory' and typed in dod@jollyrogerenterprises.com.

Then she googled Rory McDonagh.

To: Deirdre O'Dare
From: Nutcracker PR
Re: Kilrowan Arts Festival

Dear Deirdre,

Your friend Cleo Dowling very kindly passed on your e-mail address to me. I am sorry that you will be unable to participate in the Kilrowan Arts Festival this coming August, but we would be delighted if your husband, Rory McDonagh, might spare some of his time.

Allow me to fill you in on what we have in mind for the festival this year. We have decided to run with a specific theme, and the heart of this year's festival will beat to the rhythm of all things 'maritime'. I've hit upon the idea of a screening of his film, 'The O'Malley' (its subject matter being piracy, it lends itself well to the flavour of the event). If Rory was available to speak after the screening, that would be fantastic.

I look forward to hearing from you.

With very best wishes,

Hazel MacNamara, Nutcracker PR

From: Deirdre O'Dare
To: Cleo Dowling
Forward: re: Kilrowan Arts Festival

Hi, Cleo! You say you've met this Hazel person and she's kosher? Ahem. 'The heart of this year's festival will beat to the rhythm of all things 'maritime' ';-) How come she doesn't talk the talk?

Love, Deirdre

From: Cleo Dowling
To: Deirdre O'Dare
Re: KAF

Helloo!

She's fine, really. I suppose she's just talking in 'PR' mode.

If Rory's available, Deirdre, it would be great. Kilrowan's been languishing of late, and it needs a good shot in the arm to get it up and running again. The village is still a Mecca for tourists in summer, but it's not enough to keep us going all year round. Business are closing — if I didn't have independent means the bookshop would have shut down by now. Run it by Rory, see what he says.

Kisses,

Cleo

From: Deirdre O'Dare
To: Cleo Dowling
Re: KAF

Oh, all right then. I sugared the pill for Rory by telling him that Eva would have wanted him to do it. So he's said yeah.

It's weird, really, the connections. I remember visiting Eva on location in Galway when she was making 'The O'Malley'. She'd just had baby Dorcas, and it was just before I got pregnant with Aoife. That part of the world holds bitter-sweet memories for me, so I might stroll west with R, revisit Kilrowan & Lissnakeelagh. And you, of course!

Kiss your ride of a husband from me.

Love, Deirdre XXX

From: Deirdre O'Dare
To: Hazel MacNamara
Re: Kilrowan AF

Dear Hazel,

Do go ahead with your idea for screening 'The O'Malley'. Rory will be glad to make an appearance as a tribute to Eva Lavery, who, as you probably know, made her last ever movie — 'Mimi's Remedies' — in Kilrowan. She considered Connemara to be her spiritual home, so it

140

will be a poignant occasion. I hope all goes well for you.

V best,

Deirdre

The next day, Hazel re-read the latest message she'd sent.

To: Deirdre O'Dare
From: Hazel MacNamara
Re: Kilrowan Arts Festival

Dear Deirdre,

I am delighted that you have been able to confirm Rory's availability. I will let you know further details nearer the time, and will be sure to keep you updated on all future developments to do with the festival.

With every good wish,

Hazel MacNamara, Nutcracker PR

The phone rang.
'Hey, Hazel! How's it goin'?'
It was her mother's voice.
'Oh, hi, Mum.'
'Jesus! Why do you always call me *Mum*? I've spent my entire life telling you to call me Angel, and you still insist on calling me Mum.'

'Sorry, Angel. How are things?'

'Things are groovy. *But . . .* ' (Why did this '*But*' sound so ominous? wondered Hazel) ' . . . I hear you're organizing the Kilrowan Arts Festival this year, baby.'

I am not your baby, Hazel wanted to scream. *I'm a sussed thirty something professional woman.* 'Well, I'm not actually organizing it,' she said. 'But I am handling the PR.'

'So you're in a position to call some shots, right?'

'What do you mean?'

'I'm staging a comeback.'

Oh, God.

'And I can't think of a better place to stage it than in Kilrowan at festival time.'

'*No!* I mean, why?'

'That Arts Festival will have kick-ass kudos, Hazel. I hear tell there's going to be a rake of shit-hot musicians at it.'

'How did you hear that?' Zoe Conway, Donal Lunny and Sharon Shannon had confirmed, but Hazel hadn't even sent out preliminary press releases yet.

'The world of Irish showbiz is a weird and wonderful place, but it's also a very *tiny* world, babe, and word travels fast. I'm told you've even lined up Rory McDonagh.'

Gulp. 'Um. It's not definite — '

'No? I got it on good faith from a good pal. Word is he wants to revisit the beach where Eva Lavery's ashes were scattered.'

'Oh.'

'Yeah. He was beyond gutted when she died. So. How about it?'

'How about what?'

'A gig at the festival.'

'For the Fazes?' The Fazes had been the punk rock band that Hazel's mother had fronted.

'Yeah. If Debbie Harry can do comeback, so can I.'

'Well, M — Angel, I'm not sure that that would be possible. You see, there's a maritime flavour to this year's festival, and there's nothing very maritime about a band like the Fazes.'

'We could reinvent ourselves. Change our name. To something like — um — Weird Fish.'

'There's a clothing brand called that,' said Hazel quickly.

'Oh, yeah, so there is. So that's where that came from!'

'What do you mean?'

'I'm wearing one of their T-shirts.' There came the sound of a loud inhalation.

Oh, Jesus. The image of her mother wearing a surfer dude T-shirt and toking a joint while talking on the phone was almost unendurable.

'Well, if we can't call ourselves Weird Fish we could call ourselves something like . . . um, let's see . . . Angel Fish,' resumed Angel. 'With a 'Ph'. Yeah.' A loud exhalation. ''Angel *Phish*'. That sounds *good*.'

Hazel felt like crying.

'So see what you can do for us, babe.'

'Angel, I really can't do anything for you. It would look awful if I lined up my own mother as one of the 'happening' events of the festival.'

'I don't have to be your mother, babe.'

'I don't understand.'

'No-one need know I'm your mother. We don't even share a surname.' Angel's stage name was Angel Kestrel. 'Don't worry. Your secret will be safe with me.'

'Look, I don't think Scar would go for it — '

'Scar? Who's Scar?'

Shit! 'I mean Hugh. He's the guy who runs the festival.'

'Why did you call him Scar?'

'It's a nickname he was landed with, Mum.' She couldn't help it. Angel would always be Mum, despite the fact that she'd been challenged in the mothering skills department from the moment Hazel was born.

'I didn't think it would be his *real* name, babe! Ha! Imagine some poor eejit of a priest leaning over a font and saying: 'I christen this child Scar'!' And Angel went off into a wild peal of best-Lebanese-black-induced laughter.

'His real name is Hugh Hennessy,' said Hazel when the cackle subsided.

'Hugh Hennessy, eh? Just let me write that down.'

What? 'Why?'

'I'll give him a bell myself.'

'Mum — '

'No worries, baby. I'll keep shtum about the mother/daughter thing. What's his number?'

'He's not easy to get hold of. Um, he's — '

'Ex-directory?'

'Yes.'

There was a longish pause. Then: 'No he's

144

not,' said Angel. 'I've just googled the Kilrowan Arts Festival. There's a contact number.'

'Oh? I seem to remember he told me he was ex-directory,' lied Hazel, 'because he was fed up with acts phoning him up and looking to see if they could get a slot in the festival.'

'No worries. I'll sweet-talk the sonofabitch, just see if I don't.'

'You'll probably just get a machine.'

Angel affected a Dietrich-esque accent. 'I'll ask him in my throatiest purr to return my call.'

Oh, God. It was clear that there was no deterring her mother. Hazel made one last valiant attempt. She put on her most categorical voice. 'Well, I wouldn't hold your breath,' she said. There was every chance, Hazel, knew, of Angel doing just that while she had a joint between her fingers.

''Angel Phish',' said Angel. 'I've just written it down, and waddya know — it reads as good as it looks. I'll get on to this dude right away. Spin him a spiel about comebacks. Comebacks . . . Hey, that looks good written down too! Yeah! Especially with an 'x'. How about this? 'Angel Phish Cumbax!' ' She spelt it out so that Hazel could see the amazing play on words, then: 'Or should that be 'The Fazes Cum Back?' Or 'Phazes', with a 'Ph'? Ow. This is starting to wreck my head bigtime.'

It was wrecking Hazel's head, too. Time for another lie. 'Sorry, I have to go, Mum. I've a call on the other line.'

'You go, girl. Oh, there's one other thing.'

'Yes?' breathed Hazel in a teeny voice,

145

uncertain whether she could take any more.

'Your father's going to volunteer his services as a living street statue. Bye, babe.'

The line went dead, and so did Hazel's expression.

★ ★ ★

Before she finished work that afternoon, she picked up the phone to Hugh. She could just as easily have e-mailed him, but she wanted to hear his voice on the end of the line.

'Hugh Hennessy,' he said.

'Hi Hugh. It's Hazel.'

'Hazel. Hello. What can I do for you?'

'Well, I was just phoning to let you know I've had a coup. Rory McDonagh has agreed to attend a screening of *The O'Malley* as a tribute to Eva Lavery.'

'Well done. Our line up of celebrities is taking shape nicely.'

'What do you mean?'

'Well, we've Colleen, Pablo, Pixie Pirelli, Rory McDonagh, Sharon Shannon, Zoe Conway, Donal Lunny and — '

Hazel's heart plummeted. She knew with a blinding and ominous certainty exactly who Hugh was going to list next.

' — Angel Phish,' he said.

'Angel Phish?' she parroted, feeling as if she was in some grim 'wacky' movie. 'What's Angel Phish?'

'It's a punk rock revival band. They used to be called the Fazes, but they're reinventing themselves as Angel Phish.'

'Never heard of them.'

'They were big in the late seventies, early eighties. I have a vague memory of some TV show they were on. They're fronted by a dynamo called Angel Kestrel.'

Oh, God. This *couldn't* be happening to her. 'She phoned you?' Hazel tried to keep her voice featherlight.

'Yes. She's a persuasive lady. She's convinced me that they'll rock Kilrowan.'

Hazel slumped so much she was in danger of hitting her head on the desk.

'So they're going to be part of the Kilrowan Festival?'

'Yeah. And she came up with another great idea.'

'Yeah?'

'Have you heard of a guy called Mondo MacNamara?'

'No. Ow.' Hazel's head hit teak.

'Are you all right?'

'Yes. I just dropped a book on my desk.'

'Mondo MacNamara — no relation, I gather — specializes in a form of street theatre known as 'living sculpture'. He's actually known as Mondo the aMazing — that's with a small 'a' and a capital 'M'.'

'Oh?' Why, oh why, did her parents insist on this particularly juvenile form of wordplay?

'You know what a living statue is.'

'No.'

'I'm surprised. I know they'd have scarcity value in an out-of-the-way spot like Kilrowan, but aren't they all over Dublin? You must know the mime artists who paint themselves silver, or whatever, and stand completely still so you'd almost think they were statues until they wink at you, or make some unexpected movement.'

'Oh, you mean those *losers*!' said Hazel with great vehemence.

'I wouldn't call them losers, Hazel,' said Hugh, with mild reproach.

'They're little more than buskers.'

'Maybe, but some of them are extremely talented. And Angel tells me that this Mondo man is one of the most highly respected of them all.'

'I doubt *that*!'

'What? Why?'

'Because no city in the world does living sculpture like Paris,' improvised Hazel. 'If you're really thinking about that kind of an act for the festival, you should hire a French mime. Paris is the home of mime, after all. Think of Marcel Marceau.'

'Hazel, we'd blow the budget if we started importing mimes from Paris. And we can't have Yanks going back to the States raving about the French mime they saw at a solid Irish festival. Everyone involved so far is Irish. This Mondo MacNamara sounds the business. He was quite famous as a clown on television once, apparently.'

'Pixie Pirelli's not Irish,' pointed out Hazel. 'And Colleen's originally from Kilburn.'

'Ah, but Pixie will be a well-established Kilrowan resident by then. And Colleen's more

148

Irish than the Irish at this stage.'

Hazel thought hard. 'What about the maritime connection?'

'You've lost me.'

'Well, you know my idea for a maritime theme? How does a street sculpture fit in with that?'

'Oh — Angel came up with a great idea. This Mondo bloke could paint himself all over with scales.'

'What?'

'You know, silver scales. And Angel says she knows an incredible theatre designer who could rustle up a head and tail.'

'I'm still not with you.'

'A fish head and tail.'

'Da — I mean, this Mondo's going to dress up as a fish?' Hazel felt faint with horror.

'Oh, not just any old fish,' said Hugh. 'He's going to represent that quintessentially Irish fish, *an bradán feasta* — the Salmon of Knowledge.'

'Sorry, Hugh — I've a call on the other line. Gotta go.'

Hazel put the phone down on Scar and picked it up again immediately to Erin.

'Can you meet me now? This minute?'

'I thought you wanted to delay dishing your dirt until the weekend?'

'But I had no dirt to dish when I made that arrangement!'

'And you do now?'

'Yes. Loads.'

'Yay! Whose is it?'

'Mine,' said Hazel, verging on tears again. 'I've been dumped on bigtime.'

★ ★ ★

Erin was no help at all. She just kept bursting into uncontrollable gales of laughter. By the time Hazel had finished telling her sorry story, Erin had tears rolling down her cheeks, and they weren't tears of sympathy.

'Oh, God, Hazel, I'm so sorry!' she managed finally. 'Oh!' Another merry peal of mirth escaped her. 'Angel Phish! And your dad dressed up as a salmon! Oh, Christ! What are you going to do?'

'I have no idea. That's why I felt the need to share this with you in the hope that you — as an old and trusted friend — might offer me a shoulder to cry on. It was clearly an unwise move since the only thing your shoulders appear capable of doing right now are shaking with fucking laughter.'

'Sorry.' Erin compressed her lips resolutely and tried to look grave. 'And you really denied them both?' she asked.

'Yes. I was a complete Judas.'

'So how on earth are you going to cope?'

'I haven't a clue. At least Mum's not supposed to be my mum, but what the hell will I do if Dad lets the cat out of the bag?'

Erin sniggered. 'It's a fishy tale, all right. Sorry, again.' This at Hazel's unamused expression.

'The really awful irony is that I kind of visited

150

it upon myself. I was the one who dreamed up the feckin' 'maritime' theme for the festival.'

'Couldn't you un-dream it? Come up with a better idea?'

'Such as?'

'Um. 'The *Phestival* of *Phantasmagoria*'? Sorry again.'

'You're useless, Erin. Some feckin' pal you are. I'm in a seriously sorry mess and you're doing nothing to get me out of it.'

'Couldn't you just tell this Hugh person the truth?'

'What? After pretending I'd never heard of Angel Kestrel and Mondo the aMazing who just happen to be my own parents?'

'OK. Telling the truth is clearly not an option. This is a fine kettle of fish you've got yourself into, Haze. Sorry.'

The waiter approached. 'Are you ready to see the dessert menu?' he asked.

'No need. Death by Chocolate for me,' said Hazel. 'And another glass of wine, please.'

'Very good, madam.' He turned an enquiring eye on Erin.

'I'll have another glass, too. But no dessert, thanks.' The waiter inclined his head and beat a retreat. 'He's got a great ass,' observed Erin.

'Mm.' Hazel was abstracted. For some reason she'd been reminded of Hugh Hennessy's ass. In blue jeans, the way he'd worn them the day they went walking together. Not too tight, but not builder's bum loose, either. Just right, really. She wondered what it would be like to go walking with him with her hand tucked into the back

151

pocket of his jeans, and he with an arm slung over her shoulder . . .

'Maybe you could ask your dad not to reveal his identity,' said Erin now.

'Oh, Erin, I couldn't! He may be a mime, but he's still my dad and he loves me to bits. I can't inflict hurt on him.'

'Why not tell him that you're delighted he's going to be part of the festival, but unfortunately you're going to be so busy organizing events that you won't be able to meet up?'

'That has potential,' said Hazel. 'I suppose I could just avoid him.'

'I saw him and your mum in Grafton Street the other day.'

'Oh, God. What was he being?'

'Just himself. He wasn't performing. They're still great friends, aren't they?'

'Yeah. They look out for each other.' Hazel's parents had split up — amicably — when she was eighteen.

'Is she still seeing that scenic artist?'

'No. He bored the arse off her.'

'She was looking good. I'd say her comeback could be a big hit.'

'Don't depress me, Erin.'

'Don't you want it to be?'

'Well, yeah — of course I do, for her sake. But it's just so incredibly embarrassing. Why couldn't I have had solid, middle-class parents like yours, Erin?'

'Hey! I envied you your parents when I was at school. My parents were so fuddy-duddy by comparison. And it so used to piss me off that all

152

my boyfriends fancied your mother.'

'Please don't, Erin.'

'Death by Chocolate,' said the waiter.

'Death by my own hand, more like,' muttered Hazel.

'And your wine is on its way.'

'Bring it on.'

'Now that you've got your parents off your chest,' said Erin, sticking a finger in Hazel's Death by Chocolate, 'it's time to tell me about Mr Hugh Hennessy. Do you fancy him?'

'No,' said Hazel.

'You said that too fast. That means you most definitely do fancy him. What would you do if he came on to you?'

'He's not going to come on to me, Erin. Ours is strictly a business relationship.' Her phone rang. 'Mother' was displayed. 'Hi, Mu — Angel,' said Hazel.

'Hey, Hazel! I just got a phone call. From Hugh Hennessy.'

'Oh, yes?'

'Yes indeedy! You know he's coming up to Dublin tomorrow?'

'Um. Yeah. He mentioned something about that.' He hadn't. The bastard! Why hadn't he?

'Well, he's meeting me for lunch, to discuss the comeback. He's staying in the Hamilton Hotel, and I don't really have any Hamilton Hotel-type threads. Can you lend me something classy? That black cashmere dress of yours with the slit up the side would be good. There's no harm in showing a bit of leg.'

'Mum — '

'Hey, cut that out! I'm not meant to be your mum, remember? I'm Angel Kestrel of Angel Phish. And I'm making my comeback in style!' And as Angel started singing 'The Boys are Back in Town', Hazel depressed the 'off' switch on her phone and took a large spoonful of Death by Chocolate, hoping that it might do exactly what it said on the tin.

8

On a Monday morning in April, Pablo and Cleo were having breakfast when the doorbell rang.

'Who could that be?' said Cleo. 'No-one ever rings our doorbell this early in the day.'

Pablo shrugged. 'Maybe it's the Jehovah's Witnesses. I saw a couple of them doing the door to door thing in the village yesterday.'

'Jehovah's Witnesses in Kilrowan? How weird. They must be desperate, to come all this way. I'll go and shoo them.'

'Tell them you're a Satanist.'

'No. That'll only encourage them to try even harder to convert me, and I don't have time to be converted. I have a shop to open up.'

Cleo ran up the stairs and put on her best 'I've no time for this' expression as she opened the door. But there were no Jehovah's Witnesses standing there. Two strikingly beautiful women stood on Cleo's doorstep, and one of them was Pablo's princess. The other, to judge by her age, was the queen.

'Good morning!' said the queen, extending a diamond-bedecked hand. 'I'm Davina Jay, and this is my daughter, Abigail. She's here for her sitting.'

'Sitting?' said Cleo, before realization dawned. 'Oh — *sitting!* You're here to sit for your portrait.'

'That's right,' said Abigail.

155

'I'm sorry,' said Davina with a regal smile. 'We're a little early. Pablo said ten o'clock, but I have to push off sharpish.' She glanced at her Rolex. 'I'd better get cracking. I just wanted to make sure Abigail had the right place. Have fun, darling! And — don't forget this.' She handed her daughter a carrier bag. The big, glossy kind with silken cord handles — the kind that even *smelt* expensive.

'Bye, mother,' said Abigail.

'Byee!' And Davina Jay click clacked down the pathway, diamonds all aglitter.

'Well. Come in, Abigail,' said Cleo, stapling on an overly bright smile. 'We were just finishing breakfast. We're down here.' Cleo led the way downstairs. 'Forgive the mess,' she said, as she saw Abigail's eyes slide towards the wineglasses and takeaway cartons that still littered the coffee table from the night before.

'It's only what I'd expect from an artist,' said Abigail. 'Divine decadence.'

Ow.

'Did you get rid of them?' said Pablo. He was still sitting at the kitchen table, bare-chested in his sarong, and unshaven. His attention was on the previous day's paper.

'It wasn't the Jehovah's Witnesses,' said Cleo. 'It's Abigail Jay, here to sit for you.'

Pablo lowered the paper and looked hard at Abigail. Then he smiled at her, and Cleo felt her gut twist with jealousy. 'Hi,' he said, holding out a hand. 'I forgot you were due today. Sit down, have a cup of coffee.'

Abigail took his proffered hand and shook it. If

she was put out by the fact that he was wearing nothing but a sarong, she certainly didn't show it.

Cleo found herself fetching a mug from the cupboard. 'Milk? Sugar?' she asked, standing by the stove where the coffee pot was, and feeling like the maid in a bad farce.

'Just milk, please.'

'Take off your coat. Have a seat,' said Pablo. Princess Abigail did as he commanded and sat down, casually draping the soft swirl of her cashmere coat over a kitchen chair. Under the cashmere she was wearing a plain white shirt and Ralph Lauren jeans. 'Is that what you intend to wear in your portrait?' he asked.

'No.' Abigail reached into the expensive carrier bag and unfurled a length of gossamer chiffon. 'Daddy wants me to wear the gown I'll be wearing at my twenty-first birthday party.'

'And when might that be?'

'Next month. He's anxious that the portrait be finished by then. He wants to unveil it at the party.'

'No worries, Abigail,' said Pablo. 'It'll be ready well in time.' There was the hint of a smile playing round his mouth, which had the effect of making his mouth look very kissable indeed.

Cleo came forward with the coffee, resisting the temptation to spill it all over the sea-green chiffon that Abigail was pouring back into the bag. She sat down and picked up her own mug, wrapping her hands around the warmth of it for comfort.

Pablo looked at her. 'Shouldn't you be making

tracks?' he said. 'It's nearly ten o'clock.'

There was no way Cleo was going to run the risk of this bootilicious young thing changing into gossamer silk chiffon in front of her husband.

'I'm the boss. It's my privilege to run late.' She staged a 'relaxed' yawn, then turned to Abigail and said: 'Are you staying here in Kilrowan?'

'We're in the Glebe House, a couple of miles outside the village.'

Cleo knew the house. Actually, it wasn't a house — it was a virtual mansion.

'Oh. You're the new owners?'

'Yes. Daddy wanted somewhere he could retire to.'

'And what does 'Daddy' do?' asked Pablo.

Cleo shot him a warning look. It was out of line to overtly send up a client. It was all very well being subversive by putting pigs and orang-utans in his portraits because that was part of his 'quirky' style, but it was quite another thing to take the piss.

It didn't seem to faze Abigail, however. Her blue blood was clearly of the *froid* variety. 'He owns a computer manufacturing company in Dublin.'

'Do you manage to spend much time in the West?' asked Cleo.

She shrugged. 'Not really. There's not much to do, here, is there? I was actually meant to go skiing this Easter, but the friend I was going with got sick, so I decided to cry off and keep Daddy happy.' She deliberately looked Pablo in the eye as she said the 'D' word. This princess was composure personified. No coy Diana looks or blushes for *her*!

Pablo leaned back in his chair and flexed his fingers. 'Do you want to go get changed?' he said. 'I feel an overriding urge to get started.'

'Certainly,' said Abigail. She took a couple of sips of her coffee, then rose to her feet and picked up her carrier bag.

'I'll show you to the downstairs bathroom,' said Cleo, standing up likewise. The girl had fantastic posture, she noticed as they moved towards the door — the kind that comes with ballet training. But of course. This girl would have had it all! Ballet, tennis, piano, Thai Bo — the works. She wouldn't be surprised if Miss Abigail Jay had attended finishing school.

She led her down the corridor and held open the bathroom door for her.

'Thank you,' said a gracious Princess Abigail, as she stepped across the threshold.

'You're welcome.' With a polite smile, Cleo shut the door behind her, then legged it back to the kitchen. Pablo was pulling a T-shirt over his head: he always wore loose cotton trousers and T-shirts when people came to sit for him, in case they found the sarong unsettling. He gave her a wicked smile as she came through the door.

'Do you think she's intacta?' he asked.

'I have *no* idea, but I am adamant that you're not about to find out. Hands off, MacBride.'

'Hey, baby.' He was regarding her with laughing eyes. 'You know I wouldn't do the dirty on you.'

Cleo sent him a petulant look. 'Well, you're

not having MTV on while she's sitting for you.'

'Why not? I always have MTV on when I'm painting. It gets the creative juices flowing.'

'It also makes you horny as hell. I'm going to take the plug off the telly if you don't promise me not to watch it.'

'All right, all right.'

He was laughing out loud now as he stood up. Cleo's eyes went to the bulge under the cotton trousers. 'You'd better start thinking about cold custard,' she said.

'Cold custard,' he said, moving towards her and taking her in his arms, 'could actually be quite interesting. We might experiment with it when you come home from work.'

'Why do you always come up with new ideas just when I've changed the sheets?' complained Cleo. She stood on tiptoe to kiss him — once, twice, and then she felt him slide a hand up her back and cup the back of her head, putting pressure on her to kiss him more deeply.

A discreet cough caused them to draw apart. 'I do beg your pardon,' said Abigail. She was standing in the doorway, and the light from behind her made the chiffon of her gown so diaphanous she might have been naked. In fact, she very nearly was naked. The only garment visible under the chiffon was a miniature thong.

Oh, *God*!

Pablo narrowed his eyes at his subject, and Cleo knew he'd gone straight into painterly mode. 'OK,' he said, as she walked into the room. 'I want you barefoot. Lose the heels, please.'

She stepped out of them and stood there, barefoot and motionless, looking a little less like a princess now, and rather more vulnerable. Pablo strolled towards her, then circled her, his eyes taking in every detail.

'And the earrings.'

She raised a perfectly manicured hand and removed the jewels that hung from her earlobes.

'Let your hair down.'

Abigail released her glossy Pantene hair from the jaws that held it in place on the crown of her head.

'And mess it up a bit.'

She shook her hair about, then tousled it some more with her fingers.

'That's better,' said Pablo, and Cleo felt like crying. She was remembering the first time he'd ever painted her. She'd posed nude for him, and he'd claimed it was the most time he'd ever spent working on a portrait because the pair of them just couldn't keep their hands off one another. They'd spent many, many hours riding each other's arses off.

'OK,' said Pablo, flexing his fingers again. 'It's time to go to work.' He moved to the door that led to the garden and held it open so that Abigail could precede him through. 'Bye, sweetheart. See you later,' he said over his shoulder to his wife.

Cleo moved to the window and watched as the fairytale princess floated down the garden towards Pablo's studio. For some reason an illustration from a book she'd had as a child came into her head, of a princess walking towards her destiny. What had that been from? she wondered now. And then it struck her. It had been Iphigenia, daughter of Agamemnon, on her way to the temple where she was to offer herself up as a virgin sacrifice, to placate an angry god.

*　*　*

Pixie Pirelli watched from her window as a barefoot Pablo in cotton trousers and T-shirt escorted an exquisite young woman down the next door garden towards his studio. She supposed he must be painting another portrait.

Pixie had decided to treat herself to a day off. She had worked the past six days in a row, and had notched up a further twenty thousand words on her novel. Its working title was 'Away with the Fairies', but Pixie wasn't entirely happy with that. It would do, she decided, for the title of her autobiography in the unlikely event of her ever feeling the urge to write such a thing.

The door to the studio opened and closed, and Pixie caught a glimpse of Pablo looking up towards where she stood framed in her big picture window. She hoped he hadn't seen her. She hated the idea of being misconstrued as a nosy neighbour. But of course, being nosy was part of her job. Being curious about other people fuelled her novels.

Pablo was the first person she'd seen in a couple of days, now. She remembered how, when she had first come here, she had on one occasion felt so isolated that she had had to pick up the phone to Deborah for reassurance. She hadn't seen a human being for three entire days, and she just wanted to make sure that the world was still out there.

She could, of course, have turned on the news to make sure that humanity hadn't been blown away, but Pixie rarely listened to news. She found it too depressing, and she knew that she wouldn't be able to write if she allowed herself to get depressed.

What to do today — on her holiday? A walk. There was a beach nearby, and any time Pixie had visited it, she had been the only person on it. She felt so privileged! There was something infinitely pleasurable in seeing nobody's footprints but her own on a long expanse of golden sand. But first she needed to check her mail.

Oh, good. She learned from Natalie that translation rights to *Hard to Choos* had been sold to France. She wondered how they'd translate the title. 'Difficile à Choisir' would mean the pun would be lost. Nat also told her that she was holding her own in the bestseller lists despite some extremely tough competition: since Pixie had started writing, novels in the chick-lit domain had multiplied sevenfold. Humming a little tune, she clicked on Internet Explorer, and set sail to Amazon to check out her status for herself. As it shimmered into view the little tune faltered and died. Oh! How had this happened? Her beloved five stars had gone plummeting to four! Why?

A new, one-star review of *Hard to Choos* had been posted. Uh-oh. Something in Pixie's tummy lurched. She braced herself to read it.

One of the silliest, most irritating books I have ever wasted money on [it began]. Who reads crap like this? I wanted to murder the vacuous heroine, who would appear to possess at max 2 brain cells. I would have sent it to my local charity shop, but didn't want to inflict this rubbish on anyone unfortunate enough to pick it up, so I dumped it in the bin instead. The only reason it gets one star is for the Italian sex scene. Avoid at all costs.

Pixie was quite unprepared for the effect the words had on her. Her hands flew to her face. She started to shake. Her pulse rate accelerated, and she went first hot, then cold. How utterly horrible! How — how *unnecessary*. She knew she should shut the lid of her laptop so as to avoid exposing herself to the awful, creepy vibe that emanated like Kryptonite from the screen, but a morbid fascination kept her eyes glued to it. She re-read the review. It had been posted by someone called Tabbitha. Why? Why had Tabbitha been so cruel?

Pixie scrolled down the other reviews. They were five-star, all of them — complimentary, upbeat and positive. One of them simply read: 'Loved this book — loved it, loved it, *loved* it!!!'

She sat inert for a moment or two, then some impulse made her move her mouse and click on the 'used' section. Pixie hated this section — she had been appalled when she'd seen second-hand copies of her books available to buy at just one penny — but she'd learned that this was a scam by second-hand dealers to encourage readers to patronize them. These books were sent out with ads inserted in them, extolling the advantages of buying from this dealer or that one.

She scanned the list of used titles, and the descriptions of their condition — until something made her stop short. 'Buy used for 1p. Mint condition. Never read, unwanted gift. A bit dusty. Tabbitha.' Sweat broke out under Pixie's armpits and on her palms. Who *was* this Tabbitha, and why was she out to get her?

Feeling as if she was under the spell of a bad fairy, some sixth sense compelled her to visit her other babies. Without exception, her routine five-star dazzle had been tarnished. This is what confronted Pixie on each click of her mouse.

As the famous Dorothy Parker once said, this is not a book to be picked up lightly. It should be hurled, with great force. Which is exactly what I did after reading seven beyond abysmal chapters . . .

This book is highly recommended as a birthday present to be given to your worst enemy . . .

If you're having problems sleeping, I can heartily recommend that this book be read at bedtime. Believe me, it's the only cure for insomnia you'll ever need . . .

Running short of loo paper? No worries! Pixie Pirelli's lumpen effort at a novel . . .

Each review was more excoriating than the last, and by the time Tabbitha had finished with her, Pixie felt as if she'd been flayed alive.

What had she *done* to merit such vicious treatment? It wasn't as if she had any pretensions to being a lofty literary type. She simply wrote to make herself, and, by proxy, the reader feel *good*, to help effect escape from the vicissitudes and general awfulness of real life for an hour or two. A prestigious broadsheet had once dubbed her the 'Queen of Feel-Good Fiction', for heaven's sake!

And then she remembered the words she'd read in the SAS manual Deborah had given her. *Islands are especially challenging to the survivor. The feelings of loneliness and isolation are acute,* and Deborah's voice came back to her: *I'm always at the end of a phone . . .*

Pixie picked up the handset and speed-dialled her editor's direct number.

Deborah's assistant picked up.

'Hi, Pixie! Deborah's in a meeting. I'll get her to call you when she gets out.'

'How long is she likely to be?'

'Um. Another half-hour or thereabouts.'

'Could you please ask her to call me as soon as she can? It's rather urgent.'

'Sure. Can I help at all?'

'No, thank you. I really need to talk to her myself. But you might ask her to check out my titles on Amazon before she phones.'

'Will do.'

Pixie put the phone down and picked it up again immediately to phone her agent, then remembered that Natalie was off on holiday. Oh, no. Who else could she talk to? Mariella. Of course. Praying that her friend would be in, Pixie hit speed dial again.

The answering machine picked up, and Mariella's recorded message played down the line. 'Mariella and Timothy can't come to the phone right now, but please leave your message and we'll get back to you.' *Beeep.*

Pixie knew that if Mariella was working she very often put the machine on so that she wouldn't be disturbed by calls. 'Mariella?' she said into the receiver, her voice sounding breathy with shock. 'It's Pixie here. Are you there? If you are, could you please pick up? I'm terribly sorry to disturb you, but something horrible has happened and — '

'Pixie, hi! What's wrong, darling? You sound a bit shaky.'

'You're there! Thanks for picking up, Mariella — and if I sound a bit shaky, it's because I *am* a bit shaky. More than a bit, actually. Someone's got the knife out for me on Amazon.' And Pixie filled Mariella in.

'Jesus. Have you spoken to Deborah?'

'Not yet. She's in a meeting, but I've asked for her to call me back as soon as she finishes. You don't think I'm being paranoid, do you?'

There came a pause as Mariella considered. 'I don't, actually,' she said. 'If just one review was involved I'd tell you to forget it. But someone clearly bought and read every single one of your books with a view to unilaterally trashing them. It's plain vicious, that's what it is.'

'Is there anything I can do? Could I ask Amazon to remove them, do you think?'

'I don't know. You'd have to ask Deborah. Those reviews are in the public domain, after all, and everyone's entitled to an opinion. Even horrible people.'

'Could I sue?'

'Amazon?'

'No, no — I mean Tabbitha.'

'Unlikely. Anyway, you don't even know who she is.'

'Or he. It could be a he masquerading as a she.'

'No. I doubt very much that it's a man. This is specialist all-woman bitchcraft. Hey, I have an idea. Why don't you try googling her?'

'Googling's a jolly good idea, Mariella. I'll do it now while I'm waiting for Deborah to phone back.'

'Let me know what happens.'

'Of course I will. Thank you for listening. You go back to work now — I'll call you later.'

Pixie put the phone down, then went straight back to her laptop on the desk in her study and clicked on favourites. Google sprang into life. Pixie typed in 'Tabbitha', and then she clicked on 'Search'.

Oh, God. What a joke. Google told her that there were thousands of Tabbithas to be found on the world wide web. She scrolled down. There were requiems for cats, there was a lesbian poet, there was a Tabbitha offering website designs and a Tabbitha Fox offering DVDs of hardcore honeys. There were cat breeders and endless

168

family trees. How could she narrow it down? 'Tabbitha — Nasty Reviews Amazon.co.uk', unsurprisingly enough, did not match any documents.

Brrrring! At last! Deborah. Pixie grabbed the phone and said: 'Well?'

'Well. Someone's got it in for you, darling, and that's a fact. But you *mustn't let it get to you*.'

'It already has.'

'Now, listen up, Pixie. Those reviews were penned by someone who quite clearly resents you and your success, and this is how I suggest you handle it. Are you listening carefully?'

'Yes.'

'Good. This Tabbitha has seen you on the telly and heard you on the radio and read about you in magazines, and she's decided that you need taking down a peg or two. She knows very well that what she has done will get inside your head and make you unhappy and insecure, and if you allow her to make you feel this way, Pixie, Tabbitha has won. And you mustn't let her win because you are a better person than she is. Only a low bitch would resort to the kind of tactics she has chosen, and you must rise above her. You are a fighter, Pixie, and you must not let her get to you.'

'She put my book in the bin,' said Pixie. 'I can't bear to think of it in a bin. I can't bear to think of someone turning the pages of my book and sneering at my characters and then — '

'Then don't. Don't allow yourself to think about it. Think instead of all you've got going for you, of everything your books have done for you.

Think of your lovely house, and your new extension and the holidays you've been able to take on the proceeds of your books, and think of how much happier you are than Tabbitha. You earn a living doing the thing you love best, and how many people in the world are able to say that? This Tabbitha probably doesn't have a life at all. She probably has a deadly dull job working behind the cash register at — '

'No,' said Pixie. 'I know what she does. She's a lavatory attendant.'

'That's the spirit! Transcend, transcend, transcend! Think positive, Pixie. Now, go and look out of your window and tell me what you see.'

'I see my lovely view.'

'Is the sun shining?'

'Yes.'

'So take yourself off for a walk. Go visit that beach you told me about. Paddle! Kick up sea spray! Take a picnic — a bottle of champagne! How many people in the world have jobs that allow them to leave their desks and hit the beach? Celebrate, Pixie!'

'Yes, Deborah,' said Pixie in a categorical voice. 'You are absolutely right. I have every reason to celebrate. Especially since Tabbitha's stuck in a lavatory.'

'That's my girl — oh.' There came the sound of a receiver being covered and an urgent exchange. Then Deborah's voice came back on the line. 'Pixie, are you feeling OK now? It's just that an emergency's come up and I have to get someplace five minutes ago.'

'Yes, thank you, Deborah. I am feeling much better now that I know Tabby's in the toilet.'

'Good. Just cling onto this maxim at all times. Living well is the best revenge.'

'Living well is the best revenge,' repeated Pixie. 'Thank you for that, Deborah. Goodbye! I'm definitely off to the beach.'

And Pixie put the phone down feeling stronger.

★ ★ ★

The walk on the beach helped put things into perspective. Deborah had been absolutely right. Those reviews had been motivated by spleen and envy, and weren't worth wasting grief on.

Living well is the best revenge. Living well was indeed the best revenge, and Pixie was going to live her life to the max. Tabbitha would see her in *Hello!* and *OK!* and in *Heat.* She would see her quaffing champagne and laughing with other celebrities and wearing designer threads. She would see her emerging from limousines and walking up red carpets and receiving awards and airkisses and bouquets. And every time Tabbitha saw one of these photographs, it would be as if Pixie was holding up two pretty, piss-elegant fingers at her.

The beach was all hers today. The water was pellucid, inviting — even the sound of it was seductive, intimate as a whisper — and Pixie wished she'd brought her swimsuit. Of course she could go in without one, but the incident in her latest book — when Charlotte's clothes had gone missing while she swam — still had the power to make her cringe, and she was loath to invite a similar quandary upon herself. Above her, the sky was cerulean from horizon to horizon, with wisps of white cloud that might have been brushed onto blue-washed canvas by a feather from an angel's wing. A flock of vociferous gulls — terns? She'd check it in the bird book when she got home — were diving for fish. They would drop out of the sky like kamikazes before surfacing and swooshing up again, looking as if they were doing it just for the sheer thrill of it, like a fun fair ride.

Yes! Life *was* good. And, yes, she, Pixie Pirelli, was winning.

★   ★   ★

On her way along the stretch of coast that flanked the Blackthorns she had to pass Pablo's studio. He was there, now, regarding the subject of his latest portrait with inscrutable eyes. He had positioned the girl sitting in the centre of a chaise-longue, bare feet together, hands folded in lap. Her demeanour was modest — demure, even — but there was something indefinably sexy about the pose. Maybe it was the way the strap of her gown had slipped down her upper arm, exposing a golden shoulder? Maybe it was the tousled just-got-out-of bed appearance of her hair? Or was it the slightly parted bee-stung lips, or the sleepy, unfocused expression in her beautiful eyes?

Pixie walked past on the shingle, pretending she hadn't seen.

★ ★ ★

The next day Pixie did her SAS exercises as usual, juiced carrots and apples (adding a little ginger for energy), booted up her laptop and opened a new file. 'Save as,' the computer instructed her, and Pixie typed in CHAPTER NINE. Then she sat back and waited for her heroine, Jodie, to come to her and take her by the hand and lead her to wherever it was she was headed. And she waited. And waited. And waited. And nothing happened. 'Come on, Jodie,' Pixie found herself saying out loud. But Jodie didn't answer. Where was she hiding? This was most peculiar. None of her characters had ever done this to her before.

Maybe she needed another blast of juice. She went into the kitchen and slung chunks of pear and banana and some grapes into the juicer. Then she moved to the sitting room and stood at the window to drink her concoction and admire her view. She cast her mind back to Chapter Eight. What had happened? Let's see. Jodie had been packing to go to a house party in Scotland, and she had just made an arrangement to meet up with her friend Susannah, who would be doing the driving. She knew that they were going to get to the stately home where the house party was being held, but after that it was really up to Jodie to make the story happen.

OK. Enough procrastination with juice and

view. Back to the keyboard, Pixie! She sat down in front of the blank screen and willed the words to come. 'The drive took them six hours,' she typed. Well, that was a start, but it was a frightfully dull start. Try some dialogue, instead. That was often a good way to begin a new chapter. Pixie deleted 'The drive took them six hours' and substituted: ' "Oh, what a lovely day!' said Jodie.' Oh, God. That was worse. Jodie would *never* say 'Oh, what a lovely day!' What was happening?

Pixie got up and went to the window again. She watched Pablo and the girl he was painting walk down the grassy slope of next door's garden, as they had done yesterday. What had she written yesterday? Nothing. It had been her day off. What had happened yesterday? That hateful Tabbitha had spat all over her novels.

Oh. God. Was there some connection between Tabbitha's bile and what was happening to her now? What *was* happening to her now? Block? She remembered the last time she'd talked to her fellow chick-lit cohorts, Dominique and Dilys, and how Dilys had chastised Pixie for making writing sound so easy. What else had she said? *I hit a wall last week and I can't unblock myself.*

Oh God, oh goodness. Was she blocked? She'd thought she'd had the entire plot of her new novel in her head when she'd come here to Ireland to write, but she knew she couldn't write the story without Jodie's help. Jodie was like the trail of crumbs that Hansel and Gretel leave behind them on their way through the forest so that they can find the way back out. She was

Pixie's narrative compass, and without Jodie's voice in her head, Pixie was as lost as the fairytale children after the birds peck away their breadcrumb trail. Oh no! Lost in the forest was as bad as it got, because there was a witch's house in there somewhere.

What if that witchy Tabbitha had been right? What if her books *were* rubbish? What if her heroines really were irritating and vacuous, not endearing and lovable as she imagined? Could her readers all be wrong when they wrote her fan mail and heaped her with praise on Amazon? Maybe they were all deluded, and Tabbitha was the one who was clear sighted and clued in?

Pixie felt terribly cold. She walked into her bedroom, took her favourite cosy cardy from a drawer and wrapped herself up in it. Block was worse than being stuck in a jail cell in solitary confinement. Block was worse than being Norma No Friends. Block was like finding out that the fairies had substituted a changeling child for the real thing. She felt as if she'd been bereaved.

Oh, God! What if she could never again fly off to the fantasy land where her heroines lived, and laugh and cry with them? Never again allow the prince to get the girl? Never again write 'The End' with tears streaming down her face because she was missing her characters already? Tabbitha had committed genocide in Pixie's world of make-believe, and Pixie felt incapable of resuscitation. That her beloved characters might never live and breathe again was a monstrous thing.

Tabbitha was winning. She had just succeeded in pulling Pixie down to a level of wretchedness so debilitating that she wondered if she'd ever be able to write another word. At least condemned prisoners in jail cells had access to pen and ink. She might have access to the electronic equivalent, but without her make-believe characters to confide their secrets in her, her laptop was redundant.

She walked back into her study and sat down in front of the screen again. She tried to conjure Jodie and her friend Susannah, tried to hear their voices as they drove across the border into Scotland, but it was as if she had received a blow to her head that had rendered her deaf. She could hear absolutely nothing.

★ ★ ★

Pixie spent the rest of the day mourning her lost voices, and hating Tabbitha, and then she came to a decision. She'd go Tabby-hunting. Revenge was sweet, after all — especially to women — and she was going to exchange her gossamer fairy wings for the muscled pinions of an angel of retribution. She was going to track down that horrible Tabbitha and make her pay for what she'd done to her.

There may be thousands of references to Tabbitha out there on the world wide web, but she was certain she could narrow it down. The reviews had been posted on Amazon UK, so the UK was where she should start. And the most obvious city in the UK to get started on was London.

As she clicked on the search engine she reminded herself that she was a fighter, as her scuba instructor had told her. Her war zone was the Internet now, and there she would duck and dive with the dexterity of a guerrilla warrior, and use words as her weapons. Whoever coined the maxim 'Sticks and stones may break my bones, but words can never hurt me' had got it *so* wrong! She'd learned today that words could be as powerful as weapons of mass destruction, but she, Pixie Pirelli, would have the last laugh. She hummed a little song — *Oh, the shark has pretty teeth, dear* — as she typed in 'Tabbitha, London'.

Well! This looked more promising. This was manageable. There were the usual family searches and ancestral files and pen pal postings. The absolutely adult Tabbitha Fox turned up again, and a glamorously monickered Tabbitha de Goussencourt. And there, under 'Tabbitha, London by a Londonista', she read: 'Hi, darlings! Well, it's been all go in Tabbitha's weird and truly wonderful world . . . Description: daily blog from London, penned by Tabbitha, a genuine Londonista. http://www.tabbitha.blogblaggers.com.'

Pixie clicked.

It was a blog to beat all blogs.

Hi, darlings! Well, it's been all go in Tabbitha's weird and truly wonderful world lately. Shopping, socializing and shooting the breeze with *you* know who! Took in some serious theatre at the RSC — David Lawless's production of 'Uncle Vanya' is absolutely the most definitive production I've ever seen of the Chekhov classic, with a nonpareil performance from Finbar de Rossa in the eponymous role . . .

Pixie read on. And on. And on. The blog was endless, with comment boxes and links to archive blog dating back over a couple of years. There were also links to Tabbitha's favourite sites, which were all media-oriented. Names were dropped on an irritatingly regular basis. Tabby clearly fancied herself as a major player in Celebville.

'When a man is tired of London, he is tired of life.' I 'fess up to feeling a tad tired of my beloved capital — the *traffic*, my dears! — but, of course, I never tire of *my* life!

My dinner party last night was a fabulous success, if I say so myself, and I do. L does a mean bouillabaisse. We spoke of, *inter alia*, Guy Ritchie, Rory McDonagh, the cast of 'Desperate Housewives' (L could tell you a tale or two!), and the latest literary offerings from Jonathan Safran Foer and the divine Colleen. (Rumour has it, incidentally, that the aforementioned McDonagh was the inspiration for the protagonist in Colleen's latest *oeuvre*.) P told us a hilarious story about a cock-up at the studio . . .

I ran into SL in the Harvey Nicks lingerie department. We met at the cash desk, and were handing over our plat cards when we realized that we were buying identical La Perla bra and panty sets . . .

My ongoing cosmetic orthodontist work means that I am obliged to spend a lot of time in the waiting room. What a blast to have dozens of back-dated gossip magazines to read! To read about the antics of some has-beens makes yours truly very glad indeed that she's Tabbitha!

My agent is *loving* my new novel —

What?
Pixie read it again to make sure she'd read it right. My *agent is* loving *my new novel* . . .
A clue!
OK, she read, the agent was *loving* the new novel, but it transpired that it needed more work before she could send it off.

Yawn! What a bore [observed Tabbitha]. Sometimes I feel so lazy that I just wish I could get someone to ghost the thing. Although lazy writing clearly pays off for other authors. I picked up a novel at the airport recently, by a chick lit practitioner. My dears! 'Hard to Choos', by someone who goes by the ludicrous moniker of Pixie Pirelli (how porn star is that!), is *not* hard to choose at all. Just do *not* choose it! Leave it

179

languishing on the shelves to gather dust until it's relegated to the 'Remaindered' section and thence to the pulp processors.

Pixie felt two emotions simultaneously. One was a stab of searing rage; the other was a rush of triumph. She saved 'Tabbitha, London by a Londonista' to her 'favourites' file, and logged off.

'Gotcha, Tabby!' she said to herself. And then she picked up the phone to Mariella.

★ ★ ★

Later that day she went outside into her garden to get a blast of fresh air, to feast on the view, and to see if her errant muse might come calling. She meandered down to the very bottom of the sloping lawn, where a bench in an arbour provided privacy and shelter for anyone intent on admiring the sea and landscape. But the view hadn't a chance. Pixie's attention was diverted almost immediately by the sound of voices. They were fierce voices — raised in argument — and they were coming from Pablo's studio.

Pixie couldn't help herself. She craned her neck in the direction of the next door garden, and watched through the open studio window as the girl sitting for Pablo rose elegantly to her feet and assumed an arrogant stance.

'You may despise everything I represent,' she was saying in a clear, cut-crystal voice. 'But I know for a fact that you'd fuck me if I gave you the slightest encouragement. You'd actually love to do that, wouldn't you, Pablo? You'd love to fuck a bit of posh totty, because by fucking me you'd be fucking an entire conservative ethos, *n'est ce pas?*'

The two of them stood facing each other, and the sexual tension that shimmered between them was so evident that Pixie could almost strike it, see it. Pablo had a wineglass in his hand. He drained it, then set it down and said: 'Take your dress off.'

The girl smiled, and Pixie was aware that there was triumph in the smile, as well as arousal. She took hold of one slender strap of the silk chiffon gown, and slid an arm from under it. Then she did the same with the other strap. But she didn't let go of the chiffon: she held it against her breasts, challenge in her eyes, mocking him.

'Drop it,' he said.

She raised an eyebrow, then removed her hands. The chiffon slid down her body like water off a sea nymph. It pooled at her feet and she stood there naked but for a thong. Her hair was lifting a little in the breeze from the window: she looked like the subject of Botticelli's *Birth of Venus*. She and Pablo regarded each other without speaking for five — maybe six — seconds, and then they moved swiftly towards one another and united in a savage embrace.

Pixie got to her feet and backed soundlessly away, wishing passionately that she hadn't seen what she'd just seen, wishing even more passionately that there was some way of rewinding her life and erasing the past five minutes.

9

Cleo came back from the bookshop that Tuesday evening feeling dog tired. She'd had to do stocktaking after shutting up shop today, and that always did her head in. And business had been sluggish, which did nothing for her morale, *and* she had a bitch of a period. She let herself into the house and called Pablo's name. Pablo didn't answer, but Fluffy did, trotting to meet her with a big sympathetic smile because feminine intuition told the bitch at once that her mistress was exhausted.

'Hello, Your Fluffiness,' said Cleo, bending to pet her pet. 'Where's your master got to?' She knew by the expression in her beloved doggie's eyes that Fluff would without question have told her if she could. 'Oh — bad dog! Your hair accessories have gone all skew-whiff. Here, let me do your fringe. Tch, tch. I don't know how you can see where you're going, with all that hair in your eyes. There!' She bestowed a kiss on Fluff's forehead, then went downstairs to the kitchen, faithful hound following at her heels.

The kitchen was a mess, with plates left unscraped in the sink, and an empty bottle of Burgundy by the bin. There was a jar of olives without a lid on the table, and pâté with a knife stuck in it. There were two wineglasses with lees, and beguette crumbs everywhere. Brie oozed on a plate.

'Well, fuck him, Fluff!' said Cleo. 'This is the last thing I need. I really do *not* need to come home from work to be confronted with more bloody work. There'll be a row, now, mark my words, and I don't have the energy for that, either. Oh — this isn't *fair!*'

Cleo trudged upstairs to the bedroom and changed into comfies, and then she started gathering together bits and pieces of laundry to put in the wash. Pablo had left stuff lying around on the bedroom floor and in the *en suite* bathroom. In the downstairs shower room, towels were overflowing from the laundry basket.

'Bloody hell, Fluffy! Why does he never seem to notice when the laundry needs doing? He's the most shiftless househusband in the world.'

Fluffy nodded in agreement.

'I'll go down to the studio now,' Cleo told her, 'and give him a bit of grief.'

You do that! said Fluff's expression.

Slinging the towels on top of the pile that was already mountainous, Cleo turned to leave the room. There was a coat hanging on the back of the bathroom door that she recognized immediately as the one belonging to Princess Abigail. Her street clothes and effects were slung over an adjacent chair. Cleo couldn't help noticing that a particularly pretty lace-trimmed bra nestled among the more pedestrian items of clothing.

Oh. She couldn't go down to the studio, so. She never interrupted Pablo when he had someone sitting for him. But people rarely sat till this hour of the evening: it was way too tough on them. So why was Abigail still there? Cleo felt something a little chilly clog the air.

As she turned to leave the room, she caught sight of herself in the full-length mirror. She looked like shite. Haggard, limp-haired, harried, and with a bloated belly that strained against the elastic of her sweat pants. Fluffy looked more svelte than she did.

'Oh God, Fluff. I can't go down there like this. Can you imagine how I'd look in comparison to that lissom thing who's more than likely preening on a bloody pedestal right now?' She stomped towards the utility room to dump the laundry. 'Well, he can clear away his own fucking dishes,' she said as she passed by the kitchen. 'I'm damned if I'm going to tidy up after that pair. Bloody bastard!'

Fluffy's lead was hanging from a peg in the utility room. Take me for a walk, the dog pleaded, moving towards the lead and wagging her tail. Take me for a walk and we can have a good old chinwag and you can get it all off your chest. The fresh air will do you good, mistress!

'I'm sorry, Fluff. I'm too tired to go for a walk. I know you're one of the best shrinks going, but I actually feel the need to talk to another human being right now.'

Cleo located the phone — the 'search' facility told her it was under a cushion in the sitting room — and punched in Pixie's number. 'Hi! Are you doing anything right now?' she asked.

'Not a lot. I'm just responding to e-mails. But — whoosh! — there goes the last one.'

'I could do with some company.'

'Well, in that case, would you like to come

184

over for a cup of char?' She pronounced it 'cha'.

'Yes,' said Cleo. 'I'd love that. I'll be there in five.'

A cup of 'cha' was actually the last thing Cleo wanted. She wanted a stonking great big glass of wine, but she could hardly walk into Pixie's house and demand to be served alcohol instead of tea, so she nipped back into the kitchen where she and Pablo kept their stash. The wine rack was looking severely depleted. They'd done a big shop last week, and had come home with an entire case of Burgundy. How had it flown so fast? She helped herself to one of the two remaining bottles, then let herself out of the house, trying to avoid Fluffy's pleading eyes.

'Hello!' Pixie came to the door dressed in her pyjamas. 'Come in. Oh — wine! How kind. Maybe I'll take a glass with you as a reward for all my hard work.'

Cleo followed her down into the sitting room.

'Sit down, sit down,' said Pixie. 'I'll be back in two shakes with two glasses.'

'You've been working hard on the book, have you?' asked Cleo when Pixie reappeared.

There was a beat before Pixie answered. 'Not today. Today I had detective work to do — you know, research. So I spent most of the day online, and then I dashed off some mail.'

'How's the book shaping up?'

'Great. Yes — great.'

'It was obviously a good idea to come here to Kilrowan, then.'

'Yes.'

'Have you investigated getting a car yet?'

'Do you know,' said Pixie, 'I don't think that I shall bother with a car. There's a bike in the shed that I use to get to and from Lissnakeelagh, and Shanley's have very kindly agreed to deliver my fuel. I'm quite content to stay pootling around the village — I have everything I need here. Kilrowan may be small, but it's perfectly formed.'

'Well, if you ever need a lift to Galway, you've only to ask.'

'You're very kind.' Pixie popped the cork, and poured. 'I see Pablo's working on a portrait,' she remarked.

'Oh,' said Cleo, moving to the window. 'I didn't realize you could see into his studio from here.'

'You can't. But I passed the window that overlooks the beach yesterday, and spotted him at work.' She sat down on the couch and took a sip of wine. 'I've often wondered why people want to have portraits done of them. I'd hate to be confronted with a picture of me every time I walked into my sitting room, or wherever people hang portraits.'

'People do it for all sorts of reasons,' Cleo told her. 'Prestige, power — vanity, mostly. Pablo did a nude of me once. It hangs in our bedroom.'

'Oh, I can understand *that* — that's rather romantic. It must be quite a sexy thing to do — to sit for a painter when you're involved with him.'

'It is.'

'And the portrait he's working on at the moment? Who's that of?'

'It's a twenty-first birthday present for an 'It' girl, commissioned by her wealthy daddy.' Cleo took a gulp of wine so greedily that she immediately felt self-conscious. It was in marked contrast to Pixie's genteel sip.

'I see.'

The image of Princess Abigail barefoot in gossamer chiffon flashed across Cleo's mind, and a bright idea came to her. 'Hey — why don't you put an artist in your novel, Pixie? Then you could do hands-on research. I'm sure Pablo wouldn't mind you sitting in on a few sessions.' Ensconcing Pixie in Pablo's studio would be as good as hiring a chaperone.

'Nice idea. But I've already done an artist, I'm afraid,' said Pixie.

It had been worth a try. 'So. What's this one about — the novel you're writing at the minute?'

Pixie looked pensive. 'Well, my heroine is a solicitor who is taking an action against the owner of a chain of lap-dancing clubs. She's attracted to the defence lawyer, but then an old boyfriend turns up out of the blue and invites her to a house party in Scotland.'

'Ah. And which one does she end up with? The lawyer or the boyfriend?'

'I don't know,' said Pixie. 'She has to decide, and for some reason she's taking her time about it. Maybe she ends up with neither of them.' She gave a brittle little laugh. 'Maybe she kills herself.'

Cleo was astonished. 'But that's so *un*-Pixie Pirelli!' she said. 'Wouldn't you completely alienate your readership if you did that?'

'Yes. It would be a form of professional suicide.' There was something about Pixie's demeanour that made Cleo scrutinize her more carefully. She appeared perfectly sanguine, sitting there straight-backed on her couch, but there was an uncertain look in her eyes that Cleo had never seen before.

'What's this book going to be called?' she asked.

'I don't know yet. Because my heroine's a rather scatty individual I had thought of 'Away with the Fairies' — '

'I love it!'

'But then I thought again, and the title just kept suggesting to me that Yeats poem. You know, the one that goes: 'Come away, oh human child'?'

'Um. Remind me?'

Pixie stood up and moved to the window, and as she looked out over the darkening garden she recited the verse in her sweet, light voice.

'Come away, oh human child!
To the waters and the wild
With a faery, hand in hand,
For the world's more full of weeping
Than you can understand.'

There was a silence, and then: 'There's Pablo, coming out of his studio now,' she added.

At *last!* thought Cleo. The wine had mellowed her: she was feeling less tired now, and less pissed off with him. She'd give him time to get rid of Abigail, and then she'd go back home and rebuke him for the mess in the kitchen. They'd have a bit of a tiff before kissing and making up. And after that they could tidy the place up together, perhaps head down to O'Toole's for a nightcap.

Pablo and Abigail, both barefoot, were making their way back up the garden. Pablo usually bantered with the people who sat for him, sending them up with blatant irreverence, but there was something grave about his deportment this evening, and his gait was verging on the unsteady. It reminded her of Johnny Depp's sea-legged swagger in *Pirates of the Caribbean*, and as soon as she made the connection, she realized that Pablo was very drunk.

Oh, fuck. There wouldn't be a bit of a tiff, there'd be a blazing row — she knew there would. There'd be no kiss and make up, no quality time in bed, and no cosy tête-à-tête in O'Toole's. And she, more than likely, would end up cleaning the kitchen while Pablo went upstairs and slept it off. It had been happening more and more often that Cleo would go to bed in the spare room, because when Pablo was drunk he snored and kept her awake. And she was so tired today that the last thing she needed was a sleepless night.

'Sometimes it's really hard,' she said now, 'being married to a guy who's as drop-dead gorgeous as my husband.'

'D'you know, I was just thinking that the other day!' said Pixie. Cleo shot her a look. Something about her tone was wrong — it was overly bright. Pixie was picking lint off the sleeve of her

189

pyjamas, not meeting Cleo's eyes. 'Does it happen often, that he's sequestered in his studio with beautiful women?' she asked.

Cleo shook her head. 'No. Generally speaking his portraits are of couples, or families, or CEOs who are mostly men. This is a first, and I have to admit that I am madly jealous.'

'That's perfectly understandable,' said Pixie.

'That girl's a stunner,' said Cleo morosely. 'Did you know that the Pre-Raphaelites coined the term 'stunner'? It was what they called those fantastically beautiful women who sat for them, and who they all rode rotten.'

'You don't think Pablo . . . ' Pixie trailed off, but the implication was clear.

'I don't know,' confessed Cleo. 'He's been in strange form recently. Restless, as if he's not sure where his painting's taking him.'

'Like the painter's equivalent of writer's block?'

'I guess. His paintings have become darker, and that's not good for business. If he adds many more symbolic animals, people will stop commissioning him. He put a slug in the portrait of an eminent actor recently, and a snake in one of a prominent politician. I had to make him take them out. God knows what he'll put in the one he's doing now. He's threatened to do an orang-utan.'

'Yikes. I doubt the 'It' girl's daddy would like that. What did he put in his portrait of you?'

'He put,' said Cleo, 'a little parakeet.'

'How sweet! What does a parakeet symbolize?'

'Well, parakeets are the original lovebirds.

190

They're famously faithful to their owners — even more faithful than dogs, apparently. So that's a symbol of the strength of our relationship — Pablo's and mine. And, of course, parakeets never shut up, and I'm a terrible one for talking. So it was a way of taking the piss, really. I was going to buy one once — a beautiful white cockatoo — but then I realized that I'd be stuck with it for ever. They've fierce long lives.'

'I had a friend who kept a parakeet. Dinner parties at her house were always awful — the bird was so jealous that it pecked at anyone who tried to talk to her. It even drove away a lover or two.'

Maybe, thought Cleo, she ought to buy one as a present for Pablo. She could park it in his studio, and then it wouldn't matter how many beautiful girls sat for him. What an excellent idea! She'd go online this very evening and investigate the possibility of ordering a parakeet on the Internet.

Just then Cleo's phone rang. Pablo's name gleamed neon on the display. 'Hey. Where are you?' he asked.

'Next door. I'm having a glass of wine with Pixie.'

'In that case I'll come and join you.'

'No, don't.' Cleo didn't want him coming over to Pixie's house if he was pissed. 'I'm just about to leave.'

'Stay there and shoot some more breeze, why don't you? I'll be over in five minutes.'

'No. I have to come home now.'

'What's so urgent, Cleo?'

'Um. Fluffy needs a bath,' she improvised.

'Jesus Christ! How many times have you bathed that dog this month? She'll be fucking waterlogged at this rate.'

Better waterlogged than wine-logged, Cleo wanted to say, but didn't. 'Anyway, Pixie wants an early night,' she said, sliding Pixie a look that said, *Is this white lie cool with you?* Pixie nodded. 'I'll see you at home in five minutes, all right?'

'OK. Bye.'

Cleo depressed 'end call', then: 'Sorry to use you as an excuse,' she said, 'but if Pablo had rolled up here you mightn't have got rid of us till all hours.'

'No problem.'

Cleo put her phone back in her bag, and an awkward silence descended.

'It's a beautiful evening,' volunteered Pixie.

'Yes. It is. The lovely thing about the scenery in Kilrowan at this time of the year is . . . '

And Cleo and Pixie spent the next five minutes making small talk about the weather while Cleo finished her wine. Pablo's phone call had wound her up again, and she was dreading going home, dreading the row that they would inevitably have. Maybe she could avoid it by simply getting into the bath with Fluffy and locking the door?

She put her empty wineglass down and got to her feet. 'Thanks for the chat,' she said.

'Any time,' Pixie said. 'I mean it. A problem shared, and all that.'

'And, of course, the same applies to you.' Cleo

kissed Pixie on the cheek. 'It's lovely having a like-minded neighbour. It's the first time I've ever had one — apart from when Pablo was living here, of course. Good night, Pixie.'

'Good night, Cleo.'

Outside, the dusk was deepening. There was no moon tonight, and the wind had got up, dragging a ragged cloak of cloud across the stars. The sound of a dog panting made Cleo look round. There was Fluffy, standing at the garden gate, smiling her most engaging smile. 'Aren't you coming in, Flufflet?' said Cleo, unlocking the front door and holding it open.

But Fluffy laughed, and indicated with a meaningful nod of her head the handsome retriever who was waiting for her across the road. The daisies attached to her bobbin danced becomingly.

'All right, point taken,' said Cleo. 'But you're not to stay out all night, is that understood?'

The dog gave her an oblique look. Then: Byee, Cleo! she said with her eloquent eyes as she turned and trotted over to where her date stood.

Pablo was in the sitting room, lounging on the couch with his bare feet up on the coffee table. He was nursing his accessory *du jour* — a glass of red — and perusing a copy of *Circa*, the Irish arts magazine. Well, fuck him! He might have done something about the kitchen before sprawling about the place reading magazines. But she wasn't going to start. She was too tired for a row and the mess could wait until the morning. So instead of laying into him, she helped herself to a glass of wine and sat down on the couch opposite.

'How's the portrait going?' she asked.

He narrowed his eyes at his magazine, clearly concentrating very hard on focusing on some article of enormous import. 'It's going OK.'

'Is it going to be good?'

He shrugged.

'And what's Abigail going to say, do you think, when you put your pig and orang-utan in?'

His lip curled. 'Oh, I have no doubt that she'll say 'How amusing!' in that upper-crust drawl of hers.'

Something was wrong. His eyes hadn't met hers once since she'd come in. 'Do you talk much?' she asked.

He gave a big sigh, then closed the magazine and sent it skidding across the coffee table. 'No. We don't talk much. We realized very early on that we had absolutely nothing to say to each other.'

An awful, awful silence descended. Then: 'You've fucked her, haven't you?' Cleo found herself saying.

Pablo responded to the accusation by closing his eyes and resting his head against the back of the couch. Then he lifted his head again and looked at her. 'I'm sorry,' he said.

Oh, God. He had fucked her. He *had* fucked her. Even as she had levelled the charge at him she hadn't really believed it. Cleo stood up, and as she did so she felt something surge inside her, and some superhuman force take hold of her.

And then someone who wasn't Cleo was hurling herself at Pablo and lashing out. Crack!

— a slap, then 'crack' again — another. And another. And the someone who wasn't Cleo was screaming — screaming at the top of her voice: 'Get out! Get out! Get out of my fucking house!' she heard, and then Pablo was stumbling for the stairs, trying to cover his head with his hands as blow upon blow fell down upon him, and then the someone who wasn't Cleo barged ahead of him up the stairs, and wrenched the front door open and she heard again the voice scream 'Get out! Get out!' And the someone watched as Pablo lurched to grab his car keys from the table by the front door, and saw that he banged his shoulder off the jamb as he blundered through and down the garden path.

And then Pablo was in the car, and the ignition started up and the headlights came on, and the car took off with a grinding of gears. But it had travelled no distance at all before it came to an abrupt stop with a screech of brakes and a squeal of rubber. There came the sound of a startled yelp. And then silence.

Cleo came to herself. She stepped off the doorstep, ran down the garden path and out onto the road until she reached the place where the car had come to a halt at a crazy angle. And she saw, in the unreal light cast by the headlamps, a bobbin with daisies attached to it lying on the ground. Her eyes searched until they lit upon the dog that lay on the road some yards away in the darkness, beyond the pool of light cast by the headlamps, where she'd been flung by the force of the blow that had struck her.

'Get a vet!' she screamed, turning to where

Pablo sat immobilized behind the steering wheel. 'Get a vet, you fucking bastard!'

Cleo ran to the dog, and hunkered down over her. Blood was seeping from Fluffy's ear, and a bone was sticking through the flesh of her leg. The expression on her face was one of stark incomprehension. She attempted to get to her feet when she saw Cleo, but her short legs buckled under her and she fell back onto the tarmac. 'Don't move, don't move,' begged Cleo. 'Wait — wait until the vet comes, Fluff. The vet'll be here soon.'

She turned her head to see that Pablo had got out of the car — he'd had the sense to put the hazard lights on — and was racing back towards number 5, the Blackthorns. He evidently didn't have his phone on him. 'Hurry up!' Cleo shouted. 'Tell them it's an emergency!'

A light rain had begun to fall, and Fluffy's coat was misting with it, the way grass mists with dew. Cleo reached out to touch the dog's face, and Fluff licked her hand.

'Oh, Fluff,' said Cleo. 'Please don't die! Please don't die!' Her tears were coming now, big, hot splurty ones that dropped onto Fluffy's belly. 'Oh — I'm sorry, darling! I'm making you even wetter. Oh, do hang in there, sweetheart! You're not to go and die on me! Good dog, good little doggie — no! You're not to move. Stay still, sweetheart, the vet'll be here soon. Will I sing you your favourite song while we're waiting? Let's do that — we'll sing until the vet gets here.' And Cleo started to croon the song Fluffy loved most to hear — over and over again — stroking her face with one hand, holding her paw with the other.

How much is that doggie in the window?
  Woof, woof!
The one with the waggly tail?
How much is that doggie in the window?
I do hope that doggie's for sale!

Fluffy gazed up at her mistress with a smile on her face, and eyes that were brimful of love, and then something happened behind her eyes, and Cleo knew that Fluffy was gone from her.

'*No!* I told you you weren't to die, Fluffy! I told you!' Cleo lifted the lifeless body of her best friend and held it to her breast, then buried her face in her fur, and kissed her and kissed her, as if hoping to kiss dear life back into her.

And some minutes later the only sound you could hear there, in the rain on the road that led down to Kilrowan, was the worst sound in the world. It was the awful, raw keening sound of someone whose heart has been broken.

10

Hazel's phone rang. The number in the display read: 'Scar'. She took a deep breath, and smoothed her hair — even though he wasn't there to see her — then she picked up and said: 'Hazel MacNamara, PR,' in her crispest, most efficient voice.

'Hi, Hazel. Hugh here.'

'Hugh. How are you?'

'Fine. I'm in Dublin.'

'Oh?'

'Yes. I'm meeting Angel Kestrel from Angel Phish for lunch, and I thought you might like to join us?'

Oh, sweet Jesus! What could she do?

'Let me just check my organizer.' It was open on the desk in front of her, with a big blank between one o'clock and half-past two. 'Well, I'm afraid that's not going to be possible, Hugh. I've a lunch meeting scheduled.'

'Might you be free later? Perhaps you could come for a drink after work?'

'Why not? You're staying at the Hamilton?'

'How did you know that?'

'I — guessed. How long are you there for?'

'Just overnight. I've some business with an equestrian supplies distributor tomorrow, and then I'm going back down to Kilrowan.'

'Lucky you. This city's shot to hell. I heard recently that it's the second most congested city in the world after Calcutta.'

'I can believe that. What time do you think you can make the Hamilton for that post-work drink? Around midnight, given the traffic?'

She laughed. 'I've no appointments after half-past four. I'll leave my assistant to man the phones and I'll be with you around five.'

'It really takes half an hour to cover that distance by car?'

'No. It would actually take longer by car. I'm walking.'

'Sensible woman. See you later.'

Hazel put the phone down. 'I'm clocking off early today,' she said to her assistant, Renée. 'You can manage on your own for an hour, can't you?'

'Sure I can.'

Hazel didn't really need to ask. Renée was ultra-efficient and super-reliable, and Hazel was very lucky to have her. The rare days when Renée went sick were colossal nightmares.

At around 3.30, Hazel went to change. That was one of the advantages of working in a home/office duplex — if something came up unexpectedly, you could shower, change and make up without the hassle of having to get back home first.

She strolled into her bedroom and studied the contents of her wardrobe. What a bummer that she'd lent her mother her elegant black cashmere number yesterday evening! She selected a discreetly sexy Gucci top that she had seen in a *très chic* boutique in Paris with a price tag of over 500 euros (and that she had bought a couple of months later in the Brown Thomas sale for less than fifty), and teamed it with a pencil skirt that she knew made her ass look great. And heels. These were, of course, inadvisable since she was going to be walking, but she couldn't resist them.

Then she cleaned her teeth, retouched her make-up, and spritzed herself with scent.

Renée wolf-whistled when she walked back into the office. 'Ooh! Dressed to impress! I hope it works!'

Oh, God. Might she be sending out the wrong signal? Should she rethink the outfit? But there was no time to change now. 'Well, the Hamilton is a pretty classy joint,' she told Renée, keen to disabuse her of any — well — *notions* she may have been entertaining about her boss and Hugh Hennessy.

She wondered, as she checked the contents of her handbag, what impression her mother had made on Hugh at lunch. She had looked pretty damn fit last night, when she'd tried on the black cashmere. Angel was in fantastic shape for her age, and had the advantage of a flagrantly sexy voice and a completely contagious laugh.

The office phone rang just as she was about to leg it through the door. Renée put the caller on hold. 'Paul from Grant & Wainwright?'

Oh, no! If she took this call she'd be on the phone for another half an hour and she'd be running very late for her meeting. She shook her head at Renée, mouthed 'Tomorrow', and twinkled her fingers in farewell. As she backed through the door she heard her assistant say: 'I'm sorry, Paul. She's in a meeting. I'll have her

200

call you first thing tomorrow.'

Renée was not only reliable, she also lied convincingly, and sometimes that was more important.

She arrived five minutes early, and decided to buy time in the loo. The loos of the Hamilton were pretty damn sumptuous, with all sorts of little treats on offer. She was just pumping Molton Brown hand cream from a dispenser when the door to the Ladies' opened, and Angel walked in.

'Mum!' said Hazel, hurtling straight into shock. 'What are you doing here?'

'Sh!' said Angel, holding a finger to her lips. 'I'm not supposed to be your mum, remember? I'm here having lunch with the delectable Hugh.'

'*Still*? But it's nearly five o'clock.'

'I know,' said Angel equably. 'We're running late. I gave myself loads of time to get here by cab, but of course it took twice as long as I thought it would in the bogging traffic, and I didn't get here until almost two o'clock. And then we had such fun at lunch — '

'You had *what*?'

Angel gave her a look of mild surprise. 'I said, we had such fun at lunch that I suggested a bottle of champagne in the drawing room. Come and join us for a glass.'

'Mu — *Angel* — this is outrageous! You *know* I can't join you.'

'Of course you can. You scoot upstairs now,

and I'll come up after I've had my pee, and Hugh can introduce us.'

'Jesus — Mother! You're behaving like something out of a French farce!'

'I know! It's great gas, isn't it?' Angel gave one of her trademark throaty chuckles. 'I have to say he's one of the most divine men I've encountered in ages,' she continued, when she'd finished gurgling. 'And those old-fashioned good manners of his just make him even more drop-dead sexy.'

Hazel flailed around for a way out of this. 'Look, I'm going to phone him,' she said, 'and tell him I can't make it.'

'Don't be daft, darling. We're all three of us going to have to meet at some juncture. We might as well get it over with.'

'Oh, *God*, Mum. This is one of the most grotesque situations I've ever been in.' Hazel wanted to bang her head against the marble basin.

'Take it easy, Hazel. Everything will be cool! Just make sure to call me Angel, OK? Banish the mother thing to the outermost recesses of your brain. Now, off you go upstairs. You look great, incidentally.'

'Gucci,' muttered Hazel automatically.

'Maybe I should have borrowed that outfit instead,' remarked her mother. 'Although, I have to say, this cashmere feels *goood* against the skin.'

Angel regarded herself in the full-length mirror, and Hazel noticed with a big fright how similar they were physically.

She walked to the door feeling the way her dad might when he was being Frankenstein's monster, or C3PO.

'Don't worry. I'll be up in five minutes,' hissed her mother conspiratorially, as she ducked into the loo.

Hazel made her way up to the drawing room. Hugh was sitting on a couch, talking on his phone. There were two champagne flutes on the table in front of him, and a bottle in an ice bucket. He got to his feet and smiled when he saw Hazel, and indicated the empty armchair opposite.

The one-sided telephone conversation she was privy to was all about amps and sub-woofers and other arcane sound stuff. Then finally: 'I'd better go,' Hugh said into his phone. 'I've a meeting with our PR. Yeah — she's just fantastic, Jimmy.' Hazel gave him a coy smile. 'And I'd have to say she's easily as gorgeous as she was twenty years ago.' Hazel tried to pretend that the smile was a kind of contemplative expression. 'Yeah.' A laugh. 'OK. I can leave all that in your capable hands, then? Excellent.' He ended the call, then sat back down on the couch and turned his phone off.

'Sorry about that. I had to check up on something. How are you, Hazel?' he asked.

'Fine. How was your lunch with — er — what's her name again?'

'Angel Kestrel. It was great. She's a real live wire — great fun. In fact, we hit it off so well that lunch is still happening. We ordered a bottle of champagne to celebrate the comeback of Angel Phish.'

Hazel winced.

'Will you have a glass?' he asked.

'That would be very acceptable, thanks.'

Hugh indicated to the waiter to bring another glass. 'I was just talking to Jimmy, the guy who does the sound for the festival. Angel Phish — ' Hazel winced again — 'need a high-spec sound system, and I wasn't sure if we could deliver. But Jimmy seems to think we can.' He rubbed his hands together with satisfaction. Hazel had never before seen him looking so — so, well, *animated* was the only word for it. 'Angel was right when she said she was going to rock Kilrowan. She and the Phish — ' Hazel couldn't help it. She *flinched* this time — 'are just the act we need. Ah, here she comes now.' Hugh rose to his feet again.

It was the moment Hazel had been dreading. She watched as her mother sashayed across the carpet. A group of businessmen at the next table watched too, sidetracked from their visions of CEO-dom by Angel Kestrel in full come-on, comeback mode.

'Angel — I'd like you to meet Hazel MacNamara,' said Hugh. 'She's handling PR for the festival.'

'Hazel. How lovely to meet you,' said her mother in her throatiest purr. She proffered a languid hand, and Hazel shook it peremptorily. 'You'll join us for a glass of champagne, I hope?'

'Thank you.'

'You're welcome.' Angel sank onto the sofa,

and Hugh sat down beside her. 'Champagne in the afternoon is one of the most sinfully exquisite indulgences, dontcha think, Hazel?' she said, crossing her legs so that they were displayed to their full advantage. A hint of black lacetop was visible high on the thigh exposed by the slit in the black cashmere, and Hazel saw Hugh's eyes go there.

'I have to say I don't often do champagne in the afternoon,' said Hazel, feeling like a pedestrian frump beside this scintillating sex goddess that was her mother. 'I have a business to run.'

'Hey, lighten up! A gal's gotta live a little, Haze!'

Hazel gave a tight smile. 'I love your dress, by the way,' she said, wanting to remind her mother of the sartorial debt she owed her. 'Is it a Jean Muir?'

'This old thing? Ta, muchly, but I haven't a clue who designed it. I don't set much store by labels.'

The very fit-looking waiter approached with a glass, and Hazel saw Angel slide him a sexy, oblique look that actually made the boy blush as he filled Hazel's flute with champagne, and topped up the other two.

Hugh raised his glass and smiled. 'I would like to propose a toast,' he said. 'To the successful comeback of Angel Kestrel and her Angel Phish!'

'And to the Kilrowan Arts Festival,' Hazel put in, with a hint of reproach.

'Oh, yeah,' said Hugh. 'And to the Kilrowan Arts Festival.'

'Well, cheers,' said Angel, with a foxy smile. 'Let's have another bottle.'

★ ★ ★

It was categorically the worst evening of Hazel's life. She tried her hardest to bring the central focus of the meeting back to the Arts Festival, but her mother kept attracting attention back to herself and Hugh seemed quite happy to let her do it. He laughed at all her jokes and listened entranced to all her anecdotes and appeared so fascinated by her life story (most of which Hazel knew for a fact was fabricated) that he told her she should write an autobiography. She regaled him with backstage stories about U2 and Bob Geldof and the Boomtown Rats, and told him about the time Mick Jagger had asked her to be the mother of his baby and she'd turned him down.

'Do you have any children?' Hugh asked her.

'One. A daughter from a former marriage. She must be in her early twenties now.'

'You have a twenty-something daughter? I don't believe you!'

Hazel's mouth dropped open in disbelief. Her mother had just sliced a decade off her age.

'It's true,' said Angel. 'I had her when I was very young.'

How clever! By Hazel's calculations — and presumably Hugh's — that made her mother not much older than forty, and not too many years past her sexual prime. Jesus! She was flagrant!

'What does your daughter do?'

'Oh, she has some kind of real-life boring office job,' said Angel dismissively. 'She lives in — ah — Auckland.'

'I'm sure I read somewhere that she was very successful,' said Hazel.

'Did you? How weird.'

'No — I *definitely* read that she — '

'Hugh! Let me tell you about the time . . . '

On and on it went like some grotesque nightmare until Angel flitted off to the loo again to 'powder her nose'. Oh, Jesus. If her mother was caught doing cocaine in the loo of the Hamilton Hotel, all would be lost.

'She's great *craic*, isn't she?' said Hugh, regarding Angel's retreating rear, along with every other man in the drawing room.

Hazel made a noncommittal noise.

'Oh. You're not impressed?'

'No. I mean I am.' Hazel didn't want to diss her mother, but she was stung by the way Angel had referred to her as a boring real-life person, even in a fictional scenario. She also had the uncomfortable feeling that she, Hazel, might be just a tad jealous. How absurd! 'Don't you think she's a bit — you know — mutton dressed as lamb?' she asked him.

Hugh shook his head. 'No. Some women never lose it. Think Jane Birkin, Marianne Faithfull, Debbie Harry. When I told Jimmy that I was meeting up with Angel Kestrel, he got very hot under the collar indeed.'

'Oh.' Hazel tried not to sound disappointed. She reached for her glass.

'And she came up with some amazing ideas

for new songs for the festival, all with a maritime flavour to them. She's going to call any ballads she writes 'Siren Songs', and the more upbeat ones will be 'Sea Shanties'. Hey — are you all right?'

Hazel had choked on her champagne. 'Yes, I'm fine,' she said, when she finally recovered. She took a tissue from her bag and wiped tears from her eyes.

'And she's going to get her designer friend, Carmen somebody — apparently she's quite famous: she's the one who's doing the Salmon of Knowledge costume for the Mondo bloke — to design her a mermaid dress.'

'A mermaid dress?' echoed Hazel, feeling faint.

'Yes. With a 'fishtail skirt' — does that mean anything to you?'

Hazel nodded, and swigged back more fizzy anaesthetic. She knew exactly the kind of frock her mother had in mind. Carmen, her mother's designer friend, had come up with a similar outfit for Hazel's twenty-first birthday party. It had been of tight sequined stretch satin, with a bra top made of scallop shells. It had been very revealing, and Hazel had spent most of the night wearing a cardigan. She pictured her mother gyrating on stage like Cher in a low-slung fishtail skirt and a bra top, and she thought that this evening wasn't really happening to her and she was simply going mad.

Make that truly mental. Because whaddaya know! Yes, indeedy — things had just got worse. A woman sitting on the other side of the room had risen to her feet and was preparing to leave. 'Hazel MacNamara!' she exclaimed, as her gaze lit on Hazel. 'How lovely to see you!'

It was Rosemary Clotworthy, her old headmistress.

'Mrs Clotworthy!' Hazel sprang to her feet and stood there stiffly, gripping the stem of her champagne flute between white-knuckled fingers and thinking fuck fuck fuck.

Mrs Clotworthy crossed the room, took Hazel's hand between hers, and pressed it warmly. 'You don't have to stand to attention. You're not in school now!' she quipped. 'Goodness, you haven't changed a bit, dear. Apart from the clothes, of course. That's a rather more elegant get-up than your old school blazer!'

'Ha ha!'

'I hear tell you've set up your own PR business?'

'Yes.'

'I knew you'd do well for yourself. How could you have gone wrong — a high achiever like you. And this is — er?'

'Hugh Hennessy.' Hugh introduced himself, extending a hand.

Mrs Clotworthy dimpled at him. 'I haven't seen Hazel for years,' she said. 'She was head girl of my school, St Brigid's.'

'Oh?' said Hugh politely.

'An all round star pupil, was Hazel — captain of the netball team, star of the drama club, president of the debating society! Hazel was the most articulate president we ever had.'

'Really?'

'Oh yes. You could talk your way out of a paper bag, Hazel MacNamara!'

'Ha ha ha,' went Hazel.

'How's your mother keeping?'

'Um. She's OK, thanks.'

'And your father? I saw him on Grafton Street recently — '

Oh fuck. 'Oh, fuck!' said Hazel, and Rosemary Clotworthy looked rather taken aback. 'I mean — oh dear! I must go and feed the meter before I get clamped! May I escort you to the door, Mrs Clotworthy?'

'Why, yes — of course.'

'I thought you said you were walking, Hazel?' said Hugh.

'Are you mad? In these shoes? Come on, Mrs Clotworthy.' Hazel took her former headmistress by the elbow and tried to steer her towards the door.

But Mrs Clotworthy wasn't budging. She had been distracted by the click clack click of heels on the tiled floor of the lobby, and her gaze was now fixed upon Angel, who was strutting her stuff past the reception desk. 'Oh, look!' she said. 'Isn't that — '

'Come *on*!' said Hazel, gripping Mrs Clotworthy even more firmly by the elbow. 'Those clampers are cunning and vengeful! They'll be on my case any minute.' Mrs Clotworthy hadn't heard her: she was riveted by Angel Kestrel, who was bestowing smiles on everyone she passed.

'*DESPERATE MEASURES*' flashed in neon capitals across Hazel's mind. Since Hugh, too, was transfixed by the vision that was her mother listing across the lobby, Hazel decided to take advantage of the diversion. She lurched into the ice bucket and sent it flying. *Yes!* Champagne and ice went everywhere. For good measure, the gesture of alarm she made as she leapt backwards sent her champagne glass shooting across the room to come to rest with a splintering of shards on the tiles round the fireplace. 'Oh, dear — look what I've done!' she exclaimed. 'We really must go now, Mrs Clotworthy.' As she propelled Mrs Clotworthy across the carpet and through the door with a firm hand she could see in her peripheral vision a bewildered-looking Hugh raise a hand to summon the waiter.

In the lobby, she passed her mother high-heeling along, sniffing happily.

'Hey, Hazel!' said Angel. 'What's happening? And hey — it's Mrs Clotworthy, innit? How the hell *are* you?'

'Tell Hugh I forgot I had a really urgent appointment elsewhere.' Hazel threw the directive over her shoulder as she skidded to a halt at the front entrance to allow the automatic doors to open and spew her and Mrs Clotworthy finally from the maws of hell that all this afternoon had been masquerading as the Hamilton Hotel. They clattered down the steps, the liveried porter regarding them curiously.

'Goodbye, Mrs Clotworthy,' Hazel managed, as they hit the pavement.

And she wrenched the door of a taxi open and piled herself into the back seat before you could say Angel Phish.

* * *

The next morning, while Renée was out of the office, she phoned Hugh to apologize.

'I'm so sorry, Hugh,' she said. 'I was standing there, happily shooting the breeze, and then I remembered about the meter. And then I remembered that I'd promised to send a really urgent e-mail. Then the disaster happened with the champagne and I was so frazzled and so cutting things fine that I simply couldn't hang about. It was wildly unprofessional of me, and I apologize unreservedly.'

'No problem,' said Hugh. He sounded a bit remote.

'Are you really pissed off with me?' she asked anxiously.

'No, no. Not at all, Hazel. I'm just suffering from a pretty nasty hangover. I ended up in the Sugar Club last night with Angel and a friend of hers called the Sheikh. I didn't get back here until nearly four o'clock this morning. That Angel sure knows how to party.'

'Yes,' said Hazel, through very tight lips. 'She does.'

'The Sugar Club was an eye-opener. I haven't been in a nightclub for a long time. Angel says she goes every week. I don't know where she gets the stamina.'

'What a live wire she is,' said Hazel, even more tersely. 'Anyway, about the Arts Festival, Hugh — '

There came the sound of an electronic beeping.

212

'Oh. I'm sorry, Hazel, I've got to go,' said Hugh. 'I'm running seriously late for my meeting.'

'Oh — of course. Goodbye, Hugh — and don't worry — I've everything under control!'

'Thanks, Hazel. Talk soon.'

Bummer.

The next thing she did was to phone her mother.

'Oh, darling,' said Angel in a cigarette voice when she picked up. 'It's a bit early in the day for this.'

'It's eleven o'clock in the morning, Mother.'

'Jesus H. Christ! It's *that* early?'

'I've been in work since nine o'clock.'

'Yes — but you're a real-life person, darling.'

'A boring real-life person who works in some office in Auckland, according to you,' said Hazel huffily.

'What? What are you *on*, darling?'

'You told Hugh that I was a boring real-life person who works in Auckland! That was below the belt, Mum!'

Angel's tone was plangent with incomprehension. 'But you're *not* a boring real-life person who works in Auckland.'

'*I* know that! But you could have made me sound a bit more interesting.'

'I had to get rid of you somehow, didn't I? And Auckland is about as far away from Ireland as you can get. Anyway, that person doesn't exist. You mustn't take umbrage, darling, just because I turned you into a work of fiction. Anyway, wouldn't you prefer to be a boring

213

person in Auckland than the sort of crazed diva who sends bottles of champagne flying and shatters glasses to smithereens in the Hamilton Hotel? That was some exit, sweetie-pie. Even I was impressed.'

'I had to do something. It was a diversionary tactic. I needed to get out of there.'

'In my experience, it's no hard thing to get reasonably gracefully to one's feet and say: 'Please excuse me. I must leave now. I forgot I had a prior engagement.''

'What? And run the risk of Mrs Clotworthy clocking you and saying: 'Good evening, Mrs MacNamara! Hasn't your little Hazel turned out nicely?' Come on, Mum!'

Her mother sniffed down the phone. 'Oh, do stop hissing at me, Hazel. My head's wrecked enough without you giving me more grief.'

'Well, I'm not surprised your head's wrecked. The nerve of you — snorting lines in the Hamilton Hotel and then dragging Hugh off to the Sugar Club.'

'I didn't drag him. He came willingly.'

'Did you dance with him?'

'Of course I did.'

Oh, God. Could it get worse? She couldn't help herself — the next question waiting to be asked was the itch you know you shouldn't scratch. 'Did — did you snog him, Mum?'

'No. That fucking Sheikh turned up and cramped my style.'

'You mean you would have snogged him if the Sheikh hadn't been there?'

'Well, darling, what do you think?'

'You would! Oh! You would!'

'Sweetheart, what's wrong? Why have you gone all whimpery?'

Another, even more compelling itch. 'Would you have gone back to his hotel with him, Mum?'

'Um. Yes.'

Hazel put the phone down, and then she put her head in her hands. She couldn't bear to think of her mother cavorting with a man who was quite possibly young enough to be her son.

Brnnng! *Brnnng! Brnnng! Brnnng! Brnnng!*

Hell's teeth. She obviously wasn't going to go away. Hazel picked up. 'What?' she said, testily.

'You fancy him, don't you?'

'No.'

'Of course you do. You'd be mad not to.'

'I do not fancy him, Mother.'

'You're sure?'

'Absolutely.'

'Honest injun?'

'Yeah yeah yeah.'

'Oh, good. I wouldn't have been able to live with myself if you did fancy him.'

'What do you mean?'

'You're my little baby, Hazel. I couldn't do the dirty on you.'

'How charitable of you.'

'It's not charity. It's called motherly love.'

'Oh. Is that why I'm feeling so uncomfortable?'

'What do you mean?'

'Unaccustomed as I am . . . '

'Don't give me lip. And listen to me. You

215

might want to lighten up a bit.'

'What are you talking about?'

'Well, get back to basics, anyway. You're making this Arts Festival sound so fucking *worthy*.'

'It's an important event in the social calendar, Mum. It needs an element of gravitas if we want it to be taken seriously. I mean, how are we to reconcile the fact that Pablo, a painter of renown, and Colleen, a writer of international repute, are going to be appearing alongside a punk rock revival act called Angel Phish and a mime artist masquerading as a salmon?'

'Well, you can either look on that as an example of dumbing down, or you can see it as a way of lightening up. Have you a dictionary there?'

'Yes. Of course.'

'Then may I suggest that you look under the letter F for the definition of the word 'festival'? Now. I'm going back to bed. Love you! Bye! And *stop calling me Mum*!'

Hazel put the phone down, then went to her bookshelves to locate her *Concise Oxford*. She bypassed C, D and E, and got to F. *Favour, Fenestration, Ferrule.* Then: 'Festival,' she read. 'Feast day, celebration, merry-making. Performance of special import.'

Performance of special import . . . Cue ominous music. Hazel realized rather ruefully that she'd been so fixated on the 'import' aspect that she'd forgotten that merry-making was part of the equation. Merry-making? It sounded so *antiquated*, somehow, but — but . . .

Maybe her mother was right? Maybe it *was* time for Hazel MacNamara to lighten up a little.

As she put the book back on the shelf, she forced herself to hum something, in a serious attempt at lightening up. Um. What was it she was humming? She couldn't for the life of her think what it was.

It wasn't until much later in the day that she realized that the tune she'd been humming had been one of her mother's greatest hits.

11

Pixie sent a round robin to her writers' group in London, telling them of her plight. It went like this:

From: Pixie Pirelli
To: Mariella Sweetman
cc: Dominique Masterson, Dilys Morgan, Isabel Whitty, Marian Murray and Cathy Dylan.
Subject: My plight.

Hello from Connemara!

Look what I found on Amazon! She's blocked me, the horror. Go look at her poisonous site — here Pixie typed in the web address — and let me know what you think. I am going to get her.

Love, Pixie XXX

From: Mariella Sweetman
To: Pixie Pirelli
Subject: Re: Your plight

```
I'm logging on every day to see
if she drops some clue as to
her identity. Will keep you
posted if I find anything.

Love, Mariella. XXXXXXXXXX
```

From: Dilys Morgan
To: Pixie Pirelli
Subject: Re: Your plight

Oh! Poor you! Have to say her site made me LOL. How solipsistic can you get? I wouldn't allow her to get to you. Incidentally, I can't think of a better place to be blocked than the West of Ireland. Lucky you! Enjoy it!

Kisses. Dilly.

From: Pixie Pirelli
To: Dilys Morgan
Subject: Re: Your plight

Dear Dilys,

Sorry — make that MY plight. Not sure if being blocked anywhere in the world is a good thing, but at least I have no deadline. Have decided to take up fly-fishing!

Love, P XXX

From: Dominique Masterson
To: Pixie Pirelli
Subject: Tabbitha

Darling Pixie,

You poor thing — you must have got such a shock — I'm not surprised you're blocked. If I were you,

I'd visit her site on a regular basis to check her out. That way you should get some idea as to who she might be.

All love, Dominique. Xxxx

PS: The film rights to FALSE FRIENDS have been optioned! I've suggested Rory McDonagh for the lead!

From: Pixie Pirelli
To: Dominique Masterson
Subject: Re: Tabbitha

Dear D,

Rory McDonagh?! ♥

XXX

Pixie finished sending mail, then phoned Ballynahinch Castle to book her fly-fishing lesson. She'd loved the first one, the time she'd jumped off the PR treadmill and booked herself in there. There had been something so *serene* about sitting in a rowing boat in the company of a ghillie who only spoke when it was absolutely necessary. That placid, glass-smooth lake at Ballynahinch had to be the ultimate stress-free zone. She hadn't caught anything, and she was rather glad of that. She wasn't sure how she'd feel if she actually *did* land a fish — would she really have the *cojones* to knock it over the head as per the ghillie's instructions? But she reminded herself that she always had the option to let it go. When she'd mentioned this to her ghillie, he'd looked at her with genuine pity, as if she were completely barking.

What to do today? Should she try accessing her novel again, see if perhaps Jodie wanted to come out and play? No. Something told her that Jodie was still determined to continue playing hide-and-seek, and Pixie wasn't interested in that game. Sitting in front of a blank screen and waiting for Jodie to jump out at her and go 'Surprise!' was not her idea of fun. Maybe she should take a look at Tabby's blog, as Dominique had suggested? Maybe Tabby would drop the name of her agent, or give some other clue to her identity.

She'd saved Tabby's blog to her 'favourites' (huh!) under 'Hissy Tabby Cat', and clicking on it now took her straight there. Bingo! Tab had updated it only an hour ago. But the bingo buzz didn't last long.

According to the bestsellers' list in today's *Guardian*, Pixie Pirelli's classic of modern day literature, 'Hard to Choos' (sic! Or should I make that 'sick'?) is still hanging in there. The following is an example of Ms Pirelli's wit & wisdom: 'The water felt like silk that had been left in the fridge. Charlotte knew that when she got to the island her skin would be so pimply with goosebumps that even her Aveda scrub might not be able to shift them.' Hello? Is there anyone in there? Who in their right mind would leave silk in the fridge? And when was the last time you tried to get rid of goosebumps with a proprietary brand? Writing such as this makes me sigh with exasperation. Nay — it makes me want to give said Ms Pirelli a slap or two as a wake-up call. (If you're interested in trivia, incidentally, Ms Pirelli's real name is plain Jane Gray.)

Talking of wake-up calls, my beloved pussy cat — my beautiful Birman — woke me this morning by licking my perfectly pedicured toes (Jessica Nails, damson red, and smelling not of feet, natch, but of Dr Hauschka's Rose Day Cream. I know it's for the face, but I can't resist spoiling myself sometimes, and rubbing it on my tootsies as an inducement for L to worship at my feet). Anyway, this Birman is the sweetest puss imaginable . . . '

Pixie didn't — couldn't — read on. Click! Tabbitha went pirouetting straight back into the ether. Feeling as if she'd just been decked by Mike Tyson, Pixie picked up the phone and speed-dialled Mariella.

F — *fiddlesticks!* The machine picked up, and she didn't want to leave a message, didn't want to disturb her friend if she was at work. Should she try Deborah? But Deborah was always so busy. Pixie didn't want to bother her with her petty woes and paranoia. Anyway, she knew what

Deborah would tell her. She would tell her not to go there, not to go to the bad place that was Tabbitha's site. Any sensible person would avoid it like the plague sore it was, but in Pixie's experience, sores were there to be picked. Her mother had always scolded her for not leaving scabs alone when, as a child, she'd cut her knees. Pixie's knees were criss-crossed with tiny scars as a result.

She needed something to make her feel better. At times like this she wished she were a smoker. A stiff drink? No. In her experience, alcohol rarely helped. A sugar rush? Equally transient. A cup of tea? Company? Yes. She'd put the kettle on, and then she'd phone Cleo and ask if she was available as a counselling service. But first she'd have to scrub her teeth to get rid of the bile that had accumulated in her mouth while reading Tabby's blog. She ran into the bathroom and grabbed her toothbrush, wishing it was a whetstone that she could sharpen her incisors with, all the better to bite her adversary. If Londonista Tabbitha wanted a cat fight, the gloves were off and Pixie's pretty little claws were showing.

★   ★   ★

Cleo needed company. She had spent the days since Fluffy's death living in a vortex. Pablo had been banished from her life. His calls had gone unanswered; his e-mail went straight into the recycle bin.

She had buried her doggie alone, the night

after she'd died. She'd dug a grave at the bottom of the garden at midnight, and she'd wrapped Fluffy in her blanket, and put her favourite teddy in with her. She'd brushed her coat, but had buried her *au naturel*, with no hair accessories and no nail varnish. She'd sat by the grave for nearly an hour before she summoned the courage to lift the spade and shovel earth over her beloved.

Now she needed to talk to someone. She took the last bottle of wine from the rack and went to call on Pixie.

Pixie answered the door with a toothbrush in her mouth. 'Oh, hi! I was just thinking about phoning you,' she said through her toothbrush. 'I really need to t — oops!'

And Pixie raced to the bathroom to spit.

Cleo stepped into the hall and shut the front door behind her, waiting for her to come back.

'Sorry about that,' Pixie said, coming back into the hall and gesturing to Cleo to precede her downstairs.

'Thanks,' said Cleo. 'I hope you don't mind me dropping round without phoning first? It's just that I really need to talk. I remember what you said, about a problem shared and all that, and thought I'd take you up on it.'

'Oh. Oh — of course.'

Cleo reached the bottom of the stairs and held out the bottle to Pixie. 'Here's wine, as an inducement for you to listen to me.'

'I don't need inducements, Cleo. You know that. But thank you for the wine.' She took the bottle and made for the kitchen. 'You're not working today?' she asked over her shoulder.

'No. I shut up shop. I haven't been open for a couple of days now.'

'Oh? That's not like you.'

'I haven't been myself.'

Pixie paused and gave Cleo a curious look. 'Oh, God. You've been to a horrible place, too, haven't you? I can tell. I've just come from one.'

'Yes. Give me wine, please, before I spill the details — and very possibly some tears as well. What was your horrible place?'

'I'll get round to giving you the guided tour after I've listened to you.'

Pixie flicked a switch on the kettle, then busied herself with wine and corkscrew. 'Here,' she said, pushing a glass towards Cleo.

'Aren't you having some?'

'No. Tea is my stimulant of choice today.'

'You're so wise. I shouldn't be swigging alcohol. It's a depressant.'

'There's no harm in numbing the edges — maybe that's what you need right now. Conversely, I need to keep my edges very sharp indeed to get through the labyrinth I'm in.'

'Oh, Pixie — I'm sorry! The last thing you need is me bending your ear if you're going through the mill too . . .'

'Don't worry. We'll get there together.'

Something about the way she said it made Cleo burst into tears.

'What is it, Cleo?' asked Pixie.

'Fluffy — Fluffy's dead,' she said, gulping for air. 'Fluffy's dead, and Pablo killed her.' And then she couldn't talk any more. She sat at

Pixie's kitchen table with her head on her forearms and cried and cried until she was all cried out, and when Pixie said: 'Tell me all about it,' Cleo cried some more.

Half an hour later, she'd told Pixie everything. She told her about Princess Abigail and Pablo's drunken infidelity, and she'd told her about the accident that had killed Fluffy, and how she'd buried her all on her own. She told her how she had told Pablo to pack his bags while she had locked herself in the spare room with the body of her dog, deaf to his pleas, and to his apologies — and deafer still to his attempts to persuade her to reconsider. And she told her how shaken she had been when she'd emerged from the spare room to find that he seemed to have taken nothing with him when he'd departed, and how the half-dozen or so canvases that had been in his studio had been destroyed by great random brush-strokes.

'Including the portrait of the princess?'

'Yes. You should have seen the look on her face when she turned up for her next sitting. I escorted her down to the studio and watched as she took it all in. Then I told her to get her cheap ass out of there and to *never* come back.'

'Good girl,' said Pixie approvingly, pouring herself another cup of tea and refilling Cleo's glass.

Cleo had reached the level of intoxication that is just right. She hoped that another glass of wine wouldn't tumble her over into the realms of the maudlin, that she wouldn't be tempted to tell Pixie how much she still loved Pablo, in spite of

226

everything. She craved reasons to hate him. She had spent sleepless nights praying for the strength to get through the dark place she had found herself in, and praying that once she came out the other side she would have no feelings at all for the man she had married. Right now she needed the support of wise little Pixie to help her get there.

But, she reminded herself, she'd talked enough about *her* troubles. Now it was time to lend an ear to her neighbour.

'Let's change the subject,' she said. 'We've been talking about me for far too long, now, and my problem's well and truly halved. Well, reduced, anyway. What's yours?'

'Well,' began Pixie, taking a deep breath.

Cleo listened appalled as Pixie filled her in on somebody known to her only as Tabbitha, the self-styled Londonista.

'Can you bear to show me?' she asked, when Pixie had finished. 'I mean, can you bear to go back there?'

'Yes,' said Pixie, in a steely voice. 'I can. Come with me.'

She stood up from the kitchen table and led Cleo to the study, where her laptop sat on her desk.

'You see,' said Pixie, booting up the computer, 'I am determined to track her down, and to do that, I have to accumulate as many clues as I can. And the only way I can do that is by visiting her site on a regular basis to see what she lets slip.' Pixie tapped her beautifully polished nails on the wood of her desk while she waited to be connected. 'Goodness! It does get tedious having to log on all the time. When will broadband come to Connemara? Dear old Tabby is most certainly connected — she updates her blog on practically an hourly basis. I wonder if she's penned anything choice about me since the last time I checked?'

'Doesn't it wreck your head? Reading stuff like that about yourself?'

'Yes,' said Pixie. 'It's excruciating. But I have to be strong, because otherwise I'd go to pieces. We're in very similar places, you and I, and it's lucky that we're here for one another. Aha! Behold! La Londonista in all her glory!'

Cleo focused in on the myriad words. Her jaw went slack as she scrolled down Tabbitha's blog. 'Dear Jesus. Dear *Jesus*, Pixie. The woman's a complete nutter! What on earth makes her think that people are interested in reading about her and her fucking pedicure and her *cat* for Christ's sake!'

'I'm acting on the assumption that she's writing for a privileged few web browsers. I came across her blog almost by accident, just acting on a hunch. But sooner or later she's bound to include some detail that'll give the game away — the name of her agent, for instance. And that's when I pounce. I have friends in high places, and if Tabby wants her novel published she might find that some doors will close in her Dr Hauschka day-creamed face.'

'She's a sorry bitch,' said Cleo. 'That's for sure. And if her agent's so *loving* her novel, why doesn't she just get on and write it instead of barfing out all this junk?'

'Maybe she's blocked,' said Pixie. 'I have a friend who says she writes a diary when she's blocked. Most writers would prefer to write anything rather than nothing.'

'Is that how you cope with it?'

'No. My preference is to write nothing rather than risk writing rubbish. But I'm at an advantage because I don't have a deadline. Most editors would be breathing fire down their writers' necks and sending them into even more of a tizzy.'

'So what do you do while you're waiting for the muse to descend?'

'I'm going to take up fly-fishing. I have a session booked for later in the week.'

'What fun! You could put a sexy ghillie in a book!'

'I had thought of that. Sadly, my ghillie last time I was here was about seventy, and a man of few words.' Pixie closed her laptop and turned to Cleo. 'Have you thought about what *you're* going to do?' she asked. 'About Pablo?'

Cleo shook her head. 'No. I'm still too raw. I don't want to think about it now.'

'Good. For what it's worth, my advice is — do nothing. Talk about it as much as you like, but take no course of action until the hurt starts to wear off. Do you know where he's gone?'

'I got a postcard with a London postmark this morning. It just said 'From the Edge'.'

'So he's hurting too.'

'I hope so. I *so* fucking hope so.' Cleo said the words with such ferocity that she almost regretted them. 'Ow. I sound like an embittered bitch.'

'Why shouldn't you sound like an embittered bitch? He's made you feel that way, and you don't have to apologize. It's perfectly under-standable, Cleo. But do remember this — no matter how bitter you're feeling. 'Love makes bitter things sweet.''

'Did you write that?'

'No. Jalal Al-Din Rumi did.'

'Jalal Al who?'

'He was a Persian sage and poet, and he wrote that in the eleventh century, so it's stood the test of time. You'll get through this, Cleo. That cliché about time healing is an accurate one. Every day I think fewer bad thoughts about my ex, even though his brand of betrayal was unforgivable. Pablo's was *unforgettable*, but that's a very different thing. You've got to remember that there was drink involved, and that there are two sides to every story.'

'What do you mean?'

'You're assuming that he seduced that girl. How do you know it wasn't the other way round?'

Cleo drooped. She didn't want to think about it any more, and she was all talked out. It must have showed in her expression, because Pixie hurriedly added: 'Look, I'm sorry to come on like Oprah, but I have learned a lot about what makes people do the things they do. My advice to you is just to allow life to happen, and allow yourself time to mend. Then what is *meant* to happen *will* happen.'

Cleo sat quiet for a moment or two, contemplating, and then she said: 'You're really very wise, Pixie, aren't you?'

'Not wise enough to save my own skin,' Pixie said ruefully. 'My own gullibility *vis-à-vis* my ex never ceases to appal me. I find that other people's problems are always easier to solve than one's own. I solve other people's problems all the time when I'm writing. I'm a great lateral thinker.' She looked pensive. 'I'd love to know what Tabbitha's problem is. That's what's intriguing me most at the moment.'

'You might even get a book out of it.'

'I might.'

'There's your revenge!'

'And there's my phone,' said Pixie, picking it up and glancing at the display. 'Sorry, Cleo, I'll have to take this. It's my editor.'

Cleo jumped to her feet. 'I'll make myself scarce,' she said. 'Thanks so much for the agony aunt stuff, Pixie.'

'You're welcome. Give me a ring any time — I really mean that.'

'Likewise.' And Cleo twinkled her fingers at Pixie and was gone.

When she let herself into her house the first thing she saw as she hung up her coat was Pablo's scarf. She unhooked it from its peg, and stood looking at it, rubbing the fine wool between her fingers. Then she held it against her face and breathed in his smell. Longing washed over her — a longing to touch his skin, taste his mouth, hear his voice. Should she phone him? It could do no harm to initiate contact. It would have to be done at some stage, even if said contact was via a solicitor's letter . . .

No!

Then: 'No,' she told herself, more rationally. Calmly she hung the scarf back on the peg. Pixie was right. Do nothing, take no action until the wound is mended. In the meantime, just take the bitter with the sweet, and let life happen.

★ ★ ★

'Deborah! What can I do for you?' Pixie was glad to hear her editor's voice: it always sounded so reassuring.

'The first question to be asked, of course, Pixie,' said Deborah, 'is: how's your block?'

'Still there,' said Pixie equably. 'But I'm not worried, so you needn't be.'

'How would you feel if there was a squeeze on?'

'But there isn't.'

'But if there *was* a squeeze on how do you think you might feel?'

'I don't know. I've never worked to a deadline.'

There came a pause, then: 'We have a problem, Pixie,' said Deborah.

'Oh?'

'I've had to make changes to next season's list.'

'What's the problem? I'm not listed for next season.'

'I know. But I was hoping you might deliver early.'

'Goodness, Deborah! Why?'

'Dominique Masterson's title's been held over until next year.'

'Oh? Why?' asked Pixie.

'Plain and simple. It was sub-standard.'

'Oh, dear. Poor Dominique.'

'She's a friend of yours, isn't she?'

'Well, she's in the writers' group that Mariella organizes. I wouldn't call her a special friend, but we e-mail occasionally.'

'You know her last book was panned?'

'Yes.'

'She was trying to write something literary, and it didn't work. This one's even worse. That's why we've had to postpone publication.'

'Oh, *dear*. How awful for her! What makes the book so bad?'

'There's no story.'

'Can't you help her redraft?'

'No. It's far too flabby. It can't be put right in time. That's why I'm phoning you. To ask you a favour.'

'You want to bring my pub date forward?'

'Ms Perspicacity Personified!'

'But Deborah! I'm blocked.'

'You're blocked on the current book, I appreciate that. But couldn't you start something new? I know it's asking a huge amount of you, Pixie, but you're the only author I could dream of approaching with a request to have a new novel ready in time for next season.'

'That's a really tall order, Deborah.'

'I know. We'd make it worth your while financially.'

'Pooey. Talk money to Natalie. The main

reason for doing it would be as a favour to you.'

'You are such a Goody Two-Shoes!'

'I know I am.'

'So. What do you think the chances are that you might come up with something new?'

Pixie didn't even pause for thought. 'I think there's every chance, actually. Somebody suggested an idea for a new novel just this afternoon. If I get cracking on it right away, and cancel all invites to friends to come and stay here, I could let you have a hundred thousand good words in a couple of months.'

'You complete star! Star, star, star!'

Star? Pixie couldn't help thinking of how *un*-stellar she'd felt when she'd read the things Londonista Tabbitha had said about her writing. Poor Dominique must be in agony. 'Does Dominique know yet, Deborah?' she asked. 'That her novel's . . . um . . . '

'Unpublishable? No. I wanted to run this idea by you first.'

'Will you tell her that I'm likely to be replacing her on the list?'

'No. But she'll find out pretty soon, I've no doubt.'

'It won't be easy for her.'

'No, it won't. And I know this won't be easy for *you*, but perhaps you should tell her.'

'What? That her book's being replaced by something of mine that hasn't even been written yet?'

'Well, think about it. How would you feel if you were in Dominique's shoes? Wouldn't you rather hear the news upfront from a friend than in a hugger-mugger Chinese whispers way? She almost certainly won't thank you for keeping it from her.'

Oh, dear. Deborah was right. There was nothing worse than imagining that everyone else out there knew something about you that you didn't. 'You're right,' said Pixie. 'I'd absolutely hate that. The *schadenfreude* would be unbearable. When are *you* going to tell her that her pub date's been deferred?'

'I'll make the phone call now.'

'In that case I'll phone her tomorrow, to commiserate first and deliver the bad news second. I do hope she won't hate me for it.'

'She will do, initially. That'd be only natural. But she'll respect you all the more for being straight with her. Remember — you're just being cruel to be kind.'

Pixie nodded, even though Deborah couldn't see her. 'Well. Yikes. Good luck with the phone call,' she said. 'I'd hate to have to drop a bombshell like that.'

'I know. I'm dreading it. It's put a pall over the entire afternoon.'

Pixie heard Deborah sigh down the phone, and she thought: Oh, please God, may I never provoke a sigh like that from anyone.

'What are you up to for the rest of the day?' resumed Deborah. 'I suppose you're off to walk on some idyllic beach?'

'No. I'm off to don my thinking cap and exercise my fingers.'

'Exercise your fingers?'

'Four thousand words a day is a *lot* of words,

Deborah. That's what I'm going to have to produce if you want your book on time. And I've research to do on top of that.'

'What are you researching this time round?'

'Fly-fishing.'

'I won't ask.'

'No, don't. Let it come as a surprise.'

Pixie put the phone down feeling thoughtful, and a little excited, for she knew that fly-fishing wasn't going to be the only area of interest that her new novel would explore. She had another source of inspiration in the unlikely form of Londonista Tabbitha. Because Pixie wouldn't commit Tabby to the toilet just yet. She could, for the next few months, put her to *much* better service . . .

She booted up her computer and opened a new document. 'Save As', Microsoft Word asked her.

'Save as:' answered Pixie, 'Untitled. First draft.' Then she started to type.

CHAPTER ONE

Talitha Parker led a charmed life. She was a luminary on the London social scene, and she wasn't shy about letting people know this. Every day she detailed fascinating snippets about her fascinating life in an on-line journal, and every day that journal was requisite reading for le tout Londres. But pride really does come before a fall, because one day Talitha made the mistake

of letting slip her real identity.
It happened like this . . .

Five hours later, Pixie was still typing.

★ ★ ★

The next morning, after doing her SAS exercises
and drinking her juice, Pixie accessed Tabbitha's
site via her 'favourites'. Ironically, Tabbitha really
would become one of her favourites now, she
thought, as Internet Explorer winged its way
towards London.

Good morrow, people! [purred Tabby.]
More cosmetic dental work yesterday meant
that I was able to peruse back issues of the
gossips. There was a delightful feature on
some 'It' girl's wedding (a pretender to the
throne of yours truly. There's only room for
one 'It' girl at the top of the pile,
dontchaknow). There was also a spread on
porn-star monikered pop fiction author,
Pixie Pirelli.

Result! She'd struck lucky! Tabbitha hadn't
finished with her yet.

Pretty Pixie — clearly airbrushed — was
pictured in the sitting room of her pretty
Notting Hill house 'arranging flowers'. She
was pictured in her pretty kitchen 'drinking
coffee'. She was pictured in her pretty
bedroom, 'relaxing'. She was pictured in her

pretty garden 'potting plants'. She was pictured at her piano 'playing Chopin'. Gimme a break, Pixie, while I stick my fingers down my throat! However, the most nauseating picture of all was the one of Pixie sitting at her pretty bureau 'writing a novel'.

Speaking of which, I'm still at the coal-face. My agent wants rewrites — sob — but I . . .

Ha! Tabbitha didn't know it, but she was digging her own grave more efficiently than Pixie could. She scanned the rest of today's blog perfunctorily, then clicked on some of the 'comment' boxes. So people did actually comment on Tabbitha's crazed musings! This was interesting . . .

Tabbitha! How kick-ass are you! JK

Hey, Tabbitha! Concur entirely with your sentiments regarding PP. Hasn't her publishing house heard about the despoliation of the rain forest? Regards, Prima.

Tabbitha — I love the idea of your Birman pussycat kissing your tootsies! Also, an exhibition that I suspect might intrigue you. Check out Prada Simone in the Gerhardt Hess Gallery, and let me know your thoughts . . . E. XX

Pixie clicked and clicked for another hour, making notes to herself and doing loads of lateral thinking, and when she'd researched to her satisfaction she knew it was time to open the file named 'Untitled. First draft.' But before she did this, there was a chore nagging at her, and she knew that she *had* to get it out of the way before she could type the magic words 'Chapter Two'.

She accessed her organizer, and then she picked up the phone and dialled Dominique's number. She wanted to break the news to her friend as gently as possible, and it wasn't going to be easy.

'Hello? Dominique Masterson's residence?' These were not the sveltely cultured tones of Dominique: it was a cheery-sounding East Ender who had answered.

'Hello,' said Pixie. 'Is Dominique there, please?'

'Sorry, no. She's had to take Tabby to the vet. She should be back in an hour or so, though. I'm Dominique's cleaning person. Can I take a message?'

Pixie could hardly leave a message with the cleaning lady telling Dominique that she was usurping her place on Deborah's list. 'Um, no. I'd rather speak to her personally,' she said. It was half past eleven now. 'So she should be back at around lunchtime?'

'Yeah. You'll get her then. Oh — wait. Better to leave it till later. She said she might take in some exhibition this afternoon. Hang on, I'll just ask Leonard.' Pixie heard the phone being set down, and the echoey sound of receding footsteps. Then: 'Mr Marshall!' she heard. 'There's someone on the phone for Ms Masterson. Did she say something about going to some exhibition this afternoon?'

'Yes,' came a man's voice. 'She's going to the Prada Simone exhibition. She should be back around four.'

Warning bells had started to sound in Pixie's head. *Prada Simone . . . Tabby . . . Leonard Marshall . . .* Leonard Marshall! She knew that name!

She heard footsteps march back to the phone, and then the cheery voice was in her ear again.

'Leonard says she's going to the Prada Simone exhibition. She'll be back around four.'

Pixie felt cogs whirring rapidly in her brain. 'Um — I'm sorry. But you said something about a vet?'

'Yes. Tabby needs her teeth cleaning and her feli-flu.'

'Oh. Poor — poor Tabby. That — ' Pixie hazarded a guess here — 'that kitty must be — what age now?'

'Oh, Tabbitha's over two now. She's not a kitten any more! You know her, do you?'

'I've never actually *met* Tabbitha. But Dominique talks a lot about her.'

'She's a pampered puss, all right. Real exotic lookin'.'

'She's a Persian, isn't she?' Pixie tried to sound conversational, but she could hear the strain in her own voice.

'Oh, nothing as common as a mere Persian! No, Mistress Tabbitha's a Birman.'

A Birman! 'A Birman? Are . . . are you sure?'

'Yep. Hermann the Birman, I call her. But

don't tell Dominique. Who shall I say called?'

'Oh — it's nothing important. I don't need to leave a message. I'll call again another time.'

'OK. And a good day to you!'

'Good day,' said Pixie.

She put the phone down and sat motionless and expressionless for many moments. Then she speed-dialled Mariella.

'You picked up! Thank you,' she said when her friend answered.

'I saw your number on the display. How are things?'

Pixie told her.

There was a big silence while Mariella digested the information. Then: 'Hang on,' she said, 'you're telling me that Dominique Masterson is Londonista Tabbitha?'

'Yes.'

'But how can you be sure?'

'The key words were Leonard Marshall.'

'Leonard Marshall? Who he?'

'He was the producer of *Celebrity Castaway*.'

'And he's Dominique's partner?'

'So it seems. I've only ever heard her refer to him as 'Lenny'. Or 'darling Lenny'.'

Pixie heard a gasp of outrage, then: 'So you reckon Dominique suggested the Sophie/Jonah set-up to him?'

'Yes. She'd have known that it had the potential to be incendiary.'

'Oh, Pixie — you must feel gutted.'

'I'm not, actually. I'm really rather relieved. It was too horrible for words thinking that there was some anonymous person out there ranting

241

away about me in a kind of stalker-spooky way. At least I know what motivates her now. It must have been tough on her when I started outselling her, and I always had the feeling that she hated having to share editors. In a funny way I'm even rather grateful to her. She's provided me with some plot pointers. There's a novel here somewhere, Mariella.'

'Ha! That would be the ultimate irony, wouldn't it? If Dominique had inadvertently supplied you with material for another best-seller!'

'The ultimate irony, yes. And the ultimate revenge.' *Oh, the shark has pretty teeth, dear* . . . 'Oh *boy* will I make her suffer!'

'How?'

'I'll give her body odour. I'll give her bad hair, and I'll give her even worse shoes.'

'Give her one from me, too. Put spinach on her teeth.'

'Nice one. Thank you!' Pixie laughed, then heaved a huge sigh of relief. 'Oh, I'm *itching* to get back to work now. And I can't wait to get reacquainted with my new man.'

'You've a new man in your life? Tell!'

'No. You'll only laugh.'

'Go on. I promise I won't.'

'I've fallen for one of the characters in the book I'm working on.'

Mariella did laugh. 'You sad bitch. What's he like?'

'I'm not quite sure. Byronic, possibly, with a tragic past.'

'A Mr Rochester!'

'I guess.' Pixie shot a look at her watch. 'And I'd better get back to him. I'm missing him already.'

'Bye, Jane Eyre. Take care.'

When Pixie put down the phone to Mariella she minimized her organizer and left-clicked twice on 'My Documents' before right-clicking. In the box that bore the legend 'Untitled. First draft', the cursor invited her to 'Rename'.

The words: 'Sex' and 'Death' took shape in the box.

There came a tiny beat, and Pixie's eyes narrowed before she typed in the words that came next.

'And Revenge.'

She opened the file, and continued from where she'd left off work the previous day.

As she inspected her face in the mirror in the toilet, Talitha saw that she had spinach stuck to her front tooth. Oh! Had she been sitting at the dinner table for the past hour and a half looking like Shane MacGowan? How profoundly humiliating! To make matters worse, she had sweat stains under her arms, her hair was rebellious and the heel had come off her pointy orange Mary Janes.

Life had done her no favours recently. She certainly had more enemies than friends these days, and her charmed existence seemed to have lost its lustre . . .

12

'Since you came out as a bisexual, your life has been much easier, hasn't it?'

Hazel was listening to an interview with the writer Colleen on some arts programme on the car radio. She was on her way to Kilrowan, and she was not in a good mood. She'd been stuck behind a tootling Toyota for the past ten miles.

'It has,' agreed Colleen, in her throaty brogue. 'I no longer feel the need to pretend. My life is no longer a sham. I have transcended the confines of heterosexuality, and this has, of course, had an impact on my creativity. In my last novel — *To the Island* — '

'Oh, shut up!' said Hazel out loud. She changed the channel with a jab of her finger, and lit on a music station where some feel-good reggae was playing. She had felt she ought to listen to Colleen since the writer was participating in the Arts Festival, but really there was only so much guff she could take.

She was travelling to Kilrowan because she wanted first-hand details of the village hall, which was where the major events of the festival were to be held. She could, of course, have had said details supplied to her by Hugh, but she knew from experience that it was always advisable to check things out personally. Anyway, a break in Kilrowan would do her the world of good. And she was curious to know exactly how smitten Hugh Hennessy was with her mother . . .

Oh, no! As she negotiated the Galway ring road she saw that the tootling Toyota was indicating left. It was clearly heading in the direction of Kilrowan, also. Hazel couldn't stick much more of the gonk tormenting her from the rear window; she'd stop for lunch in Galway City.

She headed for the city centre and parked in a multi-storey car park. As she passed by the Spanish Arch, where a busker was belting out 'The Fields of Athenry', she was reminded of visits to Galway as a child, when her parents had gigged during race week and the festival fortnight. Nothing much had changed since then. Quay Street was still coming down with hippies and crusties and tin whistle players. And living statues, of course. Speaking of which —

'Hi, there, Dad.'

Her father was standing in a shop doorway, and — thank God — he was wearing ordinary street clothes, not some *outré* get-up. Hazel was taken aback by how — well — *nondescript* he looked. He was just another overweight, middle-aged man. To look at him you would never think that Mondo the aMazing was lurking under the unprepossessing exterior.

'Hazel! Hi!' he dropped a kiss on her cheek. 'What brings you to Galway?'

She filled him in.

'Then allow me to buy you lunch,' he said. 'You look like you could do with feeding up.'

Hazel had really just intended to have lunch on the hoof, but there was something about her

245

father's demeanour — something needy — that made her acquiesce. She hadn't seen him in months, hadn't sat down to a meal with him for years.

'OK. I'd love that,' she said.

They progressed along Quay Street, Mondo muttering many 'Hey! How's it goin'?'s to people he passed. A Grim Reaper saluted him, and a clown pinged her red nose at him.

'You're not working today, I take it?' asked Hazel, as they passed through a door into the gloom of an Irish-themed pub.

'No. I'm working nights. There's a publishing forum on in the Great Southern Hotel and I'm providing the entertainment.'

'As?'

'A human dictionary.'

Hazel repressed a shudder.

'I saw that,' said Mondo.

'Saw what?'

'I think it could be described as 'your barely concealed expression of distaste'. Don't think I don't know how you feel about the whole living statue thing, Hazel.'

'I don't know what you're talking about,' she said, with an attempt at disingenuousness. 'What 'expression of distaste'?'

Mondo mimicked the 'Ew' expression that was her knee-jerk response to any reference to clowns, mimes or living statues. Then he laughed. 'Hazel, love, there's no point in disguising the fact that your parents are failed practitioners of the performing arts and that it's been the bane of your life.'

'It has?'

'You know it has.' Then: 'Quick! Grab that table,' he said, pointing to a corner table that had just become available.

Hazel shouldered her way through the heaving lunchtime throng, trying to think of some positive spiel to spin her dad.

'That's not strictly true,' she said as she sat down, 'about you being the bane of my life. I was actually really proud of you when you were on *Bunny Brown's Way*.'

'Yeah. *Bunny Brown's Way* was the highlight of my career, all right.'

Bunny Brown's Way had been a daily afternoon children's programme. Mondo, its resident clown, had been hugely popular. Once it was axed, his career as a clown had hit the skids, which was how he had ended up as a living statue on Grafton Street.

'I'll never forget that birthday party you gave me,' Hazel reminded him, 'where you turned up dressed in your *Bunny Brown* costume. All my friends were so impressed.'

'Yeah, but you were only about six then. It was later that the rot set in. I used to feel so sorry for you when your friends sniggered and threw bottle tops into the hat on Grafton Street.'

'Oh. Poor Dad.'

'Poor *you*. My fucking heart used to break for you.'

'Oh, don't, Dad!'

They waited as the bus boy cleared away the detritus on the table, and then Hazel said: 'So

247

you knew all along that my friends used to take the piss?'

'Of course I knew.'

'Sorry,' said Hazel in a small voice.

'No need. It can't have been easy for you, getting that kind of grief. Now, love. What are you having?'

The waiter had rolled up, and was standing with his pen poised over his order book. He glanced at Mondo, and then he looked again. Hazel's heart sank as she saw recognition dawn in his eyes. Even after all these years, Mondo still wore his trademark amber *Bunny* earring with emerald chip eyes. Twiddling it anxiously had been one of his most endearing foibles. 'Hey, you used to be Mondo the aMazing, didn't you?' said the waiter. 'On *Bunny Brown's Way*?'

'That's right,' said Mondo with an attempt at a bright smile.

'Whoa, man. You were so *funny*!'

'Thanks.'

'I used to get real excited when the *Bunny Brown* theme tune started up. And I saw every panto you ever did. I told my ma that I was going to be a clown when I grew up.'

'You did?'

'Yeah. I still dream about running off to join the circus sometimes. Get away from *this* circus.' He indicated with a contemptuous nod the throngs of harried-looking punters.

'It's not as easy as you might think, clowning,' said Mondo. 'I trained for two years.'

'Did you?' asked Hazel, surprised. She'd had

no idea that her father had actually trained as a clown.

'Yes. With Lecoq. In Paris.'

'Well. Respect,' said the waiter. 'I can't think of a better way of making a living than by making people laugh. Are you still clowning?'

'No. I'm a living statue.'

'Cool! So. What can I get you, Mondo, sir? Oh — I beg your pardon. Ladies first.'

'I'll have the smoked chicken, please,' said Hazel. 'And still water.'

'And I'll have the pasta and a pint of Guinness,' said her father.

'Coming straight up.' And the waiter saluted Mondo and sailed away.

'What made you decide to train as a clown?' Hazel asked her dad. She was genuinely curious. She'd never wondered about his life before — she'd been too caught up in her own stuff.

'I had a talent for it. I originally wanted to be an archaeologist.'

'Seriously?'

'Oh, yeah. I was studying archaeology at Trinity when the whole clown thing came about.'

'So you gave up archaeology to become a clown?'

'Yep.'

'But why? I mean, what on earth made you *do* that?'

'I was good at it. I used to make people laugh at parties, and it just kind of evolved from there. Clowning and mime and all the rest were very much in vogue then. And people really showed you respect for your craft. That's gone. People don't have time to stand around looking at living statues any more.'

'I thought you loved being a living statue?'

'Are you mad, Hazel?' Mondo's expression was one of mild incredulity. 'Do you know what being a living statue is really all about? It's about standing around in all weather, being 'kooky' in the hope that someone might sling a coin into my hat. It's about being made fun of by drunken louts, and being told to 'Move along' by the Feds. But it was fun in the old days,' he conceded. 'And there was good money to be made, too, back then. I cleaned up on *Bunny Brown's Way*.'

'Funny,' said Hazel. 'I never thought that money was an issue for you. You've always been so — well — *alternative*.'

'Not when I started out. Money was *really* important in those days. I had a family to support, remember. You'd just arrived, and Angel's career never took off in the way she'd expected.'

'Had she such high hopes for it?'

'Oh, yes. She even had an invitation to tour the US of A, but she turned it down.'

'What? Why?'

'Because it would have played havoc with your schooling.'

'No!'

'Oh, yes. She'd seen what happened to some rock stars' kids. She didn't want you ending up in rehab.'

Oh, God. How completely selfish she'd been! She'd never had an inkling of any of this. Hazel reached out a hand and touched her father's. 'What top parents I have,' she said.

'Well, we must have done something right, me and Angel. Just look at how you turned out, love.'

There was something so poignant about his smile that a lump came into Hazel's throat. 'Do you mind me asking this, Dad? Do you love her still?'

'Oh yes. I'm solid cracked about her. I've never stopped loving her, even when she ran off with the acrobat. She's the love of my life, and there'll never be another.'

'You know that she's stopped seeing that scenic artist?'

'I do.'

'Might there be a chance — you know — that you could get back together?'

'Ah, no. I wouldn't even begin to think that way. Anyway, I'm sure she has her sights set on higher things, now she's planning her comeback.'

This was so *sad*. Hazel wanted to cry for the parents she had never known, the parents who had once been so young and so in love that they'd brought her into the world, and had sacrificed their own hopes and dreams in the process. 'Why don't you try, Dad?'

'No, darling. I'm too old to be trying to woo a top-class chick like your ma.'

'Excuse me? And *she's* not too old to make a comeback as a punk rock queen?'

'That's different. Your mother will always have that aura of glamour about her. Sure she's so gorgeous no man could resist her.'

'You're partisan, Dad.'

Their food arrived.

'Ah! Grub's up!' said her father, rubbing his hands, and Hazel remembered how irritating she'd found that expression when she was growing up. He'd said it before every meal, and Hazel used to mimic him to her friends behind his back, because she knew that if *she* didn't, they would. She was reminded of how Hugh had instructed his friends to call him 'Scar' to his face, as a defence mechanism. The thought of Hugh made her think too of how she had denied her parents to him, even now, even as a supposed 'grown up'. What a prize cow she had been! What did it matter if her mother was a past-it punkette, and her father a living statue? Would she have preferred it if her parents were civil servants like Erin's, made cranky by pen-pushing? At least her parents had had *fun* in their lives.

'How come you never told me any of this before?' Hazel asked.

'It didn't seem important.'

'But it *is* important. Your life is just as important as mine.'

Mondo shook his head. 'You don't feel that way when you have a child. I know you think your mother was flighty and that, Hazel, but she fought like fuck to give you the best things in life. Don't ever tell her I told you, but she used to take jobs recording the naffest advertising jingles imaginable when times were hard, so that she could keep you in the style to which you had become accustomed.'

252

'Poor Mum! I must have been a completely spoilt brat.'

'No. You were our princess. Anyway, she was never afraid of hard work, your mum. Look at her now, trying her damnedest to climb back up on the career ladder.'

Hazel felt full of self-loathing. She should be proud of her parents. She should be embracing them publicly instead of trying to pretend that they didn't exist. She remembered how she'd told her first boyfriend at summer camp that her father was a doctor and her mother a solicitor. She remembered going to another boyfriend's house one Patrick's Day, when the parade had been on the telly, and how she'd joined in the jeering at the 'loser' living statue perched on a float. And the awful pain she'd felt when the boyfriend had said: 'Look at that fat wanker', and she had laughed and said: 'Yeah'. She remembered that her favourite poem had been that one by Philip Larkin that starts 'They fuck you up, your mum and dad', and how wholeheartedly she'd agreed. Well, her mum and dad hadn't fucked her up. She'd fucked herself up. She, Hazel MacNamara, was a mealy-mouthed, ungrateful, tight-arsed cow who didn't deserve the parents she'd been blessed with, and she was going to make it up to them.

'You know something, Dad?' she said now. 'I'm really glad that you're going to be part of the Kilrowan Arts Festival.'

'Are you?' he said, and he went a bit pink with pleasure. 'Well, that's a turn up for the auld books!'

253

'And Mum, too,' she said with an effort. 'I'm actually really proud that she's going to be making her comeback as part of something I'm organizing — and I'll do my best to make sure she wows them!'

Mondo laughed. 'D'you know something? I never thought I'd hear you say that. I had this image of me and your mum at the festival having to pretend we didn't know you so as not to embarrass you!'

'Ha ha, Dad — don't be ridiculous! I think your Salmon of Knowledge idea is inspired. How did you dream it up, and what exactly will it involve?'

Mondo bounced a bit on his chair, setting his *Bunny* earring a-jiggle. He was clearly quite fired up about being the Salmon of Knowledge. 'Well, this is how it'll work. I'm going to have an ear-piece that's linked up to a colleague who has access to a laptop computer. So any questions I'm asked will be relayed to this geezer who'll get the answers on Encarta . . . '

Hazel listened abstractedly as her father filled her in on his Salmon of Knowledge project, all the time thinking of a question of her own that badly needed answering.

What in hell's name was she going to tell Hugh?

★ ★ ★

She arrived in Kilrowan just after six o'clock. Hugh was busy in the stables, but he told her to make herself at home.

254

'Make yourself a cup of tea,' he said. 'Or maybe you'd prefer a G & T after your drive?' He indicated the bottle of Bombay Sapphire that stood on a sideboard by the kitchen door.

G & T it most definitely was. She needed Dutch courage more than the boy who'd stuck his finger in the dike. When Hazel pulled her finger out, the tidal wave of truth would be of titanic proportions.

She'd spent longer in Galway than she'd intended, shooting the breeze with her dad. Mondo without Angel was quite clearly wretched. She'd tried to boost his self-esteem by telling him how boring was the scenic artist her mother had been dating, and how much more amusing Mondo was, but she knew he wasn't convinced.

As she nursed her (stiff) gin she observed Hugh through the kitchen window, leading a horse across the stable yard. What beautiful animals horses were. Hazel had had riding lessons as a child, before giving it up in favour of Thai Bo. Riding, Thai Bo, ballet, flute . . . Her parents must have forked out a small fortune in classes for her! It was a measure of how dedicated they had been, and how much baby Hazel had been cherished, and her eyes went a bit misty as she pictured her father standing stolidly in the rain on Grafton Street, the butt of tittering teenagers, waiting for someone to sling him a few bob so that he could pay for Hazel's flute.

And now she was going to have to tell Hugh that actually, Angel Kestrel of Angel Phish fame was her mother, and her father was Mondo the aMazing, and she was going to look like a raving lunatic and it *served her right*.

'Hi,' said Hugh, coming into the kitchen. 'I stink of horse. I'm just going to have a quick shower, and then we can eat before we hit the pub. There's a trad gig on tonight that you might be interested in.'

'Are you going to av-check them for the festival?'

Hugh looked puzzled. 'Av-check?'

'Availability check.'

'I forgot you media types had your own kind of hip shorthand,' he said with a smile. 'Yes, I *am* going to 'av-check' them. Help yourself to a refill,' he added, with a nod at Hazel's empty glass before he left the room.

'Thanks.' She wouldn't make this one quite as stiff, she decided, as she moved to the fridge and clinked more ice cubes into her glass.

The phone rang — once, twice — then went to answer mode.

Hazel had just unscrewed the top of the Bombay Sapphire bottle and was poised to pour when she heard her mother's sexy purr come over the speaker.

'Hugh? Hi, it's Angel. Could you ask your sound man to phone me? I lost his number, and I need to know if I'll be using a radio mic or a hand-held. Although I could drive down next weekend if necessary and check it out with him personally — it would be good to get a chance to rehearse in the actual venue. And I was wondering — ' There came the sound of a polyphonic version of Debbie Harry's 'Platinum

Blonde', and: 'Hot *damn*,' her mother said, 'that's my mobile. Bad timing. Talk soon, Hugh. Byeee!'

Hazel tipped the gin bottle alarmingly, and sloshed a reckless amount into her glass instead of the two-finger measure she'd promised herself. Bloody hell! Her mother was obviously so intent on pursuit that she was prepared to travel the entire breadth of Ireland in order to get her quarry into her sights.

Oh God, she thought, swigging back liquid anaesthetic, what if it worked? What if Angel and Hugh actually became an item? Some men had a thing for older women, she knew. Look at Percy Gibson and Joan Collins, Ralph Fiennes and Francesca Annis, Ashton Kutcher and Demi Moore. The image of Angel parading glamorously around the Kilrowan Festival on the arm of the tall, dark and handsome Hugh Hennessy while her father masqueraded as a fish and looked on like a lovesick puppy made her want to weep. She recalled the soppy expression on his face when he'd spoken of Angel, how it had almost made her cry, and now she felt like crying even more. This *couldn't* happen! *How* could she distract Hugh from the charms of Angel Kestrel?

Doh. The answer was staring her in the face. What if *she* distracted him? If Hugh hooked up with her, Hazel, there was no way he could make a move on Angel, or vice versa. Could she do it? She was not without her own considerable charms, she'd been told. But when was the last time she'd seduced a man? Um, actually, never.

She'd never had to — men always ended up seducing her. But seduction was an art, and she was highly skilled in the art of persuasion, which was much the same thing. In the cut-throat world of PR you had to be.

All the magazine articles she'd ever read about seduction had stressed the importance of the five senses — and ambience. Should she attempt to seduce Hugh after dinner tonight? Here, in his kitchen? The ambience was hardly romantic, but after some good food and wine his guard would be down. That was a good word to use for Hugh, she decided, as she sipped thoughtfully at her gin. There was something guarded about him. The only time she'd seen the guard slip had been when he'd hung on Angel's every word that awful evening in the Hamilton Hotel. *Angel* . . . What had her mother said to her recently, about lightening up? Maybe Hazel should forget about using dinner with Hugh this evening as an opportunity for discussing plans for the Arts Festival. Maybe she should concentrate instead on getting to know the man behind the guarded demeanour.

But he'd mentioned that trad gig. Yuck! Sitting in a crowded pub while a crowd of musicians fiddle-dee-deed was hardly conductive to seduction. Maybe she should talk him out of going, plead tiredness after her long drive, maybe suggest an early night. She'd packed a sexy little slip of a nightdress this weekend, because all her comfy jimjams appeared to be in the wash, and the pair that wasn't had been missing a button.

As she sat at Hugh's kitchen table meditatively

sipping gin, Hazel thought about the last time she'd had sex. It had been with that tightwad, Mick, and in fact it had been rather fine sex. She was overdue a decent orgasm . . .

'Penny for your thoughts?' Hugh was standing in the doorway, leaning against the jamb. His aftershave smelt of sandalwood and he looked pretty damn hot.

'I was thinking about food,' she lied. 'Let me cook for you tonight.' She could do the Nigella Lawson thing. 'Please,' she added, tilting her head a little coquettishly at him, the way she'd seen her mother do.

'That would be a real treat,' he said. 'I'm dog tired after exercising the horses today, and to be perfectly honest, the last thing I feel like doing is cooking.'

'I'm tired, too, but I find cooking a really good way to unwind.' She staged a little yawn. 'I might cry off going down the pub, if you don't mind. Will there be another opportunity to catch this trad band?'

'Yeah. They're playing again tomorrow night. We could go then instead, if you prefer.' Hugh moved over to the answering machine and pressed play. He smiled when he heard Angel's smoky voice drift into the room. 'Hey,' he said, after he'd listened to the message. 'She's really keen, isn't she?'

'Mm,' said Hazel, fishing her ringing phone out of her bag. The display read 'Mother'. With a peremptory thumb she switched it off and turned back to Hugh. 'Have you any tagliatelle?' she asked.

★ ★ ★

She'd sent him out to the village shop to get asparagus and cream and Parmesan. The recipe she had in mind was simple and sexy, and it didn't matter that the only asparagus available was of the tinned variety. She was sure that the canning process did nothing to detract from its legendary aphrodisiac attributes.

Before starting to cook, she showered and changed out of her city girl gear into something a little more relaxed. A streamlined dress in fluid silk jersey that clung when she moved, drawing attention to the curves of her breasts and the jut of her hip. Mules that she could kick off to reveal pretty rose pink toenails. Underwear that she knew was breathtaking. She sprayed herself with scent, tousled her hair and subtly exaggerated the pout of her lips with liner. The gin had made her feel good — in fact she was feeling horny now — but she knew she would have to hold back on alcohol consumption during the meal. She'd make sure that Hugh's glass was topped up, though: she'd brought him two bottles of very good Bordeaux as a present. Hazel took one last look at her reflection in the mirror, adjusted the neckline of her dress so that a tantalizing glimpse of lace-trimmed bra strap was visible, then made for the stairs.

Hugh was sitting at the kitchen table, reading the sports section of the *Irish Times*. He glanced up when she came in, then got to his feet, looking a bit confused. 'Well,' he said. 'You look — lovely.'

'Oh? Thank you. This is one of my favourite dresses to relax in.'

'Yes, I'm sure. It's very — er — relaxing looking. Glass of wine?'

'Thanks.' She moved towards him, and smilingly accepted a long-stemmed glass of red.

Hugh raised his. 'To the Arts Festival,' he said stoically.

'Oh, pox on the Arts Festival! Let's not talk shop tonight. I want to find out all about you.' Hazel took a sip of wine, then put out the point of her tongue and licked her upper lip delicately. 'Mm. This is very good, isn't it? Don't worry! I'm not going to go all 'winespeaky' and compare its nuance to gooseberries or chocolate or whatever. I hate that kind of guff, don't you?'

She smiled at him, then sashayed across the kitchen to the work station, where all her ingredients were assembled. Excellent! The tagliatelle, she knew, from watching Nigella, was a clever touch. She'd have to taste it by dangling it into her mouth at least twice to make sure it was *al dente*.

Hugh was looking at her as if he'd never seen her before. She supposed in a way he hadn't. The persona she was wearing now was a million miles away from the Nutcracker PR Hazel, who was efficient, savvy, and driven by ambition.

'I had a boyfriend once who took a course of classes in wine appreciation,' she told him. 'He became so boring that I had to break it off. Every time we went out for dinner he'd drone on about the wine until I ended up like the Dormouse.'

'The dormouse?'

'In *Alice in Wonderland*. You know, at the Mad Hatter's Tea Party, when the Dormouse keeps falling asleep at the table? *Alice* was one of my all-time favourite books when I was a child. What was yours?'

'Um. I wasn't really into reading that much.'

'I read to escape. What do you do to escape?'

'I ride,' said Hugh. 'Um — horses, of course.' Result! He wasn't looking her in the eye, he was uncomfortable, shifting in his seat. She was clearly having a palpable effect on him.

'I did a bit of riding myself,' she volunteered. 'Not enough to achieve a very high standard of horsemanship — or should that be horsewomanship? But I had fun. Maybe you could take me for a ride tomorrow. Have you a suitable mount for someone who's been out of the saddle for so long?'

'I'm sure I could find you something.'

'Good. If you can spare the time, perhaps we might ride down to the beach? I'd love a paddle.' Hazel smiled again, then turned away so that he had ample opportunity to check out her rear view. She ran a hand over her hip for emphasis, and shook her hair back. Then: 'Have you a garlic crusher?' she asked.

'Yes. Let me root it out for you.' He moved to a drawer, rummaged and took out the implement. 'Here,' he said, handing it over.

'Thank you.' She took the item from him, making sure that her fingers made fleeting contact with his. Immediately he slid his hands into his pockets and stood watching her while she slung butter into a pan and opened the carton of cream.

'Oops!' she said, as a little cream spurted from the hole she'd made in the foil lid. She scooped it up with the tip of her finger, and sucked it off.

Hugh had his shoulders hunched defensively. He was looking increasingly ill at ease.

'What about some music?' she asked him. 'I love to listen to music while I cook.'

'Sure.' He moved to the CD rack. 'What do you fancy?'

'Got any reggae?'

'Yes. Marley?'

'Marley's perfect.'

The strains of 'Stir It Up' slid through the speakers, and Hazel started to move to the rhythm as she peeled garlic with deft fingers, then crushed it and sent it scooting into the melting butter in the pan. 'Mm. I love that smell,' she said happily as the aroma rose into the air. 'D'you like your garlic subtle or conspicuous?'

'Conspicuous.'

'So I should add another clove?'

'Why not?'

Hazel smiled. Quantities of garlic were perfectly permissible as long as both parties partook of it. She peeled and crushed again, then slid the garlic off the chopping board with the blade of a Sabatier. Asparagus next. 'Tin opener?'

'I'll do it.' Hugh opened the tin using a wall-mounted opener. She took it from him — that fleeting contact again — and he resumed his stance, leaning rather stiffly against a kitchen unit, hands in pockets, watching her still.

She concentrated hard on draining the tin, mouthing the Marley lyrics as she did so. Then she proceeded to chop the asparagus into small pieces. 'I can't resist you!' she said to one particularly tender-looking tip, picking it up between thumb and forefinger and sliding it into her mouth. Then: 'Ouch!' she said, as the edge of the Sabatier made contact with her thumb. She watched as a tiny bead of red appeared. 'How careless of me! Have you kitchen towel?'

'Here.' He tore off a wad and handed it to her.

Hazel dabbed her wound, then inspected it more closely.

'I'll get you a Band-Aid,' he said.

'Oh, it's just a nick — don't go to the trouble. I don't need a Band-Aid.'

'Just in case. It'll stop it from reopening.'

He fetched a first-aid box from a cupboard, selected a tiny Band-Aid and proceeded to coax open the packet.

'Maybe you should rinse your thumb under the tap?' he suggested.

'No,' said Hazel, licking the tiny drop of blood from the wound. 'Saliva contains a natural antiseptic. That's why animals lick their wounds. But I'm sure you knew that.'

'Yes.' He moved close to her. 'Show me,' he said, and she leaned towards him, holding her thumb out and affording him a clear view of her cleavage. He took her hand, pressed the plaster onto the pinprick, then impulsively deposited a tiny kiss on top. 'To kiss it better,' he said,

264

reddening at the liberty he'd taken. 'My mother always used to do that.'

'Sweet,' said Hazel, smiling at Hugh as he backed away in confusion, evidently very fazed by the physical contact. He made for the table and sat down again, and Hazel resumed her display of culinary expertise, turning her back to him, moving her hips to the rhythm of Marley, humming along to the melody.

'Hazel?'

'Yes?'

'You mentioned a boyfriend.'

'An ex boyfriend,' she corrected.

'Do you have a current boyfriend?'

'No. Why?'

'Because,' said Hugh. 'I should very much like to take you to bed.'

Hazel turned and looked at him.

'I'm sorry,' he said. 'I don't know why I said that. It was totally out of order.'

Without breaking eye contact, she twisted the knob on the gas cooker and extinguished the flame under the pan. Then she moved across the room to him, slid herself onto his lap, wound her arms around his neck and kissed him. And when she broke the kiss she looked down at him with a smile. 'I thought you'd never ask. I've been in chronic denial until now. I fancy the arse off you, Hugh Hennessy,' she said. 'And you can take me to bed immediately. With pleasure.'

* * *

265

Marley was playing on the CD player again and the flame had been reignited under the pan. It was now nearly ten o'clock. Hugh had lit a candle on the table, and opened another bottle of wine. Hazel was tasting tagliatelle. She had on Hugh's pyjama top, which she'd fastened with only one button. 'Mm. Perfect,' she said. 'We're in business.'

'Thank Jesus for that. I'm ravenous,' said Hugh. He was lounging bare-chested at the table wearing low-slung pyjama bottoms and nursing a glass of red. Hazel had discovered the scar on his chest earlier. It ran from his collarbone to just above his navel. She'd kissed the curve of it all the way down, and beyond.

She piled pasta onto plates, dolloped the creamy sauce on top, set the food on the table, and sat down beside him. 'I'm ravenous too,' she said. 'But it's hardly surprising. We were meant to have eaten hours ago.'

They sat and looked at each other for several moments with foolish smiles on their faces. Then Hugh leaned in to kiss her before turning his attention to his plate. 'Well,' he said. 'What a revelation *you've* turned out to be, Hazel MacNamara!'

'Are you referring to my culinary skills?' she asked, giving him an arch look.

'That too,' he said. 'Nigella Lawson has nothing on you. What highly developed taste-buds you must have!'

'You're no mean gourmet yourself, Mr Hennessy.'

That was something of an understatement.

Hugh Hennessy had tasted every inch of Hazel MacNamara with such evident pleasure that she hadn't bothered to keep count of her orgasms. That was a habit she'd got into after one of her past boyfriends had taken to asking her how many times she had come after he made love to her. He used to go into a sulk if the total was fewer than three, and that was how *he'd* bitten the dust. When she thought about it, all of her boyfriends to date had had fatal flaws. There had been Sulker, Tightwad and Bore, and there had been Giant Ego, Big Bastard and Pathologically Jealous. She wondered what Hugh would turn out to be — if, indeed, she could allow herself to dream that he might become a boyfriend. So far she could find no flaw at all — apart from the physical one manifest in the scar on his chest: but there was something very sexy about that scar. Something *manly*.

She remembered how when she'd first met him she'd made a superficial assessment of him as being tall, dark, handsome, strong and silent. She now realized that he was all of those things bar the silent. After their first bout of lovemaking this evening they had laughed and joked and talked loads. They'd found they had a lot in common. The usual suspects featured — movies, music, politics, eating out — but there were other shared interests. They had both had a childhood passion for Cluedo (she always tried to get Miss Scarlett because Scarlett O'Hara was her favourite fictional heroine; he always tried to avoid the Reverend Green because he thought he looked like a pervert), they both confessed to a sad but covert fascination with *Late Night Poker* on Channel 4, and they had both holidayed in the same small laid-back resort in Jamaica, and longed to revisit it.

'It's funny, isn't it,' he said now, 'how misleading first impressions can be. When I first met you I was scared of you.'

'What? Why?'

'I know. It's stupid, isn't it? You were this high-flying unattainable city girl and I was the village idiot. I couldn't string two words together, I found you so intimidating. I'll never forget the night we had dinner at Ballynahinch, when you were the focus of all eyes in your smart designer gear. I'd scoured the *Irish Times* so that I'd have some topics of conversation up my sleeve to impress you with, but all you wanted to talk about was the Arts Festival.'

'Oh, I'm sorry, Hugh. I must have been painfully dreary company. But I know now that the reason I wanted to focus on the festival was because otherwise I'd have gone into unseemly flirt mode.'

'Really?'

'Really. I've fancied you rotten since the minute I met you, but I haven't been able to admit it to myself because I was so convinced that you didn't fancy me at all. I thought you fancied — ' don't go there! She couldn't risk bringing up the subject of her mother — 'um . . . Pixie Pirelli.'

'But I don't even *know* Pixie Pirelli!'

'I think it was the fact that she's so feminine and pretty.'

'And you're not? Get a grip, Hazel. You're a very sexy lady. More wine?'

'Thanks.'

Hugh poured, then continued to demolish his pasta.

'I suppose we ought to talk about the festival at some stage,' he said, between bites. 'We can't spend the entire weekend in bed — much as I'd like to. We're counting down now. Only three more weeks.'

'*Three?*' said Hazel, with a sense of impending doom. 'Is it really only three?' Oh, God. In three weeks' time her mother and father would be descending on Kilrowan. She'd *have* to come clean with Hugh soon.

'I've some bad news, incidentally,' he said.

'Oh?'

'We won't be getting a painting from Pablo to auction this year.'

'Why not?'

'He's gone AWOL. He's left the village.'

'Oh! And he's left his nice wife, too?'

'Yeah. Poor Cleo. She's trying to put a brave face on it, but I think she's probably pretty gutted. They were a really fantastic couple.'

'Where's he gone?'

'No-one seems to know. But the *good* news for the festival is that Colleen has doubled the prize money for the short story competition this year, so there'll be more entries, and more media attention.'

'And she'll award the prize in person?'

'She will indeed. She loves doing that. She's like an empress distributing largesse. Mm. That was *so* good.' Hugh put his fork down, then sat back in his chair and scrutinized Hazel. 'You're a mean chef, Ms MacNamara,' he said, 'and I suspect you're a mean horsewoman too. I am longing to get a load of your seat in the saddle tomorrow.'

'I don't think you need to wait that long to find out,' she said, sliding off her chair and straddling him. 'Talking of chefs,' she added conversationally, 'you know what a very wise woman once said about being a chef in the kitchen?'

He undid the button on her pyjama top and parted the lapels to admire her breasts. 'What did she say?'

'She said a woman should be a chef in the kitchen, a hostess in the drawing room and a whore in the bedroom. I can go one better.'

'Yeah?'

'Oh, yeah. I can be a whore in the kitchen as well.'

'And in the drawing room?'

'We'll put that one off until tomorrow,' she said.

And as for revealing the truth about her parentage, she'd put that off until tomorrow too. After all, as her favourite heroine, Scarlett O'Hara, had famously said, tomorrow was another day.

13

Since Pablo had gone, Cleo had stopped writing her erotic short stories. She had no incentive any more. She couldn't even concentrate on reading, and only the most mindless television held her attention.

She had heard nothing from her husband since the postcard from London. She wondered about him constantly, and on occasion had been tempted to phone his agent, Rebecca, to quiz her as to his whereabouts. However, she had resisted the temptation because she knew she would be unable to hack the tone of *schadenfreude* she would hear in the woman's voice: Pablo's agent had the hots for him. Also — she cautioned herself — if Rebecca herself picked up the phone, word would be sure to get back to him that Cleo was asking questions, and she didn't want him to think for one moment that she was concerned about him. It was up to him to make the first move.

She had cleared out his studio shortly after his disappearance. She hated herself for going through his correspondence: she didn't like the snoopy feeling it gave her, but she wanted to know if there was evidence of further betrayal. There was none. The only curious letter she unearthed was from the CEO of a chain of very upmarket hotels that had been forwarded to him by Rebecca. A Mr P.B. Crotty wished to enquire whether Pablo would be interested in accepting a commission for a series of portraits of their regional managers. P.B. Crotty intended to hang a portrait of each of these illustrious individuals in the hotel chain nationwide. The portraits would, he assured Pablo, be displayed behind the reception desk, and would thus be the first thing guests would see on their arrival and the last thing they'd see on checking out. It would be such a fantastic showcase, P.B. Crotty told Pablo, that he might think about negotiating his rate downwards?

Scrawled across the letter were four words in Pablo's handwriting. They read: 'Go eat your Y-fronts.'

Cleo knew that word of Pablo's defection would have spread like wildfire round the village, but she didn't talk to anyone about it. The only person she felt she could talk to was Pixie and — via e-mail — her friends Deirdre and Martina.

Martina and Cleo had been friends since childhood. Theirs was that special brand of friendship that could survive months of non-communication and miles of separation. Martina had recently realized a lifelong ambition and moved to Japan, and now wrote long e-mails to Cleo, relating all the problems she was experiencing with culture shock. When there was nothing mindless worth watching on television, Cleo sat down most evenings and poured her heart out to Martina the way she'd once poured her heart out to her beloved, non-judgmental Fluffy: indeed, Fluffy was very often the subject of the e-mail.

To: Martina Cohen
From: Cleo Dowling
Subject: Fluffy

Dear Martina,

Fluff's boyfriends came calling today, looking for her. They've done it before, but today for the first time they seemed really upset, as if they knew something bad had happened. One of them sat by her dog flap and howled. Do dogs understand about death?

Still no word of Pablo. He must be OK, because otherwise his gallery would be on the phone. I am still hurting, but am determined not to contact him. Let him do any running that's to be done.

Love you. Sorry for being downbeat. Send me a joke to cheer me up.

She got a response the very next day.

To: Cleo Dowling
From: $BCH^F;!!C#X]
Subject: Joke

Dearest Cleo,

A grasshopper walks into a bar and the bartender says: 'Hey! We have a drink named after you!'

The grasshopper looks surprised and says: 'You have a drink named Steve?'

Love as ever, Martina

To: Martina Cohen
From: Cleo Dowling
Subject: Re: Joke

Made me LOL! Thank you for cheering me up.

Here's one for you.

Two blondes are on opposite sides of a lake.

One blonde yells to the other: 'How do you get to the other side?'

'You are on the other side,' the other blonde yells back.

Any love interest to report?

All love, Cleo. XXXXXXXXXX

To: Cleo Dowling.
From: $BCH^F;!!C#X]
Subject: Love interest

☹

The startling $BCH^F;!!C#X] at the top of Martina's mail had fazed Cleo the first time she'd seen it. She copied the attachment it contained to 'My Documents' before she opened it, thinking it might be a virus, but then realized that it was simply the Japanese version of Martina's e-mail address, translated into English characters. She'd immediately e-mailed Martina to tell her that her address looked like an expletive, and Martina had sent a rapid-fire jokey e-mail back. She was glad they'd resumed communication at a time when they were both in need of it. Martina was living in a foreign country with no BF, and Cleo was living in uncharted territory now that Pablo was no longer part of the landscape. She had taken to sleeping with his sarong wrapped round her pillow.

She called on Pixie so that they could share gripes, but only very occasionally. She was loath to disturb her neighbour now that she had such a punishing schedule to stick to. Cleo could see her through her window, pacing the floor sometimes, sometimes doing her army exercises, but more often sitting in front of her laptop, typing furiously.

It wasn't all work and no play for Pixie. She had decided to afford herself some amusement by embarking on an act of sabotage. In her spare time she had taken to visiting Tabbitha's blog and leaving anonymous messages for her in the comment box.

Her first salvo went like this:

Hey, Tabbitha! I am *so* addicted to your blog. What a kick-ass chick you must be! I live in Ruritania, so reading about you gives me a vicarious taste of London. It's a kind of religion isn't it? Your Fan from Ruritania.

She waited a day before checking Tabby out. Yes! She had taken the bait. There in the comment box was the following:

A big welcome, Fan from Ruritania! Nice to know you're a Tabbithaddict, and to answer your question — yes, darling. London *is* a religion!

Pixie smiled, then posted her response.

Thanx for the welcome, Tabbitha! I'm intrigued by your Amazon wish-list. Can you give me any further hints on what's hot to read and what's not?

It took less than four hours for Tabby to get back to her.

To answer your question, Fan from Ruritania, [smiled Dominique/Tabbitha], Dominique Masterson floats my boat. Her first novels were pre-eminently aimed at the much-maligned 'chick-lit' market, but her last novel shows an increasing maturity, and invites comparison with the work of the scribe Colleen. Because she is exploring the realms of Magic Realism, some of her fans may find it less accessible, but I love it! Her heroine Marla's relationship with her tiger/lover is movingly poignant and quite intriguing . . . Incidentally — talking of chick-lit — exponent of the genre, Pixie Pirelli, is devoutly to be avoided!

Aha! Pixie had baited her hook, the fish had bitten, and the reeling in was going to be gloriously satisfying!

She was pleased with her fishing analogy. Fly-fishing had turned out to be one of the most pleasurable forms of research she had ever embarked upon. In the past, research for her novels had included scuba-diving (she'd spent a bleak hour one Saturday morning ninety feet under the freezing surface of a flooded quarry), a Linguaphone course in Italian, and work experience as a gofer on a film. But this was the first such pastime to have brought her so much unadulterated delight. She spent heavenly, soft mornings listening to giddy birds warbling songs of praise above the bucolic beauty of Ballynahinch, and the world and its worries simply vanished. No taunts from Tabbitha could goad her here, no writers' block worries plague her, no self-doubt undermine her.

She tried to explain the appeal of the sport to

Cleo one evening, but she wasn't sure if Cleo understood. The mounting anticipation after a successful cast, the adrenalin rush when the fish took the bait, the sense of gratification once the glittering prize had been reeled in — so many emotions came into play while fishing that Pixie often wanted to shout with joy when she landed her catch.

Reeling in Tabbitha was proving equally satisfying.

'Hey, Tabbitha!' she wrote now.

Thanks for your literary recommendations. I happen to have read Dominique Masterson's first novel, 'Frollix', and I have to say I wasn't impressed. I mean, I know that the heroine is meant to be a 'madcap' creature, but frankly I found the 'madcap' stuff unconvincing and embarrassing. And as for the title? What can I say? She asked for it! Bollix to 'Frollix'!

The reply the next day was less than friendly.

Dear 'Fan from Ruritania'. As regards the title of Dominique Masterson's first novel. Does it not occur to you that perhaps a first-time author — such as Dominique was then — might have very little say in the appellation of her book?

Ooh! Snitty.

Hey! This is fun, Tabbitha! Like an online literary discussion forum!

The next day, Pixie took careful aim again.

Tabbitha — it's your Fan from Ruritania. I checked out Dominique Masterson's profile on Amazon. Oo-er — her last book got less than faint praise. One reader compared it to 'reading Isabel Allende under water'. Any comments?

No response was forthcoming. Tabbitha/ Dominique was clearly in a major huff.

Pixie reached for her fly-fishing manual. 'Having hooked your fish,' she read, 'it now remains to land him. Here discretion is required. Small fish may be dropped into the net as soon as the line can be shortened sufficiently, but if over ½ lb, caution must be used. Keep a firm strain on, and if the fish rushes off wildly, do not attempt to stop him, but the moment he eases, put on more pressure. Once he is exhausted, wind in the line until the fish may be brought sufficiently near to be dropped into the net.'

Hm. She estimated that Tabbitha/Dominique was easily heavier than ½ lb. It was time to allow her a little slack. Pixie decided to leave her alone while she dreamt up her next strategy.

It didn't take her long. She was checking mail one evening when she found a message that had been forwarded to her by Rufus, her web master. It went like this:

Dear Pixie,

I hope you are well. I wonder if you remember me? You signed a copy of your book for me one night in Ballynahinch Castle.

I hope you don't mind me writing to you, but I came across something on the Internet that I think you ought to know about. I entered your name in a search because I wanted to enter a competition that Princessa Publishing is running (the prize is a complete set of your backlist), and I found a blog by someone called Tabbitha. I am sorry to tell you this, but she has said some really mean things about your books on her blog, and I just thought you ought to know, in case you could sue or something.

I can't wait for your next book!

Love, Natasha

Pixie wrote back straight away.

Dear Natasha,

Of course I remember you! You were a very pretty brunette with a twinkle in your eye!

Thank you for warning me about Tabbitha. In fact, I've been aware of her blog for some time now, and am embarking on an act of sabotage. I'm hoping to get an online discussion forum going on her site — might you like to contribute? And if you can mobilize your friends and friends of your friends via a round robin, that would be fantastic. To the ramparts!

Love, Pixie XXX

PS: If we're successful, I shall name the heroine of my next book after you.

That night, Pixie resumed her offensive. 'Tabbitha, hi! It's me again, from Ruritania! I've ordered all of Dominique Masterson's backlist books from Amazon because I want to give her a chance. I'll let you know when I finish them.'

The very next day Tabby took the bait again. 'Well, 'Fan from Ruritania' — you are in for a treat!'

Result!

Pixie held off for some days before revisiting Tab/Dom's blog. Her ghillie had told her that while it was important to cast skilfully, one further attribute was essential for the successful fly-fisher. Patience.

Click! Aha. La Londonista's latest dilemma was what to wear to the theatre this evening. Her new Marni frock? Or a zesty yellow Calvin Klein? The only comment on the box read: 'You sound like someone in a Pixie Pirelli novel.'

Pixie smiled, then scrolled down several days' worth of blog to find the following:

Checked out Pixie Pirelli's website! Save our Souls! Her photo gallery is a veritable montage of Pixie-ness! Pixie receiving awards, Pixie partying with other posers, Pixie prinking at a big table covered in piles and piles of Pixie books! Shiny, happy Pixie! How splendidly Pixie-ish it must be to be her!

Three comments had been posted. 'Tabbitha, I think you're being a little unfair about PP. Lighten up. Love, Pooch.' 'Gimme Pixie Pirelli over Dominique Masterson any day! Nefertiti.' 'Hey — at least the Pirelli chik writes books not boring blogs. Hamlet.'

Could Tabbitha stay cool under pressure? Pixie made the following contribution to the comment box: 'Pixie Pirelli v. Dominique Masterson? The struggle for domination continues. Vote here.'

The next time Pixie visited Dominique's blog she found a rash of responses. Hurray! This online literary forum *was* fun! 'We love Pixie,' she read. 'Pixie.' 'Pixie P.' 'Pixie.' 'Pixie.' 'PP.' 'Pixie.'

It was like a roll-call for a Brownie convention — and it had the desired effect.

'So how come my blog has suddenly become a forum for discussing chick-lit writers?' hissed Tabby. 'This blog is *not* a promotional tool for Pixie Pirelli's unreadable books. Sweet Jesus! Weapons of mass destruction couldn't possibly compare with the effect that Pixie Pirelli has on my head!'

Open season had been declared, and the sweet smell of revenge was in the air. Pixie decided to lure Tabbitha to the surface and reel her in. She flexed her fingers, then: '"Fan from Ruritania" reporting for duty, Tabbitha!' she typed.

I have done my homework and I am sorry to have to tell you that Dominique Masterson's novels are among the very worst I have read in my life. My jaw dropped at the pretentiousness of her last one. Magic Realism? There was nothing either Magic or Realistic about it. The following extract eloquently proves my point. Listen up to this! 'The lake was awash with stars. Marla dipped her hand into the cool water and picked one up. It glistened on her palm momentarily, then faded, died, melted like ice. The tiger seemed to sense her feelings of isolation. He licked her hand on the place where the star had lingered. 'Come, Zanzibar,' she said, turning towards the horizon, where fate glowed in the shape of a misty harvest moon. 'It is time . . . "'

'It is time.' Time for what? Time to take a dump? Time to throw up at Ms Masterson's icky prose? No, it's time to shut the case on Ms Masterson, I think, and get back to some decent reading. For the record, Tabbitha, Pixie Pirelli kicks ass!

The next day Tabbitha wrote: 'The integrity of this site has been compromised by someone known as a 'Fan from Ruritania'. I apologize to my regular visitors. I have reluctantly decided that I must terminate this blog and start over using a different identity. I hope you find me. Sayonara, amigos. Love, Tabbitha. PS: I may be gone, but my link to the site of the divine Colleen remains for posterity . . . '

The fish was well and truly landed, but Pixie resisted the impulse to shout for joy. The first rule of fly-fishing was, after all: 'Study to be quiet.'

★ ★ ★

Some time later, Pixie phoned Deborah to tell her that she'd finished the first draft of her novel.

'Hurrah!' said Deborah. 'Star, star, star! Have you a title yet?'

'I thought 'Sex, Death and Revenge' had a nice ring to it.'

'Mm. I'm not convinced. It's rather a radical departure from your backlist titles.'

'There's only so much fun to be got from designer labels, Deborah.'

'Granted. But the 'D' word's a bit of a turn-off.'

'OK,' said Pixie equably. 'I'll have a think.'

'What will you do to celebrate?'

'I'm going fishing.'

'You're totally hooked, aren't you? Sorry. Bad pun.'

'I can use it. I'll write a magazine article with 'Hooked on Fly Fishing!' as the header. Maybe I can make fly-fishing the new rock 'n' roll.'

'Please explain to me, Pixie. What's so special about fly-fishing?'

'I can't explain it to people who don't do it. It's an arcane thing.'

'It's so not my idea of fun.'

'What's your idea of fun?'

'Curling up by the fire with a glass of wine and a Pixie Pirelli novel.'

'Thank you! Aren't you kind.'

'I'll get on to Camilla. See if she can use the fishing thing as a hook — sorry! — for interviews. Hang on, she's just walked past my office. Camilla!'

Pixie heard muffled discussion down the line, then Camilla's voice came on.

'Pixie, hi! Well done — I understand you've finished!'

'The first draft. Yes.'

'So that means you'll be back in London soon? I can line up some PR for the paperback pub of *Hard to Choos?*'

'Yes. But please hold off for another week or so, Camilla. There's a festival happening soon here in Kilrowan, and I want to take it easy for a while.'

'Sure. Um. I hate to put pressure on you, but how would you feel about a phone interview? *Writing Times* would like to do a quickie. One of those 'My Favourite Pen' jobs. Is it all right to let them have your number?'

'Of course.'

Camilla sounded curious. 'Do you actually have a favourite pen?'

'No. But I'll make one up.'

'Excellent! Let's see, what else? You might do a 'My Pet' for the *Sunday Satellite*?'

'I don't have a pet.'

'Couldn't you make a pet up too?'

'No. It's one thing to make up a favourite pen, but quite another one to make up a pet. There's something not quite ethical about it.'

'Fair enough. I'll hit Dominique Masterson with it. She can talk about that Birman cat of hers. Anyway, let me put you back on to Deborah. And thanks for the favourite pen thing.'

'You're welcome.'

There was a pause, then: 'Hi, again,' said Deborah. She lowered her voice a fraction. 'Have you spoken to Dominique lately?'

'Not directly,' said Pixie. 'Is she still piqued?'

'No. She's remarkably resilient. Dominique always bounces back. Anyway, she has other fish to fry now.' Pixie almost laughed. 'She's sold an outline for a reality TV show to a production company for megamoney.'

'Really? What's it about?'

'Another of those desert island thingies, except instead of calling it 'reality' TV they're ringing the changes by calling it 'magic reality', and having a magician set the tasks.'

'So there'll be lots of celebrities sawing each other in half and suchlike?'

'I think that's the general idea.'

'Sounds like fun. *I'll* certainly be watching!'

There came the ping! of an incoming e-mail, then an intake of breath from Deborah. 'Shit. I'm going to have to get on to design straight away, Pixie. There's been a major, *major* cock-up, and I have to go kick some ass. Jesus! I *hate* kicking ass!'

'I rather enjoy it,' said Pixie.

'Yes — but that's in *fantasy* land, darling. It's rather different when one has to do it in reality.'

'I suppose you're right. I used to practically hyperventilate any time I had to kick my builders' asses. What's the name of Dominique's 'reality' show, by the way?'

'Can't remember. Something bonkers to do with survival of the fittest illusionist.'

'Ha! Been there, done that.'

'What do you mean?'

'Isn't it obvious, Deborah? That's what publishing is all about.'

'You're right. It's a tough business.'

'Yes,' said Pixie. 'It really, really is. I should lend you that book you gave me.'

'What book?'

'The *SAS Survival Handbook*. Remember?'

'Oh, yes. What a lark! Did it come in useful?'

Pixie smiled down the phone, a little catlike smile of victory. 'The stuff about fishing did,' she said.

14

Cleo looked up as the shop door opened and Hugh Hennessy came in.

'Hi, Hugh,' she said. She was glad to set down the book she was leafing through. It was an interior design bible written by someone with a snobby name.

'Hi. Can I leave a pile of flyers here?'

'Sure. What are they?'

'Events guides for the festival.' He set the flyers down by the till, then hovered by the bestsellers, looking out of place. Hugh rarely came into the bookshop. 'Whatcha reading?' he asked Cleo.

'It's one of those lifestyle books. Don't you hate them? Some posh bird telling you what your house should look like.'

'I wouldn't mind that. My house is a mess. I'd love a posh bird to tell me what to do with it. Give us a gander.' Cleo passed him the glossy tome. 'Christ. It costs a fortune,' he said.

'I know. That won't put people off, though. It'll probably be a mega-seller. Books like this are a measure of how insecure people are about their own taste.'

'Why would people want to go to the trouble of *faking* woodworm on their furniture?' asked Hugh, leafing through the book with a baffled expression. 'I've accumulated masses of the stuff without having to lift a finger.'

'People are weird, Hugh. There's no accounting for tastes, and we just love being told what to do. Look at the success of Trinny and Susannah.'

'Who?'

'OK, let's not go there. You *really* wouldn't understand them. How's the festival shaping up?'

'Good, thanks. All that prep's paid off. The parade's kicking off on Monday.'

'Fun!' Cleo picked up an events guide and scanned it. 'Wow. You've some great names lined up this year. Zoe Conway, Donal Lunny, Sharon Shannon, the *Tribunals* show. I must tell Pixie to get tickets for that. She's fascinated by the Irish Tribunals. She finds it hard to believe that Ireland's such a corrupt country.'

Hugh started folding a flyer into a dart. 'People have been incredibly supportive. All these acts are appearing for free, and the school has pulled all the stops out. The kids have designed banners and flags and bunting. And lights are going up all over town tonight, and the fun fair's arriving.'

'So it's the *new! improved!* Kilrowan Arts Festival.'

'Well, it is hopefully new and improved, but we've left the 'Arts' tag off this year.'

'Oh? Why's that?'

'Hazel did some research. She found that loads of people generally found the word 'Arts' off-putting and elitist. A festival is supposed to be a celebration, not a dour convention of cerebral navel-gazers.'

'That', said Cleo, 'is a very good point.'

'She said that the last time she was at the Cork Film Festival, everybody was going round dressed in black and looking deep. She's trying to get the balance right this year, and it looks like we might succeed. We've just the right amount of the light and the heavyweight. As well as that bumper harvest of celebrities.'

'Talking about celebrities, I heard Colleen on the Pat Kenny show. I'd better drag her cut-out out of the store room if she's going to be in town. Presumably she's giving a talk again this year?'

'Yeah. And she's doubled the prize money in her short story competition. It's extremely generous of her.'

Cleo resumed her scrutiny of the flyer. 'Oh! Wow! Mondo the aMazing's performing. I *loved* him when I was a kid.'

'Ahem.'

'I remember all the kids in school wearing Bunny Brown earrings, like his.'

'Ahem, Cleo?' She looked up. Something about Hugh's demeanour had changed. He was looking a bit shifty now, like the messenger who has bad news to deliver. 'I got a delivery today of a painting. From Pablo.' He tapped the point of the dart he'd been making against the ball of his thumb.

'Oh.' Oh, God. She didn't know what to say. There was something — *significant* about Hugh's pronouncement. She watched as her fingers traced the title of a book on the counter. It was a self-help book called *The Total Forgiveness Experience* by some saint called R.

290

T. Kendall. She hadn't bothered to consult it — she'd lay a bet that even R. T. Kendall would find forgiving Pablo MacBride a challenge. 'I'll get that cut-out now, before I forget,' she said, retreating into the jumble of her back room.

So Pablo had donated a painting. Had he delivered it himself? Would he be making an appearance at the festival to present it personally to the highest bidder as he did every year? Was he in Kilrowan now? Cleo wanted to know all these things and more, but she didn't want to ask Hugh. She bought time by dithering, and then she hefted the cardboard cut-out of Colleen in her trademark crimson cloak from a shelf and trundled back into the shop with it.

Hugh was still loitering by the cash desk. 'Would you like to see it?' he asked.

'Pablo's painting?' said Cleo. She gave an insouciant shrug of her shoulders as she reached for the packets of Cif wipes and Swiffers dusters that she kept in the cupboard under the till. 'I suppose it's more of the same. 'Still Life with Pig'. 'Politician with Pig'. 'Princess with Pig'.'

'No,' said Hugh. 'There's no pig in this one.'

'Oh? So what's he put in instead of a pig?' asked Cleo, vigorously wiping dust off Colleen. 'An ape? An aardvark? A fucking sloth?'

'No. There are no animals in it at all.'

Cleo couldn't help herself: she was curious, now. She faltered in her dusting of Colleen. 'What's it of, then?'

'I think you should see it yourself, Cleo. Maybe you could call round to the house after you finish up here?'

'Is that where the painting is?'

'Yes.'

'Let me think about it.'

Cleo finished her dusting and set Colleen in the centre of the window display, and Hugh aimed his paper dart at it just as the diva herself came striding down the street. Her red hair was wild, her cloak a crimson swirl.

Cleo ducked back out of the display and faced Hugh.

'Will Pablo be at your house?'

'No. He sent the painting by FedEx. But there's a letter there for you.'

'All right,' she said. 'I'll drop by after work.'

'Cool,' he said. 'Around half-past six?'

'Yeah.'

Hugh made to leave the shop, but a volume displayed on the front table caught his attention. It was a glossy travel book about Jamaica. 'Hey,' he said, picking it up and leafing through it. 'My favourite place!'

'It's a pricy book,' said Cleo. 'But I can let you have it at a discount. It's slightly shop soiled.'

He looked thoughtful, then set the book back on the pile. 'No,' he said. 'Could you look out a clean copy for me, please, if you have one? And could you gift-wrap it? It's for a present.' He handed her a wad of euros.

'Sure,' said Cleo, counting out change. 'Will you wait while I wrap it? Or shall I bring it when I come this evening?'

'Bring it this evening,' said Hugh, looking at his watch. 'I'd better get on. See you later, Cleo.'

Before Hugh could reach the door, it was

flung open. Colleen was standing on the threshold, looking nearly as resplendent as her cut-out in the window.

'Hi, Colleen,' said Hugh. 'That was a terrific interview you gave to Pat Kenny. We were inundated with entries for your short story competition after that.'

'Do I not know it? I have been reading short stories until my eyes have become dim and weary. The standard this year has not been felicitous.'

'Will you get through them all in time?'

'I will,' said Colleen, assuming an even more magisterial air. 'It is my onus as an arbiter. But I have enlisted the help of Margot this year. She has an unerring eye for talent.'

'How is Margot?' asked Cleo dutifully. The last time she'd seen her sister had been shortly after the publication of *Proust's Sewing Machine*, when she'd come into the shop to sign stock. She'd been snitty with Cleo because she'd only ordered half a dozen copies. All these months later there were still two languishing on the shelves.

'Margot is well,' mused Colleen, nodding her head in a ruminative way. 'She is experimenting with a euphonious literary style which she expects will be comparable to the Athenian orators of the — '

'Sorry — excuse me, Colleen, but I have to dash,' said Hugh. An alarmed expression had come into his eyes. When Colleen started waxing eulogistic about matters literary it was hard to shut her up.

'*Slán*, Hugh!' said Colleen, as he exited the shop with a 'See you later!' to Cleo.

Colleen shut the door behind her, and advanced into the shop. Her bag of rust-coloured hemp was crammed and jumbled with vegetables, but some unerring instinct told her exactly where to locate her fountain pen.

Cleo automatically made for the front table and picked up a pile of Colleen's books, then teetered towards the cash desk with them. She opened the topmost book at the title page and watched as Colleen wrote 'Doubt not your soul!' in her distinctive jagged script, then added 'Colleen' with a flourish.

'So Margot's helping you get through the short stories?' asked Cleo.

'Indeed and she is. I should be lost without her help.'

Cleo braced herself inwardly. 'How's your writing coming along, Colleen?' It had to be asked.

Colleen gave a little droop of exhaustion. 'I delivered two weeks ago, with the help of Margot. She was my birthing partner. I had been over a year in gestation and the labour was a difficult one, but — with Margot to hold my hand between contractions — it was an ecstatic experience. I took the progeny to London myself just last week.'

'Wouldn't it have been easier to e-mail it?' asked Cleo, hefting another tome and turning to the title page.

A look of horror crossed Colleen's face. *Yikes!* What a gaffe! Cleo had forgotten that Colleen

294

wrote her novels by hand on hand-made Nepalese paper.

'Or post it?' Cleo added hastily.

'Would you dream of putting a living infant in a 'jiffy' bag and sending it via airmail?' demanded Colleen. She always put quotation marks around any word she found unworthy of utterance.

'No. Silly me. Of course you were absolutely right to deliver it yourself.'

'I saw Pablo while I was there,' said Colleen, slanting Cleo a catlike look as she put the exclamation mark on another 'Doubt not your soul!'

'Oh?' Cleo tried to sound indifferent.

'Yes. He has been living there for some months now. But I'm sure you knew that.'

'Mm,' said Cleo ambiguously.

'Hi!'

Cleo looked towards the door. Pixie Pirelli was standing there smiling brightly. The smile vanished when she registered the presence of Colleen, and she took a step backwards. Cleo had the impression that she would have turned tail and scarpered if she'd had the chance, but when Colleen looked up, Pixie stapled the smile on again.

'Hello, Colleen,' she said.

Colleen assumed an expression of mild puzzlement. 'Ah. Do I know you?' she asked.

'We met once, at the London Book Fair. I'm Pixie Pirelli.'

'Pixie Pirelli?'

'Yes.'

'And you were there in your capacity as a . . . er?'

'I'm a writer.'

'Oh? Oh, yes — the name does ring a bell. *Conas atá tú?*' And Colleen stretched a paw towards Pixie.

Pixie stepped forward and took the proffered hand. 'Um. *Conas atá tú*, too,' she said, and her very English pronunciation of the phrase produced a barely disguised wince from Colleen.

'What brings you to Kilrowan, 'Pixie'?' asked Colleen.

'I've been working on a novel.'

'Pixie's been living in your house for the past six months, Colleen. Remember, Pablo organized the tenancy back in March?'

'I recall Pablo mentioning it to me, yes. But I had no idea as to the identity of the resident.' She turned her green gaze back to her interrogatee and fixed Pixie with a gimlet scrutiny that a member of the Gestapo might envy. 'And have you found number 4, the Blackthorns, conducive to your writing?'

'Yes, thank you,' said Pixie.

'Pixie has written an entire novel while she's been here,' supplied Cleo.

'In six months? You wrote a novel in *six months*!' An incredulous look crossed Colleen's face and her hands shot to her face in alarm. The theatricality of the gesture caused the Tara brooch at her bosom to ping, and her cloak fell off.

Cleo wanted to laugh so much that she started to gabble as a diversionary tactic. 'Actually,

Pixie, it was much less when you think about it. Don't forget all the time you spent on the one you — ' Oh. She didn't want to say 'the one you got blocked on' in front of Colleen. Pixie's block was none of Colleen's business. She amended it to 'the one you changed your mind about'.

'Mm.' Pixie had diverted herself by diving for Colleen's cloak and brushing imaginary dust off it. 'What a lovely cloak!' she said, handing it back to Colleen.

'Well,' said Colleen, re-assuming the garment. 'You have been working very hard indeed. Congratulations. I wish you every success with your 'novel', Pixie.'

The quotation marks hung in the air, staring the two women in the face, but while Pixie could not have failed to register them she gave no indication that she had. She merely continued to regard Colleen with an unflinchingly polite expression.

'Please accept a copy of my book as a token of my warm wishes,' continued Colleen, turning back to the pile and signing another copy.

'Thank you. How very generous of you,' said Pixie. 'And I in turn would love you to have one of mine. Do you have any in stock, Cleo?'

'Of course,' said Cleo, marching to the bestsellers section and selecting a copy of *Hard to Choos*.

She watched Colleen put the finishing touches to her dedication on the title page of *To the Island*, and saw Pixie put in 'XXX' under her sparkly signature and add a ☺ for good measure.

'How kind!' said Pixie. She read the

dedication out loud. ' "To 'Pixie'. In celebration of your fecundity. Doubt not your soul! Colleen.' Lovely!'

'I'll finish off this stack for you, Cleo,' said Colleen, continuing to write her 'Doubt not your souls', 'and then I must hurry away, lest I keep the documentary people waiting. They want to set up an interview with me on Lissnakeelagh strand.'

'On Lissnakeelagh? That's a weird place for an interview.'

'On the contrary. I want to be interviewed with all my senses heightened, and there is no better place on earth for the heightening of the senses than Lissnakeelagh.'

'Are they doing *another* documentary on you?' asked Cleo.

'Not exclusively on me, no. Not this time. There is a documentary being made of the Kilrowan Arts Festival.'

'They've lost the 'Arts'.'

'I beg your pardon?'

'The 'Arts'. It's gone from the wording. It's just a plain 'Festival' now.'

Colleen looked stricken. 'Arra, no! Another instance of the 'dumbing down' of the world. Ochone, ochone to the Arts.' She shook her head lugubriously, then: 'Have you a bag for this, Cleo?' she asked, holding out the book Pixie had signed for her. 'My hempen satchel cannot accommodate it.' Colleen's hempen satchel was indeed quite overladen with organic produce. It was market day in Kilrowan.

'I'm afraid not,' lied Cleo cheerfully. 'I'm all

out of bags. There's been a run on them.'

'I see,' said Colleen. '*Slán*, then, Cleo. *Slán*, 'Pixie'.' And Colleen made her majestic exit with her head held high, carrying her hempen satchel as if it were a sceptre, and *Hard to Choos* as if it were something smelly.

When the shop door closed behind her, Pixie and Cleo regarded each other with incredulity.

'Well!' said Pixie. 'How fantastic is she?'

'She's a prize cow,' said Cleo, 'that's for sure.'

'Oh, fiddlesticks to that!' said Pixie. 'I think she's *magnificent*!' She picked up the book Colleen had signed for her and re-read the dedication. ' 'To 'Pixie'. In celebration of your fecundity. Doubt not your soul. Exclamation mark. Colleen.' Cor blimey!'

'What did you put on hers?'

'I put 'I really dig your Birkenstocks'.'

'No!'

'Oh, yes. I could have put 'Up your hole, Colleen', but I decided the reference to Birkenstocks was a better literary joke for a book called *Hard to Choos*.'

'You really would have had the nerve to put 'Up your hole'?' asked Cleo, aghast.

'Oh yes. I knew she'd never even open the book, let alone read it,' said Pixie matter-of-factly, moving to the shop window. 'And in fact, she's doing exactly what I thought she'd do. Look over there.'

Cleo looked. There, on the other side of the road, Colleen was surreptitiously sliding Pixie's book into a litter bin.

'The skanger!' said Cleo.

But Pixie looked perfectly sanguine. 'There's no great mischief done, Cleo,' she said. 'Because that's where Colleen's book will end up too. I'm not going to read her book any more than she would ever dream of reading mine.'

'But you told me how gutted you were when you read on Amazon that Tabby had dumped your book in the bin!'

'That was very different,' said Pixie, 'because Tabby had read my book and was motivated by spite. Colleen isn't being malicious. We're just two very different literary animals who speak a completely different language, but who can afford to live and let live — it's axioma — ' Pixie stopped, furrowed her brow and then smiled. 'It's as simple as that,' she said.

* * *

Later, Cleo walked down the drive to Hugh's house feeling apprehensive. There was clearly something hugely significant about this painting of Pablo's, and she wasn't sure if she was ready to take any kind of significant step either forwards or backwards.

Hugh's door was opened by Hazel, the PR person who was handling the festival.

'Hi,' she said. 'Come in. Hugh's just had to nip out and do something to some horse. He actually *uses* that thing on a penknife for taking stones out of horses' hooves. He's the only person I've ever met who does.'

'I always thought Enid Blyton made that up,' said Cleo, stepping into Hugh's hall. She'd only been in the house once before, at a housewarming party shortly after he'd moved in. Nothing much seemed to have changed since then. It was very much a man's house, but it was not without its own brand of faded charm. She wondered what the posh bird who'd written the interior design book would make of it. She'd change everything about it, probably.

'Come on downstairs,' said Hazel. 'Will you have a glass of wine?'

'I'd love one.' Cleo followed Hazel down to the kitchen, which was bright with evening sunlight. Hugh's dogs came to meet them. They'd hung with Fluffy on occasion, Cleo remembered.

'Hi, Prue, hi, Honey,' she said, hunkering down to pet them.

'You know them, obviously,' said Hazel.

'Yes.'

'I adore Honey. It took Prue a while to warm to me, but I like to think she just about tolerates me now. Red or white?'

'White, please.'

Hazel poured, then set glasses on the table. Cleo sat down and looked around the kitchen a little apprehensively, wondering where Pablo's painting was.

'The painting's upstairs,' said Hazel. 'Hugh'll take you up. He won't be long.'

Cleo nodded. 'That's cool,' she said. She took the gift-wrapped book on Jamaica out of her bag and put it on the table. 'Hugh bought this in my shop earlier today. I told him I'd gift-wrap it for him.'

'Pretty!'

'I have to say I *hate* gift-wrapping books — all those fiddly feckin' rosettes — but it's a skill I had to master. You want to see the shop at Christmas time. It's like Santa's grotto with all the gift-wrapped packages.' She took a sip of wine. 'What's the buzz on the festival?'

'Very good. There's a documentary being made, so don't be surprised if a camera crew vox-pops you.'

'They were interviewing Colleen today, I believe.'

'Yep.'

'You should have them interview Pixie Pirelli too, to help the balance.'

'That's a good idea. I'll ask them to get some of 'An Evening with Pixie Pirelli' on tape. That's booked out. Oh, hi, Hugh!'

Hugh had come through the back door. 'Hi, you. Hi, Cleo. There, *there* — take it easy. Good dogs!'

Honey and Prue had leapt up at the sound of their master's voice, and Cleo felt a little tug of pain when she remembered the way Fluffy used to come running to greet her, plumy tail waving, hair accessories dancing, and with a big smile on her face.

'Have — um — have you seen the painting yet, Cleo?' asked Hugh.

'No.'

'I didn't want to show it to her,' explained Hazel. 'I didn't really feel it was my place.'

Hugh nodded. 'Fair enough. Is that the book I

302

bought from you?' he asked, indicating the parcel on the table.

'It is,' said Cleo. 'Gift-wrapped by my own fair hands.'

'And *your* fair hands are to *un*gift-wrap it, Ms MacNamara.' Hugh picked up the parcel and handed it to Hazel.

'It's for me?' she said in surprise.

'Yes. It's a reward for all your hard work on the festival.'

'Oh, Hugh! Thank you! Oh — I *love* getting surprise presents!' Hazel unceremoniously undid all Cleo's gift-wrapping and took out the Jamaica book. 'Class! Thank you so *much*,' she said, getting to her feet and putting her arms about him. And as Hazel and Hugh exchanged a very tender kiss, Cleo realized with a rush of awful envy that they were an item.

No! She found herself thinking back to the times when Pablo had surprised her with presents, and she wanted to weep. He'd been a fantastic buyer of presents, leaving them in places where she'd come across them accidentally. Little things, like CDs he knew she'd like, or the pretty painted eggs she loved to collect. Ow! Watching another couple doing lovey-dovey stuff was about as bad as it got.

'You're obviously a big Jamaica fan,' she remarked when they broke the embrace.

'We both are,' said a smiley Hazel. 'We're going to go back there together. We both stayed in the same resort there once upon a time.'

An awkward silence fell. It was time for Cleo

to do the thing she'd come here to do. She cued Hugh. 'Um?' she said.

'It's in the drawing room upstairs,' he said. 'Would you like me to show you, or would you rather look at it on your own?'

His expression told her it would be more appropriate if she viewed the painting solo. 'I'll go up by myself,' she said. 'If you don't mind.'

'Be my guest,' said Hugh.

Cleo left the kitchen, aware that the sympathetic eyes of Hugh and Hazel would be on her retreating back, and hating the idea. She almost wished she hadn't come here now, to be viewed as an object of pity, a woman whose husband had left her. But then, she reasoned, she'd *told* him to leave her. Screamed it at him, actually.

In the drawing room the painting stood on a side table, leaning against the wall. It was covered by a sheet of bubblewrap. An envelope with her name on it in Pablo's handwriting was propped up against it. She took the envelope and steeled herself to open it. Count to three, she told herself. One. Two. *Three*. She tore the envelope open and took out a single sheet of paper.

Dear Cleo,

Please allow me to tell you where I have been for the past few months. I have been in hell. I have been in exile. I have been examining my conscience, and I have been in conference with my soul. Sounds serious, doesn't it? That's because it is.

I wronged you, and this painting is my penance. It is my way of saying sorry to you, and it is my way of begging you to take me back. If you accept it as a gift, then I will understand that you have found it in your heart to forgive me. If you are not ready, please make sure that the money raised from the proceeds of the auction goes to this year's charity — the Safe-Home Ireland programme. It's the charity for the indigent Irish in London.

Please know that I love you, that I will always love you. I am so sorry. I have been a complete shit and an utter imbecile.

Pablo

Cleo folded the letter and replaced it in the envelope. Then she took hold of the corner of the bubblewrap and pulled.

There, in a tortoiseshell frame was a landscape in oils of Connemara, and in the landscape stood two small figures — a man and a woman. The man had a stick in one hand — a blackthorn, a walking stick — and the woman supported his other arm, which seemed shrunken and insubstantial. The female figure was elevated a little by the sod of turf she stood upon. Both figures were gazing across the landscape, but it was impossible to tell if they were gazing into the past, or gazing into the future, or gazing into the middle distance.

She knew what she was looking at. She was looking at what Pablo now saw with eyes unclouded by alcohol, and a mind unjaundiced by cynicism. There were no quirky trademark touches. No pig, no snake, no monkey. The only other subject matter in the painting was a small whitewashed cottage. Home. The figures in that bleak Connemara landscape could only be himself and Cleo, a couple uncertain whether they should work hard to recapture their past happiness, or step forward into separate futures. Here, made manifest, was the powerful spirit of a love remembered. Pablo's longing to be forgiven, to come home, was almost palpable.

She imagined the painting displayed as a trophy in an ostentatious house in Dublin 4, and she thought about the kind of money that could be raised for the charity he'd stipulated. Safe-Home Ireland.

And then she covered the painting up with the bubblewrap, and went back downstairs to where Hugh was waiting for her decision.

'I'd like it,' Cleo said, 'to go to auction.'

15

Cleo was doing a roaring trade in Colleen. Paperback copies of *To the Island* with 'Signed by the Author' stickers were clearly *the* thing for the cognoscenti to be seen reading this summer.

'Thank you!' she trilled as another €10.50 registered on the till and she handed back a fifty cent coin.

She'd been busy earlier, but things were quiet now. There was only one customer in the shop — a woman with bleached blond hair, who was browsing through the second-hand section. She was wearing a ra-ra skirt, fishnet tights and vertiginous heels. She was somewhere in her forties, Cleo calculated, and the skirt was — well — *inappropriate* was the word that sprang to mind. 'Hey! Far out!' said the woman, evidently alighting on a bargain. 'Paula's book! I've been looking for this for ages!'

Cleo gave a polite smile as the miniskirted woman high-heeled up to the cash register with a copy of Paula Yates's *Blondes*.

'We have more fun!' said the woman.

There was no answer to that, so Cleo just gave her another polite smile.

'She was a friend of mine.'

'Sorry?'

'Paula Yates.'

'Really?'

'Mm. In the early days, when she was married

307

to Bob. At one stage we thought we might collaborate on a rock chick book, but it fell through.'

'Ah.'

The blond woman nodded. 'I started to write it myself, but it just never happened. I wouldn't have the discipline to be a writer.' She nodded at the pile of Colleen's books. 'Imagine sitting on your arse and writing all those words. It'd drive me mental, so it would. How much do I owe you?'

'Five euros.'

The woman handed over a twenty and started to leaf through the book while she waited for her change. 'Aw. Look,' she said, showing Cleo a full-page portrait in pastels of Paula Yates in a flame red gown. 'Doesn't she look sweet? She was an absolute honey, you know. She used to babysit my daughter before Fifi Trixibelle arrived.'

'Really? Were you a — a rock chick too?'

'Still am, sweetie. I'm gigging at the festival this week.'

'Oh! So you're . . . um . . . '

'Angel Kestrel of Angel Phish. We used to be known as the Fazes back in the seventies. You know, as in 'it's just a phase you're going through'. My mother used to say that to me all the time. And I'm still going through it.' Angel Kestrel gave a delighted gurgle. 'Oh, look! There we are on the flyer!' She picked up a flyer from the pile by the till. 'Hm. They spelled it wrong. It's meant to be 'Phish' with a 'ph', not 'Fish'. And Mondo's meant to be aMazing with a

308

capital 'M'. They've got it with a capital 'A' here. I'm surprised Hazel fouled that up, considering he's her dad.'

'Hazel? You're talking about Hazel Mac-Namara?'

'Yeah. She's my daughter. Oops!' The woman clapped a hand over her mouth. 'I shouldn't have let that slip. She's actually in quite a boring office job in — um — Auckland, I think it is.'

Uh oh. This woman was clearly on something.

'I see. And Mondo the aMazing's Hazel's dad?'

'Yup. God knows how me and him managed to produce such a sussed offspring.' That gurgle again.

'I *loved* Mondo the aMazing when I was a kid,' said Cleo. 'What's he going to be doing in the festival?'

'He's the Salmon of Knowledge,' said Angel. 'He will provide the answer to any question you care to ask.'

'Cool!' said Cleo. 'How does he do that?'

Angel tapped the bridge of her pierced nose with a finger. 'If I told you, I would have to kill you.' She started leafing through her book again. 'Oh, wow! Look at Paula all in white! And *wow*! Get a load of Debbie Harry in leopardskin! Can you believe we used to dress like that? And that *hair*!' Angel Kestrel held the book up so that Cleo could get a load of Debbie Harry with electric shock hair. 'I used to wear my hair like that. I'm not surprised that Hazel was embarrassed when I picked her up from school.' Angel laughed again, then shut the book.

'Thanks for this,' she said. 'It means a lot. I had a signed copy once, but I made the mistake of lending it to someone and I never got it back. Byee!' She twinkled her fingers at Cleo and left the shop.

Well! That was Hazel's *mother*! Hazel the grown-up with the designer threads and the real-life job had a rock chick for a mother and a clown for a father!

Her phone rang. 'Dowling's Book Shop?' she said.

'Hi, Cleo. It's Pixie.'

'Hi, Pixie. How's it going?'

'It's going very well, thank you, and I'd like to take you out to dinner tonight,' she said. 'To celebrate. I've finished the novel and it's my birthday.'

'Well, happy birthday. And yes, please — I'd love to have dinner.'

'Ballynahinch is booked out. So how about we stroll down to O'Toole's, at around seven? I know it's a little early, but I like to get to bed before eleven.'

'Seven's perfect. See you later.'

'I look forward to it.'

Cleo put the phone down, then turned her attention to the window. The display had a maritime theme to it to tie in with the festival, and all the books arranged there had covers featuring river or seascapes (luckily for Colleen *To the Island* had a fuzzy image of Clew Bay on it, so several of her paperbacks were fanned out at the front). In the centre of the window was a gigantic glossy travel book. It boasted a photograph of a coral reef on its jacket, and it was called *Great Escapes: The Dreamiest Destinations in the World*. That would make a perfect present for Pixie now that she'd finished all her hard work and could, perhaps, allow herself a holiday at last.

As Cleo lifted the book out of the window display she saw Hazel MacNamara's father coming down the main street, talking on his mobile phone. How he'd changed! Mondo the aMazing had been small and chubby, but extraordinarily charismatic — the way people are who have the ability to make people laugh. The anxious-looking individual standing outside her shop window right now could be a double glazing salesman, or a ticket inspector. She watched as Mondo the aMazing put his phone in his pocket and stood there twiddling his earring and looking uncertain for a moment or two, before registering the bookshop and making a beeline for the door.

He looked around the shop furtively before approaching her. 'Hi,' he said in the surreptitious voice favoured by the kind of men who were after titles dodgier than she cared to stock. 'I wonder can you help me? Do you happen to have the Encarta Encyclopaedia in stock?'

'You're in luck,' said Cleo, relieved that he hadn't asked for 'Spanking Nancy' or 'Slutty Secretaries' Office Party'. 'It's right there.' She indicated the stand where she kept a small selection of CD Roms.

Mondo moseyed over, helped himself to the Encarta, then made a face at the price. 'Bugger it,' he said, taking a credit card from his pocket. 'But it has to be done.'

'You're Mondo the aMazing, aren't you?' asked Cleo as she took the card that bore the signature 'M. MacNamara.'

'That's right.'

'I'm very pleased to meet you,' said Cleo, swiping his card and handing him a pen. 'I *loved* your show on the telly. I'm recording all the re-runs.'

'Re-runs? What re-runs?'

'They're re-running *Bunny Brown's Way* every weekday afternoon.'

'What? The bastards! Nobody ever bothered to tell me. I'm due repeat fees for that. I'll have to get on to my agent. Thanks for letting me know.' He scribbled his signature on the credit card slip, then slid the card into his pocket.

'Would you like a bag for that?' asked Cleo.

'Damn right!' said Mondo, taking the proffered bag and slinging the Encarta into it.

'I know your daughter, Hazel,' said Cleo conversationally as she handed him his receipt. 'In fact, I had a glass of wine with her just last night.'

Mondo looked inspired, suddenly. He clicked his fingers and said: 'Hazel! *Yes!* That's the answer! Hazel'll be able to help me out! Cheers!'

He took his phone from his pocket and speed-dialled a number. 'Hazel? It's your dad here. Can you meet me? I'm in the Kilrowan bookshop. I need to ask you a big favour. I can't tell you over the phone. There's a pub just across the road. I'll meet you there in, say, ten minutes?'

And Cleo watched as Mondo the aMazing left her shop and legged it across the road to O'Toole's pub.

* * *

Hazel was sitting at Hugh's kitchen table going through a checklist of technical equipment. Her favourite thing in the world was crossing things off lists. She had just put a satisfying line through 'mic stands', 'mixing board' and 'two-way radio mics' when her phone rang. Her dad's number was displayed. 'Hi — um — Where are you? Oh.' Oh, God. 'What is it? Ten minutes?' She bit her lip. 'OK.'

'Some problem?' asked Hugh.

'Not really,' lied Hazel, turning off her phone. 'I just need to nip into O'Toole's. I've to meet with someone about Mondo the aMazing.'

'It's incredible the number of people who remember him,' Hugh said. 'Cleo Dowling was waxing lyrical about him yesterday.'

'Mm. Well. He was pretty famous once upon a time.' Hazel picked up her bag and put her phone in it. She thought for a moment or two, then: 'Hugh?' she said. 'There's something I have to tell you.'

'Oh?'

'Yeah.' She couldn't do it. She couldn't! 'We need lecterns. I forgot to put them on the checklist.'

'That shouldn't be a problem. I can borrow

313

music stands from the school.'

Hazel wrote 'lecterns' on the checklist just so that she could have the pleasure of crossing it off.

'By the way, the gas has been cut off,' Hugh said. 'Dumb-ass me forgot to pay the bill. So book us a table for tonight in O'Toole's while you're there, will you?'

Hazel whimpered inwardly. She didn't much fancy the idea of dining in O'Toole's while her mother and father were at large in the village. 'Don't you fancy Ballynahinch?' she asked.

'There's no way we'd get a table there at this time of the year.'

O'Toole's it was, then. It looked as if her days as a parentless child were numbered.

Hazel checked that her car keys were in her bag, then kissed Hugh goodbye.

How had she allowed this sorry state of affairs to arise? she wondered, as she got into her car and drove the short distance to the village. Why hadn't she been straight with Hugh from the very beginning? Why had she woven this tissue — no, this Bayeux *tapestry* of lies? It all stemmed from being ashamed of her parents. But what was so shameful about having embarrassing parents? At least she *had* parents, unlike poor Hugh, who'd been motherless since boyhood. And from what people had been saying about him, Mondo the aMazing wasn't even that embarrassing. The really, *really* embarrassing thing for her now was that she was going to have to 'fess up: an explanation was way overdue. It had been one of those things that got more and more difficult to do the longer you put it off. She had tried on several occasions, and had even composed a speech in her head, but every time she thought she'd summoned the courage, she'd wimped out again. It was a bit like postponing a visit to the doctor's because you instinctively *know* you have some mortal illness and you don't want to hear the diagnosis; or postponing a visit to the dentist when you know you're simply allowing more rot to set in.

Hazel parked outside the pub and went in, looking around surreptitiously. Mondo was sitting on the banquette by the fireplace with a pint in front of him. He got to his feet when he saw Hazel, and kissed her cheek.

'Hi, Dad,' she said.

'Drink?'

'No, thanks.' She sat down opposite him. 'What's the problem?'

'The problem is,' said Mondo, 'that my feed's let me down. He was meant to be driving down here today, but he's got gout, apparently, and his doctor's prescribed bed rest.'

'What feed?' asked Hazel.

'Jason. The bloke who was going to be feeding me all the answers as the Salmon of Knowledge.'

Yes! Her dad was going to have to take himself back to Dublin! She could relax. 'Oh, dear. What a shame,' she said.

'But all may not be lost!'

Shit.

'You've got a laptop, Hazel, haven't you?'

Why did the question sound so loaded? 'Yes,' she said.

'Could you do it?'

'Could I — you're not asking me to be your feed?'

'Yes. Jason's got all the gear in Dublin, so I was well fucked until I hit on this idea. Look here.' He took a CD case out of a bag. 'I bought a new Encarta CD Rom, hoping I might be able to rope someone local in to help, but then I realized that if I approached a stranger and asked them to do it my credibility as the Salmon of Knowledge would hit the pan.'

'But Dad, everyone'll know there's some trick involved. There's hardly any great mystique about it.'

'You'd be amazed at the number of people who can't work it out,' said Mondo shirtily. 'Especially kids. They're gobsmacked by it.'

'You mean, you've tried it out?'

'Yeah. I've been working the circuit for a couple of weeks now. This is really going to take off for me, Hazel — there hasn't been this much interest in me since the days of *Bunny Brown's Way*. I wish I'd thought of this act ages ago.'

'So — you're actually *enjoying* being the Salmon of Knowledge?' asked Hazel.

'Damn right. It sure as hell beats being a living statue. Word of mouth has spread already — I've gigs lined up for next month — and the kind of publicity I'll get from appearing in the Kilrowan Festival will be invaluable.' Her father's enthusiasm was almost childlike. Hazel couldn't bear it. 'Yup. Things are definitely looking up, Haze. They're re-running *Bunny Brown's Way* on afternoon television, so I'll be due repeat fees

— and the exposure can't be bad for business.'

Oh God. Hazel couldn't let him down.

'I'm not sure I'll be able to help,' she said. 'But run it by me anyway.'

Mondo shot her an aggrieved look. 'I told you all about it in the pub, that day in Galway. Weren't you listening?'

'Yes,' lied Hazel. 'I just need reminding.'

'Well,' said Mondo, bobbing up and down on the banquette and rubbing his hands together. 'This is how it works. It's cunning, but it's surprisingly simple. We have a two-way radio link-up, right? I can hear you through the ear-piece that's concealed in the salmon's head, and you can hear me — and, of course, the person asking the question — through your cans. Once you hear the question you search for the answer on Encarta and relay it to me.'

Hazel wasn't convinced. 'Doesn't that take forever?'

'No. It's surprisingly fast. And if you have to prolong the search, I improvise a rap.'

'A rap?'

'Yeah. For instance, someone asked me recently for the date of Napoleon's death. When Jason performed the search he discovered that there were actually three Napoleons, so I came up with something like: 'Nappy's death date? Let me see. Would that be Napoleon one, two or three?''

Oh, God. 'What was the answer?'

' "We bade the bould Nappy Auld Lang Syne, in seventeen hundred and sixty-nine."'

'Oh-*kay*. And what happens if someone asks a

317

question so obscure that Encarta can't come up with the answer?' Hazel was longing to find a spanner that she could jam in the works.

'Encarta knows everything,' said Mondo, avoiding her eyes.

'Angel Phish?'

'OK. Maybe not,' he conceded. 'But the success rate is so impressive that people don't begrudge the occasional glitch. The bottom line is that nobody's asked for their money back yet.'

'Do you charge by the question?'

'No, no. I have a booking fee. But I'm not going to make any money on this gig. I'm donating my services for free because I want the festival to do well for you, Hazel. Now. Will you help me out or not?'

Hazel knew she had no alternative. She bit her lip, then: 'OK. I'll do it,' she said.

'Thanks Haze, you're a star!' If her dad had had a tail he would have wagged it. 'Where are you staying?' he added. 'We'll have to get some practice in.'

'I'm staying with the guy who runs the festival.'

'OK,' said Mondo. 'Tell me how to get there and I'll call over this evening.'

'No! No — I'm going out this evening. I'll phone you and we can arrange to meet up somewhere tomorrow.'

'That only gives us one day to rehearse.'

'Dad, I'll only be able to spare you a few hours. I'm meant to be organizing this festival, remember?'

'Sure, you must have most of the organization

318

done by now, haven't you?'

'Yes, but I have to stick around in case there are problems, and to meet and greet people. There'll be celebs rolling into town over the next few days.'

Mondo gave her an admiring look. 'Who would ever have thought that my little girl would be hobnobbing with celebrities? Oh, one other thing, Hazel — do you think you might persuade the film crew that's doing the documentary to include me in some of their footage? That'll give the auld Salmon of Knowledge a bit of street cred. People will be queuing up to book the act!'

'I'll see what I can do.'

'That's my girl!' said Mondo, patting her hand. 'I knew I could rely on you to help me out, Hazel. A father and daughter double act, wha'? Isn't it funny how things turn out?'

'Yeah.'

It *was* funny: not so long ago Hazel would have ridiculed the idea of her ever colluding with Mondo on one of his cracked schemes. But it was even funnier, Hazel thought, that when it came to her parents she sometimes felt so much more like a mother than a daughter.

★ ★ ★

Pixie was looking ravishingly pretty, thought Cleo, as they strolled down the main street of Kilrowan towards O'Toole's pub and restaurant. She was so used to seeing her in the pyjamas she wore when she was working that it was almost surprising to see her looking borderline glam in a little pleated chiffon dress and silver sandals.

'I know it's only O'Toole's,' said Pixie, 'but I always dress up on my birthday.'

'You look fab,' said Cleo.

'And so does the village,' remarked Pixie.

The village was indeed looking its prettiest, with fairy lights strung out all along the main street and bright bunting festooning every lamppost. A banner outside the village hall proclaimed THE KILROWAN FESTIVAL — THE WARMEST WELCOME IN THE WESTERN WORLD!

'There's going to be a fireworks display tomorrow,' said Cleo, 'to announce the official opening. It's funny. The last time there was to be a fireworks display here, it didn't happen.'

'Why not?'

'It was to be on the night of the wrap party of *Mimi's Remedies*. But that day the accident happened that killed Eva Lavery.'

'Oh, God. How horrid. Did you ever meet her?'

'Yes. I was in the film, as an extra.'

'I loved that film. Eva certainly earned her posthumous Oscar. Would I have noticed you in it?'

'You might have. I played one of Mimi's Minxes.'

'Really? I must get it on DVD and have a look for you.'

'Why don't you come to the screening in the village hall next week of *The O'Malley*? Eva's in that, too.'

'*The O'Malley?*'

'Yes. Haven't you heard of it? It's the seafaring

blockbuster that was made in Galway some time in the nineties. It's about Grace O'Malley — the famous Irish Pirate Queen. Eva played Grace, and Rory McDonagh was in it. That's what made Hazel come up with the idea of a screening for the festival, with Rory as the main attraction.'

They walked through the door of O'Toole's, the very first diners to arrive.

'Hello, Marie,' said Pixie to the waitress who greeted them. 'Did you manage to secure the window table for me?'

'I did,' said Marie. 'It's all yours.'

'Hurrah! Thank you.'

They moved across to the window and sat down. Every single table in the restaurant had a 'Reserved' sign on it.

'I love this table,' said Pixie. 'I could sit here for hours watching people. I'm going to resist the temptation to take my notebook out, though. I'm off duty this evening.'

The street outside was crowded. Two tour buses had just parked outside Shanley's shop and were disgorging tourists. 'Put him in your next book,' said Cleo, indicating a poser wearing designer shades who was sitting on the sea wall, taking pictures of himself with his phone. 'And make him fall off the wall.'

Marie approached with menus.

'Thanks,' said Pixie. 'I've actually put her in a book,' she added in an undertone as the waitress retreated, 'because she has mysterious eyes. Oh, goodie! They have scallops as the special.'

'I'm glad we're eating early.' Cleo opened her menu and scanned it. 'It's going to be manic here later. Do you always go to bed before eleven, Pixie?'

'I do try to. I like to get my eight hours' worth.'

'So you're up every day at seven?'

Pixie nodded. 'I'm boringly disciplined.'

Cleo remembered how *undisciplined* Pablo had been about his work — unless he had made an appointment with someone to sit for him. She remembered how he would come to bed in the early hours of the morning, smelling of linseed oil and wine, and how he would often wake her to make love to her, and she wondered if he really had changed. She thought of the painting propped against the wall in Hugh Hennessy's house, and conjectured how much it had cost him in terms of blood and sweat and tears, and then she recalled the words of the letter he'd written her. *I have been in hell.* Well, so had she. *I have been a complete shit and an utter imbecile.* You said it.

And as Cleo perused the menu, she wondered how much money would be raised at the auction next Friday for Safe-Home Ireland.

Then she banished all thoughts of Pablo to the place in her mind where she kept a lid on things, and reached for the wine list. 'Let's have champagne, Pixie, to celebrate,' she said brightly. 'My treat!'

'Good idea,' said Pixie. 'There's lots to celebrate, really, isn't there, aside from my birthday? I'm celebrating finishing my book and I'm celebrating being here in Kilrowan at festival time.'

'That reminds me,' said Cleo, 'I left your present across the road in the shop. Will you order for me while I run across and get it? I'll have the stuffed mussels to start, and the pan-fried sole.'

'Certainly,' said Pixie.

Cleo got to her feet and went back out through the door.

Across the road, her shop bell went ping! as she undid the locks and went through. She loved her shop at this hour of the day, when it was full of evening sun — the warmth seemed to intensify the gorgeous, booky smell of the place. She fetched Pixie's gift-wrapped present from the back room, then remembered that she hadn't written a card.

Cleo had recently come across a range called 'Quotable Cards'. On the front each bore a pronouncement made by some legend. Which was the most appropriate for Pixie? wondered Cleo, riffling though the assortment. Pixie was a fighter. How about this, then, from Winston Churchill? *Never, never, never give up.* Or this, from Thoreau? *Go confidently in the direction of your dreams! Live the life you've imagined.* Or the following, from Eleanor Roosevelt? *Do the thing you think you cannot do.*

All of these were spot on for Pixie, but she knew there was one that was just perfect. Aha! She'd got it. It was a quote from Lewis Carroll's *Through the Looking-Glass*, and it went like this: *Sometimes I've believed as many as six impossible things before breakfast.*

Cleo opened the card and wrote: 'Happy

323

birthday to a very dear neighbour. I shall miss you loads. Love, Cleo XXX'. Then she put it in an envelope and sellotaped it to the gift wrap.

Back in the restaurant, the waitress had set an ice-bucket on the table and champagne flutes were at the ready.

'Cheers,' said Cleo, as the bottle popped and fizz was poured. 'And happy birthday!' She handed Pixie the parcel and raised her glass in a toast.

'Cheers!' said Pixie, mirroring the gesture. 'Honestly, you shouldn't have gone to the expense of a present as well as champagne, Cleo. But thank you very much. It's very generous of you.' She opened the envelope first. 'It's from my favourite book ever!' she said when she read the quote. 'And what a *fantastic* travel book! It's made me go all wanderlusty. *The Dreamiest Destinations in the World*! Look — there's a whole section about Best Beaches. Heavens! Get a load of Pulinkudi Beach. And Ansa Patates. And — look, there's Lissnakeelagh! Oh, Cleo, this book is just crammed with escapes!'

'I thought you'd like it.'

'*Where* exactly is that reef?' exclaimed Pixie, gazing at the jacket. 'Take me there now, if you please!'

And Cleo wondered, not for the first time, about the astonishing appeal that books like this held for the reading public. Was it because they brought back memories of past holidays, or was it because they inspired in the reader a yearning to run away from it all? She and Pablo had shared some amazing escapes in their camper van once upon a time. She recalled now a particularly tender moment on a beach in Capri . . .

The sound of laughter came from an alcove on the other side of the partition that divided the restaurant.

'Oh,' said Cleo, 'I thought we were the only people here.'

'Some people came in while you were in the shop,' said Pixie. 'A woman and two men. One of them looked awfully familiar.'

'Locals?'

'No. I wouldn't have thought so.'

'Celebrities, probably,' said Cleo. 'It's amazing how blasé I've got about them since I came to live here.'

'One of them was terribly distinguished looking, with amazing cheekbones.' Pixie put her head on one side, thinking. 'If I put him in a book, I'd call him 'Byronic'. Oh — here come Hugh and Hazel.'

Through the window Cleo could see the pair walking towards the restaurant, hand in hand. 'Did you know they'd hooked up together?' Cleo asked Pixie.

'No! How romantic! He's so very — '

'Sh!'

The door opened and the glamorous-looking couple walked through.

'Hi, Hugh, Hazel!' chimed Pixie and Cleo.

'Hi,' said Hugh. 'Hey! Champagne? What are you celebrating?'

'It's my birthday,' said Pixie. 'Please join us for a glass.' She raised a hand at the waitress. 'Could we have two more champagne flutes, please?' she said.

'Well, thank you — and happy birthday,' said Hugh, dropping a kiss on Pixie's cheek.

'Happy birthday,' echoed Hazel, sitting down beside Cleo. She glanced at the travel book. 'An escape book. And a seriously glossy one!'

'It's a present from Cleo,' said Pixie.

'D'you mind if I take a look?'

'Be my guest.'

Hazel opened the book at random and flicked through a few pages. 'Jamaica,' she said. 'Oh, doesn't it make you so want to *be* there? Oh, those *beaches* . . . '

The glasses arrived. Hugh and Hazel raised theirs to Pixie and toasted her birthday, and then Cleo said: 'Both your parents were in my shop earlier today, Hazel. I never knew your dad was Mondo the aMazing — I used to be such a big fan of his. And as for being babysat by Paula Yates! *That* must have been something else.'

Hazel's phone had started to ring in her bag. She lunged for it, extracted the phone, checked the display, then said in a rather strangled voice: 'I'll take this outside. Excuse me.' She made for the door, looking, Cleo thought, rather distraught.

Hugh was looking at Cleo with a most peculiar expression. 'What did you say about Mondo the aMazing?' he asked.

'He's Hazel's dad,' explained Cleo. 'He came into my shop today and bought an Encarta encyclopaedia, and Hazel's mum bought a book by Paula Yates. They used to hang out together years ago, apparently.'

'Sorry — you're telling me that Hazel's father is Mondo the aMazing?'

'Yes. Didn't you know? And her mother is the front woman of that band with the truly awful name.'

'Angel Phish?' said Hugh woodenly.

'That's the one. And look — there they both are now.'

Mondo and Angel were standing outside the restaurant, chatting. Mondo gave Hazel a jaunty wave as she fled past them to the other side of the street and Angel made to follow her. But before she did, Cleo saw her clock Hugh through the restaurant window. The rock chick mouthed 'Hello, you!', blew a surreptitiously sexy kiss at him, then turned away with a twitch of the hip that made her ra-ra skirt flounce.

What was going on?

*   *   *

Some social diarist had been gibbering in her ear as Hazel watched Angel blow a kiss at Hugh through the window of O'Toole's restaurant, and she knew instantly from the cat-who'd-got-the-cream expression on her mother's face that she'd slept with him. She depressed 'end call' while the social diarist was in full flow, and stood stock still on the main street of Kilrowan feeling as if she'd been punched in the face.

'Come with me,' said Angel, cosily linking Hazel's arm. 'I've a confession to make!'

Oh God, oh God, oh God. Hazel knew with

an awful sense of premonition what was coming. She felt like wrenching her arm away from her mother's and taking off like a Greek heroine tormented by the Furies. But she could hardly go back into O'Toole's and face up to Hugh. A rock and a hard place had nothing on this: this was her very own Scylla and Charybdis. She stumbled on in dread anticipation of her mother's next words, wishing that she'd never heard of Kilrowan. Its very picturesqueness was anathema now: the boats with their cheerful blue and red paintwork bobbing away in the harbour seemed to mock her, the bright bunting fluttered festively in flagrant disregard of her predicament.

Beside her her mother was humming one of her jazzier compositions and snapping her fingers in time to the rhythm. How grimly ironic that the epic sound track accompanying this moment of high drama in Hazel's life should be the click click click of her mother's fingers as she shoo bap doo wapped along. Oh, for God's sake, Angel! Bring it on! Bring on the cathartic denouement for all our sakes. Let that sword of Damocles drop!

Hazel stopped dead abruptly, if only to put an end to the intolerable racket. She turned to face her mother, and in the ensuing silence she heard her own voice say: 'You've slept with him, haven't you?'

'What?'

'You've slept with Hugh Hennessy.'

Angel looked guilty, and rather taken aback. 'Oh. Well, that wasn't exactly what I intended to share with you. But, yes. I have.'

'Oh, God.'

'Sorry. Too much information?'

'No. You can't give me too much information because I know it all already.'

'What? What are you talking about? How could you know?'

'I've slept with him too.'

Angel unlinked her arm from Hazel's and stood regarding her with an expression of stark shock. There was silence for several moments, and then Angel said: 'You told me you didn't fancy him.'

'I lied.'

'Oh. Shit. How long have you been seeing each other?'

'Three weeks. You?'

Her mother bit her lip. 'I went to bed with him ages ago,' she said in a small voice. 'It was strictly a one-night stand, Hazel. I'm not terribly proud of it, and I haven't slept with him since. We've been kind of pretending it didn't happen.'

Hazel couldn't help herself. '*How* did it happen?'

Angel was looking stricken now. 'I was in Galway, spending the weekend with some friends, and I ran into him in the Great Southern Hotel. He was a bit pissed, made a pass. We ended up in bed.'

'Did you spend the night together?'

'No. It was strictly a one-off.' Her tone implored Hazel to forgive her. 'You've got to believe that.'

'I do believe you, Mum. But it doesn't make the situation any less excruciating. This is — oh,

God — this is just *grim!*'

It *was* grim. Nothing could get much grimmer than a mother and daughter bedding the same man except — agh! What was *almost* grimmer was that she, Hazel MacNamara, now found herself crying in public. A hot tear had dropped onto the back of her hand.

'Darling, if I'd known you fancied him, I wouldn't have gone near him,' protested Angel. 'You don't think I'd hijack my own daughter's love interest, do you? What kind of a mother do you think I am?'

An embarrassing kind, thought Hazel. Christ, how stupid had she been? Her feelings of embarrassment for her parents had made her concoct a convoluted cat's cradle of lies and omissions that had messed up her life. She'd pinioned herself with lies, lies, and more damned lies. She'd orchestrated her own fall from grace, and she had only herself to blame.

'There, there,' said Angel, taking her in her arms and rocking her. Hazel allowed herself to be rocked for a little while, to be crooned to. She even found herself taking a strange kind of comfort in the unfamiliar confines of her mother's embrace until she became aware that they were attracting some unwelcome attention. Around them, tourists were clearly intrigued by the spectacle of the sussed-looking city girl in her crisp white linen ensemble weeping openly in the arms of an ageing miniskirted glamour puss. 'There, there,' soothed Angel again. 'There, there. Cry all you like.'

Cry all she *liked!* But she didn't like crying.

Hazel MacNamara *never* cried! She was the only person she knew who hadn't cried at *Casablanca*, she was the only person she knew who hadn't cried when George Dubya had been re-elected, and she'd actually thought that Erin had been having her on when she'd told her that copious teenage tears were being shed over Bryan McFadden's defection from Westlife.

Hazel finally, firmly told herself to wise up. She took the tissue her mother offered her and dried her eyes, blew her nose. She felt calmer now, more in control. It was time to make decisions, because decisions were what she was good at. Shit — decisions were what she was paid for!

This was what she was going to do. She was going to phone Renée her assistant and tell her to get her ass down to Kilrowan ASAP to tie up any loose PR ends that needed tying. She was going to phone her dad and say sorry, but she couldn't be his feed for the Salmon of Knowledge gig after all. She was going ask Renée to pick up her stupid designer threads from Hugh's house since she, Hazel, would be unable to. Because Hazel MacNamara of Nutcracker PR had been afflicted by a mysterious virus, and was going back to Dublin. Right now.

16

Back in O'Toole's, Cleo and Pixie hadn't dared speculate on what might be going on between Hugh and Hazel and Hazel's mother, but there was clearly scandal in the air. Hugh had left the restaurant on some pretext, leaving his champagne untouched.

Cleo toyed with her starter, feeling a bit subdued now. Pixie would be gone from Kilrowan soon and she'd really miss her. She hadn't done much socializing with her because the writer worked so extremely hard, but it was nice to know that there was someone right next door who'd be there for her when she needed support or advice, or just to share a glass of wine or a cup of 'cha' with.

At a nearby table, a family of four were dining. The teenage daughter had just come back from the loo in a state of high excitement.

'Guess who's at the table round the corner?' Cleo heard her say in a stage whisper. 'Rory McDonagh!'

A succession of 'oohs' and 'wows' ensued.

'So *that's* who I saw come in earlier,' said Pixie. 'Rory McDonagh! I knew the face was familiar, but I just couldn't place it. Why don't you go and say hello?'

'I don't know if he'd remember me. I only met him once.'

'Nip to the loo and see if he shows any sign of

recognition as you go past.'

'Good idea!'

Cleo rose to her feet and prinked herself a little before heading in the direction of the loo. As she turned the corner, she stopped dead. There was her mate Deirdre O'Dare sitting at a table in an alcove with Rory and another man whom she recognized as the renowned theatre director, David Lawless.

'Deirdre!' said Cleo. 'Hey!'

'Cleo!' Deirdre jumped up, and the pair embraced with glee. 'How great to see you!'

'You evil person! Why didn't you let me know you were coming to Kilrowan?'

'I didn't know myself that I was coming until yesterday,' Deirdre told her. 'Mum volunteered to take the kids, so I dumped them in Wicklow and headed westward ho, ho, ho.'

'You look fantastic.'

'*You* look fantastic. Here — let me perform introductions. You've met Rory, of course — ' Deirdre's delectable husband took her hand and kissed it, and Cleo tried not to swoon — 'and you may remember David Lawless? He spent some time in Kilrowan when *Mimi's Remedies* was being made.'

'Of course I remember,' said Cleo. It would be hard to forget David Lawless. He was the widower of screen luminary Eva Lavery, and was obviously the man whom Pixie had described earlier as being 'Byronic'.

'Will you join us?' asked Deirdre.

'I'd love to, but I'm here with a friend. It's her birthday.'

333

'Ask her to join us for a birthday drink, then. Who is she?'

'She's Pixie Pirelli.'

'Pixie Pirelli, the writer Pixie Pirelli?' asked Deirdre.

Rory gave his wife a 'doh!' look. 'I can't imagine there's another person on the planet with *that* moniker, darling,' he said.

'Go get her!' said Deirdre. 'I'd love to meet her.'

So Cleo shimmied back round the corner to where Pixie was sitting. 'It *is* Rory!' she said. 'And my friend Deirdre's with him, and David Lawless.'

'David Lawless? The director?'

'Yes. Come and meet them. They've asked us to join them.'

Pixie looked a bit doubtful. 'But he's frightfully intellectual, isn't he, David Lawless? He directs Pinter and stuff. I'm sure he doesn't want to meet a bird-brained chick-lit writer like me.'

'I don't really know him,' said Cleo. 'But Rory and Deirdre are great fun. You'll love them!'

It wasn't really fair of her, she knew, to drag Pixie away from the birthday *dîner-à-deux* that she'd been kind enough to invite her to, and introduce her to new people. She hated it when people said things like 'Oh, So-and-So are great fun,' because you just might infer from that that you *weren't* great fun. But things had taken a bit of a downturn since the weird Hugh/Hazel incident, and it was time to kick-start the evening again. It was only eight o'clock, and even

Pixie couldn't possibly want to go home *this* early.

'OK, then,' said Pixie. 'But will I have to pretend I know about Pinter? I haven't read *The Bluffer's Guide to the Theatre.*'

'Bollix, no. And I *have* read it, so I can waffle about 'resting' and 'the green room' for both of us. Marie,' she said to the waitress, 'we're going to join some people at the table round the corner, if that's OK? Can you organize more place settings?'

'Sure,' said Marie of the mysterious eyes, taking up the ice-bucket and transporting it round the corner. Cleo and Pixie followed her.

'This,' said Cleo, effecting introductions, 'is Pixie Pirelli. Pixie, this is Deirdre O'Dare and Rory McDonagh. And this is David Lawless.'

'How do you do?' said David, and Deirdre and Rory said: 'Nice to meet you,' and then everyone was making room and small talk, and new places were being set at the table for them by Marie, and dishes were arriving.

'What do you write — er — Pixie?' asked David Lawless politely, as Pixie settled herself in the seat next to him in a wift of chiffon looking, Cleo thought, rather like a character out of one of her own books.

'I write fairytales,' Pixie replied, 'for grown-ups.'

'Fairytales for grown-ups?' said David, sounding baffled. 'I see.'

'Thank you, Marie,' said Cleo, as her fish was set in front of her. She'd forgotten to ask for the head and tail to be removed. The way its one eye looked reproachfully up at her from the plate made her feel a bit uncomfortable.

'I hate it when Rory orders lobster.' Deirdre nodded towards the enormous two-pounder on the plate in front of her husband. 'He digs out every last shred of flesh, and it takes him for ever to eat.'

An image flashed across Cleo's mind's eye of Pablo sitting across from her at this very table, dipping the choicest morsel from a lobster claw into melted butter and feeding it to her with his fingers. She'd put it into one of her erotic short stories and then taken it out again because it would have meant cooking lobster at home, and she couldn't bear the idea of putting a living creature into boiling water. Pablo had laughed and — oh! Go away, Pablo, just go! And Cleo picked up her knife and fork, feeling bereft.

At that very moment they were all distracted by a deafening crash. Marie, who had been pouring wine for them, rolled her mysterious eyes heavenward and headed for the kitchen.

'Is Robert still the chef here?' asked Deirdre.

'Yes,' said Cleo. 'And he's as accident prone as ever.'

Deirdre smiled. 'How is everyone in Kilrowan? I think about this place a lot when I'm trailing along highways in LA.'

'There's a real buzzy vibe around at the moment because of the festival, of course,' Cleo told her. 'Hazel's roped in a fair few celebrities.'

'Oh? Who?'

'Well, Pixie's giving a talk in the library on Monday evening, and Colleen's short story competition has been attracting quite a lot of media attention, and there are some brilliant musicians gigging for free.'

'Excellent. There'll be a load of trad sessions going on then, will there?' asked Rory.

'Yup. We've got Sharon Shannon and Donal Lunny and Zoe Conway. And a band called Angel Phish.'

Deirdre and Rory looked blank.

'It's a comeback gig for a band that used to be called the Fazes — '

'Not the band that was fronted by Angel Kestrel?' Rory asked.

'The very one.'

'Whoa. I remember her. She was a sexy chick, way back. But she must be ancient now.'

'She is,' said Cleo. 'It's a bit sad, really. Incidentally, Rory — Hazel managed to get a big cardboard cut-out figure of you in full pirate regalia to put outside the village hall, to advertise the screening of *The O'Malley*.'

'How profoundly embarrassing,' said Rory. 'I imagine it'll be vandalized before too long.'

'I'll put in the snot and the pimples,' volunteered Deirdre.

'Jejune as ever, my love.'

'Hey,' said Cleo. 'At this rate we could have a convention of cardboard cut-outs in Kilrowan. Rory's cut-out could get together with Pixie's and Colleen's!'

'Speaking of whom,' said Deirdre, 'we took a stroll on Lissnakeelagh earlier and saw her communing with nature. Striding through the dunes with her hair streeling out behind her. Is

337

she still as batty as ever?'

'She's very possibly battier.'

'Is she still holed up with your sister?'

'Oh, sweetheart,' said Rory with a wince. 'That was a rather unfortunate turn of phrase.'

'Why?' queried David.

'Don't ask,' said Deirdre.

★ ★ ★

Pixie was feeling nicely relaxed. She watched with amusement as a teenage fan approached Rory with a paper napkin for him to sign. He obliged with very good grace.

Her birthday was turning out to be quite an occasion. More wine had been ordered, and a cake had appeared, and the whole restaurant had joined in the singing of 'Happy Birthday to You', and she was just so *happy* that her book was finished and that she was wearing silk chiffon and silver sandals and sitting in the company of a major movie star! Hurrah!

She'd expected to have one of the quietest birthdays of her life today, and had actually been quite looking forward to taking it easy. Her last birthday had coincided with the launch of a volume of her short stories, and it had been something of a circus, with media rampant and Pixie on display in her satin and tat. She'd been required to pose sitting on a big pile of her books with a quill in her hand. A *quill*, for goodness sake! How anachronistic was that? There was no way she could produce a book a year if she used a quill and ink!

Lots of her friends had turned up to that birthday/launch party, and lots of her enemies too — including, she thought now, a little sourly, Dominique Masterson, who had just celebrated the publication of her last chick-lit novel, *False Friends*. *False Friends* . . . How apt!

Pixie was feeling a little muzzy with wine. She rarely allowed herself to over-indulge: she didn't like the way it compromised her self-control and made her lips go all tingly. But Rory had been pouring with a liberal hand and the atmosphere in the restaurant was so festive this evening that Pixie thought she might allow herself to let her hair down for once, and celebrate.

Rory was being seriously chatted up by the teenage fan. It was funny, Pixie thought, that Deirdre didn't seem to mind, but then she supposed that their relationship might be that rare thing — one based on absolute mutual trust. How terribly sad for Cleo and Pablo that they hadn't applied the same principle to their marriage . . .

The other two women were confabbing now, and Pixie heard Pablo's name mentioned. She couldn't — wouldn't — become part of a relationships analysis session when the rather scary Mr Lawless was sitting with no-one to talk to. She should really make an effort to strike up a conversation with him.

'What brings you to Kilrowan, David?' she asked, as an opening gambit.

'I'm on a sentimental journey,' he said.

'Are you from these parts?'

'No. I — I scattered my wife's ashes on

Lissnakeelagh strand last year, and when Rory told me he was going to be making an appearance at the festival here I decided to come back and revisit.'

Goodness! What an appalling gaffe. 'Oh, dear — I'm so terribly sorry,' said Pixie.

'You weren't to know.'

She felt a silence begin to dangle. 'Lissnakeelagh's such a beautiful name,' she felt inspired to say. Well, that was an utterance worthy of a bona fide bird-brained purveyor of chick-lit!

'Do you know what it means?'

'It has a meaning?'

'Oh, yes. Lissnakeelagh strand is 'the beach near the wooded fort'.'

'So there were defences there once?'

'There's no archaeological evidence to back that up. The reference is more than likely to a fairy fort.'

'A fairy fort? How lovely!'

'All Irish place names have a meaning, but a lot of compromising went on when they were translated into English. There's a play about it by Brian Friel. *Translations*. Do you know it?'

'No,' said Pixie, feeling even more inadequate.

'It's set in Donegal in the early eighteen-hundreds. One of the characters is an interpreter. He has a line that goes: 'My job is to translate the quaint, archaic tongue you people persist in speaking into the King's good English.''

'Goodness! Are you serious?'

'Yes. The Irish language is incredibly rich and ornate, and if the Brits couldn't come up with an English equivalent for a place name, the Irish pronunciation was simply anglicized. The play is set in the town of Baile Beag which in English becomes plain old Ballybeg. It doesn't have the same ring to it, somehow.'

The way he pronounced the word — 'Bawlya-baig' — sounded beautiful.

'It certainly doesn't. So we English took over not just the country but the language as well?'

'Yes. To this day Irish isn't recognized as an official European language.'

'That's shocking!'

'Yes, it is. The British considered the Irish to be savages, you see, when in fact the Irish peasantry was probably better educated than the English. They set great store by book learning, and many of them spoke fluent Greek and Latin.'

'How fascinating. Perhaps I should take a Linguaphone course in Irish. I hear them talking it in the local shop sometimes. It sounds beautiful.'

'It's not easy to learn.'

'I'm sure. But I have a facility for picking up languages.'

'Oh? What's the last one you learned?'

'Cockney rhyming slang.'

'Ah.'

Pixie took a sip of wine, sensing that another conversational kick-start was called for. 'What are you directing at the moment?'

'Chekhov's *The Seagull*.'

341

Yikes! 'In London?'

'Yes.'

'I must go and see it when I'm back there.'

'Let me have your address and I'll put you on the invitation list for the opening night.'

Well! Maybe going back to London might not be so grim after all, thought Pixie. She'd had a taste of being sociable this evening, and it had reminded her that before the Jonah débâcle she'd actually quite *enjoyed* being sociable. While in Kilrowan she'd been missing out on all the theatre and art exhibitions and dining out that she'd used to do in London. O'Toole's was all very well and cosy and friendly, but just occasionally she yearned for the opulence of a top class restaurant like the Criterion or the River Restaurant at the Savoy, and the company of people who understood how very lonely the life of a writer could be.

Across the table, Rory's fan had finally relinquished him, and he turned back to the company. Seeing that Cleo and Deirdre were still sharing secrets, he turned the beam of his attention on Pixie.

Heavens above! She found it perfectly understandable now how his fan was so smitten. Full-on, Rory McDonagh was utterly, diabolically, and quite unashamedly sexy. No wonder one of his co-stars had once let slip in a television interview that he'd spoiled her for any other man.

He smiled at her, exuding what could only be described as a 'roguish' charm. 'Tell me. If my wife were to adapt one of your novels into a screenplay,' he said, 'might there be a part for me in it?'

'Oh, yes.'

'Which book would you recommend?'

'I suggest you read them all and find out for yourself,' she said.

'Read chick-lit? A macho yoke like me? Are you mad?'

Pixie shrugged. 'You can't dismiss any kind of literature out of hand until you've sampled it. I forced myself to read some crime fiction when I started writing, but had to call a halt after forensic details of the third murder of a child by a convicted paedophile made me vomit. I trust that none of my books have such an emetic effect on people.' Apart from Dominique Masterson, of course, she thought wryly.

'Point taken,' said Rory. 'I forced myself to read something called *False Friends* recently, by a dame called Dominique Masterson, because my agent thought I might be interested in playing the male lead. It didn't make me vomit, but maybe that's because I didn't read enough of it.'

'Did you turn the part down?'

'Damn right,' said Rory.

Pixie smiled.

'I've heard that some men read chick-lit to learn more about the female psyche,' said David.

'I'm not sure I'd want to know too much more about the unfairly fair sex. Look at those two witches — ' Rory indicated Deirdre and Cleo — 'hatching some unspeakable plot.' He helped himself to more wine and took a gulp, looking at Pixie over the rim of his glass with eyes that were shockingly green. Then he set the glass down. 'Talking about sex,' he said, 'is there much of it in your books?'

'Yes,' said Pixie.

'Is it any good?'

'I'm reliably told,' said Pixie, 'that my sex scenes should be prescribed reading for men.'

'Interesting. Is that 'prescribed' with an 'e' or 'proscribed' with an 'o'?'

' 'Prescribed' with an 'e', of course,' she said with hauteur.

'In that case, I must request Deirdre to buy some of your canon.'

'I wouldn't describe myself as having a 'canon'. Only literary heavyweights like Colleen have a 'canon'.'

'Don't underestimate yourself. I wouldn't touch one of Colleen's books with a barge pole. But I'll definitely skim through yours for the sex, if nothing else.' He gave her a contemplative look. 'It's about time I played a role that had some decent sex scenes. In the last flick I made, the heroine died before I had a chance to ride her.'

Pixie was shocked. 'In real life?'

'God, no. In makey-uppy-land. But it's amazing how the parameters overlap, sometimes. I'm sure you find that in your line of work.' He gave her a lethal smile. 'I sometimes can't believe that I get paid so much for vicariously riding other men's women.' He picked up the wine bottle and made to refill glasses, but both Pixie and David put their hands over theirs.

'Not for me, thank you,' she said. 'I've had enough.'

'Goodness. What remarkable restraint you show. My wife could take a leaf out of one of your books — metaphorically as well as literally. She swigs back the stuff. Are you sure?'

'Absolutely.'

'David?'

'No, thanks, Rory,' David said, with a glance at his watch. 'I want to get back to the hotel and go over my notes. There's a technical rehearsal on Tuesday, and I'll need to have my wits about me. And if I have any more to drink I'll be over the limit.'

Pixie thought there was something a little mournful about David's demeanour as he got to his feet and extracted car keys from his pocket. She wished more than ever that her opening gambit had been a little more tactful.

'Good night, David,' said Rory.

'Good night, Rory. I'll see you tomorrow. Say good night to Deirdre from me, will you? I don't want to bother her while she's in full-flight girl-chat mode. Good night, Pixie. It was nice to meet you.'

'Likewise.'

He didn't say anything more about the theatre tickets he'd promised her, and Pixie felt a little disappointed. She was too shy to remind him, however, or to ask for his telephone number. She watched him as he moved to the door, resisting the impulse to take her notebook out. He really was awfully Byronic.

When she returned her attention to the table she realized that Rory had been studying her. There was something very knowing about his smile. 'Smitten?' he asked, raising an eyebrow.

'No,' she said, carelessly. But I might put him in a book some time.'

'So you could fuck him vicariously?'

Pixie had to laugh. 'Goodness gracious! You, Rory McDonagh, are quite one of the most outrageous men I have ever met.'

'Then you must know a lot of very boring people.'

'Touché.'

'I'm fascinated by this chick-lit lark,' he continued. 'Do you really enjoy writing it?'

'Yes. I'm a consummate escape artist, and I've found that the best way for me to escape is through writing. I like to think my novels help the reader to escape, too.'

'Escape?' said Rory, leaning back in his chair and regarding her with interest. 'That just happens to be one of my favourite words.'

'Oh? How do *you* escape?'

'I spend time in the desert, howling at the moon. Wearing nothing but Calvin Klein's Escape for men.'

She drained the small amount of wine that was left in her glass, then leaned her elbows on the table and smiled at him. 'I'm intrigued. Which desert do you go to?'

'The Mojave. The bit about wearing Calvin Klein's Escape was a joke, incidentally.'

'I thought it might be. How do you get there?'

'On my classic Norton motorbike.'

'In that case,' said Pixie, 'I think I shall have to put *you* in a book.'

He smiled at her. 'Be my guest,' he said, taking up the bottle and sticking it upside-down in the ice-bucket. 'Marie, darlin'?' he called, pointing at the bottle. 'Can you bring another one of these?'

'Right away, Mr McDonagh,' said Marie, whose mysterious eyes were suddenly looking very animated.

He turned back to Pixie and regarded her with interest. 'Have you ever tried to write a film treatment of any of your books?' he asked.

'Yes. Without much success. I don't really know much about film-making.'

'I meant it about showing Deirdre your stuff. She'll know at once if it has cinematic potential.'

'Well . . . If it's not too much trouble?'

'Not at all. We're both in the market for new vehicles — we've set up our own production company. You might be doing us — and yourself — a favour. Everyone's looking for the new Bridget Jones, but she's proving pretty damn elusive. There's plenty of dross out there, but not much 22 carat stuff. Deirdre says the problem is that no-one's writing from the heart any more. Everyone's writing to formula.'

'She could be right. It's a long time since I've seen a film that made me laugh *and* cry. Everything nowadays is so slick with production values that I feel rather joyless every time I leave a cinema.'

'Joyless,' he repeated. 'Good word. Why do you think that is?'

'I don't like feeling that I've been manipulated.'

Rory gave her a look of assessment. Then: 'Tell me this,' he said. 'How involved with your characters do you get when you write?'

'Very. I laugh with them, and I cry with them.'

'Do you dream about them?'

Pixie considered. 'Funnily enough, no. I don't.'

'Do you fall in love with your heroes?'

'Yes.'

'How sweet. Tell me something about the hero of your most recent book.'

'What do you want to know?'

'Is he, for instance, tall, dark and handsome?'

'Yes, actually.'

'Does he have a tragic past?'

'Yes. He does.'

'And if you were to describe him using just one word, what would that word be?'

Pixie looked away. She thought for a moment, and then she looked back at Rory's laughing eyes. 'Byronic,' she said.

17

Hazel and Renée passed each other on the Dublin — Galway road, talking on their hands free.

'Are you sure you should be driving, boss?' asked Renée, 'if you're feeling so unwell?'

'I'll be fine,' said Hazel grimly. 'I just need to get back to Dublin and get under the duvet. Feel free to call me if you need any help, Renée, but I'm reasonably certain that everything's under control. Mr Hennessy has a reliable team working for him, and you're well filled in on the PR schedule. Nothing can go wrong. Send your mum my love.'

Renée was killing two birds with one stone by combining the festival with a duty visit. 'Yeah,' she said a little gloomily. 'I'm not much looking forward to being on the periphery of things. I won't be able to join in any of the *craic* because I'll be driving home every night.'

'Look on the bright side,' said Hazel. 'This is fantastic work experience for you. It'll be your first real taste of hands-on PR.'

'I guess.'

Renée was hoping to set up her own consultancy in Galway some day, in order to be closer to her mother. Hazel hadn't a clue how she'd manage without her.

'Good luck, Renée,' she said now.

'Drive safely, boss!'

But Hazel put her foot down a little harder on the accelerator, intent on increasing the distance between herself and Kilrowan as speedily as possible.

She'd texted Hugh to tell him that her assistant would be replacing her as PR co-ordinator. She hadn't wanted to phone in case he picked up. She knew it was terribly unprofessional of her, but she wanted no further contact with him on the Kilrowan case. In fact, she never wanted to see him again.

She had, she knew, been in real danger of falling in love with him. If the — thing — with her mother hadn't happened, she suspected her life might have changed for ever. She'd nursed fantasies — of course she had — of maybe relocating to Galway so that she could commute from Kilrowan. That very convenient scenario had an added attraction since it meant that she might be able to hang on to Renée. She'd pictured Hugh's house as she would revamp it when she moved in with him. She'd visualized them galloping along Lissnakeelagh on two of his most beautiful horses, and having cosy tête-à-têtes in O'Toole's. She'd even — in her most cherished fantasy of all — held their baby in her arms.

But the image that arose before her mind's eye now had superseded all the rosy-tinted ones. It was the hellish image of Hugh in bed with her mother. And what made it worse was that it was all her own fault. If she hadn't lied in the first place, it might never have happened.

Hazel jabbed off the country & western song

that had started to play on the radio. No country & western tragedy could compare to what she'd just been through, no blues song put into words the depth of her humiliation. She remembered how Hugh had remarked on her song *du jour* once, on the morning after they'd first met. It had been 'Don't worry, be happy', and now Hazel found herself wondering if she would ever sing that song again.

★ ★ ★

Pixie was standing thigh deep in waders in the rushy, peat-coloured current of Ballynahinch river. It was early on Sunday morning, and she had grabbed a last opportunity to fish. None of the ghillies were available, but she no longer needed one — she'd learned all she needed to know.

Pixie had been determined to get one last shot at the river before she packed up and left Kilrowan at the end of the week. She was booked on a flight to London on Thursday, and next week was shaping up to be a sociable one. She was attending several festival events (the *Tribunals* show sounded fascinating, and she'd heard great reports about Zoe Conway's fiddle-playing), she was meeting up with Deirdre O'Dare to discuss the viability of her books being turned into a film vehicle for Rory McDonagh, and she had her 'Evening with Pixie Pirelli' tomorrow, at which the subject under discussion was 'How to Get Published'. She would also have farewells to say to all the people who'd been so good to her while she'd been living in Kilrowan. Cleo, of course, and Marie in O'Toole's, and Breda and Michael Shanley in the village shop, and the postmistress who was so chatty it took twenty minutes to buy a stamp for a postcard, and Linda the librarian in the little village library who had lent her myriad books for research purposes. She was going to be far too busy next week to spend a leisurely day on the river.

A leisurely day! She'd better cherish every moment of this sunny Sunday. Leisure would soon be the stuff of hazy memory. Once she was back in London there'd be publicity to do for the mass market edition of *Hard to Choos*, and she'd be run off her Choo-clad feet. Make that Nike-clad. She'd spoken to Camilla, who had efficiently set the publicity treadmill going full speed again.

'Hello, Pixie.'

She turned too quickly and her trusty waders slipped on a smooth rock. Before she knew it Pixie Pirelli had bumped down a little cascade and was sitting in the river up to her neck in rushing water — an expression of outraged surprise on her face — and David Lawless was wading in to help her.

'*Oh*, what an idiot I am!'

'Are you all right?' he asked, taking hold of her upper arm with his right hand and supporting her back with his left.

'I'm fine,' she said, as she struggled to her feet. 'I really am. I'm just *so embarrassed*.'

'I bet,' he said. 'Embarrassment's often worse

352

to contend with than injury, in my experience. Let's get you back on dry land.'

Together they made it back to the riverbank, their progress greatly impeded by the fact that Pixie's waders were now full of water.

'Well, that'll have scared off any trout that were lurking,' she remarked, adding a 'ha ha' at her little joke. She was feeling so unconscionably mortified that she started busying herself with her tackle immediately as a diversionary tactic. But confusion had rendered her clumsy, and under David's amber-eyed scrutiny she found herself reeling in her line so inexpertly that it got caught on some weed.

'Here. Let me help you,' said David. He took the tackle from her, and managed to free the line by dextrous manipulation of the rod.

Pixie nearly said 'You handle that rod beautifully,' but stopped herself just in time, and just said, 'Thank you very much, David.'

'It happens to all of us fly-fishers,' said David.

'You fish, too?'

'Yes. I'm passionate about it. This place — ' he indicated the river and the lake beyond — 'is one of the most beautiful in the world to fish. Swimming, however, is *not* recommended. Presumably you have a change of clothes in the car?'

Feeling even more gauche, Pixie bit her lip. She *should* have a change of clothes, of course she should — getting wet was an occupational hazard of her chosen sport, after all — but: 'Not only do I not have a change of clothes,' she confessed, 'I don't even have a car.'

'How did you get here from Kilrowan, then?' He was looking down at her, head tilted in enquiry. His tallness made her feel even smaller than she usually did.

'I hired the local hackney. He's on his way to the airport now to pick up the fare.'

'So. You're in a dilemma.'

'Yes.'

'But one that's easily resolved.'

'Oh? How?'

'I propose that you come back to my room and get dried off, and then I'll drive you back to the village.'

'I can't allow you to do that!'

'Can you think of another way out?'

She tried to apply the lateral thinking she often brought to bear on her novels, but he was right. She could see no other solution. She'd asked the local cab driver to pick her up much later in the day, and he'd been glad to agree because the airport run would take him ages. She could hardly shamble around waiting for him in Ballynahinch Castle wearing soaking wet clothes.

'You're right,' she said. 'Thank you. But how do I dry off my clothes?'

'You could ask the hotel to do it for you.'

But *that* would involve hanging around David Lawless's hotel room wearing nothing but a courtesy robe while she waited for them to dry, and she couldn't do that. She'd feel far too vulnerable. Oh, Lord! There was a certain irony here. This situation was similar to the dilemma poor Charlotte had been confronted with in

Hard to Choos, when the goats had eaten her clothes. How had Charlotte coped? The answer was: not very well.

David must have sensed her discomfort. 'Or I could lend you something to wear,' he suggested. 'Except you really are very small.'

'And you are exceptionally tall.'

'We'll manage somehow,' he said, with a perfunctory smile. 'The first thing to do is get you out of those waders. Sit down, and let me do it for you.'

Pixie sat down on a grassy tussock.

'You look like Miss Muffet,' said David, kneeling at her feet.

'Miss Muffet?'

'In the nursery rhyme.'

Pixie lifted her right leg so that David could pull off her wader. A gush of water came out, and the same thing happened when he took off the left one.

'I may look like Miss Muffet,' she said. 'But I feel like Wishy Washy.'

'Who's Wishy Washy?'

'In the panto.'

'Of course. It's a long time since I've been to a panto.'

'I go every year,' said Pixie. 'I take a friend's daughter along, but really she's just an excuse for me to go.'

'I ought to take Dorcas this year,' said David, looking thoughtful.

'Who is Dorcas?'

'She's my daughter.'

'What age is she?'

'She's fourteen. And I have a son who's quite a lot older than that.'

'Is fourteen not a little old to be going to the panto? My friend's daughter has just turned twelve and I had to practically beg her to come with me last year. She wanted to go and see Justin Timberlake instead.'

'Dorcas is different,' said David. 'She has a learning disability.'

Oh, you stupid girl! Pixie told herself crossly. That's the second time you've put your foot in it with David Lawless since you met him. 'I'm sorry,' she said.

'There's no need to feel sorry for her. Dorcas has a charmed life, really. She'll be forever young. She still believes in fairies.'

'That's funny,' said Pixie. 'So do I.'

★   ★   ★

David made himself scarce downstairs while she took a shower in his *en suite* bathroom, and got into the clothes he'd laid out on the bed for her. A T-shirt and jeans. She'd have to steal the hotel slippers, and the sash of the bathrobe, too, to prevent his jeans from falling down around her ankles. Her wet clothes went into the Ballynahinch Castle laundry bag.

Pixie took a look at herself in the full-length mirror before she went down to the foyer, which was where they'd arranged to meet up. Her hair was dishevelled, the T-shirt dwarfed her, the turn-up on the jeans was so pronounced it was almost modish. She looked about twelve. At least

356

she could disguise the unruliness of her hair by donning her baseball cap, which was the only item of her clothing that had remained dry. She stuck it on, slid her feet into the towelling slippers and slung the laundry bag over her shoulder, then she slunk out of the room and down the stairs of Ballynahinch Castle feeling like a burglar with a bag of swag.

He wasn't in the foyer.

'Excuse me?' she said to the surprised-looking receptionist behind the desk. 'Would you happen to know where Mr Lawless is, please?'

'Yes. He's in the conservatory. Through the drawing room on your left.'

Pixie flip-flopped through the drawing room in her slippers, feeling very glad indeed that the weather was so fine that no visitors had been tempted to take their ease by the fire. The conservatory was another matter. There, lounging opposite David in a rattan chair, nursing a Bloody Mary, was Rory McDonagh.

An amused glint came into his eyes when he spotted her. 'Ms Pirelli. How fetching! So this is what romantic novelists are sporting this season?'

Pixie didn't feel she knew him well enough to tell him to piss off. 'I fell in the river,' she said, 'and David very kindly volunteered to lend me some clothes.'

'Yes,' said Rory. 'David told me how he happened upon you up to your thighs in the river, wielding your rod.'

The look Pixie threw him told him to mind his own business. 'Um — can we go now, David?'

she asked. 'I really do feel terribly self-conscious in this get-up.'

'Of course.'

She shuffled back to the foyer, and David moved quickly to the door to hold it open for her. Outside on the forecourt he indicated a smart hire car. Pixie climbed into the passenger seat, and as he turned on the ignition and put the car into gear, she could see Rory McDonagh through the window of the conservatory, raising his Bloody Mary at her, and laughing.

'Are you going back to London tonight?' she enquired, as he negotiated the curves of the driveway.

'No.'

'I thought you said something about rehearsals?'

'Tomorrow's a fit-up day for the crew. There's no point in my being there — the stage director will take care of everything. I'm flying out from Galway first thing on Tuesday. I wanted to spend as much time here as I could since it's unlikely I'll ever be back.'

'But — you are Irish, aren't you?'

'Yes. But I've been living in London for years.'

'And you don't feel the need to return here, the way most Irish seem to?'

'Not since Eva died, no.'

'So this was a kind of farewell visit?'

'If you like.'

'You won't be here for the screening of *The O'Malley*, then.' It was scheduled for Thursday night.

'No. I'd find it too painful to watch that. Eva

gave birth to our daughter shortly before she made that film. There's a scene where Grace O'Malley breast-feeds her infant. The infant was our own Dorcas.'

'How immeasurably sad!'

David glanced at her. 'You use some terrific words, I've noticed. 'Immeasurably' is a good one.'

'I wouldn't get away with it in a novel, though, except under extraordinary circumstances.'

'Why not?'

'It's not the kind of word most people use in real life.'

'But your novels *aren't* real life,' he pointed out.

'No,' she conceded, with a tiny sigh. 'I sometimes wish they were.'

They drove in silence for a while, taking in the wild beauty of the scenery, and then David spoke again. 'What did you do before you became a writer?' he asked.

'I was a hand model.'

'That doesn't surprise me,' said David. 'I couldn't help noticing when you were reeling in your line that you had very pretty hands.'

'Thank you!'

'You really ought to wear barrier cream when you're fishing, to prevent your hands from getting chafed.'

'I won't be doing much fishing in the foreseeable future,' she said gloomily. 'I'm going back to London next Thursday.'

'And not looking forward to it much, by the sound of things.'

'No.'

'Here,' he said, producing a pen and a notepad from the pocket of his shirt. 'Write your address down on that and I'll make sure you get an invitation to the opening night of *The Seagull*. That might cheer you up.'

'Thank you so much. I'd love that.'

How organized of him to carry around a pen and notebook, she thought, as she riffled through it and found a blank page on which to scribble her address.

'I carry a pen and a notebook around with me wherever I go so that I can jot down any directorial ideas that come to me. I tend to get especially good ones when I'm fishing,' David told her.

'Oh, you do that too! I always carry a pen and notebook too in case ideas for a book come to me. Oh, bother! I've just realized that it'll be soaked now, after that pratfall in the river.'

'How long have you been fly-fishing, Pixie?'

'I had my first lesson around six months ago when I stayed in Ballynahinch, before I decided to come to Kilrowan to live. I love it.'

'Me too. It's my therapy.'

'It's more than just the thrill of the chase, isn't it? There's something very Zen about it.'

'There is. Have you ever read *The Compleat Angler*?'

'No, but I have taken out a subscription to *Angling Times*. What's *The Complete Angler*?'

'It's a book, subtitled *The Contemplative Man's Recreation*. It was written in the

360

seventeenth century, but it's as pertinent now as it was then. You should check it out. I never go on a fishing trip without bringing my copy with me. I'd offer to lend it to you, but Rory has it at the moment.'

'Is Rory keen on fishing?'

'No. I'm trying to convert him. He's more into horses.'

'He's a gambler?'

'No. He rides.'

'He *looks* like a gambler.'

David smiled. 'I suppose he has a Runyonesque thing going. He does play a demon game of poker. And I seem to remember he won a few bob once on a very dark horse. What kind of fly were you using today, incidentally?'

'One that my ghillie recommended. He told me . . . '

And the rest of the journey to Kilrowan was spent in discussing casting techniques, and hooks and reels, and the differences between wet fly and dry fly fishing.

'Will you come in for a cup of tea or something?' she asked when they pulled up outside number 4, the Blackthorns.

'No, thank you,' he said.

'But how shall I get your clothes back to you?' She had planned on changing into her own clothes and giving him back his jeans and T-shirt.

'Don't worry about them.'

She couldn't keep his clothes! 'But they're lovely jeans. And this is a very classy T-shirt.'

'Leave the jeans for me at the theatre when you're back in London. You may keep the T-shirt, since you admire it so much.'

'Well . . . Thank you.' Pixie opened the passenger door and stepped out with her laundry bag. 'Goodbye, David. Good luck with your show.'

'Goodbye, Pixie.' And then he drove off in his sleek car, leaving Pixie standing outside number 4, the Blackthorns, looking quite ridiculous in his outsized clothes, and feeling like a proper prat.

★ ★ ★

It was Monday afternoon, and the festival had officially started. Cleo watched from the bookshop window as the parade passed by. It was headed by a band of traditional musicians, diddly-idling away on a float. A crowd of local kids dressed as marine life drifted after them in a wifty wafty, swimmy fashion. There was lots of green and blue parachute silk being waved around, and there were a few staggery sideways-walking crabs. A mermaid wearing a sea-green wig was being towed along in a rowing boat on wheels by one of Hugh Hennessy's horses, followed by stilt-walkers, jugglers, a flame-eater and a gang of marauding pirates with cutlasses and eye patches. Bringing up the rear was Hazel's father as the Salmon of Knowledge, getting much mileage out of the fact that he was having serious problems walking in his fish tail. There was no sign of Angel Kestrel or her Phish.

Cleo was reminded of how Kilrowan had been transformed on another occasion into a festival town during the making of *Mimi's Remedies*, when, as an extra, she had had to sashay down the street in a 'village wench's' outfit, with Fluffy at her heels, and how Fluff had competed for attention with an organ-grinder's monkey.

Dear Fluff. Cleo had visited her grave just yesterday, and sat there with the sun on her face, wondering what her life would be like once Pixie was gone, and wondering if she could handle the winter living in a virtual ghost town with no neighbour to call on. She wondered, too, if maybe it wasn't time to think about finding a dog to replace her beloved Fluffy, and the thought had made her feel guilty because no dog in the world could have a sense of humour like Fluff's, no dog could look so flirtatiously at her, no dog make her laugh the way Fluffy had done. No dog could be so faithful to her.

The parade streeled by, and the music faded as the band floated further and further away. The tune they were playing was one that Pablo and she had used to listen to in the car on their drives through the insane beauty of the Inagh Valley, laughing out loud at how happy they were, and how very lucky. In her mind's eye she saw the painting he'd made for her of the couple in the Connemara landscape yearning, yearning for home . . . And now his gift was going to auction, instead of her accepting it in the spirit of love in which it had been offered and inviting him back into her life.

The music had faded away completely now.

Back to business, Cleo! She turned away from the window and headed for her store room. Inside she was confronted by Colleen, majestic in her cloak, leaning up against shiny happy Pixie. They'd been banished to the store room because they'd finally slid off the bestseller list. Maybe Cleo should take the cut-out of Pixie home to keep her company? Even a cardboard Pixie would be better to talk to than no-one, she thought, as she rummaged amongst the stacks of titles for the one that Colleen had ordered: *The Celtic Book of Living and Dying*. The author had told her she'd be in to pick it up later.

Outside in the shop, the bell sounded that announced a customer. 'In a minute!' she called, finally locating the book. But when she went back into the shop, there was no-one there.

She stashed Colleen's book on the shelf under the till, sat up on her stool and reached for the book she'd been reading: *A Thousand Days in Tuscany*.

And then a voice said something that made her nearly fall off her stool. She had thought that she was quite alone in the shop. 'Who's there?' she asked, looking around, baffled.

'Pretty you,' came the voice again.

'I beg your pardon?'

'Pretty, pretty you.' It was a strange voice, like something badly recorded — the kind of voice a horror-movie actor might use. What was going on?

Cleo put her book down and slid off her stool. Cautiously she moved away from the counter and craned her neck to see if somebody might be hiding round the corner. No-one there. Feeling a bit spooked, she went back to her stool.

'Cleo Dowling's a kick-ass ride.'

A Thousand Days in Tuscany went tumbling to the floor.

'Who the hell's there?' said Cleo, shaken now.

There was no answer.

She sat there motionless, breathing rapidly, shallowly, all her senses heightened by adrenalin. What was going on? Had some crazy joker from the festival sneaked into her shop as a hoax? Was it some kind of sex pest, or stalker? Should she phone the police? Go out on to the street and get help?

As she sat there dithering, a sudden fluttering movement caught her attention. Something, someone was hiding under the front table.

Cleo slid soundlessly off her stool again and approached the table with the stealth of an Indian tracker. She knelt down on the floor, and angled herself so that she could see what was there.

For a moment or two she thought she was hallucinating, or suffering from the DTs. But hey — she hadn't drunk *that* much last night. She blinked at the vision that confronted her. Eyeing her back coquettishly, preening itself shamelessly, was an outrageously pretty white cockatoo. *What?* What was it doing there? Where on earth had it come from? This was insane! The cockatoo cocked its head at a flirtatious angle and regarded her with an intelligent eye. 'I love you,' it said, and Cleo had to laugh.

'Where did *you* come from, you bold thing?' she asked.

As if in response to her question, the bird emerged from under the table and marched across to a cage that had been placed just inside the shop door. It was of intricately wrought white painted metal — the kind of cage you might see in a Victorian conservatory. A packet of bird feed was attached to it, and its door hung open. The bird walked into the cage, then turned and gave Cleo another coquettish look. 'Take me home,' it said.

'Home? You want me to take you home?' she answered, laughing.

The bird hopped on to a little swing and made a rocking motion that set the swing in action. 'Cawwhawwhawwhawhaww,' it sang, swinging to and fro, clearly having the time of its life. 'Cawwhawwhawwhawhaww, *hawhawha aaww!*'

'What a little show-off you are,' said Cleo, hunkering down and admiring the display. 'What's your name?'

'Cawwhawwhawcawwhawwhawwhawhaww, *hawhawhaaaww!*' The swing had gathered momentum now and was rocking so wildly that Cleo thought the bird was in danger of falling off, but it appeared to be as thrilled as a small child at a fun fair. Its cawwhawwhaw-ing was evidently the cockatoo equivalent of a 'Wheeeeeeee!' or a 'Yaaaaaaaaay!'

'No, no. Cawwhawwhaw's way too long a name for you!'

'*Dia duit!*'

The shop bell pinged, as Colleen made her entrance. '*I gcuntas Dé!* What is it you have there?' she asked. 'A parrot?'

'It's a kind of a parrot. A cockatoo,' said Cleo, looking up at Colleen from her hunkered position on the floor.

'But what is it doing here?' said Colleen. 'To whom docs it belong?'

'I'm — minding it for a friend,' improvised Cleo. 'Isn't it fun?'

'Alas, no,' said Colleen, backing away from the cage. 'I suffer from ornithophobia. A fear of birds. Please shut the cage door in case the creature flies at me, and pecks me.'

'I'm not sure it can fly,' said Cleo, shutting the door on the swinging cockatoo. 'I imagine its wings have been clipped.' She got to her feet and moved to the cash desk. 'I have your book here for you, Colleen.' She reached under the counter and put *The Celtic Way of Living and Dying* into a paper bag.

'How much do I owe you?' asked Colleen, taking a purse from her hempen satchel.

'Fifteen euros, ninety-five, please. How's Margot?'

'She is well. She is still doing last-minute reading for the short story competition.'

'Have you had many entries?'

'We have. We have entries from all over the world. They have come by land, sea and air, and some have even come by 'e' mail.'

Cleo watched as Colleen laboriously examined the notes she'd extracted from her purse, to identify their denomination. She still hadn't got used to the euro.

'I didn't know you had a telephone line on the island,' she remarked.

'We do not. But I have, alas, been obliged to have a line installed in my house in Kilrowan. My editor insisted.'

In Kilrowan, Colleen resided in the kind of house the Addams family might find old-fashioned. Cleo wasn't surprised that Colleen's editor had insisted that she get her techno finger out.

Colleen put money on the counter. 'Ochone, Cleo!' she said, wrapping her cloak tighter around her even though evening sun was streaming into the shop. 'I fear the twentieth century may be breathing down the back of my neck at last, and I am fearful of its chill, ill wind.'

'It's actually the twenty-first century,' Cleo pointed out.

'No, no! I will never live there. I shall never write except by hand, and I shall never, ever send the 'e' mail.'

'So Margot does all that stuff for you?' How convenient!

'Of course. Margot has a flair for 'techno-communications'. I sometimes believe she speaks with alien beings when she is communing 'on-line'. I saw on her computer screen a submission that had come from someone known simply as — let me see, it was such an intriguing hieroglyph that I felt compelled to write it down — ' Colleen rummaged through the vegetables in her hempen bag — 'Ah, yes! I have it here.'

And she placed a sheet of handmade Nepalese paper on the counter in front of Cleo that bore, in Colleen's ostentatious black script, the legend: $BCH^F;!!C#X].

'I have, of course, no idea as to its significance,' resumed Colleen. 'But it is a glittering stitch in the rich tapestry of life, is it not? To think that somewhere out there in the world resides a soul who has aspirations to being the winner of the Colleen/Kilrowan short story competition, known only as — ' and Colleen traced the characters of the hieroglyph with a pensive finger — $BCH^F;!!C#X].

★ ★ ★

As soon as she got home from work, Cleo went online and saw from her instant messaging service that Martina was online, too. Ha!

Hey you — you're up late, she typed.

Was out partying . . .

Listen up — did you send a short story off to the Kilrowan competition?

Yeah. And look what I got back! Hang on — let me just access e-mail . . . There!

From: Margot d'Arcy

369

To: $BCH^F;!!C#X]
Subject: Re: Kilrowan/Colleen short story competition.

```
Dear $BCH^F;!!C#X]

This is to acknowledge the
receipt of your short story.
Please furnish me with further
details of your name and address
in the event of your winning the
competition.

Yours in the spirit of literature,

Margot d'Arcy
```

Dig that 'Yours in the Spirit of Literature'!

Wow! Did you reply?

Are you mad? If I'd 'furnished' her with further details she'd remember that I was your best friend at school who was big into practical jokes.

Practical jokes?

Yeah. I sent in a plagiarized version of 'Little Noddy Goes to Toyland' that I claimed had been written by my inner child.

Glad to know you're as juvenile as ever, darlin'. That inner child just won't let go. Hey guess

370

what? I have a cockatoo — a bona fide lovebird — and all's well with the world!

A *cockatoo*?

Will send more detailed e-mail nxt wk. Sorry — have to dash. Thanks for making me laugh!

Love you!

Cleo XXX

Ha! Life had loads of glittering stitches in its rich tapestry, Cleo decided, as she got ready to go to Pixie's talk in the library. She had a quick shower and retouched her make-up, talking non-stop all the while to the white cockatoo who was fiddling around on her dressing table, playing with various cosmetic items. It appeared to find her lipstick particularly fascinating, and had been mesmerized earlier by its own reflection in the mirror. Cleo had decided to call it 'Polly' because it was so pretty.

'Well, Polly! Shall I tell you a little about myself?'

'Cleo Dowling's a kick-ass ride,' pronounced Polly.

'Well, yes, there is that, but what else? Um — Let's see . . . I used to be a city girl, dontcha know, but I moved to the country when I won the lottery — which is how I could afford this lovely house — and then I met a man called Pablo who was so very sexy he inspired me to write erotic short stories. I fell in love with him and married him, and then he did something so heinous that I had to throw him out. He needed to learn a big lesson, you see. He needed to learn a very big lesson about life . . . ' Cleo's eyes went to where Pablo's sarong was draped over the foot of the great big double bed. She allowed her gaze to linger there for several moments, and then she turned back to her new pet. 'Now!' she said. 'Put down that lipstick, and get back into your cage, lovebird. I have to go out. I have to go and listen to my friend Pixie talk a load of crap about 'Getting Published' in the library.'

She shut Polly back up in her cage and set it on the chest of drawers above which hung the portrait that Pablo had painted of his wife with no clothes on. And then she blew the cockatoo a kiss, and waltzed out through the door.

★   ★   ★

Pixie had showed up at the library with a pile of her books for Deirdre O'Dare, who had agreed to have a look at the novels with a view to checking out their screenplay potential. Pixie was feeling a bit fluttery because it was nearly time for her authorial talk.

'Has there been any interest at all, in this talk?' she asked the librarian.

'Oh, yes,' said Linda the librarian, pouring red and white wine into glasses. 'Masses! It seems that everybody thinks they can write a bestseller these days, and they're counting on you to tell them how.'

'It's not as easy as it might seem,' said Pixie.

'It's a bit like winning the lottery, really. The competition is ferocious.'

And as she checked out the lectern that had been set up for her, she thought of fearsome, fearful Tabbitha, red in tooth and claw, and wondered if she'd conceded defeat and had reverted to writing for the chick-lit market, or whether she was persisting in her efforts at clubbing the editor they shared over the head with her Magic Realism.

Pixie looked at her watch. She'd arrived early, and Linda had made her welcome by giving her the cup of tea she'd asked for in preference to wine, but it was after seven o'clock now. There wasn't even any evidence of the film crew that had been promised. 'Are you sure they said seven on the flyer?' she asked.

'Oh, yes. Look. I have one here. 'Pixie Pirelli, author of six bestselling novels, will give a talk on 'Getting Published' in the Kilrowan Public Library at seven o'clock',' Linda read out loud.

'It's five past, now,' said Pixie, and just then the door opened and a little old lady walked in carrying a weighty-looking shopping bag.

'Is this the talk on 'Getting Published'?' she demanded.

'Yes,' said Linda.

'Good.' The little old lady made for one of the three dozen or so moulded plastic chairs that had been ranked round the small room, and plonked herself down on it.

Oh, God. Pixie had read a book recently called *Mortification: Writers' Stories of their Public*

Shame, in which some very famous authors indeed had 'fessed up to having had their fair share of humiliating public appearances. Anecdotes abounded about no-shows for book signings, people asking for their money back 'because the book was crap', and readers mistaking less well known authors for someone much more famous. It was clear that this was not going to be 'An Evening with Pixie Pirelli'. It was going to be the occasion of 'Pixie Pirelli's Taste of Public Shame'.

The door opened again. Thank goodness! Someone else!

It was David Lawless.

'Hello, Pixie,' he said.

'Oh. Hello.'

Oh, God. Why was the prospect of David Lawless being an onlooker at 'Pixie Pirelli's Taste of Public Shame' so keenly embarrassing? She felt like dropping to the floor in a feigned faint.

'I would have thought you'd prefer to spend the evening fishing rather than listening to me rabbit on,' she said.

'No. I wanted to show you some support.'

'It looks like I'm going to need it.'

The door opened again and two more people came into the room. Cleo Dowling and Deirdre O'Dare. They looked — unsurprisingly — a little uneasy as they took in the spectacle of Pixie standing on her own behind a lectern over which she could barely see.

'Pixie?' said Cleo, 'I hate to have to tell you this, but you've got major competition in the village hall.'

'Zoe Conway?' Pixie bleated. Cleo had raved about the fiddler.

'Well, it's not just Zoe Conway. Um. Rory just phoned to tell me that she has a surprise guest appearing with her — someone who's been staying with friends in Kilrowan.'

'Oh?' said Pixie. 'Who?'

'Bono,' said Cleo.

★   ★   ★

In fact, the occasion turned out to be neither an 'Evening with Pixie Pirelli' nor 'Pixie Pirelli's Taste of Public Shame', because no other members of the public showed up. The event actually turned out to be an 'Evening with Mrs Martin', which was the name of the little old lady who had fetched up at the library wanting to know how she could get her novel published.

She had, she told Pixie, written a novel which was some three hundred and fifty thousand words long — which made it nearly as long as *Gone With the Wind*. It was, she said, warm, generous and human, and it was full of the lyrical beauty of love.

'So tell me how I get it published,' she said. 'Do I get myself an agent?'

'Well,' said Pixie, 'that's always a help.'

'Ah, but then the agent'll want their percentage, won't they? Aren't they the scavenging merchants?'

'Well, they'll be able to tell you whether your novel is any good — '

'Any good? Any *good?* Of course it's good!

Look at it!' And she withdrew from her shopping
bag reams of closely written manuscript. And a
single ream, Pixie knew, was 500 pages. 'Would
you like to read it yourself, perhaps?' asked Mrs
Martin, giving her a sly look. 'You'd be welcome
to — as long as you don't steal any of my ideas.'

'I'm frightfully sorry,' said Pixie, 'but I simply
wouldn't have the time.'

'Well, give me the address of your publishing
house and I'll send it off to them, so.' She
handed Pixie a biro. 'You can write it on here,'
she said, indicating the title page of her novel.
'Who's the best person to send it to?'

'Um, well, my editor's Deborah Millen.'

'Is she any good?'

'Well, yes, actually, she's one of the best in the
business.'

'And if I send it off to her, what will she do
with it when she realizes that she has the
publishing sensation of the century on her
hands?'

'Well . . . ' Thank God for the word 'Well',
thought Pixie. It was the most useful stalling
word she knew. 'Well, she'll help you edit it — '

'You mean cut bits out of it?'

'Well, yes — '

'Haha! No-one's tampering with *my* novel. No
two-bit editor's going to cut a word of it without
my say-so! My book's . . . '

And so it went on. And on. And on. Mrs
Martin's massive tome was evidently the best
book written since Dave Egger's self-proclaimed
Heartbreaking Work of Staggering Genius, or,
indeed, the Bible.

By the end of the 'Evening with Mrs Martin', Pixie felt as drained as an empty bath. She finally saw her audient out of the library with a very weak smile and a 'The best of luck with it!' as well as a promise to let her know when Deborah received the manuscript.

She shut the library door and saw Cleo and Deirdre and David Lawless sitting in a row on their plastic chairs, stiff with the effort of trying not to laugh and looking like the three monkeys in the parable.

'You were magnificent,' said David.

'Better than Bono,' said Deirdre.

'Well, hey! Here's to Pixie Pirelli,' said Cleo, raising her empty wineglass at her, 'the incontrovertible hit of the Kilrowan Festival. But — ' she indicated the serried ranks of red and white that the hapless librarian had poured out earlier — 'who's going to drink all the wine?'

'I am,' said Pixie.

18

Hazel hadn't phoned Erin with the news that she was back in Dublin because she didn't want to tell her the reason. She didn't think she could bear to tell anyone.

The last thing Angel had said to Hazel before Hazel had run away from Kilrowan was: 'I just wish there were more ways to say sorry, darling. I just so wish that I could undo what happened.' Hazel had kissed her on the cheek, and said 'I know, Mum.' She knew that Angel was genuinely stricken with remorse, but that didn't make Hazel's burden of knowledge any easier to bear.

She was trying to keep herself busy by doing the thing she loved most — crossing things off lists — except she wasn't enjoying it as much as usual because she was distracted. Not just because of the Hugh/Angel thing, but because she'd had to let her dad down. When she'd told him on the phone that she was heading back to Dublin because she had a 'virus', he'd sounded genuinely upset — and the worst thing was that he wasn't upset for himself, he was upset for her.

'I knew you'd been working too hard,' he scolded her. 'You've lost weight, and that means you haven't been eating properly. And that leaves your immune system open to everything that's going, Hazel. You take some time off, and look after yourself. And eat organic and *no* MSG. Take lots of vitamin C and echinacea — '

'Dad, I'll be fine,' said Hazel. His concern for her only made her feel guiltier. 'Don't worry. And I'm so sorry about the Salmon of Knowledge.'

'Don't you worry about me,' he said. 'I'm as resilient as India rubber. I bounce back.'

It was true. Both he and her mother had always bounced back, going from one gig to the next with hope being the only thing to keep them going. How had they managed to survive for so long? They said that hope springs eternal, but what would her mother do when Angel Phish bombed at the festival and she came to the stark realization that she was past it? Her parents had started to remind her of that couple in the Beckett play, living out the rest of their lives in bins.

The phone rang. It was Renée with an update on how the festival was progressing. Hazel had asked her to put in a call every day.

'Well,' said Renée, 'you'll be glad to know that the parade went without a hitch yesterday. And I've some good news and some bad news. Which do you want first?'

'Oh, God. The bad news, I suppose.'

'The bad news is that nobody turned up at Pixie Pirelli's talk.'

'What? But that looked like it was going to be a major draw!'

'But the really *excellent* news is that the reason nobody turned up at the talk was because Bono rolled up out of the blue and gigged with Zoe Conway.'

'No shit! That's *fantastic* news.'

'So you can expect to see Kilrowan all over tonight's *Evening Herald*.'

'Well done, Renée!'

'I had nothing to do with it. You've the beneficent Bono to thank for that. But the downside is that the highlight of the festival has happened so soon. Nobody can best Bono.'

'We've still got Rory McDonagh and Donal Lunny and Sharon Shannon and the *Tribunals* Show. And, er . . . Angel Phish,' said Hazel.

'Yes. Chin up, Hazel.' Renée knew how Hazel felt about her mother performing at the festival.

'Couldn't you sabotage that gig somehow?' Hazel asked piteously.

'But they might be *good*,' reasoned Renée. 'You never know.'

'Yeah.' Hazel did *not* sound convinced. 'Let's change the subject. What's the weather like over there?'

'It's fantastic. Big blue skies, and everybody in T-shirts, smiling.'

'No shit. It's lashing down here, and everybody in rain gear, looking frazzled. Any other news?'

'No. Everything's under control.'

'I knew I could count on you, Renée. Phone me again tomorrow, will you? What's the forecast like for the rest of the week, incidentally?'

'More of the same.'

'Yippee.'

Hazel put the phone down and was just about to resume work on her lists when it rang again. Renée was back on the line.

'Well, do you want the good news or the bad news?' she said.

Oh Jesus! Talk about *Groundhog Day*! 'Not again, Renée!'

' 'Fraid so.'

'The bad news, then.'

'Your mother's pulled out of the Angel Phish gig.'

Hazel felt a surge of pure relief. 'Whoa. That's the *bad* news?'

'She's lost her voice.'

'Oh. Poor Mum.'

'The good news is that she approached someone else to front the band in her place.'

'Oh? Who?'

'Bono.'

'And he *agreed*?'

'Yeah. He said that the Fazes were one of the reasons he founded U2. That's how much respect your mother's band had back then.'

'Oh.' Hazel felt small now. 'Maybe I misjudged her. Maybe this really would have been a triumph for her.'

'I dunno. There's something very sad about ageing rock chicks. The blokes can get away with it, but I'm never convinced by the women. I know it's unfair and sexist, but you kinda feel they'd be better off retiring gracefully.'

'I'd better give her a ring.'

'She won't be able to speak to you. Apparently her vocal cords are in ribbons from all the rehearsing she's been doing.'

'I know, but *I* can speak to *her*. Make sympathetic noises down the phone.' Her mother was probably still feeling like shit over the Hugh Hennessy débâcle. This was a double whammy for her.

'Oh — by the way, the other good news, Hazel, is that the Salmon of Knowledge is a big success.'

'What?'

'Yeah. Your dad's set up a booth on the seafront, and there are queues of people who want to test his wits. He's especially popular with the American tourists. Everyone wants to ask him a question that he can't answer, and apparently that's only happened a few times. And when he's stuck for an answer he improvises this astonishing rap. I don't know how he does it. Oh — hang on, Hazel — there's Rory McDonagh. I need to ask him whether he's definitely going to make a speech after the screening of *The O'Malley*. I'd better dash.'

Hazel put the phone down feeling a bit redundant. Maybe she shouldn't have run away from her responsibilities in Kilrowan after all. She knew that Renée was well able to handle everything — and she seemed to be having a brilliant time hobnobbing with celebrities — but really Hazel should be there to console her mother. How awful for her not to make her comeback! And how on earth had her father managed to find a feed?

She picked up the phone and speed-dialled him. 'Hi, Dad,' she told his voice mail. 'I understand from my assistant Renée that you're up and running, and that you're a big success. Well done! How did you manage it? Give me a bell when you've a mo.'

Then she braced herself to dial her mother.

'Hi there, Haze!' came her mother's bright voice down the line.

'Mum? I thought you'd lost your voice?'

'Phooey, no. That was just an excuse to get out of doing the gig. When I heard that Bono was in town I thought that I could do the festival a big favour, so I pretended to lose my voice and asked him if he'd oblige by stepping in.'

'How could you ask him if you'd lost your voice?'

'I wrote him a note. He very sweetly wrote back 'Yes! I'd be glad to! Love, Bono.''

'How generous is that!' For Bono to guest with a band called Angel Phish was an act of such extraordinary generosity it merited canonization.

'And he put in a PS, which went 'On one condition only. That you refer to the band as 'The artists formerly known as the Fazes'.' I'm not surprised he put that in. Angel Phish is a truly tragic moniker. I only dreamed it up because I was stoned, and the next thing I knew, it was on the flyer and *fait accompli*. How did you let me get away with it, Hazel?'

'I don't think,' said Hazel, very gently, 'that I ever dreamed the day would come that Angel Phish would actually happen.'

'And you're right, it didn't. Phew! What a relief. I could have been an ageing rock chick like the one who shall be nameless who was on *The Late Late Show* the other night. I think that's what made me get cold feet. She looked like a dog, and I found myself thinking about what would happen if I went on *The Late Late Show*, and viewers all over the country were going 'Wise up, love!' to the screen. I'm going to start behaving in a more dignified fashion from now on.'

Hazel tried to picture her mother looking dignified, and couldn't.

'I'm going to keep that note from Bono,' Angel continued. 'It'll be worth a fortune some day. D'you know how much his autograph fetches on eBay?'

'I've no idea.'

'Neither have I, but I'm sure it's worth masses. Oh — there he is now! Hi, Bon — oh. I'd forgotten that I'm meant to have lost my voice. I'd better not let him see me jabbering away on the phone. I'll take you round the corner, Hazel.' Her mother sounded like a kid playing hide-and-seek. 'D'you know something, darling? I'm *soo* glad I had that wake-up call. I'm too old to be prancing around on a stage wearing revealing outfits. That's what I was going to tell you, you know — the day you left Kilrowan. I was going to 'fess up to you that I wanted out of the festival and say sorry for letting you down. And then the whole thing about — um — Hugh came up and proved to be something of a . . . Well, whatever . . . ' Angel's voice trailed off.

' 'Whatever' will do nicely.'

There was a longish pause before Angel resumed. 'I've been thinking a lot about that, you know,' she said in a sudden rush, 'and I'm going to say something very wise to you. I've undone it. It never happened.'

'What do you mean?'

'Like in *His Dark Materials*.'

'I'm sorry, Mum. I'm not with you.'

'The Philip Pullman trilogy. Think about it, because it's the only sense you can apply to a straight-from-hell scenario. If we were in parallel universes it would never have happened. If I'd known what I know now then, I would never have come on to Hugh. If he knew then what he knows now, *he* would never have allowed it to happen. So put it out of your head. You don't even need to *pretend* that it didn't happen because in that parallel universe it *didn't* happen.'

There was some kind of vague, New Age plausibility to her mother's argument. But Hazel didn't want to think about it now. She changed the subject.

'How did Dad find a feed for his gig?' she asked.

'Oh — *I'm* it. It's great gas!'

'You're feeding him?'

'Yeah. We make a great team. I sit in the back of the van and zoom around Encarta. Nobody's worked it out yet. The Yanks are especially impressed by it, and he's had av-checks from all over the country about Christmas parties.'

'Well, good for him!'

'Oh! Christ! Is that the time? I'd better go, Hazel. I'm late for lunch.'

'Who are you having lunch with?'

'Your dad, and Deirdre O'Dare and Rory

McDonagh. It turns out I knew his mother, way back.'

'Really?'

'Yeah. She's a musician too — although she was more into trad. She'll be showing up for the screening of *The O'Malley*. It'll be great to see her after all these years. Bye, darling!'

'Bye, Mum.'

Hazel put the phone down and thought about her mum and dad having lunch in O'Toole's with Rory McDonagh, and she thought about Bono coming to the rescue of the Fazes and rocking Kilrowan, and she thought about the queue of people waiting to ask questions of the Salmon of Knowledge, and she thought about Hugh Hennessy at the helm of it all — and she wished she was there.

The phone, again.

'Nutcracker PR, Hazel MacNamara speaking.'

'Ms MacNamara? I'm Bob Hughes from Bespoke Wines. I know it's a bit early, but I'm planning our Christmas party.'

'It's never too early to plan your Christmas party, Bob!' said Hazel, putting on her most efficient PR voice.

'Especially since we're out to impress this year. We've decided to hold a party for our most honoured clients — around fifty people — and I'm hoping that you can help us out.'

'I'd be glad to, Bob.'

'We'd like some kind of entertainment, obviously, and I thought you might recommend something kinda — well — zany.'

Hazel didn't miss a beat. 'I certainly can,' she

said. 'There's a fantastic act on in the Kilrowan Festival right now, but you'd have to book him right away because I know his diary around Christmas time is pretty full already.'

'Oh? Who is he?'

'The Salmon of Knowledge.'

'The Salmon of Knowledge?'

'Yes. He used to be Mondo the aMazing of — '

'*Bunny Brown's Way*! My favourite programme when I was a kid! Well, whaddaya know! I didn't know he was still around.'

'Oh, yes, Bob. He's still very much around, and easily as entertaining as ever,' said Hazel, smoothly.

'Well, I'm much obliged to you for this. Book him immediately, Hazel!'

'Will do, Bob! Give me your e-mail address and I'll get back to you.'

When Hazel put the phone down, she picked it straight up again, and left another message on Mondo's voice mail. 'Dad?' she said. 'It looks like I may have got you another gig. Love you!'

Then she dialled Renée. 'Renée?' she said. 'You know I asked you to pick up my stuff from Hugh Hennessy's house?'

'Yeah?'

'Don't bother. I'm going to do it myself.'

'You're coming back down?'

'At the weekend, yeah.'

'So you're feeling better?'

'Yes,' said Hazel. 'The pain's all gone. It's weird. I don't even feel as if that virus happened to me.'

'What do you mean?'

'I dunno. It's hard to explain. It feels — it feels — oh, this is stupid! I *never* come out with guff like this!'

'Go on, weirdo. Spit it out.'

'It feels as if it happened to someone in a parallel universe,' she said.

★ ★ ★

Today, Wednesday, was Pixie's last day in Kilrowan. She was on her way to the village hall, where the announcement of the winner of the Kilrowan/Colleen short story competition was to be made by the revered author herself. As she tripped down the be-buntinged main street, her ring tone — 'Always Look on the Bright Side of Life' — went off. Private Caller turned out to be Deirdre O'Dare.

'Hey! You kept me up until after four o'clock in the morning, you bitch!' said Deirdre.

'I beg your pardon?'

'*Hard to Choos.*'

'Oh!' Pixie prinked. 'That's a wonderful compliment. Did I really?'

'Yes. Rory was seriously pissed off, though. I was so immersed in your book that he didn't get a ride last night. But he got one this morning after I made him read the Italian sex scene out loud.'

Pixie pinkened.

'So,' said Deirdre. 'Do I have the go-ahead from you to approach your agent about optioning your novels?'

'All of them?'

'We'll see. I'll have to read the others first, and decide which of them most merits a treatment.'

'Oh, Deirdre,' said Pixie. 'That would be just amazing!'

'And Rory's interested. You know we've set up our own production company, Jolly Roger Enterprises?'

'Yes.'

'Well, Rory needs a new star vehicle if he's to afford the ranch he's set on buying, and he thinks this might just be the new *Bridget Jones*.'

Pixie felt so faint that she had to stop and sit on the sea wall. Goodness! How fast things were happening! She could barely take it all in.

'He also,' continued Deirdre, 'finds the idea of vicariously riding some bootilicious starlet decked out in Coco de Mer lingerie understandably appealing. I'm thinking of cutting that scene.'

Pixie giggled. She didn't often 'giggle', but there was no other appropriate response to the news she'd just heard. She was floating in a bubble of pure happiness. 'So what do we do now, Deirdre?'

'Who's your agent?'

'Natalie Remington.'

'Lucky you. She's top notch. I'll give her a bell and we'll talk.'

'You are such a star! Thank you.'

'You're welcome, Pixie.'

After she put her phone away, Pixie continued to sit on the sea wall, staring at the horizon and trying to make sense of things.

Cleo Dowling sat down beside her. 'You look like that lunatic who works for Hugh Hennessy.'

'I beg your pardon?'

'You know, the one who sits around on gates staring into the middle distance.'

'Do I? I suppose I must appear a bit doolally. I've just had the most fantastic news.' And Pixie filled Cleo in on the telephone conversation she'd just had.

'How cool is that! Rory McDonagh in one of your books!'

'It's like a dream come true,' said Pixie. 'I feel like Cinderella when the glass slipper fits.'

'Well, Cinders,' said Cleo, looking at her watch, 'if we're to make it to Colleen's gig in time, we'd better make tracks.'

They arrived just in time, passing Colleen who was doing yoga exercises outside the village hall, prior to making her entrance. Pixie and Cleo slid into the back row of the audience and sat down on those ubiquitous moulded plastic chairs that are so very uncomfortable to sit in for long. Pixie wondered if her bottom would be able to endure the time it would take for Colleen to make her speech, which, she suspected, was likely to be endless.

'Look, that's my sister, Margot,' said Cleo, nudging Pixie.

'Where?'

'There. Walking in Colleen's wake.'

Colleen had flung open the door to the hall and was now striding up the aisle looking like Boudicca, or Maeve, Queen of Connaught. Her handmaiden, Margot, sported an identical cloak to the one worn by Colleen, but hers was in a rather less ostentatious shade of forest green. She was one of the most beautiful women Pixie had ever seen.

'Goodness,' she said. 'She's awfully beautiful!'

'I know,' said Cleo. 'She used to be a top model here in Ireland.'

Colleen had reached the top of the hall and was standing behind her lectern, with Margot on her left (distaff) side but maintaining a discreet distance behind the Titaness herself. There was a theatrical silence, and then: '*Céad Mile Fáilte*, Fellow Worshippers at the Shrine of Literature!' trumpeted Colleen.

'Uh-oh,' said Cleo in an undertone to Pixie. 'We're in for it now.'

'My speech today has been inspired,' said Colleen, 'by something that came to me out of the blue. It came out of the blue, and it is still out there.'

She drew a sheet of nubbly handmade paper from the pocket of her cloak, and consulted it. Then she took up a felt-tip pen and turned to the whiteboard that had been set up behind her. There was a pause before she wrote anything, and then, with a flourish, she penned the following:

$BCH^F;!!C#X]

'What on earth?' said Pixie, and Cleo started to snigger.

'You may wonder about the significance of these characters. What do they imply? What do they denote? For me, this hieroglyph is a glittering stitch in the rich tapestry of life. Somewhere out there in the world resides a soul who might one day descend from the clear blue sky of anonymity, but who until then will be known only as an enigma.' And Colleen traced the characters of the hieroglyph with a pensive finger. 'Oh, enigmatic one — we sympathetic souls salute you! We know what it is to be anonymous, we know what it is to be oppressed, we know what it is like to seek liberation through the spoken or the written word. The obscurity of the authoress has been the stuff of literary debate for centuries. Allow me to quote from Margot d'Arcy's poem, 'Penumbra'. Colleen cleared her throat.

'Lament her loudly, ululate!
Did Delphic Sibyl see her fate?
Parnassian Pierides intimate
Her elegy? Her time in hell?
No hwyl or complex villanelle
Dare flesh out spectres such as dwell
In groves of Cypress under glass;
No sciomantic art foretell
The mumchance that would come to pass.'

Colleen swallowed, wiped a tear from her eye, then practically ululated:

'Larks' tongues! Once passerine, unheeded
    now.
Take flight again! The only riddle: How?'

The diva bowed her head. She had been quite overcome with emotion. 'I will be brief, now,' she said, 'I will be as brief as this hieroglyph — ' she gestured at the whiteboard — 'as brief as a haiku.' A pause to end all pauses before Colleen declaimed: 'The winner of the Kilrowan/Colleen short story competition by a woman in this Year of our Lord two thousand and five is — ' another dramatic pause ' — Jane Gray.'

'Oh!' said Pixie, jumping to her feet. 'What fun!' she sang. 'That's me!'

⋆ ⋆ ⋆

'Oh, oh, *oh*!' said Cleo. 'I'll never forget it! I'll never forget the look on her face when she said '*You?*' ' Cleo imitated Colleen's stentorian tones. ' 'But *you* cannot be Jane Gray! *You* are Pixie Pirelli!' '

They were in Pixie's house, because Cleo had volunteered to help her neighbour pack.

'It was pretty priceless all right,' agreed Pixie. 'Good old 'Miching Mallecho'!

'Miching Mallecho?'

'Yes. That's the name of the short story. I wrote it when I attended a writers' workshop, years ago, before I started writing popular fiction. I tried to turn it into a novel, but that just made it worse. Goodness! I shudder to think of all the big pretentious words I used.'

'I'm not surprised that Colleen loved it, then. She's *really* into big words. They do my head in when I try to read her books — it's a bit like reading a foreign language. What are you going to do with the prize money, incidentally?'

'Hm. I hadn't thought about that, because I honestly never dreamed in a million years that I'd win the competition.'

'What made you enter it, then?'

'I didn't. My mother entered it. She found a hard copy that I'd left lying around and posted it off, hoping that it might confer some literary kudos on me. But I'm glad she did now — a charity's a great idea. Preferably an Irish one, since Ireland's been so good to me.'

'Safe-Home Ireland.'

'What's that?'

'It's a charity that brings people home — the Irish who had to emigrate to the UK back in the fifties and sixties, when Ireland was practically a third world country. They're old men now, but they were the ones who really helped us become contenders in Europe because they used to send most of their money home to their families. They can't afford to come home now. Safe-Home Ireland brings them back to their loved ones.'

'What a worthy charity,' said Pixie. 'That's exactly what I'll do.'

'I saw a documentary on it recently. They actually built Britain, those men. They were mostly labourers.'

'So the Brits stole your workforce as well as your land and your language?'

'Effectively, yes. But they gave us something very precious in return.'

'Oh? And what was that?'

'They gave us Colleen,' said Cleo.

19

The village hall was crowded with people wearing Rolexes and Patek Philippe and Cartier. It was also crowded with locals wearing Swatch, and Lorus and fakes, who were dying to know how much the Dublin 4 elite would fork out for a painting of a couple standing in a bog.

Cleo had taken extreme care with her appearance this evening. Her hair was shinier than My Little Pony's, she was wearing fascinating underwear, and she was fake-tanned to within an inch of her life. Her dress was of pale-blue wraparound silk jersey, which required no special skills to take off.

The only free seats were in the front row. Cleo hated sitting in front rows because it made her feel conspicuous, but she had no choice in the matter. Across the aisle was the mother of the princess Abigail, wearing Gucci-something. Cleo simply pretended she wasn't there.

At the very top of the hall, Pablo's painting was displayed on an easel. Even though it was inexpertly lit, it was evident that this was his most exquisite, poignant work to date. The figures in the landscape seemed to be saying in unison — almost as clearly as Polly the cockatoo had the first time Cleo had met her — 'Take us home'.

The chattering classes shut up as the auctioneer stepped up to the lectern. He was a foppish man, wearing what resembled a smoking jacket and a floppy bow-tie.

'Good evening, ladies and gentlemen,' he said in an educated accent. 'Welcome to the annual Kilrowan art auction. As you all know, local painter, Pablo MacBride donates a work of art to the Kilrowan Arts Festival each year.'

Aha! thought Cleo. The Arts is back in there tonight to mollify the cognoscenti!

'Pablo has achieved international recognition for his painting, and his work is much sought after,' continued the auctioneer. 'So we trust that you will bid generously this evening. The money raised by auctioning this painting will go to Mr MacBride's charity of choice, which this year is the Safe-Home Ireland programme. Safe-Home Ireland has been set up by Mayo TD, Dr Jerry Cowley, in order to build accommodation for those expatriate Irish living in the UK, whose most heartfelt desire is to come home to their native land. I'm sure you will all agree that it is a most worthy cause.'

A smattering of applause flittered round the room as the Celtic Tiger put its paws together.

The auctioneer looked around at the expect-ant throng, smiled, and rubbed his hands in satisfaction. 'I see some people here tonight who have sent the bidding rocketing in the past. Let's hope we can achieve a record figure for Pablo MacBride's — ' he made a theatrical gesture towards the easel — '*Figures in a Landscape.*'

'I doubt that,' Cleo heard the man next to her say in a low voice to his companion. 'His style has changed. Why didn't he put a pig or something witty in?' Cleo felt like digging the man in the ribs with her elbow, but he was so well fed he probably wouldn't feel it.

'To judge by the palpable sense of anticipation in the air,' resumed the auctioneer, 'we should get things under way without preamble. May I start the bidding at, say, twenty thousand euros? Twenty thousand anyone?'

An awful silence took root, and stretched. Oh, God, thought Cleo. Maybe the man sitting next to her was right. Maybe there would be no interest in Pablo's work now that its commercial appeal was diminished?

The auctioneer looked unsettled. It was unheard of for bids to proceed downward at a charity auction. Lots of people here could afford to be generous to the tune of twenty thousand euros. 'No bids at twenty? I would ask you not to force me to start the bidding any lower, ladies and gentlemen. Aha! You, sir! Twenty thousand to the gentleman in the navy shirt.'

Cleo glanced round. The gentleman in question was a well-known art *aficionado* and collector. Thank God! This was endorsement enough for Pablo — a real vote of confidence. Beside her saw the man who'd dissed the painting for not having a pig in it sit up and take notice.

'Any advance on twenty thousand?'

In her peripheral vision, Cleo saw Abigail's mother give a nod.

'Twenty-one thousand, to the lady in the red suit. Twenty-two to you, sir?' Cleo's lardy-arsed neighbour had raised a finger. 'Twenty-two it is.

Do I hear twenty-three? Twenty-three to you, sir. Twenty-five? Thank you, madam. And it's thirty to you, sir. Increments of five only from now on, I think, ladies and gentlemen. Thirty-five. I thank you. Forty. Forty-five. Fifty thousand euros. Fifty-five.'

Cleo looked round. The heads of the members of the audience were swivelling between bidders as fast as if they were keeping an eye on the ball at the Wimbledon finals. Finally, it appeared that there were only two bidders left.

One was the Red Queen, the other was the art *aficionado*.

'Sixty. Seventy. Eighty,' intoned the auctioneer.

Cleo knew that the *aficionado* was a strong contender. A seriously wealthy building contractor, he owned several paintings by Pablo already, and it appeared that he was keen to get his hands on this bold new departure by the artist. But the Red Queen was being tenacious. It was clear that since she'd been thwarted in her attempts to have her daughter immortalized by Pablo on canvas, she was *determined* to own this painting. But she was nervous now, Cleo could tell. The nods of her beautifully coiffed head that had started out being gracious had become brusque little jerks, and her hands were gripping the handles of her Hermès bag as if they were the reins of a steeplechase champion completely focused on winning.

'Ninety thousand euros,' the auctioneer announced in imperturbable tones. 'One hundred thousand. Have I any advance on one hundred thousand?'

It felt as if the entire assembly was holding its breath. But the building contractor was looking bullish. He had evidently set his limit at one hundred thousand, and was refusing to budge.

'One hundred thousand, to the lady in red. Going, going — '

'One hundred and twenty thousand,' said Cleo, and the auction room gave a collective gasp.

'One hundred and twenty thousand euros, to the lady in blue. Have I any advance on one hundred and twenty thousand euros?' A silence fell. 'No advance on one hundred and twenty thousand euros . . . Very well. Going, going — '

'One forty,' said the lady in red.

Fuck, thought Cleo. She hadn't been expecting this. 'One hundred and sixty thousand,' she said, feeling sweat break out under her armpits.

'One hundred and seventy.'

Sweet Jesus! The gloves were off, now! Cleo gazed intently at the painting on the easel at the top of the hall. *Can we come home?* the couple asked piteously, isolated and lonely in the Connemara landscape.

'One hundred and eighty,' she said.

'One hundred and ninety.'

'Any advance on one hundred and ninety? One hundred and ninety thousand euros to the lady in red. Going, going . . . '

Can we come home?

Yes! Of course you *must* come home! 'Two hundred thousand euros,' said Cleo, and blood rushed to her head.

'Any advance on two hundred thousand

euros? Two hundred thousand euros to the lady in blue. Going, going — '

Oh, God. The moment lasted for ever. In slow motion, she saw the Red Queen's husband lay a restraining hand on his wife's arm.

'Gone.'

She'd done it. They were coming home.

The hall was in uproar, but it was nothing to the roar inside Cleo's skull. Whoah! she thought, shaking the adrenalin out of her head. That had been — kinda fun! She rose to her feet, and as she did she heard a clearly audible voice behind her say: 'You daft bitch.'

Turning, she saw Pablo standing at the door, leaning against the jamb, hands in his pockets. They regarded each other for a moment or two, and then Cleo was pelting up the aisle to him, and into his outstretched arms, and they were kissing and kissing, and the people in the auction room were all cheering and whistling, and when Pablo and Cleo stopped kissing she heard his voice in her ear say: 'Thank you for allowing us to come home.'

'Us?' she echoed.

'Me and my cockatoo,' he said, smiling down at her.

★ ★ ★

They decided to go to O'Toole's for a celebratory drink before going home to bed. It felt a bit strange to be sitting in a pub with a seriously valuable painting swathed in bubble-wrap on the banquette beside them. It would have to be insured first thing in the morning.

'It's a beautiful painting,' said Cleo. 'Thank you.'

'And thank *you* for bumping up the price. How fucking insane are you — to fork out two hundred thousand euros for something you could have had for free?'

'I couldn't have accepted it for free, Pablo. If I'd done that I would have deprived Safe-Home Ireland of a chance to make loads of money. It would have been a most uncharitable thing to do. Anyway, I decided you needed to sweat a little. And I hope you did, when Hugh told you that I wasn't keeping the painting.'

'Damn right, I sweated. But I wasn't going to give up. I was determined to get your attention by hook, crook or cockatook. I spent an entire week teaching that damn bird to say the right things.'

'The bird was a pretty good tactic,' conceded Cleo. 'Polly and I fell in love at first sight.'

'So the cockatoo is Polly, is he?'

'Yes.'

'For the amount of cash I forked out for him you might have given him a more grandiose moniker, darling.'

'Like what?'

'I dunno. Tarquin, or something. Peregrine.'

'You can't call a bird that silly Peregrine,' Cleo told him. 'He's pretty Polly.'

'And he's for life. You do know that? They live to an advanced old age, those birds. And he will cleave to you till endsville.'

'You too?'

'Me too.'

They smiled at each other, and then Cleo took hold of his hand. 'We'll have to hire a babysitter every time we go away. Or stick to camper van holidays so that Poll can come too.'

'How about,' said Pablo, 'hiring a sitter for a baby, as well?'

'A real one?'

'Yes.'

'You think we should try?'

'I do.'

Cleo slanted him a sideways look. 'In that case,' she said, drawing an envelope out of her bag. 'I have something for you.'

'What is it?'

'It's a short story.'

'Oh?' he smiled at her and raised an eyebrow. 'When did you write it?'

'This morning.'

'Should I read it now?'

'Why not?' Cleo sent him her most provocative smile and crossed her legs so flagrantly he had to look at them.

'Stay-ups?' he asked.

'Of course.'

'Clever girl,' he said. Then he took a swig of his pint, set it down, took the envelope from her and tore it open.

' "The Auction",' he read out loud. 'Not a very inspired title, is it?'

'Read on.'

She watched as his eyes scanned the pages, watched his mouth curve in a smile. 'So this lady's wearing a pale blue dress in silk jersey that clings to her breasts?'

'Yes. And she looks absolutely lovely,' said Cleo.

'Hm. It says here that nipples are very prominent. Are they?'

'Why don't you look for yourself?' she asked.

Pablo ran his eyes over her blue jersey dress. 'Well. She's obviously in a fairly advanced stage of sexual arousal. Why's that, I wonder?'

'Read on.'

'Aha! She's seen this rough Spanish-looking painter staring at her, and from the bulge in his jeans, he's clearly sporting a hard-on.'

'Is he?'

'Why don't you look for yourself?' he asked.

'Ooh. I think he just might be.'

'So,' he said, resuming his perusal of the manuscript, 'she wants to take this rough-looking painter back to her very posh house so that he can ride the arse off her?'

'I think she probably does. But there's the auction to be got through first.'

'Oh kaay.' Pablo read on. 'Hey! It says here that she only paid a hundred thousand euros for the painter's landscape. What kind of an underestimation of the painter's talent is that?'

'A pretty accurate one, I'd have thought. How many ex-pats will Safe-Home Ireland be able to bring home for two hundred grand, incidentally?'

'A fair few.'

'I should bloody well hope so. Carry on reading.'

403

'They go to the pub, blah, blah, blah. She's feeling so horny after the adrenalin rush of the auction that when he touches her leg, she gives a little gasp.' Pablo laid a casual hand on Cleo's thigh.

'Oh, sweet Jesus!' she said.

'They return to her house. They're so hot for each other that as soon as they walk through the front door he rips her dress off and rogers her unceremoniously on the hall floor. I see.' He gave her an interested look. 'How easy is that dress to rip off?'

'Extremely.'

'OK,' said Pablo, draining his glass. 'I think it's time we went home to number 5, the Blackthorns. That *is* the address of the lady in question, isn't it?'

'It certainly is. And the lady has the key secreted on her person.'

'Where?' said Pablo, giving her a lazy smile.

'That,' said Cleo, smiling back at her husband, 'is for the painter to find out.'

★ ★ ★

After the lady in the pale blue dress had been frisked for the key and ravished to her satisfaction on the hall floor, she and the painter retired to bed to talk.

'How was it for you?' asked Pablo. He was lying against a bank of pillows, his right arm round Cleo, his left hand toying with a strand of her hair.

'Gorgeous, thank you.'

404

'No, I mean how was it for you living on your own here?'

'Pretty awful. If it hadn't been for Pixie I probably would have moved out. How was it for you?'

'The pits.'

'Where did you go?'

'London. Shall I tell you a story now?'

'Does it involve a rough Spanish-looking painter?'

'It does.'

Cleo took his hand. 'Once upon a time . . . ' she prompted him.

He took a deep breath, then: 'Once upon a time,' he said, 'there was a painter who loved his work so much that he whistled while he painted. He was very, very poor, but he didn't give a fuck because his work made him the happiest man in the world. But then he struck lucky — at least that's what he thought.'

'How?'

'He got rich. He became a society portrait painter — a prolific one. He painted every day, canvas upon canvas, and he laughed at the people who paid him stupid money for their portraits. And for a while life was a blast, especially when he married a beautiful girl who loved reading and fucking.'

'What was her name?'

'Her name,' he said, 'was Beauteous Beloved Honey-tongued Ride.'

'That'll do,' she said, with satisfaction. 'Continue.'

'But one day the painter realized that he

wasn't whistling while he worked any more, and he began to hate the fat cats who bought his talent as carelessly as if he were a rent boy, and he began to *feel* like a rent boy. And then he began to drink too much.'

'Why did he do that?'

'He did it because he was bitter and twisted with self-loathing. He did it to drown out the sneering voices in his head that told him over and over again that he had sold out, and that his work was facile crap. And finally he got to a stage where he could barely bring himself to look at the canvas he was working on without opening a bottle of wine. And one day he got so very, very drunk that he betrayed Beauteous Beloved, and she banished him from her life. And that's how he ended up in London.'

'What did he do there?'

'He walked the streets endlessly, looking for people to paint.'

'What kind of people?'

'The first person he asked to sit for him was a homeless child. He paid her well, and she told him all about her life as she sat, and he learned all about her hopes and dreams and her frailties, and he *loved* the painting he made of her. But his agent didn't.'

'Oh? What did she say?'

'She scolded him, and told him to go back to doing what he did best.'

'And did he?'

'No. He couldn't, because he knew that if he did that he'd be living a lie. So he sacked her. And then he found a new agent and lots more people to paint — people who had no fine clothes or jewels or chains of office, but who were richer than the fattest fat cats he had ever painted, even though most of them lived in hostels. And do you know why they were richer?'

'Why?'

'They were richer,' he said, 'because their souls were full of hope.'

'What did they hope for?'

'The future. The men in those hostels live in hope that one day they might return home to their native land, and they dream that one day they might regain their dignity. And when the painter heard them talk of home, something miraculous happened to him, even though it seems like a small thing.'

'What happened?'

'He started whistling again, while he worked.'

'Oh! Was he too hoping that he might come home?'

'He was. And he stopped hating himself. And after a while his self-esteem was such that he dared to go to Beauteous Beloved Honey-tongued Ride and offer her inducements to take him back.'

'What inducements did he offer her?'

'He offered her the best painting he had ever made. He offered her a symbol of undying love in the shape of a beautiful bird. And he promised her he would worship at her feet in the power shower any time she commanded him to.'

'Cool! I love that bit!'

Pablo turned his head on the pillow and looked at her.

'Is that the end?' she asked.

'It's the story so far.'

'Is he going to live happily ever after?'

'I hope so.'

'With Beauteous Beloved Honey-tongued Ride?'

'If she'll have him.'

Cleo slid out of bed.

'Where are you going?' he asked.

'I'm going to fetch Polly.'

'Why?'

'He wants to tell you something. Wait there.'

Cleo scampered downstairs. The bird was playing with his new toy — one of Cleo's old eyeliner brushes. 'Hello, darling!' she said, as she hefted the cage. 'You know what to say, don't you?'

'Cleo Dowling's a kick-ass ride.'

'No, no! Not that! The one I taught you.'

She whispered something to the bird and then she carried the cage up to the bedroom and set it down at the foot of the bed.

'What's that he's playing with?' Pablo asked.

'It's one of my old make-up brushes.'

'Hey! Inspired. Maybe we could teach him to paint. We'd stand to make a fortune flogging Paintings by Pablo's Parrot. They'd fly off the gallery walls easily as fast as my quirky stuff did.'

'Sh. Listen to him.' Cleo leaned in to the parrot and whispered through the bars again. 'Go on, Poll,' she urged him.

Polly regarded her with a sagacious eye.

'Go on, darling! Cat got your tongue?'

The bird turned to Pablo and squawked, as if

408

clearing his throat. Then: 'Pablo MacBride has the biggest dick in Ireland,' said Polly.

★ ★ ★

Much later they were sitting at the kitchen table. Cleo had made her best dish of egg and rasher sandwiches, and had opened a bottle of wine.

'By the way,' she said, 'I noticed when I cleared out your studio that it looked like a wino had been living there. You could have built a conservatory with all the bottles I dumped in the recycling bin.'

'Poor you having to endure the shame of dumping them. I hope no-one saw you.'

'I took care to do it at dead of night. You were putting away a *lot* of booze, Pablo.'

'I know. I did wonder if I had a problem. I even thought about checking myself in some-where, and then I realized that actually, alcohol wasn't the problem. The problem was me. Once I took things into my own hands and started living my life the way I wanted I didn't need to drink any more.'

'Can you handle it now?'

'For sure. I could stick a cork in that bottle now and put it back in the fridge, no problem. I could go to Ballynahinch and drive home well within the limit. I could take you to bed and not have to worry about brewer's droop.'

She gave him a 'Doh!' look. 'You never had to worry about that anyway.'

'Thanks to you, Beauteous Beloved Honey-tongued Ride. *God* — I'd love to paint you now.

409

You're wearing that fantastic 'wrecked from sex' look. Shall we go down to the studio?'

'No. You won't be able to find anything, and you'll start giving out. Why did you destroy all your canvases, incidentally?'

'You know why. I destroyed them because they were cynical and shallow and slick and worthless. I shall never paint a pig again in my life, Cleo, no matter how much money I'm offered.'

She remembered the last commission he'd been offered, from the man who wanted portraits for his hotel lobbies. 'By the way — I found a letter in there from someone called P.B. Crotty.'

'P.B. who?'

'Crotty. He's the CEO of some hotel chain — he wanted to commission a series of portraits by you.'

Pablo laughed. 'Oh, baby, am I grateful to him!'

'But you'd scribbled 'Go eat your Y-fronts' across the letter!'

'That's what I mean. Good old P.B. was responsible for giving me my wake-up call.'

'What do you mean?'

'That's when I realized that if I painted another 'quirky' portrait I'd be selling my soul to the devil.'

'So there's nothing quirky about any of the portraits you did in London?'

'No. Nothing quirky at all. Most of them are of expat Irish.'

'I'm dying to see them.'

'My new agent's lining up a show for me there. You'll come over, won't you?'

'Sure.'

'You've no idea the kind of sacrifices those men made, Cleo. In those days it was tough to find accommodation — you know that B&Bs used to post signs saying: 'No blacks, no dogs and no Irish'? Once upon a time it was — incredibly — *untrendy* to be Irish. So lots of those men ended up on the streets, and they had *nothing*. No money, no hope, no prospects. And now they're on the slag heap, and most of them drink to blur reality, as I did, and it scared me to think that I could have ended up like them.' He topped up her glass, then stuck the cork back in the bottle. 'And I thought of what I'd thrown away, and of how insane I'd been. And that's when I painted *Figures in a Landscape*, for you.'

The look he gave Cleo turned her heart over. She regarded the painting now, where it sat propped against the wall by the kitchen door.

'You see how I raised you up,' Pablo said, 'so that you're on a higher level than me?'

'Yes.' She smiled. 'I'm on a little grassy tussock.'

'That's your pedestal. And see how I've put you supporting my arm? That's an indication of how good you've been to me. And a reminder of how I can't live without you.'

'You won't have to. As long as you keep your promise about worshipping at my feet in the power shower once in a while.' She smiled at him. 'Why is your arm withered?'

'That's my fatal flaw. My venality. And the

411

crutch is my salvation. My passion for painting.'

'And the cottage is home, and you're home at last!'

There was a longish silence, and then Pablo said: 'I'm so sorry, Cleo.'

'What are you sorry about now?'

'About Fluffy. I did think about buying you a replacement, but I knew that no other dog could ever replace Fluff in your affections. That's why I opted for a cockatoo.'

'The cockatoo,' said Cleo, 'was an inspired present.'

Pablo stood up from the table and gave her his slantiest smile. 'Come here,' he said. 'I want to give you another present right now.'

'Goodie,' she said, taking the hand he had held out to her. 'What are you going to give me?'

'I am going, Cleo Dowling,' said Pablo MacBride, 'to give you a baby.'

And that's exactly what he did.

20

Hazel drove to Kilrowan on Saturday, the last day of the festival.

Before she took the turn-off to the Hennessy house she pulled over, spritzed herself with a little scent, reapplied her lipstick and double-checked that she had everything she needed in her small overnight bag. Change of underwear, toothbrush, condoms. All the manifestations of her wishful thinking were present and correct.

There was no sign of life when she pulled up in the courtyard to the rear of the house, apart from Prue and Honey, who were barking at her over the half-door of one of the stables. Hugh's car was there, but that didn't mean he was at home — he could be out exercising the horses. She'd half expected the batty stable hand to be lurking around, and she was glad that he was nowhere to be seen. She didn't want her tryst with his master to be interrupted by more queries about baulky horses, whatever they were.

As she shut the car door, she was aware of movement beyond the kitchen window. A curtain twitched. Someone was watching her. She felt painfully self-conscious as she zapped the locks, and regretted instantly that she was carrying her overnight bag. It smacked so of presumption. However, she couldn't very well turn round and sling the bag back in the car. That would look even worse.

As she made her way across the courtyard the door to the kitchen opened and Hugh stepped out. The sight of him made her stop in her tracks. He too stood very still, assessing her, and then he adopted a casual stance, leaning against the jamb and regarding her without any trace of the contempt she'd feared she might see there. She had, after all, been guilty of a gross deception. There was no dismay there either, nor even any surprise. Indeed, her erstwhile lover didn't seem to be wearing any expression at all: his face was a *tabula rasa*. But when she said: 'Hugh', something behind his eyes flickered into life, and a smile moved the corners of his mouth.

'Hi,' he said.

Hazel still stood motionless in the centre of the courtyard. She didn't want to move any closer to the house until she got the absolute green light that everything was A OK. 'Hi,' she said, in a very small voice. And then she said: 'I'm sorry. Can you forgive me? I misled you abominably.'

'What's to forgive?' he said in a low voice. 'Come on in.'

She took a step towards him, then another, and then she was standing on tiptoe, closing her eyes and proffering her mouth for a kiss.

He obliged by brushing her lips with his and then he stepped back inside the house, holding the door open for her. She walked through, inhaling the scent of aftershave as she passed him by, thinking abstractedly that there was something new about the way he smelt, then allowing the thought to drift away into the ether

414

as he moved up behind her and slid his arms around her waist.

He dropped a kiss on the nape of her neck, another on the place behind her earlobe. 'Hi, gorgeous,' he said, nuzzling her. And when she felt the heat of his breath in her ear and the rasp of his tongue against her cheek, she knew that her own breath was starting to sound ragged with arousal. Hugh gave a low laugh, and his hand glided smoothly from her waist to her breast.

'I didn't expect that you'd be so glad to see me,' she said in a voice that was shaky with both relief and desire. 'I thought that perhaps you might — '

'Ssh,' he said, turning her to face him, caressing a nipple through the silk of her blouse. 'Let's not talk now.'

'You're right,' she said with a smile. 'There are more important things to be doing.' She released her hair from its chignon and shook it out. 'We can't allow the thing with Angel to — '

'Ssh,' he said again, winding his fingers in her hair and pulling her head back so that he could kiss her throat. 'Don't talk. Don't talk unless you wanna talk dirty.'

'I'm a nice girl,' she said with jokey hauteur. 'Nice girls don't talk dirty.'

'In my experience,' he murmured, as his tongue traced the line of her collarbone, 'the nicest girls like it down and dirty. How hot are you?'

'I'm hot,' she said, with a little laugh. 'But you know how to make me hotter.'

'Maybe you should tell me how.'

'You could start by kissing me.'

Hazel smiled as he lowered her to the floor and proceeded to kiss her with agonizing expertise. She'd forgotten what a silky kisser he was. Oh, God! *How* could she have forgotten? She wound her arms around his neck and clung to him, ardent, responsive, drinking him in.

'Oh, baby, you are *hot*,' he said, sliding a hand under her blouse and unhooking her bra. 'You are one slick, hot chick. Come on — talk dirty to me, baby. Tell me what you want me to do with my tongue. This? How about this?' And then his tongue was in her mouth again, probing, sinuous, sexy as a snake.

Hazel responded with mounting urgency. She had never before heard Hugh talk this way — she wasn't sure she liked it — but the sensations he was conjuring were quite mind-blowing. He had pulled her blouse open and was caressing her breasts, making low sounds of appreciation in his throat. She reciprocated by sliding her hands up under the fabric of his T-shirt. Christ, how gorgeous the feel of bare muscled flesh against her palms! She wanted — no, she *needed* him naked. Gyrating her hips against him, she pulled his T-shirt up so that she could experience the thrill of his skin against hers.

Hugh's voice was in her ear again. 'You hot bitch. I know what you want. You want this, don't you?' He grabbed her hand and thrust it against his groin, and as she looked down at the smooth expanse of his lean, tanned chest she saw that there was no scar there.

There was no scar there.

She pulled her hand away. 'Hugh — I — '

'Ssh. I told you to shut up.'

'Hugh — '

'I said *shut up*! Don't call me that.'

'The scar! Your scar — '

'Shut the *fuck* up!' Suddenly his hand was covering her mouth and Hazel knew that something was going dreadfully wrong. She struggled to get up, but his full weight was on her now, pinioning her to the floor, and the more she twisted, the more he seemed to enjoy it.

'What's up, sweetie-pie?' he said, his voice sounding unfamiliar, like a rasp in her ear. 'Don't tell me you don't like a bit of rough stuff?' He thrust his thigh between her legs, ruching up her skirt.

'Stop!' she whimpered from behind the hand that was covering her mouth. 'Please — stop!' But no sound came. She was seriously frightened now. If Hugh was playing some kind of sex game, she wasn't up for it — she just wanted out of there. Oh God, dear God. What to do what to do what to do. *Fight or flight!* Adrenalin surged, and she bit down hard against the skin of his palm.

It was a wrong move.

'You fucking bitch!' He slapped the side of her head, then rammed his knee against the inside of her thigh, spreading her legs further apart. 'What's got into you, bitch? You were gagging for it minutes ago. Don't tell me you're a pricktease?'

One of her arms was pinioned under the weight of his elbow, the other was trapped in vice-like fingers. Hazel had never imagined that she could be rendered so completely powerless. The only time she had ever experienced such helplessness in her life had been when caught in the grip of one of those awful waking nightmares when you scream and scream for help, but no sound escapes you, and the straitjacket of the dream holds you ever tighter.

He reached down, fumbled with the buckle of his belt. Hazel shut her eyes. He was panting now like a dog, she could feel his spit on her face. Tears seeped out from between her eyelids as his tongue darted into her ear.

'Oh, you're going to love this, sweetheart. You're really, really going to love this. Is this how Hugh does it, is it? Slaps you about a bit, does he? What does he call you? Does he — '

Thwack! There was a sudden sickening crack of bone on bone, but Hazel felt no impact. Her assailant's weight shifted; she heard an animal grunt.

Then: '*Fuck you!*' came a roar. 'Get off her!'

A tall figure was bending over her, and the demon was being dragged away. Instinctively Hazel curled herself into as tight a ball as she could manage, covering her head with her hands and sliding herself into the corner of the room.

'You fucking *shithead!* Get the fuck out of my house!' It was Hugh's voice. Another cracking sound, a groan. 'Get the fuck *out!*' Then came the sound of stumbling feet, a thump, a yowl of pain.

Hazel dared to look. It was a surreal sight: two men were laying into each other, and they were both Hugh. The man in the T-shirt was bleeding from a wound to the side of his head: he was staggering and clearly dazed, but the swing he took at his opponent struck home. Hazel had never seen Hugh look anything other than sanguine: the expression he wore now was terrifying. Mad with rage, he aimed a blow to the jaw so forceful that the other man fell to his knees. Spitting blood at Hugh's feet, he muttered something guttural, then crawled to the door. Hugh stood over him, fists clenched, breathing hard, clearly having trouble resisting the impulse to kick a man who was down. The other man spat again, then pulled himself up by the handle and stood swaying in the doorway.

'She's all yours, now, bro,' he said, with a malicious smile. 'But remember this. I'm the one who warmed her up for you.'

Thwack! Another vicious blow from Hugh drove the man through the door. He stumbled down the steps into the courtyard, and Hazel heard the dogs bark as he disappeared from view.

Then Hugh was kneeling beside her, saying: 'Hazel! Hazel — are you all right?' and his hands were on her shoulders, and she was crying and crying, and clinging to the sleeve of his suede jacket and breathing in the familiar sandalwoody smell of his aftershave.

★ ★ ★

419

He ran her a bath, made her hot sweet tea, wrapped her in his big towelling bathrobe, and cooked her an omelette. She wasn't hungry, but she ate it to please him.

'Brandy?' he asked when she'd finished the omelette.

'Brandy would be good.' Her voice was still shaky, but she felt preternaturally calm. She knew she was still in shock.

Hugh moved to the sideboard and poured two stiff brandies into balloon glasses. He set hers in front of her, then sat down opposite Hazel at the kitchen table and took hold of her hand. She saw that his knuckles were raw, and made a little sound of sympathy.

'Don't worry about me,' he said. 'It's you I'm concerned about. Are you going to press charges?'

She shook her head. 'No, no, no. I'm not injured.'

'That's not the point, Hazel. That was a serious assault.'

'Hugh. I know this is cowardly of me, but I couldn't hack it. I couldn't hack the humiliation. I feel so dirty. I feel so — I feel that I was partly to blame . . . '

'Don't say that!'

'And I don't want people to know that I was so fucking *stupid*, that I was so easily gulled.'

'Hazel, if anyone's to blame, it's me. I should have warned you about Harry. But I honestly never dreamed he'd have the nerve to show up here. The fucking bastard. The fucking *shithead* deserves — '

420

'Ssh. Be calm and tell me now,' she said, stroking the back of his hand. 'Tell me all about him.'

Hugh took up his brandy glass, swirled the contents, and took a swig. 'Harry,' he said, 'is pure evil. Always has been. He was the first to be born. He barged his way out in the delivery room, according to my father, leaving me stuck with the cord around my neck. It was war at first sight.'

'It's funny — you always imagine identical twins to be soulmates.'

'We may be identical on the outside,' he said, 'but I like to think that I'm as different to him as it's possible to be on the inside.'

'Can someone be pure evil?'

'Oh, yes. Harry is what's known as a sociopath. He doesn't care about anyone in the world except himself.'

Hazel took a sip of brandy. It burned all the way down. 'I read a novel about a sociopath once,' she said. 'It was called The Bad Seed.'

' 'Bad Seed' just about sums it up. I thought that he might act different around me after the accident, after our mother died. But if anything, it made things worse. I know it's unchristian to hate a member of your family, Hazel, but I loathed Harry so much I wished him dead. The day he finally upped and left was the best day of my life.'

'How long has he been gone?'

'He left on our seventeenth birthday.'

'Where did he go? What did he do with himself? Or do you know?'

'All I know is that he's spent his adult life in prisons all over Europe.' Hugh looked at her levelly. 'He could go back to prison if you pressed charges, Hazel.'

'No, Hugh — please don't make me.'

'Of course I won't *make* you.'

Hazel took another hit of brandy. The prospect of having to stand in a dock and testify against the stranger who'd tried to rape her filled her with horror. And oh, God — it filled her with shame, too — shame at the way she'd responded to his kisses, caressed his bare skin, pressed herself against him . . . No. *No!* The incident was in the past now, and it was going to stay there, locked away like a guilty secret. But . . . what if he targeted some other woman? What if her reluctance to press charges put someone else at risk?

'Do the gardí know that he's at large?' she asked.

'For sure. I notified them as soon as I knew he was back. They'll keep an eye out for him as long as he's in the country.'

'But he's already broken the law! Didn't he break into the house?'

'No. That was my fault. I left the door unlocked. They can't charge him with breaking and entering.'

'And I can't charge him with assault, Hugh. I'm sorry.'

He nodded. 'Fair enough.'

'What is he doing back in Ireland?'

'Cashing in on my father's death. My sister was the executrix of the will, but he had to come

422

sniffing around — see if there were any more pickings going.'

'What'll happen to him now?'

'I don't imagine he'll hang around. He didn't get what he was looking for, so there's nothing to keep him here.'

'Has he been living in the area?'

'Yeah. He's been sponging off some woman in Galway.'

Galway. Angel had slept with a man she'd assumed was Hugh in the Galway Great Southern. Oh, God. It was time to bring up the subject of her mother. 'Has he been done for — ' she was almost afraid to say the words — 'sexual assault before?'

'Not to my knowledge. He's a charming motherfucker by all accounts — most sociopaths are. Women are happy to go to bed with him until they get to know him.'

'I think — I think Angel may have gone to bed with him, Hugh.' Hazel couldn't meet Hugh's eyes. She wanted to cringe when she anticipated the confession she was going to have to make.

'Angel. Your . . . ?'

The question mark was implicit in his tone.

'My mother. Yes.'

'What on earth makes you think she slept with Harry?'

'She told me that she'd run into — um — you. In the Galway Great Southern . . . '

'Me?'

'Yes.'

'I haven't been in the Great Southern for years. I didn't sleep with your mother, Hazel.'

She bit her lip. 'I'm so sorry. I have some explaining to do as well.'

'You do.'

'Angel said that you — I mean, *Harry* — made it clear it was a one-night stand.'

'So now I have to take the rap for that! Jesus! How am I going to handle her now that she thinks I've slept with her?' Helplessness was scrawled all over his face. 'I've had experience of this kind of shit before — women coming on to me after they've been seduced by my brother. But my girlfriend's *mother* . . . '

'I'm so sorry, Hugh. About the deception.'

'What on earth made you do it?'

She didn't — couldn't — admit that she'd been brimful of shame at having a joke for a mother, and a jackass for a father. She took a deep breath. 'Well. It would have smacked of nepotism if I lined both my parents up for the festival. It would have looked as if I was using my influence as PR to wangle gigs for them. It was Mum's idea,' she added lamely, passing the buck.

And then she thought: No. That's not fair. She couldn't heap blame on her mother. The ultimate reality was that *you* took responsibility in your life for the actions that you took, the decisions you made, the talk that you talked and the lies that you told — no-one else. Hazel MacNamara was the author of her own destiny, and she couldn't allow anyone else to take the rap: not her mother, not her father.

'I remember,' she said, 'walking into the kitchen at home once, and there was coffee

424

gushing out through the electric percolator onto a work surface.'

'Um. Sorry — but what has this to do with your parents?'

'Not a lot. It has more to do with me. I put on my best face of thunder and stamped my foot when I saw the mess. I couldn't believe that this was yet another example of my parents' arrant fecklessness. Until I remembered that *I* had been the one to turn the machine on, *I* had been the one who'd forgotten to put the coffee-pot under the percolator.'

'And the moral of the story is?'

'Everyone makes mistakes. Even me, so-sussed Hazel MacNamara of Nutcracker PR. I landed myself in this one, Hugh.'

'You sure did.'

'And actually, all the lies I told had nothing to do with worries about charges of nepotism, and everything to do with the fact that I was deeply ashamed of them.'

'You were *ashamed* of your parents?'

'Yes.' Her voice was very small.

'Why on earth would you be ashamed of them? Your parents are fantastic.'

She hid her face behind her hands. 'I've been ashamed of them for as long as I can remember. It's difficult having parents who are in the public eye. And I never dreamed that you and I would get involved. And then after we became an item I just stuck my head in the sand and hoped that the plot would work itself out. I was going to come clean with you that evening in O'Toole's, but then we got waylaid by Cleo and Pixie and everything started to unravel and I just legged it.'

'And you're telling me you masterminded this lie fest because you were ashamed of your parents?'

Hazel looked down at her lap. 'Yes,' she said.

'Jesus!'

She didn't want to look at him, didn't want to see the contempt that was sure to be there on his face. But when she plucked up the courage to meet his eye, Hugh was wearing a puzzled frown.

'There's a lovely absurdity,' he said, 'about a woman who seems so sussed and smart on the surface making a complete arse of herself. I'm rather glad you have a silly side to you. I can use it to blackmail you.' He gave her a slow smile.

She managed a smile back. 'You won't ever tell anyone about — what happened with Harry, will you? I made a complete arse of myself today.'

'Of course I won't tell.'

'I am so glad you came in when you did.' Her voice faltered.

Hugh moved to her, took her in his arms and rocked her a little, and she was reminded of the way her mother had comforted her so recently on the main street of Kilrowan. It felt rather blissful to have someone take charge for a change. She was feeling drowsy now, from emotional fatigue and brandy, and the rocking was threatening to send her to sleep. Then a thought struck her that jolted her wide awake.

'Oh, shit!' she said. 'The screening! The ceilí!'

'Don't worry. Renée's got everything under control. She's nearly as sussed as you are, Ms MacNamara.'

'But shouldn't you be there? You *are* the Kilrowan Festival, after all.'

'I'm not going anywhere, sweetheart. I'm going to put you to bed and tuck you in.'

'Oh. And then?'

'I'm going to watch over you.'

'You're gorgeous!'

'Come on,' he said. 'Bed for you. You've had a bitch of a day.'

Hugh scooped her up in his arms, and made for the hallway.

'Oh,' she said. 'No-one's done this to me since I was tiny. I feel like Scarlett O'Hara, when Rhett carries her up the stairs.'

'Your favourite heroine.'

'My favourite heroine.'

'Hugh?' she said as they reached his sister's bedroom. 'You know that movie, *The Lion King*?'

'Never heard of it,' he said, tumbling her on to the bed.

'It's about these two lion brothers, one good, one evil. Except in the movie the evil one is called Scar. And in real life — our real life — the good brother is Scar. Funny how things get reversed when art holds a mirror up to life, isn't it?'

'You're rambling now. Under the duvet you go.'

'Can't I sleep in your bed?'

'No.'

'Why not?'

'Because you had a shocking thing happen to you earlier, and if I allow you into my bed you

427

won't get any sleep. You're going to need your eight hours tonight.'

And the next day Hazel woke feeling as refreshed as Sleeping Beauty, to find her handsome prince drawing back the curtains.

★ ★ ★

She stayed in Kilrowan for most of Sunday. She didn't want to leave. But she had to be back in Dublin for work on Monday.

Hugh waved her off, making her promise to phone the minute she got home. Halfway back to Dublin she stopped to access her phone, and found a text message from him. 'Fancy spending nxt wkend in B'nahinch Castle?'

'Yes please!' she texted back, just as her ringtone sounded.

'Hello, darling! How are you?' trilled Angel when she picked up.

'I'm much better, thanks, Mum. How are you?'

'We're grand!' It was her father's voice. Angel clearly had her phone on conference mode. 'We're in Ballynahinch Castle. In a dead posh room.'

'Your dad remembered out of the blue that it's our wedding anniversary,' explained Angel.

'But you're not married!'

'We are. We could never be arsed getting divorced. Too much palaver.'

Was there no end to the list of things she'd never bothered to find out about her parents?

'Well, congratulations!'

'It's feckin' lovely here,' said her dad. 'River view, room service, four-poster bed. Oh. Sorry. I know you find the whole notion of your mum and dad — erm . . . '

'No, I don't. I don't find it 'erm' at all! I think it's fantastic. Congratulations all over again!'

Hazel heard the sound of a distant rat-a-tat.

'Ah, there's room service now,' said her dad. 'Grub's up!'

'Wait, Dad. I just want to say — I don't know when was the last time I said this, but I love you two very much. I really, really do.'

'We know that,' said Angel. 'Go, Mondo. Let the lad in. And don't forget to tip him!' She lowered her voice. 'Now. Tell me, darling. How are things with Hugh?'

'Well, you might like to know that we're following your excellent example and spending next weekend in Ballynahinch.'

'Far out! So the parallel universe thing worked!'

'Er — not exactly,' said Hazel.

'Oh? Elaborate.'

'He has an identical twin, Mum.'

'So?'

'Are you still on conference mode?'

'No.'

'Are you sitting down?'

'Yes.'

'You didn't sleep with Hugh, Mum. You slept with his twin brother.'

There was a beat or two as Angel took in this new development, then: 'What a relief!' she said. 'And what a blast! It's like something out of a

429

Pixie Pirelli novel. You should sell her the story. Just think — you and I could be the stars of her next bestseller, Hazel. And I could play myself in the film version!'

'I thought you were getting out of show business?'

'I thought so too. But I got a call from my agent the other day. They want me to play Gypsy Rose Lee in the Sondheim musical, and they're offering the kind of money no gal in her right mind could turn down.'

'Gypsy Rose Lee?'

'The famous stripper. She invented the fan dance. Isn't it fabulous? And don't worry — I won't be naked all the time. I'll get to wear some *über*-glam frocks. Gypsy was glamorous well into her fifties, you know. And I get to sing some real ballsy numbers.'

And as her mother launched into 'Everything's Coming up Roses', Hazel switched her phone off.

21

The final shot of *The O'Malley* was a guaranteed tear-jerker. The camera lingered on the face of Eva Lavery — the dying Grace O'Malley — as she unhitched the hawser of her favourite galley — the one she loved so much that she kept it moored to an iron ring set into the wall of her tower room — and watched through her window as it drifted towards the horizon. As she gazed after it, the audience saw by the expression on her face that the further away the galley drifted, the closer the Pirate Queen came to death.

Cleo had never seen the movie before. As the credits rolled, so did the inevitable tears down the faces of just about every member of the audience. Everyone in Kilrowan had their 'Eva story'. It must be worse for Deirdre, she knew, and of course, when the lights came up in the village hall, she saw that her friend's cheeks were wet, too.

'There, there,' murmured Cleo, taking hold of Deirdre's hand.

'It's going to get worse,' whispered Deirdre. 'I'm so glad that David's not here. He wouldn't be able for this.'

The last strains of the theme tune echoed round the village hall, and then Rory rose from his seat, and moved to the top of the hall.

'Good evening, ladies and gentlemen,' he said.

'Thank you all for coming here tonight to pay tribute to a great lady.' He took a deep breath, steeling himself. 'I made this movie with Eva in Galway, not far from here, over a decade ago. The baby in the film is Eva's own daughter, Dorcas, and I would like to recite to you something that Dorcas herself recited on Lissnakeelagh strand on the day that Eva's ashes were scattered. It's a speech of Prospero's from *The Tempest*.'

Rory looked laid-back, casual even, as he put his hands in his pockets.

'He looks relaxed,' Deirdre whispered to Cleo, 'but he's not. This is one of the toughest things he's ever had to do.'

The following words rang out, in Rory's resonant voice.

'Our revels now are ended. These our
   actors,
As I foretold you, were all spirits, and
Are melted into air, into thin air:
And, like the baseless fabric of this vision,
The cloud-capp'd towers, the gorgeous pal-
   aces,
The solemn temples, the great globe itself,
Yea, all which it inherit, shall dissolve,
And, like the insubstantial pageant faded,
Leave not a rack behind. We are such stuff
As dreams are made on, and our little life
Is rounded with a sleep.

'You all know what a special place this part of the world was for Eva,' he resumed. 'It's a special place for me, too. Eva made it possible for me to be reconciled with my girl here, not once, but twice. Our first baby was conceived in Connemara. Without the advice and the wise words of one of the most clued-in women I have ever known, my beautiful daughters, my son, would not be in the world today.

'In the last movie she ever made — and it was made here in Kilrowan — Eva played a white witch. It is my firm belief that she was, in life, a white witch. And you in Kilrowan must consider yourselves fortunate that some of her magic will linger here, for ever. I know it sounds insane to hear a grown man speak this way, but on the evening of the scattering of her ashes I felt as if fairy dust was being scattered over Kilrowan. Eva has bestowed a blessing on this place, and I thank you all once more for honouring her memory. May I call upon you people to rise in a standing ovation to one of the greatest actresses this country has ever known, an actress whose spiritual home was here in the wild and wonderful west of Ireland?'

As the audience in the village hall rose to its feet, Cleo recalled that the last time the hall had been this crowded had been when Eva had given a talk here one evening. She remembered too the words that Eva had spoken to her when she'd gone to the actress one night for advice, when she'd been feeling insecure and unhappy . . .

You do have someone to be proud of you, you know, Cleo. You have Pablo. You don't have to be embarrassed at showing him your gift, your propensity for happiness. It's the greatest gift there is . . .

She reached for Pablo's hand now, as if by holding on to it she could make their bond stronger, and he smiled at her and said 'Penny for them?' and Cleo just said: 'I was remembering Eva. This has been such a special festival, hasn't it? I wish she could have been here.'

'I'm sure she is here, in spirit. But as the poet says, 'Our revels now are ended'. The festival's over, sweetheart.'

'No it's not,' said Cleo, smiling back at him. 'We've still got the ceilí to look forward to!'

'Oh, fuck,' said Pablo.

'Don't you want to go?'

'Sure I do. It's just that I'm dreading being subjected yet again to Colleen and Margot's impersonation of Michael Flatley and Jean Butler in *Riverdance* . . . '

★ ★ ★

The plastic bucket seats had been unceremoniously stacked against the walls of the hall, and the local ceilí band had taken to the stage.

Cleo was straining her ears to hear something Deirdre was trying to say to her over the decibel level of the music. 'What?' she had said at least three times now.

'D'you mind if I dance with Pablo?' Deirdre shouted in Cleo's ear. 'Rory and I have never been able to dance with each other.'

'Why not?'

'We had to dance together in a Restoration

434

comedy once, and we just creased each other up every night on stage. We haven't been able to dance together since. Will you give him the pleasure?'

'Of course!'

Cleo watched as Deirdre turned to Pablo and shouted to him, and then the two of them took off into the swirling throng of dancers. Shouldering her way through the crowd, Cleo went off in search of Rory, who, she suspected correctly, was leaning up against the bar, being chatted up by someone. It was the Princess Abigail.

'Hi!' said Cleo, standing on tiptoe so that her mouth was on a level with Rory's ear, loving the fact that Abigail was there to witness the intimacy of the action. 'Your wife's dancing with my husband. Will you come and dance with me?'

'It would be my pleasure,' said Rory, executing a smart, military-style bow. Then: 'Excuse me,' he shouted at Abigail. 'Enjoy the rest of the evening.' He took Cleo's hand and led her into the centre of the room. 'How boring was she?' he said into her ear. 'I'm very glad you came to my rescue.'

And then Rory McDonagh took Cleo Dowling in his arms and they danced polka-time round the floor of the village hall, and Cleo felt so happy! This is what a festival should be, she thought. It should be — well — festive! With bands and bunting and babies staying up late, being breast-fed by their mothers with no-one looking disapproving. And pretty girls prinking in pretty frocks, and young men to ogle them, and old men tapping their feet to the music, and some of them taking to the floor with their wives and showing off how they can dance still, and dance better than some of them youngsters! And flushed faces, and hairstyles ruined in the heat, and the smell of soap that can't disguise a more animal smell, and bodies pressed close, and the pressure of hands on backs, and the merry-go-round madness of it all. And the music, the beat, the rhythm that comes up through the floor and thrums through you and makes you feel like the girl in the fairytale who can't stop dancing, the girl with the red shoes.

Cleo laughed as she saw Deirdre O'Dare swirl past in the arms of her beautiful, prodigal husband — one, two three! one, two, three! — and she looked up at the face of the drop-dead film star in whose arms she herself was spinning round the floor, and she thought: All's right with the world. I am happy and healthy, I am secure and lucky, I am dancing with one of the handsomest men in the world, and tonight I shall go home and make love with my husband. He doesn't know it, yet, but *I* know that I am already pregnant, and need no test to tell me that I have, beyond the shadow of any doubt, conceived the baby that Pablo made me a gift of on the evening he came home.

And, as happens in all the best fairytales, I am, beyond the shadow of any doubt, going to live happily ever after, thought Cleo Dowling. And in her head she heard Eva's voice again saying: *Happiness. It's the greatest gift there is . . .*

★ ★ ★

Back in London, Pixie couldn't keep from moving around her revamped home, admiring it. She'd spent over a week admiring it now. She would sit down at her laptop and tweak, tweak, tweak away at the redraft of her novel, and then some irresistible impulse would come over her to fetch a glass of water so that she could admire the new units in her kitchen, or go and brush her teeth so that she could admire the new fittings in her bathroom, or go and change into fresh pyjamas so that she could admire the cupboards in her walk-in-wardrobe. It had been her most cherished dream since childhood to one day own a walk-in-wardrobe!

She had arrived home the previous Thursday and that her housekeeper had been thorough. There were fresh flowers in vases, there was food in the fridge. Every last trace of builder had been eliminated. There was no brick dust, no sandwich box with ageing sandwich crust, no pornographic magazine in the loo. The dust sheets had come off the furniture, her clothes had been re-hung in her wardrobe, and a sheaf of mail was neatly stacked on the bureau in the study. Her home had been restored to her, and she was happy.

There was another reason for her to be happy today. She was going to the theatre this evening, with Deborah, her editor, to the opening night of David Lawless's much anticipated production of *The Seagull*. An invitation had arrived last Friday, and Pixie had chosen her opening night

437

outfit with extreme care. She was going to wear a very simple white satin bias-cut frock — short, but not too short — and team it with black stockings, black heels, and a little black bolero jacket with a faux ermine trim. Black and white was always eye-catching, and she wanted to stand out so that the press photographers would home in on her. The engine of the media merry-go-round had been cranked up, and Pixie was spinning around again.

★ ★ ★

She emerged from the Merc into a blur of white light. Press photographers were flashing away, seemingly at random. Every time a car pulled up and disgorged its celebrity contents, a battery Canons and Leicas and Nikons made t distinctive whirring, clicking sound.

'Who's she?' she heard a journalist ask as posed obligingly on the red carpet.

'She's that chick-lit writer who got dumped *Celebrity Castaway*,' came the response.

Pixie high-heeled the gamut, Kylie smile glu firmly in place and finally, finally she reached t haven of the theatre foyer, where Deborah w waiting for her.

'Ew,' she said, with a shudder. 'That wa horrible!'

'But you do it so well,' Deborah reassured he 'And you look particularly fetching tonigh Mwah, mwah.'

'Mwah, mwah, yourself. We're in the dre circle.'

'Cool!'

'Do you know this play, Deborah?'

'Yes.'

'Is it any good?'

Deborah shrugged. 'It's Chekhov,' she said. 'What else can I say?'

★ ★ ★

The Seagull started out with a couple mooching onto the stage.

'Why do you always wear black?' asked the man of the woman.

'I'm in mourning for my life. I'm unhappy.'

Nobody else sniggered, so Pixie resisted the impulse. As the play progressed, she found herself resisting the impulse more and more. Maybe she was wrong. Maybe this wasn't meant to be funny? Maybe it was the kind of High Art that Dare Not Provoke a Smile.

The character Pixie found most interesting in *The Seagull* was that of the flamboyant actress Arkadina. Aside from that, the other characters were a mostly miserable bunch. She felt like telling the moany juve male lead to get a life, and when the heroine trailed onto the stage at the end of the play, she knew she was in for a major dose of *Weltschmcrz*. How the actress in question managed to say the line 'I am a seagull' with a straight face was beyond her. She nearly cheered when the male lead finally got up the gumption to shoot himself.

At the curtain call, Pixie rose to her feet along with the rest of the audience, and applauded loudly. The cast all took their curtain call looking as if they'd rather be at the dentist's, having their teeth pulled. The actor who'd had to kill himself looked particularly upset with the audience for repeatedly dragging him back onto the stage for standing ovations. Perhaps he was just desperate to get to the pub. And the actress who'd called herself a seagull looked as if she could do with a stiff drink, too. She appeared to be on the verge of fainting with exhaustion.

'Goodness,' said Pixie, as she and Deborah traipsed out of the theatre, following all the other punters in the direction of the bar. 'What a brilliant bunch of moaning Minnies!'

'More moaners than *EastEnders*,' said Deborah.

'And as for the fellow who shot himself! Did you hear what he said in that last scene?'

'About getting published?'

'Yes! How, ever since he'd finally had his work published, his life had become intolerable. I felt like giving him a jolly good slap!'

'I thought I heard you gasp in indignation at that bit.'

'I liked the Arkadina character, though. She reminded me of Colleen. In fact — ' Pixie narrowed her eyes thoughtfully — 'that play within the play might have been written by Colleen. It sounds just like the kind of sententious stuff she comes out with.'

All around them text alerts were sounding. Pixie turned her phone on, and it rang almost at once.

'What's that ring tone?' asked Deborah.

'It's 'Always Look on the Bright Side of Life',' said Pixie.

'They should have played it at that curtain call.'

'Hello?' Pixie said into her phone. 'Cleo! Thank you for your e-mail — I got it just before I left the house this evening. You'll be in London next week? Yes — I'd love to meet up. And I received Pablo's invitation, so tell him yes thank you very much, I'd love to go. Mm. I'm at the theatre, darling.' Pixie invested her tone with a kind of stoicism. 'Yes. Back in the thick of things. Better go. Love you!' Pixie depressed 'end call' and stuck her phone back in her bag. 'That was Cleo, my Irish NBF. Her husband's having an exhibition of his paintings here next week.'

'In London?'

'Yes. At the Gerhardt Hess Gallery.'

'Hip.'

'He's very collectable, Pablo. I bought one of his canvases.' Pixie looked thoughtful. 'Now there's an idea . . . ' she said.

'What?' demanded Deborah.

'Cleo mentioned the title of his latest painting in her e-mail — *Figures in a Landscape*. Good title for a novel?'

Deborah waggled her hand. 'A little *comme ci, comme ça*.' Then: 'Yikes,' she said in an undertone. 'There's Dominique Masterson. We've dropped her, you know. Hello, Dominique!'

'Hello,' said Dominique, clearly not the happiest to have happened upon her ex-editor and ex-rival.

But the ritual went on, anyway. Mwah. Mwah! Mwah. Mwah!

'Back from Ireland, Pixie?' asked Dominique. 'How did you get on?'

'I loved it.'

'But you must be glad to be back in the Smoke for a fix of culture?'

'There's plenty of culture in Kilrowan. There was an arts festival happening just as I was leaving.'

'Oh? Featuring the usual parochial iddly-diddly suspects, I've no doubt.'

'Yes. Bono ripped the joint.'

'*Bono*?'

'Yes. And Rory McDonagh rolled up with David Lawless.'

'David Lawless? Who directed this show?'

'The very same.'

There was a silence as Dominique digested this information. Bono, Rory McDonagh and David Lawless were the kind of celebrity scalps that La Londonista would *luuurve* to blog about, and the fact that Pixie had run into such luminaries in a remote village in the West of Ireland must be making her feel sick as a parrot.

'What did you think of the play?' asked Dominique stiffly, clearly anxious to change the subject.

'Well, I have to say that that 'I am a seagull' line has to be one of the most hilarious ever penned,' said Pixie.

Dominique adopted an incredulous expression. 'You found that funny? I found it profoundly moving.'

'But isn't the play supposed to be a comedy?' asked Pixie.

'I don't *think* so,' said Dominique, looking at Pixie pityingly. 'It's Chekhov.'

'Maybe I got it wrong. I was certain it was meant to be funny. Oh!' In her peripheral vision Pixie could see David Lawless moving in their direction, meeting and greeting pressing the flesh. 'There's the director,' she said to Dominique. 'Why not ask him?' She turned — timing spot on — to receive him.

'Pixie. Glad you could make it.' He took her hand, kissed her on both cheeks. 'What did you think of the show?'

'I thought it was hilarious. Was I not meant to? I couldn't understand why there weren't more people laughing.'

'I know. Not many people realize that Chekhov wrote it as a comedy. They were even flummoxed at the very first performance in 1896.'

Pixie slid Dominique a look. Then: 'May I introduce you,' she said, 'to my editor, Deborah Millen? This is my friend David Lawless. And this is Dominique Masterson, who is a foe — ' Dominique shot her a look ' — midable writing talent.'

'Pleased to meet you, both,' said David, shaking hands.

'What a fantastic production,' said Dominique, gushily. 'Your actors worked so hard. They appeared quite wrung-out at the curtain call.'

'That's because they didn't get the laughs they were expecting.'

Dominique looked uncertain. 'Some of the humour's a little — er — on the obscure side.'

'Chekhov himself described it as a comedy,' said David. 'He actually described it as: 'a comedy with three female parts, six male parts, four acts, a landscape, much talk about literature, and five tons of love'. Sounds like the stuff of one of your books, Pixie!'

'David? Can you spare a moment?' An elegant brunette laid a hand on his arm.

'Sure. Excuse me. I'd better go and face my public,' he said.

'Ádh mór ort, David,' said Pixie.

He hesitated, then turned back to her.

'Go raibh míle maith agat. You've been learning Irish?'

'Yes. It's a lot more difficult than cockney slang, but much more beautiful.'

'I'm impressed.'

'David?' A second, even more elegant brunette approached him. 'I'm very sorry to interrupt, but may I remind you that you have a post-show interview scheduled with BBC radio?'

'Of course. Excuse me, Pixie.' He went to follow the brunettes, then turned to her again. 'By the way. Did you ever find that book I recommended to you? The Compleat Angler?'

'No,' she confessed. 'I keep meaning to go on Amazon and check it out.'

'You won't regret it. It's a classic. Goodbye, Pixie.'

'Goodbye.'

And then he was gone, sucked into the maw of fawning well-wishers.

'Why on earth,' said Dominique, with an offhand little laugh, 'would you be interested in a book called *The Compleat Angler?*'

'I took up fly-fishing when I was in Ireland. David and I adore it. It's our mutual passion.'

'*Fishing?* Are you serious?'

'Yes. It's astonishingly therapeutic.'

Dominique shuddered. 'Have you ever actually caught anything?'

Pixie remembered the thrill that had rushed through her when she'd felt that tug on the line, the playing out that had ensued, the luring in, and the joy as the trophy was landed. 'Oh yes,' she said.

'Minnows, I suppose,' remarked Dominique, smirking down her patrician nose at Pixie.

'Well, no, actually. I caught mostly trout.' Pixie looked Dominique directly in the eye. 'But funnily enough, the sweetest satisfaction I ever had was when I landed a catfish. Called Tabbitha.'

Sweet is revenge!

But Dominique's attention had been diverted to a prominent social diarist, who was hovering nearby.

'Hi, Dan!' she said, twinkling her fingers.

'Oh, hi — um — Dominica. Pixie! D'you mind if I steal you for a couple of minutes? I was just talking to Deirdre O'Dare — '

'Deirdre's here?'

'Yes. And she tells me that she's hoping to adapt one of your novels with a view to Rory McDonagh playing the lead. Would you mind posing for a photo with him?'

445

'Rory's here too? What fun! Of course I wouldn't mind!'

She turned back to Dominique to take her leave of her. Malice emanated from her adversary's every pore. Pixie could practically smell it. It had the reek of rotting fish.

'Oh, Pixie?' said a gimlet-eyed Dominique.

'Yes?'

'I thought I ought to warn you that your ex is here. The one who jilted you on *Celebrity Castaway*?'

'Oh, Dominique, gimme a break.' Pixie gave her a look that drawled indifference. 'You think I give a fuck? Him dumping me was the best thing that ever happened to me. And thank you so very much for facilitating it.'

'What? What do you mean?'

'Sorry, Pixie. D'you mind if I hurry you a little?' The journalist was looking anxious. 'I don't want to miss this photo op.'

'Sure, Dan.' But Pixie couldn't resist one final tease. She turned back to Dominique and smiled a sweetly disingenuous smile. 'Hey — big thanks are also due for the beauty tip!'

'Beauty tip?'

'Yes. I've taken to using Dr Hauschka's rose day cream as a foot cream just as you suggested!' And Pixie adopted the kind of pose favoured by Sarah Jessica Parker, sliding one foot forward a little in order to display to advantage her pretty pedicure in her barely there Jimmy Choos.

'What — what are you talking about?'

'www.tabbitha-blogblaggers.com mean anything to you?'

Result! She flashed Dominique her best *Hello!* smile, then turned and danced away to where her celebrity NBFs were waiting for her.

★ ★ ★

She got revenge on more than just one person that night. After she'd obliged the photographers by prinking picturesquely between Deirdre and Rory, she found herself face to face with Jonah Harrington. It was the first time she'd seen him since the *Celebrity Castaway* débâcle.

He pretended he hadn't seen her and tried to slink past, but Pixie said: 'Hey Jonah!' so brightly that he had to stop.

'Hey,' he said, clearly fazed by her friendliness.

She was aware that around them people were looking, curious to see how things would pan out between the celebrity ex-couple.

Jonah was aware of the interest, too. He gave her his famously charming smile, then spread his hands in a gesture of regret. 'Pixie, what can I say? I'm sorry.'

'No worries. How's your balding lap dancer girlfriend?' Pixie replied.

'Lap dancer?'

'Sorry.' A careless laugh. 'I meant actress.'

'Oh — er — Sophie? We split up ages ago.'

'Of course. I seem to remember reading something about it in a subdued four-page spread in *Heat*.'

Pixie had actually rather enjoyed reading about that. Sophie had put on so much weight from stuffing her face with Ben & Jerry's ice-cream while on the island that the headline had read: JONAH AND THE WHALE. Now she allowed a silence to develop, unnerving Jonah further by giving him the benefit of her most charming quizzical smile. Finally: 'Erm. How's the writing going?' he asked her.

'It's going fantastically. I think my next book might be my very best yet.' Pixie's radar told her there was a photo op imminent. A flash went off as she turned to twinkle at a photographer.

'Blow's a kiss, Pixie!' came the matey directive.

She obliged, glad to see that Jonah had pulled on his 'public' face too late.

'Tch, tch.' Pixie shook her head and gave him a pitying look. 'You're going to look like a real prat in that pic. And I'm sorry to have to tell you this, Jonah, but you're also going to end up with a chronic case of crabs.'

'I'm sorry?'

She shrugged. 'That's what happens when you mess with lap dancers, mate.'

Then, smiling at his totally clueless expression, she turned on her heel for the second time that evening and high-heeled back to where Deborah was waiting for her, singing her favourite song under her breath:

> Oh, the shark has pretty teeth, dear,
> And she shows 'em pearly white.
> Just a pen knife has Jane Gray, dear
> And she keeps it way out of sight . . .

The next day a courier called at Pixie's house with a delivery. Inside the padded envelope she found a calfskin-bound copy of *The Compleat Angler*, and a business card with 'Enjoy this!' scrawled on the back in jagged black italics. The book bore the patina of age, and was indubitably a rare edition. When she opened it she saw that the title page had been inscribed with the words: 'For Pixie, from your friend David' in the same black italic script. She couldn't accept it! She was sure that a volume such as this must be worth a small fortune.

Pixie turned the pages with reverent fingers. The book was illustrated with engravings of bucolic scenes celebrating the art and spirit of angling. It was a little gem, containing not only practical advice on the sport, but nuggets of wisdom and philosophy. One sentence that had been underlined in black ink caught her eye. 'He that hopes to be a good Angler must not only bring an inquiring, searching, observing wit, but he must bring a large measure of hope and patience . . .'

Pixie set the book down, and looked at the business card again. Then she picked up the phone, feeling nervous and a bit silly.

'David Lawless.'

'David? It's Jane Gray here.'

'I'm sorry? Who?'

'Um — I mean Pixie. Pixie Pirelli.'

'Oh, Pixie! Who did you say first?'

'Jane Gray. That's my real name. Pixie Pirelli's my *nom de plume*.' Or should she have made that *nom de guerre*?

'I see.' There was a smile in his voice. 'How are you? Did you get my package?'

'Yes. And honestly, David, I can't accept such a generous gift. I'm sure that book is worth a lot of money.'

'Its worth is immaterial. Some books are written to be passed on. *The Compleat Angler* is one of them.'

'Well,' Pixie bit her lip. 'It's a treasure. If you really intend for me to keep it, please be reassured that I shall value it always. How can I thank you?'

'You're right. It is a treasure. And you can thank me by signing copies of your own books for me.'

'Oh, I don't think so — I'm sure you wouldn't be interested in any of my books!'

'We shall have to wait and see. They're on their way from Amazon. Rory told me that I might enjoy them.'

The bastard!

'Well. If you've already forked out the retail price for them, the very least I can do is sign them for you,' she said. 'That's one way of increasing their value.' She looked at the beautiful leather volume lying on her coffee table, and thought wryly of the discrepancy between the value of this single book and her entire 'canon'. 'Thank you so much, David,' she said again. 'You've been so good to me. First theatre tickets, and now this beautiful book.'

'You're most welcome to it. I mean that.'

'Thanks.' She cast around, trying to think of something more to say. She didn't want to say goodbye just yet. 'Um . . . How were the reviews in today's paper, incidentally, for *The Seagull*?'

450

'Uniformly excellent, I'm pleased to say. After another couple of nights I can hand over the baton and leave my actors to it. I'm due a break. The preview week was punishing.'

'Why don't you take yourself off on a fishing holiday?'

'You read my thoughts.' There was a pause, then: 'I hope you won't consider this forward of me, Pixie — or perhaps I should call you Jane? I feel a bit ridiculous calling you Pixie.'

'Please do! The only other people in the world who call me Jane are my parents. It's a blessed relief to be called plain Jane sometimes.' *What was he going to say that could be construed as 'forward'?*

'I wonder . . . Might you come with me?'

Oh. Oh heavens! 'On your fishing holiday?'

'Yes. I — um — I'm not propositioning you — please don't get me wrong. It's just that it's a long time since I took a holiday with anyone other than my daughter and her nanny, and it would be a pleasure to have like-minded company. I know a rather lovely hotel in Buckinghamshire that specializes in fishing weekends. It does fantastic food, too, and they provide hampers for anglers. We could spend an entire weekend on the river.'

There was a longish pause while Pixie contemplated the implications of his offer.

'Please don't think I'm hitting on you, Jane,' he put in quickly. 'I'd hate you to think that my intentions were — well — less than honourable.'

'Oh — of course I don't think that! And I

451

should like very much to come with you,' she said.

'Really?' There was a smile in his voice again. 'That's terrific. I'll make some phone calls and get back to you, shall I?'

'Please do.'

'Talk soon.'

'Yes. Goodbye, David.'

'Goodbye, Jane.'

Pixie set the phone down and reached for *The Compleat Angler*. She sat there with her hands in her lap for many moments, tracing the embossed letters on the spine, and then she opened the book. Turning to the page that contained the sentence that had been under-lined, she read again the following words: 'He that hopes to be a good Angler must not only bring an inquiring, searching, observing wit, but he must bring a large measure of hope and patience . . . '

⋆　⋆　⋆

The hotel was a seventeenth-century castle set amidst woodland and open fields. It was like something out of a Georgette Heyer novel, and Pixie wished that she could waft down the drive in sprigged Regency muslin instead of trudging along in waders and sensible waxed jacket. Pixie and David had booked into their separate rooms earlier. Pixie's room boasted vaulted beam ceilings and a French sleigh bed made up with crisp white linen and piled with masses of cushions. On the walls were paintings of rural idylls, and one rather erotic one of a naked Hera being ravished by Zeus.

The hotel had packed a picnic for them, and a boy had delivered the hamper down to the river with the assurance that he would pick it up again later in his jeep. Pixie was glad to hear it — the hamper probably weighed more than she did. It contained no namby-pamby delicacies like quails' eggs or caviare. This picnic basket was crammed instead with big doorstep sandwiches wrapped in grease-proof paper, hard-boiled eggs, gingerbread, a packet of shortbread biscuits, a flask of tea, bottles of mineral water, a flagon of cider and a noggin of Scotch whisky.

Once they'd unpacked their tackle, David generously allowed Pixie to fish upstream of him, which meant that she had the advantage. She felt self-conscious as she prepared to make her first cast, trying hard to remember all she'd learned from her ghillie in Ballynahinch.

She chose a spot in the river where a tree cast its shadow. This was so that her own shadow would not hit the surface of the water and alert any fish below to her presence. Taking careful aim at a point two or three feet above where she wanted the flies to fall, she prayed that they would land softly, so as not to frighten off any trout that might be lurking. Result! They landed with barely a hint of a plash.

She began to extend her line a yard at a time, wading smoothly further upstream. Before long, a movement in the water alerted her to the presence of her quarry. Raising her wrist, saying another prayer, she hooked him with a smart jerk and reeled him in with care, more prayers, and a great deal of patience. He was hers — all hers! — and she did not want to run the risk of losing him. She drew him up out of the water into her net and deftly extracted the hook from his mouth, and then she clamped her eyes shut as she banged his poor surprised head against the edge of the creel and dropped him in.

When she opened her eyes, she dared look downstream. David was standing with a hand shading his eyes from the sun, and he was smiling.

★   ★   ★

They lunched late, and hungrily, and Pixie hoped she wouldn't spoil her appetite for dinner later. She'd be feasting on freshly caught river trout this evening!

'More cider?' she asked David, as she returned the detritus of their picnic to the hamper. 'There's a little left.'

'Thanks,' he said, draining his plastic cup. 'That would be good.'

She poured, then settled back against the bole of a tree. Sunlight dappled the surface of the water, a thrush was singing in the wood, and the cadence of the river was like a lullaby. Contentment swelled within her. She had landed two trout, David three.

'I haven't felt this carefree in a long time,' said David. 'Not since I last went on holiday with Eva.'

'Where did you go?'

'Mexico. We stayed on the edge of Zihuatanejo Bay, on one of the most beautiful beaches in the country.'

'You're a beach person too, then?'

'Yes. I find beaches are the ultimate escape. Apart from fly-fishing, that is.'

Pixie smiled to herself. She thought of how, when she had first met David Lawless, she had imagined that they would have absolutely nothing in common. How strange to think that they shared more than just a few interests!

A silence fell, then: 'Have you read *The Compleat Angler* yet?' he asked.

'Most of it. It's a brilliant book for dipping into.' She steeled herself. 'Have you read any of my books?'

'I've — erm — likewise, dipped into them,' he said. 'I have to confess that I didn't really understand them.'

'I'm glad to hear it. I'd be a little worried if you did. I didn't write them for men.'

He smiled at her. 'Eva would have loved them.'

In the wood beyond the river a thrush performed a cadenza that Kiri Te Kanawa might have envied.

'You must miss her terribly,' said Pixie.

'Yes,' he said. 'I do. Since her death my life has been a kind of sham. I sometimes think that I only keep going for Dorcas's sake.'

'How long is it since she died?'

'Over two years. I kept her ashes in the urn for a year before I could bring myself to scatter them.'

'On Lissnakeelagh.'

'Yes. It was actually rather a joyous occasion. If you're going to be scattered to the wind, you might as well be scattered to the wild west wind that blows in off one of the most beautiful beaches in the world.'

'Yes. Lissnakeelagh really is something special.'

They sat on in silence for several more moments, and the silence felt good, not embarrassing at all. Pixie closed her eyes, relishing the ozone-rich air, and she might have drifted off to sleep had not a drop of rain landed on the back of her hand.

'Oh!' she said. 'Rain. Great — the fish'll rise to this.' She spoke without any real enthusiasm. The imminent rain might be good news as far as fishing was concerned, but it was seriously bad news for her hair.

David must have registered her rather glum tone, because he looked at her and said: 'Maybe we've done enough for today. We've done well — five trout between us. What do you say we head back to the hotel and take it easy by the fire for the rest of the day?'

'I'd really rather like that,' said Pixie.

The rain was coming in fast from the north, but it wasn't of the heavy variety, it was more of a light drizzle that drifted intermittently on the wind. David got to his feet, and Pixie did likewise. 'Oh look,' she said. 'Over there!'

She pointed to where a rainbow hung in the air above a stretch of the river that cascaded over a rocky falls.

David turned and looked in the direction she had indicated. He gazed at the rainbow for several moments, then: 'Hello, Eva,' he said.

Pixie looked at him.

'I'm sorry,' he said, with an apologetic smile. 'Talking to rainbows is one of my more eccentric habits. They remind me of Eva. I always think she's trying to tell me something when a rainbow appears in the sky.'

'I don't think that's eccentric at all,' said Pixie. 'I think it's really rather lovely. What do you think she's trying to tell you now?'

'I don't know. She often moves in mysterious ways. Like Mimi.'

'Mimi?'

'The character she played in the last film she ever made was a white witch called Mimi, who made good things happen.'

'Of course! *Mimi's Remedies*. I loved that film.'

'She had a feeling that it would be her last film. That's what makes it so special. The final shot is of her walking towards a rainbow on the horizon.'

'I remember.'

Lost in thought, David regarded the rainbow for several more moments before turning and hefting his rucksack onto his back. Pixie followed suit.

'Can you manage?' he asked.

'Oh, yes. I do SAS training exercises every day. You need stamina to be an author.'

'So it's not about lying around on divans eating grapes while you wait for the muse to descend?'

'Damn right it's not.'

They smiled at each other, then picked up their fishing rods and set off up the hill in the direction of the hotel. There was mist rising from the damp earth, and the landscape had an other-worldly appearance about it, like something illustrated by Arthur Rackham.

'It looks like a fairytale castle,' he said.

'Yes,' agreed Pixie, 'that's just what I was thinking.'

'Careful!'

David reached out a hand to steady her as Pixie stumbled over a treacherous bramble that lay hidden in the long grass. She clutched at his hand gratefully. The last thing she needed was to go arse over tit while laden down with tackle! The rain was easing off into a fine mist, and behind them the rainbow shimmered and faded over the river.

David took one last look at it over his shoulder. 'If we shadows have offended,' he murmured.

'I'm sorry?' said Pixie.

'It's Puck's speech from *A Midsummer Night's Dream*. I directed it once, with Eva as Titania, the Queen of the Fairies.'

'How does it go?'

'If we shadows have offended,
Think but this and all is mended,
That you have but slumber'd here
While these visions did appear.'

David looked down at her and smiled, then he and Pixie continued on their way, walking over the wet grass hand in hand, in silence.

Epilogue

A couple of weeks later, Pixie was checking out Rufus's most recent link on www.pixiepirelli.com when her phone rang. She was relieved to see from the display that it wasn't her publicist, for a change. She'd been doing so much posing recently that her jaw muscles ached from smiling for photographers.

She'd also done a load of newspaper interviews, including 'My Favourite Shoes', 'My Favourite Handbag' and 'My Favourite Sandwich'. She'd been so obliging that she might even have considered doing 'My Favourite Builder', if she'd been asked. And she genuinely hadn't minded doing 'My Favourite Painting' because she was able to give Pablo's exhibition — which went under the title 'Figures in an Urban Landscape' — a big plug.

It was Natalie, on the phone.

'How was your weekend in Buckinghamshire?' she asked.

'It was lovely, thank you, Nat.'

When it became clear from the ensuing silence that no more information was likely to be forthcoming, her agent said: 'Good! Now — I have some news for you. You'll be getting a call from the film rights department soon. Jolly Roger Enterprises want to option your entire backlist.'

'Yo ho! Will I have a say in the casting?'

'Unlikely.'

'Bum.'

'Why?'

'I'd love to see Sophie Burke play the stripy-haired slapper in *Hard to Choos*.'

Natalie laughed. 'How's the redraft of the new book going?'

'Jolly well, I think. I've tweaked here and there so that it makes chronological sense. I've brought a little research to bear. I've renamed the heroine Natasha — '

'After me?'

'Yes,' lied Pixie.

'Thank you, darling!'

'And I've reworked the ending.'

'I liked the ending.'

'We can go back to it, if you like. No worries.'

'I trust you. Thought of a title yet?'

'No. But I've found a lovely quote for the epigraph. It's from *A Midsummer Night's Dream*.'

'Fab. When will I be able to have a look?'

Pixie smiled. 'I'll e-mail it to you this evening.'

'Star!'

And Natalie put the phone down, sounding happy.

Pixie looked at her computer screen. 'Happy Endings,' she typed. 'Happy Ever After,' she tried. And then — not for the first time — 'Figures in a Landscape'. Her favourite, next. 'Sex, Death and Revenge'. She *loved* the 'R' word, but her editor had had a point about the 'D' word. It *was* a bit bleak. 'Sex,' Pixie typed again. '*Sex* . . . '

She thought hard, flexed her fingers, and then she typed:

Sex, Lies and Fairytales

A Novel
by
Pixie Pirelli

Epigraph

Now, until the break of day,
Through this house each fairy stray,
So shall all the couples three
Ever true in loving be.

(William Shakespeare,
A Midsummer Night's Dream)

Pixie re-read the last two lines of the verse. And then she reached for her *Compleat Angler* and consulted the words of wisdom contained therein.

'He that hopes to be a good Angler must not only bring an inquiring, searching, observing wit, but he must bring a large measure of hope and patience . . .'

She smiled to herself. Hope and patience?

She had them in spades.

461

We do hope that you have enjoyed reading this large print book.

Did you know that all of our titles are available for purchase?

We publish a wide range of high quality large print books including:
Romances, Mysteries, Classics
General Fiction
Non Fiction and Westerns

Special interest titles available in large print are:
The Little Oxford Dictionary
Music Book
Song Book
Hymn Book
Service Book

Also available from us courtesy of Oxford University Press:
Young Readers' Dictionary
(large print edition)
Young Readers' Thesaurus
(large print edition)

For further information or a free brochure, please contact us at:
Ulverscroft Large Print Books Ltd.,
The Green, Bradgate Road, Anstey,
Leicester, LE7 7FU, England.
Tel: (00 44) **0116 236 4325**
Fax: (00 44) **0116 234 0205**

Other titles published by
The House of Ulverscroft:

LIVING THE DREAM

Kate Thompson

For Cleo Dowling the dream becomes a reality. She comes into serious money and takes herself off to the pretty village of Kilrowan in the west of Ireland to write a novel. But what happens when she becomes obsessed with her sexy neighbour? Dannie Moore's love life has always been complicated, but when film director Jethro Palmer chooses Kilrowan as the location for a blockbuster movie, the effect on her life is cataclysmic. Deirdre O'Dare leaves her husband Rory behind in LA to accompany her friend, movie star Eva Lavery, to Kilrowan. When the cat's away and all that . . . And although Deirdre is writing Eva's biography, it would appear that the actress is not telling the truth, the whole truth . . .

THE STARTER WIFE

Gigi Levangie

When her husband dumps her (by cell phone) just before their tenth wedding anniversary, Gracie Pollock is left reeling. Though her role as the wife of a semi-famous studio executive often left her cold, she had become accustomed to the unique privileges extended to Tinseltown's elite. Gracie really believed that she and Kenny were different from other Hollywood couples. She never thought she'd be a *Starter Wife*. But now that her marriage is over, she's a social pariah and things go from bad to worse when she learns (via her florist) that her husband has upgraded: Kenny is dating a famous blonde pop starlet. What will Gracie do next?

AT FIRST SIGHT

Nicholas Sparks

Jeremy Marsh had always vowed he'd never do certain things: leave New York City, give his heart away again after barely surviving one failed marriage and, most of all, become a parent. Now, Jeremy is living in the tiny town of Boone Creek, North Carolina, married to Lexie Darnell, the love of his life, and anticipating the birth of their daughter. But just as his life seems to be settling into a blissful pattern, an unsettling and mysterious message reopens old wounds and sets off a chain of events that will forever change the course of this young couple's marriage . . .

LEFT BANK

Kate Muir

Olivier and Madison Malin are glittering inhabitants of Paris's exclusive neighbourhood, the Left Bank. The Malins' life in their grand apartment with their daughter is the stuff of dreams. Madison is an American film star: she's beautiful and talented. Her husband, Olivier, darling of the sophisticated Left Bank, craves adoration (and is a little too willing to return it) . . . Everything seems perfect, until a new English nanny, Anna, appears at the doors of their Rue du Bac apartment. Gamine and artless, Anna unwittingly sets in motion a chain of events that will gravely endanger the Malins' daughter and their charmed lives — in ways no one could have foreseen.

OLD SCORES

Bernardine Kennedy

At sixteen, Maria Harman feels confused, resentful and bitter. She has always known she was adopted — a longed-for daughter amid three sons — but she has never understood her mother's disdain for her. Finola Harman's abuse, her older brothers' bullying and her father's lack of intervention have led to a life of misery. For, although hardened to her mother's contempt, Maria craves her love. Her solace comes from her warm-hearted, slow-witted brother Eddie, and her involvement with local bad boy Davey Allsop, until a tragic accident destroys even that ... And slowly, as the truth of Maria's true parentage is revealed, the dysfunctional Harman family is thrown into chaos with potentially fatal consequences.

BRAND NEW FRIEND

Mike Gayle

When Rob's girlfriend asks him to leave London and live with her in Manchester, it means leaving behind his best mate in the entire world. Believing that love conquers all and confident that he'll meet new mates, Rob takes the plunge. Six months in, and yet to find even a drinking buddy, Rob realises that making friends in your thirties is not easy, so his girlfriend places an ad in the classifieds. Three excruciatingly embarrassing 'bloke dates' later, he's on the verge of despair . . . until his luck changes. There's just one problem. Apart from knowing less than nothing about football and the vital statistics of supermodels, Rob's new friend has a huge flaw. She's a girl . . .